I0611774

From Cornwall to Moonta: migration and resettlement

Dianne Griffin

Glass House Books
Brisbane

Glass House Books
an imprint of IP (Interactive Publications Pty Ltd)
Treetop Studio • 9 Kuhler Court
Carindale, Queensland, Australia 4152
sales@ipoz.biz
http://ipoz.biz/

© 2023, Dianne Griffin (text) and IP (design)
eBook versions © 2023

All rights reserved. Without limiting the rights under copyright
reserved above, no part of this publication may be reproduced, stored
in or introduced into a retrieval system, or transmitted, in any form
or by any means (electronic, mechanical, photocopying, recording
or otherwise), without the prior written permission of the copyright
owner and the publisher of this book.

Printed in 12 pt Adobe Caslon Pro on 14 pt Avenir Book.

ISBN: 9781922830302 (PB); 9781876819319 (eBk)

 A catalogue record for this
book is available from the
National Library of Australia

Glass House Books

From Cornwall to Moonta: migration and resettlement

Dianne Griffin lived in Moonta, South Australia, as a child. She loved the town and its people, especially her grandparents, Charles W and Eleanor B Bowden.

At 25, Dianne set out to see the world, and re-immigrated to Cornwall and Britain. She married in 1970 and, settling in Ireland, raised three children.

Never one to shy away from telling a great story, Dianne published short stories and dabbled in journalism.

Moving back to Australia in 1989, she settled in Brisbane near family. She retrained as a Registered Nurse, and, at the age of 50, completed her Bachelor of Science. Dianne's nursing career gives her great insight into the experiences of women, and the inevitable health issues faced by immigrants to Australia in the 19th century.

Continuing her lifelong desire to learn, Dianne completed a post-graduate certificate in creative writing, focusing on Life Writing.

Dianne's office began to overflow with books, diaries of immigrants and newspapers of early South Australia.

With inspiration from her grandfather, who wrote in his preface to *History of Agery*, "Being blessed with a fairly retentive memory, and having in my possession much authentic information, I have a duty to pass it on – now that I have lived the allotted life span."

Dianne discerned the mantle had passed to her, and that the voices in From Cornwall to Moonta should come back to life.

Glass House Books
Brisbane

No pains should be spared to teach the labouring classes to regard the colonies as *The Land of Promise*, which it should be their highest ambition to be able to reach.

    – Edward Gibbon Wakefield. *A Letter from Sydney*, Sydney: Royal Australian Historical Society, 1829.

This book is dedicated to my late grandmother, Eleanor Beatrice Bowden. She loved us all. Grandma also heavily assisted my grandfather in writing *A History of Agery*. The booklet provided dozens of stories about Emma and Ben's children, tales that set this process in motion.

Acknowledgements

Front cover image: "Port Adelaide" by George French Angus from the 1847 edition of *South Australia Illustrated*. Lithograph by W. Hawkins, courtesy, South Australia State Library, B15276/7.
Back cover image: Solomon's Store, c. 1870, South Australia State Library, B3780
Book design: David P. Reiter
Author photo: Katelnd Griffin

I am deeply indebted to publisher Dr David Reiter and James Devitt of Interactive Publications, for their editorial skills.

Thank you also to my husband Lynn for his genealogical skills, his endurance, encouragement and editorial assistance. And many thanks to my children, Alison, Katelnd and Adam for their suggestions, patience, proofreading, and computer *HELP*.

Many others have contributed to the work. Cousin Gerald Trethowan, late of Constantine, Cornwall, 1928-2014, escorted us around Constantine, showing us where each family in the story had lived. Gerald and I also perused the museum together, the churches and chapels, and my favourite exhibit, a floor-sized tithe map of the various farms in Constantine. Marilyn Philbey, National Trust of South Australia, helped in many ways, making freely available her database of indexed names, and articles from early *Yorke Peninsula* newspapers. John Weyland, my brother, assisted me greatly during my research in the State Library of South Australia.

Contents

1. Plymouth Harbour, England

March 15, 1864

At last, the *Eastern Empire* had arrived, and a smile broke over the face of twenty-two-year-old Ben Bowden. The 993-ton wooden sailing ship was anchored just inside the breakwater at Plymouth Harbour. Ben wiped the damp from his mouth and beard. It was a misty day, and the three tall masts pierced the low grey cloud.

Many more emigrants, cheering, crying, and pointing, swarmed around Ben and Emma, but as the rain grew heavier, the young couple ran back for shelter inside the depot.

Later in the evening, the emigrants were told they would board in the morning. It was to be their last night in England.

The next morning, Ben and Emma, with heavy hearts, joined the queue for boarding the *Eastern Empire*, and, in what seemed hours later, arrived at the base of the *ship's* gangway. Ben hauled their traps and bundles, while Emma gripped the ropes and walked up the steep walkway. When Ben reached the deck, he gratefully grasped the rails. At last, they were on-board. He still couldn't believe he and Emma had been chosen.

'Mr Vicary was right,' Ben said, his face almost hidden by his battered felt hat and fine black beard. 'I thought we should be on one of those shiny new iron ships. But this is grand and solid.'

The 380 or so straggling migrants continued to arrive on the deck, pushing Emma and Ben forward slowly, until they could go no further. They eased their belongings down to their feet.

Ben looked up at the neatly rolled sails. 'So easy,' he said. 'No horses to feed. We'll just float our way around the world, for thousands of miles.'

Emma doubted it would be that easy. She covered her nose, as the smells of fish and chloride of lime, clawed at her nostrils. Wondering if her family missed her as much as she missed them, she jumped when a seaman yelled an order to another seaman. 'What are they saying?' she asked Ben, tensing when she felt the gentle tipping of the ship from side to side.

1

The bellowing continued, from one seaman to another, from stem to stern. She had been used to noise, when she was younger, living with twelve brothers and sisters, but, in the last six years, when she served as a kitchen maid in Nansloe, Mr Tyacke would have none of it.

'Look, over there,' Ben said, as the seamen stomped on the downbeat of an old sea shanty. Emma smiled, pushing her tight dark curls from her face, and tightening her bonnet strings against the rising wind. Ben slipped his arm around her.

The constable for the voyage, Isaac Kimbly, rang the ship's bell. A cool breeze blew the stack of papers in his hand. 'Attention please,' he shouted. 'These are your berth numbers.' He nailed the flapping list to the hatchway. Ben and Emma squeezed their way towards the list with another young couple, James and Amelia Vicary.

'Here we are,' James said, running his finger down the page. 'Let me see – Ben, you are berth number 45, and Amelia and I are 46.'

Both couples headed down to the between decks cabin.

'You are so lucky,' Emma confided to Amelia, 'travelling with your whole family.'

James Vicary's brother, John, pulled away from the group. 'I don't know about that,' he said. 'We signed up to get away from them, and they followed us!'

Emma laughed and said to Ben, 'That fellow is cheeky, but no worse than my brother. And a bit of leg pulling might be just what we need right now.'

Ben and Emma kept an eye on James's chocolate-brown cap, and his matching beaverteen jacket. They didn't know which way to go.

'It's quite dark down there,' Emma said.

Ben took her hand, and Emma trod carefully, her eyes gradually focusing on the roughly hewn deck below. All four walls were lined with rows of double bunks. Down the centre was a long mess table. This area was to be their bedroom, dining, and living room for the next three months. She couldn't wait to tell her sisters. Then Emma remembered that she wouldn't be telling them anything, until she learned to write.

Ben and Emma continued across the third-class cabin, apologising as they collided with other passengers trying to settle into their small spaces. When Ben and Emma reached their bunks, they gratefully let go of their bags.

Emma was tired after their travel and goodbyes, but she was also surprised at how weary Amelia looked, as she eagerly lay back on their bunk, only to land on the handle of a heavy bag.

'There is no headroom,' Amelia said to Emma.

'Here, let me,' James removed the bag and helped Amelia back onto the bunk.

Amelia was pretty in an English Rose kind of way. Her high-necked gown, although well worn, was adorned with ribbons and lace. She smiled at Emma. 'Hope I'm not going to be a misery for long.'

Emma smiled back. 'You'll be better soon.'

Ben and Emma's bunk was only three feet wide. Emma opened a bundle and took out a towel, her nightclothes, and a change of clothes each.

Ben suspended the ham and the bag of their remaining clothes and linen on the nails provided. 'It's a juggle,' he muttered, stuffing the tin plates, pickles, and molasses into one corner of the bunk, and his writing materials into the other. He put the Bible under his pillow, and the bowl and marine soap at the foot of the bed – now to hide the chamber pot.

As the ship's bell rang, Kimbly stood on the hatchway steps. 'Listen carefully,' he shouted. 'Migrant ships only have a skeleton staff. They are the seamen, the captain, surgeon-superintendent, matron, and the water distiller. You, the migrants, are responsible for the rest, collecting, cooking, and serving of food, and keeping your cabin clean. The adult males will form groups of ten, or thereabouts, and make a roster, nominating a sweeper, who will act as your captain for each week. It is your captain's responsibility to see that everything in your area is done.'

Emma's brother, William, had told Ben about the cleaning, but Ben only realised now what a chore it would be. The deck was already caked with bird droppings, mud, biscuits, and rubbish. Ben would have to take a knife to it – although William said they were provided with holystone, and broomsticks. Ben grimaced and rubbed his forehead.

The emigrants' mutterings grew to a grumble.

'Quiet please!' Kimbly continued. 'You will rise at seven and roll up your beds. Wet beds must be aired on deck.'

Ben eyed the narrow steps. He envisioned eternal bottlenecks of passengers trying to go up and down to the deck with mattresses and bedclothes.

Kimbly looked back at his notes. 'Breakfast is at eight, and dinner at one, but only after the surgeon and matron's inspections. You will wipe down the tables, sweep out the cabin and throw dirt overboard.

Supper is at six, fires out at seven, and bedtime is ten.' He softened his tone as he spoke to the women. 'Ladies, you will prepare some meals, but you are not permitted in the galley.'

Mrs Temby, mother of seven young girls, smiled at Emma, and whispered, 'The less galley work for me the better.'

The constable's voice rose again. 'And absolutely nobody must tamper with the lamps.' He nailed the list of rules near the hatchway. 'Read the rest at your convenience. Now, choose your sweepers and ready yourselves for the muster.'

Back in the between decks area, James's father, John Vicary senior, sat at the table. He looked world weary, and all of his fifty years, with his greying moustache and beard. However, he put his hand up and offered to be their first sweeper.

Ben stretched his neck and elbows. 'Praise the Lord,' he whispered to Emma. 'I would have no idea where to start.'

Mr Vicary held up two lists and tapped his spoon on a tin mug. 'Hello, can you all hear me? We have enough for two groups. The families that hail from St Blazey are keen to stay together, so that means the Vicary, Hore, Curtis, and Bice families are in one group. The second group is the Breens, Matthews, Tembys, Bowdens, and Sarah Murley. Oh, and the Rowes. Sorry Danny and Rachel.'

Mr Vicary continued. 'Mary-Ann and I will visit upon the purser and prepare your supper tonight. And, it being our first meal on board, everyone will wash their own tinware.' His voice was drowned out when Constable Kimbly shook his brass handbell.

'Everyone immediately on deck,' Kimbly announced. 'It's time for the muster.'

Ben imagined they'd be sitting around on the ship, waiting out the days. Now it seemed the orders would never end. He and Emma followed everyone, cramming for the steps.

The surgeon superintendent, Doctor Isaac Baker-Brown, was barely thirty. He pulled out his gold watch and waited on the poop deck.

'I wish he'd hurry up,' Emma complained, not comfortable with the side-to-side movements of the ship.

Susan Hore winked at her and said, 'The surgeon is quite a looker. I wonder what he's doing on a ship like this. It can't be fun, working at sea.'

'Quiet, please,' the surgeon boomed in his best Harley Street voice. 'I am responsible for both your health and well-being.' He twirled the tips of his fine moustache. 'We must have strict order. Punishment for infringements will be severe. As Constable Kimbly told you, we are supplied with a minimum of staff on board. And I have chosen the following constables to assist them. Perform your duties well and you could receive three pounds sterling on arrival.' He read the names from his list, and each man stepped forward, proud of his selection.

Ben noticed that John Vicary's sons were listed. Lucky them, he thought. Three pounds would come in handy. After the surgeon finished reading, the passengers began discussing his choices.

'Quiet, please!' the surgeon repeated. 'For your good health, you must spend as much time on deck as possible. However, at no time should single males and females be on deck together.'

This raised a titter and the surgeon glowered. 'Quiet!' he demanded yet again. 'The roster for single male, and female deck times is available from Mr Kimbly. Now, single men to the stern, which is at the rear of the ship, and single women to the bow.'

The first-class passengers now boarded – including the Reverend Mr Stanton and his large family. Emma gaped at their finery. She caught Susan Hore's eye. Susan grinned, as she heaved baby William onto her hip.

Captain George Jury greeted the new passengers. He was splendid in his dark, braided, gold-buttoned suit, and a flat seaman's hat, with the title *Eastern Empire* and its royal insignia embroidered on the band.

Ben was pleased the master was a middle-aged man. They would need his experience on such a long journey.

The customs officer briefed and saluted the master. The surgeon left the poop deck, and the seamen, in a straight line, saluted the captain, and returned to their duties.

Ben found the orderly ceremony of departure reassuring.

Seamen scaled the masts, while others pushed on the splaying handles of the capstan, raising the ship's anchor. They trudged around, singing an old shanty and stomping their boots to the beat.

'Tis when a Black Baller's preparing for sea
to my way haye, blow the man down,
You'd split your sides laughing at the sights that you see.
Give me some time to blow the man down.

Clouds of smoke belched from the tugboat, and the *Eastern Empire* moved slowly from the port. There was no propitious wind to fill the sails.

'So, we continue like this till the wind comes up?' Ben asked.

'Ay,' Mr Vicary replied, 'Let's hope we get one soon. We don't want the tug to run out of steam. We could be here all day – or until tomorrow.'

'Tomorrow?' Ben almost spluttered.

After nearly an hour, gusts of wind were greeted with a rousing cheer, as the *Eastern Empire* took off at speed. It was like magic, Emma thought.

The seamen's shouting increased, as the sails filled, and the English emigrants, hands on their hearts, sang the well-loved anthem.

> God save our gracious Queen...
> Long to reign over us,
> God save the Queen.

Emma shivered as the splendid tenor voices, including that of her husband, rose up. Tears ran down her cheeks and she leaned into Ben. He put his arm around her.

'It's difficult to believe I'll never see everyone again,' Emma cried, twisting Grandma Philley's silver ring on her forefinger. 'And little Jane, she's only six, she doesn't even know where I'm going.'

'Oh, sweetheart,' Ben said, wiping her eyes, and hugging her tighter. 'Think about it. We'll be with William and Eliza again.'

Ben only had one sister, Elizabeth. All of his brothers had died in infancy. But no matter the size of his family, it had been heartbreaking saying goodbye – forever. He tried not to dwell on the look on his mother's face. It had surprised him, the extent of her pain.

But he would make his parents proud. He would write to tell them all about the new country. Australia was a place they and their friends knew little about. And, in a small town like Constantine, new knowledge was highly prized. Surely that would compensate somewhat for his leaving.

2. The Voyage

The tugboat separated from the ship, and the *Eastern Empire* left the harbour at speed. It was about half past two, and the sun momentarily glinted through the clouds.

As the hollering and stomping of the seamen intensified, Emma, hands again on her ears, turned to Amelia and said, 'There must be somewhere quieter. Let's try over there.'

Amelia and Mary Ann Vicary, Susan Hore, and Rachel Rowe followed Emma to huddle beside deeply packed bales.

'My boys can stay with their father,' Susan said, waving to her sons. She opened the buttons of her tousled blue jacket, loosened her chemise, and began to feed baby William.'

Emma thought of all the men around and blushed a little.

'You are brave, Susan,' Rachel whispered. 'This one,' she said, indicating 12-month-old Mary Ann, sitting in her lap, 'is going to wait until I'm back on our bunk – not that there is much privacy down there either.'

'I'm not so much brave, as worn out,' Susan quipped. And smiling intensely at her baby, she whispered, 'We're well covered up, aren't we, bubby?'

Emma sympathised. 'I can't imagine setting out with two children and a baby. All of that packing. I remember Mama, even trying to get to chapel. Most of us older ones worked three Sundays out of four, so she had the littlies to herself. Getting them fed, looking for shoes, clothes, caps… It was always a rush.'

The girls nodded vigorously. Emma grinned; her friends knew what she meant.

When the English coastline became significantly distant, Ben moved toward the bow. He strained forward, looking into the sea, as the ship ploughed through the light green water. A gust of wind blew a foul smell towards him, and, when the bow dipped steeply, he saw the row of six men's water closets. He drew back. While the seawater would wash away much of the waste, there was obvious spillage around the seats. And at times there would be too many people waiting. What would they do? Squat where they were?

The *Eastern Empire*, built in New Brunswick in 1857, looked powerful. But was the big ship actually strong, Ben wondered. He could see now it had been freshly painted. What was under the paint? Ben looked closer at the capping. A small section was lumpy. Had a sail smashed into it?

Like any impoverished farm labourer, Ben had painted over many a crack in a house or a barn. Now he recalled the terrifying, roof-raising westerly winds in Cornwall. There would be no protection from such gales at sea.

Once in the Atlantic Ocean, the ship rolled more steeply from side to side, and Emma clutched her stomach. Ben began to stagger, too, steadying himself by every rail and rope he could find as they retreated to their beds. Emma already looked wretched, Ben thought, and they'd only just left England. He frowned as he recalled the hecklers and chants at the emigration meetings, talking of storms, shipwrecks, and death.

'I'll be all right once I lie down,' Emma said. Suddenly, she retched, her vomit partly missing the bowl and lightly staining the clean towel. She looked apologetically at her husband. Turning to the two rungs at the foot of their bunk, Emma tried to climb but fell back as the ship lurched. Ben caught her.

'I keep stepping on my skirt,' she complained. James Vicary offered Emma a foothold, allowing her to look over the bunk, but she couldn't get her knee up to climb in as her head was pressed firmly against the ceiling. She turned into it on her side, hunched over, and worked fold by fold to free her skirt until she was able to lie on her back and wiggle into position. She sighed as her head found the pillow, her dark curls falling around her face. 'I am definitely staying here until we get to Australia.'

Ben smiled. Here was the real Emma, the courageous girl he'd fallen in love with. Her bravery would be a great asset on this journey.

With Emma and Amelia resting, James and Ben were determined to go back on deck. Ben nodded and they set out, staggering from post to post, until they finally sat, braced against the crates on the deck. Ben breathed in the fresh sea air and congratulated James on becoming a constable.

'I am pleased,' James replied. 'It should increase a man's prospects. I mean, look at Isaac Kimbly. He arrived early – and he has no children – so the surgeon had him trained as the journey constable. That will set him up as a hotel manager in South Australia, or he could run a shipping depot. There's money in that.'

'So, they paid his passage?' Ben asked.

James nodded. 'But the really lucky one is John Gale, assistant surgeon, if you please. Like Kimbly, he's only a labouring man like us. Gale could become a doctor.'

Ben was quickly envious. If only he could climb the career ladder, too. As for being instantly important, that was never going to happen. Ben pulled his legs up and looped his arms around his threadbare trousers. He had planned to acquire newer clothing before the voyage was underway. Now, he watched the deft movements of the seamen as they reefed the sails. Poverty had long eaten into him.

Isaac Kimbly, in his smart, brown, wide lapelled, knee-length jacket, and matching brown trousers, shouted at the passengers. 'Everyone go below. The hatch will be closed.'

The men relieved themselves over the side of the ship and returned to the steps.

'Argh,' Ben groaned as he gulped the warm turgid air from the deck below. 'Everyone seems to be vomiting – already.'

The ship tilted and Ben almost fell. Luckily, he was near his berth, able to throw himself at the bedpost and heave his way up. Lying back and breathing heavily, he again wondered just how sound the *Eastern Empire* really was as the block and tackle above him groaned and creaked. And the pounding boots of the seamen were only inches away. Why had he left home? What had he been thinking?

It was a visiting preacher at the Constantine Wesleyan Chapel who had sealed his fate. It wasn't until the clergyman looked straight into Ben's eye and told him that God wanted young men like him, strong and able, to choose emigration, that he took the notion seriously. If he, Ben, emigrated, those who were less able could remain in Cornwall.

Now that God had shown him the way, Ben felt he should be thankful.

An eerie wind howled and rolled the ship ever more steeply from side to side. Emma moaned, and when the crying and shouting in the cabin increased, Ben wondered if they would ever find sleep.

'God is with us,' Ben said, wrapping his arms around Emma.

March 17

The ship's bell jangled at seven in the morning.

Ben yawned, rubbed his eyes, and snuggled back into his pillow. 'We must have slept a little,' he murmured to Emma, who was lying on her back, staring at the girders above.

'Thank God that wind has dropped,' she said.

The hatch was opened and buckets of saltwater fetched to clean the fouled cabin. At eight o'clock, with everywhere still damp, breakfast was served.

'The smell is vile,' Emma groaned softly. 'The sick has soaked into the wood, and there's spilled chamber pots.'

'We'll go on deck as soon as we can,' Ben said. 'A little bit of tea?'

Emma nodded, hoping she would feel better.

Mr Vicary appeared from the galley with a cloth over his arm, pretending to be a serving man. Mrs Bice laughed and nudged Emma.

'He is a one,' Emma said, giving a wan smile. Elizabeth Bice, although much older than Emma, had become a good friend at Plymouth, and Ben was pleased.

A wave dashed against the hull and Mr Vicary staggered. But he held fast and deposited the pan of oatmeal safely. However, everyone's spoons, pannikins and empty bowls slid across the table.

'Only for that lip tacked on the edge,' James said, 'our things would all be on the floor.'

Emma warily sipped her tea. As soon as breakfast finished Ben took her arm and they headed for the deck, reaching carefully from one anchor point to another. At the top of the steps, Ben and Emma blinked into the sharp light of day and breathed in the fresh sea air.

'Praise the Lord,' Ben said. 'And listen. Is that music I hear?' he tilted his head. 'There's a fiddler. Over there.'

The music was a joyful sound to Emma after the terror of the storm.

'And here's a tin whistler,' James Vicary said. 'Of course, it's the Feast of St Patrick. The Irish are out in force.'

A hand-clapping crowd with patterned ganseys and green shirts quickly surrounded the group, and more musicians arrived.

'It's the men and boys this morning,' James said. 'They will have to be safely in their cabin before the young ladies arrive.'

'It's a pity the young men and women can't dance together; it's so unnatural,' Emma confided to Susan. 'As if the journey isn't long and tedious enough. What a silly rule – in broad daylight.'

Susan nodded. 'Yet they can mix with the married men and women. I mean, couldn't that be worse?'

The musicians, cheered on by the crowd, played many a lively tune.

'It reminds me of Helston's Flora Day,' Emma said, clapping along to the music.

'This is a jig,' Mary Griffin said, welcoming the English girls.

The dancers, breathless now, kicked their heels high. After several jigs, the girls clasped hands and swung out widely. The crowd whooped, gave them space, and tapped their feet in time.

In the evening, the passengers returned to the deck, singing and dancing. Emma sat with Elizabeth Bice, Catherine Temby, and a woman from Cheshire named Margaret Standring.

'You said your Mr Tyacke led the dancers on Flora Day last year?' Catherine Temby asked Emma.

'Ah ha,' Emma nodded. 'Led them all the way from the Guildhall, right through the town. He steps out real fine, too. It was the only reason I had the day off. But the servants' dance was better. Our frocks weren't as grand, but we had a lot of fun. And the Mock Mayor, how we laughed, him in his fools cap and chequered suit, trying to get the asses to move his carriage.'

With Ben beside her, their arms tingled as they touched. 'But I had to be back at work by four,' she went on. 'They had a party that evening. Right jovial lot they were. But I was tired. So much to do.'

Emma, fetch the Claret... Cigars... Draw the curtains.

'And all of those dishes to wash.' Emma turned to Susan and asked, 'Do you think they will celebrate the arrival of spring in Australia?'

'I doubt it,' Susan replied.

'It's my mother I miss already,' said Emma. 'You just don't think you'll miss your mother. I only saw her every three weeks...'

The ladies nodded and helped themselves to another of Mrs Bice's sweet treats. Emma grinned as she munched. 'Mmm. This journey might be bearable after all. Parties on deck. Food with friends below. Better than rising every day before the sun and emptying the slops.' There would be no more tears, either, she vowed to herself. She was a grownup now.

Ben, who was standing with Samuel Bice, near their wives, discussed the matter of celebrating the feast days in South Australia.

'I think they might,' Ben argued. 'There are a lot of Cornish out there. And the Irish, they're a merry lot. We must remember... What is it? March seventeenth?'

John Vicary, senior, squinted at Ben. 'I doubt all your countrymen would agree. Feelings between the Irish and English go deep.'

Ben grinned. 'But I saw Englishmen drinking stout too.'

'That's different.' Mr Vicary nodded, tapping his nose.

It had been a perfect day, but, by nightfall, the wind was up with a vengeance, the ship lurched violently, and the hatch was to be closed. Ben and Emma struggled onto their bunk, and, while sharing the one bowl, they both vomited.

'Listen to those poor babies,' Emma said, wondering if her stomach was empty yet, 'there must be at least thirty of them screaming. It breaks my heart.' She lay back, her elbow over her eyes. 'And with no lamps, how are we going to find the water closets?'

She padded herself with old sheeting material, and after some deep thought, handed a piece to Ben. He was mortified and prayed it would only be soaked with urine.

Thus, it was that they endured one of the worst nights of their lives.

The next morning, Ben praised the Lord for the men's saltwater shower on deck. He returned with a bucket of saltwater for Emma, and she gratefully washed in it.

They forced themselves to sit at the table, nodding with a faint 'good morning' to all. Ben liked the oatmeal. It gave him the strength to help Emma, who accepted only a spoonful.

She groaned quietly, 'It's only been two days. How will we bear this, for months, and months...'

Ben handed Emma a handkerchief. 'It's calmer this morning,' he said, smoothing her hair. 'And Kimbly said there will be times when the sea is as smooth as glass, for days on end.'

'It's difficult to imagine, with everything tilting every which way.'

Ben took her arm. 'I really need some fresh air.'

They battled their way above deck to join Mr and Mrs Vicary at the rail.

Mr Vicary, shading his eyes, pointed to the horizon. 'Look,' he said, 'it's a steam ship.'

'How can you tell?' asked Emma.

'It has one sail and two black funnels.'

'I think you're right,' said Ben, peering out under his own hand.

'They go twice as fast as we do,' said Mr Vicary, wistfully.'

Emma could barely see the two small plumes of black smoke. 'Twice as fast? Why aren't we on one of them?'

'Hardly any go to Australia,' said Mr Vicary. 'It's too expensive just for migrants.'

Emma clenched her fists. It was so unjust. When they'd eased away from the Vicarys, she turned to Ben and asked him, 'Why would we spend a day longer at sea than necessary?' Emma wiped the drip hanging from her nose. 'We could die in one of those storms.' Fortuitously for Ben, the midday dinner bell clanged, and he was already nudging her toward the smell of a tasty mutton stew that wafted up from below deck. Emma planted her feet. 'No. Answer me, Ben.' But he had no answers. If only he had asked, Emma thought. He had gone to the meetings. And it was probably in that little book, *The Emigrant's Friend*. She turned away from him. 'I can't believe it. We could be there in six weeks instead of three months. It doesn't bear thinking about.'

In the evening, when the gales returned, Kimbly again rang his bell. 'Prepare yourselves for a real storm tonight; anchor everything and tuck your children in firmly.' He withdrew and bolted the hatch.

'A real storm! What was that last night?' Emma sputtered. 'I can't trust anybody to tell me the truth.'

Ben bit his lip, regretting ever leaving home. He lay tense as the howling wind increased. A loud crack caused Emma to scream. Ben reached out for her.

'Leave me alone,' she shrieked.

After several rolling thunderclaps, Ben began to tremble. When the first enormous wave thumped the hull, the entire cabin of men, women and children screamed.

Emma turned to him. 'It's all your fault.' She looked fierce with her hair and nightrobe in disarray.

'Emma – I never imagined – I'm sorry.'

Riding high on the crest of a wave, the *Eastern Empire* dipped sharply, and two or three people fell from their beds. Ben watched them roll from one side of the deck to the other, screaming amongst the pots, pans, and pickles.

Emma rose herself immediately. 'Somebody will be hurt,' she said.

'Emma, stop...' Ben watched her climb down and stand steady, amazed she was able to move at all. 'Be careful.'

'Are you all right, Mrs Bice?' asked Emma.

'My husband is helping that poor mother; she has three little ones,' answered Mrs Bice. 'I'm so cold, Emma, can you pull my...'

Emma had found Mrs Bice's rug lying in a dirty puddle. Susan Hore quickly handed Emma a spare rug, and, while fighting against the ship's stagger, Emma laid it over Mrs Bice and moved over to help her husband.

'Emma,' said Mr Bice, looking relieved to have found another hand. 'Help me get this young lady back to her bed?'

'Yes, of course,' said Emma, not allowing the ship another moment to test them.

They quickly had the mother back into her bunk, and Emma was left to make her way back to Ben. She clawed herself up the ladder and onto the bed, exhausted. Enough heroics for this night, she thought. Ben was gone. He'd gotten himself up at some point and cleared some of the rubble, pushing it under the nearest bunk. When he'd shortly returned, Emma gave him a fiery look.

'William didn't tell us it was going to be like this,' she said, 'Wait until I see him!'

They drifted in and out of sleep. In the early morning, Ben vaguely remembered Kimbly and the surgeon helping those who had fallen. He had relaxed when he saw the surgeon. He felt safer.

However, sometime later, the storm resumed, and continued on until Ben and Emma were watching torrents of water pour around the coaming of the hatchway. Emma was right. They were going to die.

'What's happening?' Emma cried out, as seawater soaked everything on the floor.

Ben groaned and began to pray. 'Our father which art in heaven…' Mopping his eyes, Ben waited for the sea to take them. He had never cried in front of Emma before, and he tried to hide his face from her. He listened for what seemed an hour, until the sea calmed.

The between-decks cabin had taken in gallons of water. There would be no bailing down here with their small basins; there was nowhere to throw the water, and the bowls near the lower bunks were floating with vomit anyway.

He peered over the edge of the bunk. 'Emma, I think the water is running away through the cracks – into the hold, maybe.'

'But what about the next wave?' Emma insisted. 'It's past breakfast time, and the children are hungry, of course.'

They put their pillows on their ears and dozed lightly, until the seamen finally opened the hatch and began to clean the cabin. They used giant towels to mop their deck, and, although it was still damp, the slipping hazard was much reduced.

Matron and her two assistants arrived and administered a powdery white mixture to the ailing.

The surgeon, his face pale and taut, called for attention. His dark-blue, double-breasted jacket was crumpled. He checked the fastenings for two of his sixteen gold buttons. 'The storm is passed,' he said. 'You are perfectly safe.'

Ben looked at Emma. 'That's reassuring.'

'How can you believe him?' she countered. 'Look at him. He's as white-faced as you are.'

They were offered magnesium-carbonate, and gin. Several passengers, including Amelia, were assisted to the hospital.

For breakfast, the families were offered only bread or cold oatmeal, after which the few able captains removed the dishes.

The seamen left and battened down the hatch. The noise and smell were unbearable. Ben desperately wanted to get out of there and walk. He prayed for daylight and fresh air. But all he had was the foul odour of the swinging, flickering tar lamp. His head throbbed and ached.

Once the hatch was opened again, Emma, flushed and exhausted, slept. Ben pulled heavily on the top post and swung himself down. He joined a small crowd of men on deck.

Mr Vicary was talking to a sailor. When the seaman returned to his post, Mr Vicary turned to Ben.

'The seaman says we were caught on the edge of the Bay of Biscay, the biggest cove of them all. He says there is no land mass between here and America, and by the time a good storm rolls all the way from there, the waves have become gigantic. Well, you felt them for yourself.'

'Are any more of those bays coming up?' Ben asked.

'He said no.'

'That's a relief,' said a stranger.

Ben nodded at the man who joined them.

'Charles Marsden,' the fair-headed stranger said. 'I'm from Stalybridge, near Cheshire.' He shook Ben's hand.

'You a miner, too?' Ben asked.

'No, I'm a weaver from the manufactories. There's eighty-one of us on board. One shipment has already gone. We're all from the North. Cheshire.'

Ben heard there was plenty of work in factories. In fact, his father had suggested he seek employment there, instead of 'going to the other end of the earth.'

'Why are you leaving?' Ben asked Marsden.

'We refused to weave cotton picked by slaves. We even wrote to the President to share our support.'

Ben stared, overwhelmed. 'You wrote to President Lincoln? You've no jobs; that was mighty noble of you.'

'He wrote back, too. Said our actions were *an instance of sublime heroism.*'

'As indeed they were,' said Ben. Ben tried to click his heels to the man, but his ill-fitting old boots didn't click.

Marsden bowed, 'But we are all in debt. Rev Hoare raised money through the church – for our fares, new clothes, and a Bible. And we all have jobs promised out there. We hope to repay our debts.'

'Of course,' Ben said.

Marsden continued, 'And there are no slaves, or convicts in South Australia. We're happy with that. Well, I must go, I've had hardly any sleep and I have two babies waiting for attention down below.'

When Ben returned to the cabin, he told Emma about the weaver and his two babies. 'They had no choice really, and it must be difficult with two little ones under two.'

Emma forced herself to be civil. 'Susan told me that mothers had to bring enough diapers for the whole journey. Mostly, they are old sheets and cut up towels. Even at one diaper a day, that means, what – ninety for three months? For your weaver, that's nearly two hundred. Susan's bunk is overloaded with stuff.'

'Where do they dry them?' Ben asked.

'They don't,' Emma said wrinkling her nose. 'They don't wash them either. They are to throw the fouled ones overboard, when the hatch is open of course. If they try to re-use them, they could spread dysentery.'

'That's terrible,' said Ben.

It didn't bode well for the newlyweds when the surgeon called an emergency muster on March 19.

'It is my sad duty to report,' the surgeon said, 'that we lost a seaman early this morning. He was washed overboard. He was a Swede, named Henry Thomson, twenty-six-years of age. We put out a lifeboat, with four others, but they saw nothing of him.

'Now, let us pray. Bless those who mourn, eternal God, with the comfort of your love, that they may face each new day with hope and certainty.'

Later, when they were sitting on deck, Ben moved closer to Emma, but she turned away from him. 'If the seamen aren't safe, what hope have we?' she said.

'The seamen are out in the weather, Em. The surgeon said we are perfectly safe if we follow orders.'

Emma shook her head. 'How can he be so sure? People were rolling on the floor. Mr Temby broke his leg, and his nose.'

'It's true,' Ben said. 'Let's thank the Lord for our safety, and pray for good weather.'

'That won't happen overnight,' Emma snapped.

Remarkably, the following day dawned with the sea flat, and the sky a perfect cornflower blue. While Ben firmly believed the Lord watched over them, he was more than surprised that He had acted so quickly.

But as Ben looked at the horizon, left and right, he paled at what he saw. Nothing but water. Deep blue sea wallowed around him in every direction, to the very edges of the earth. So much water, such a small ship.

If anything happened to the *Eastern Empire* – and there was plenty of evidence that it might – the few lifeboats would not fit all the passengers.

'Water. Nothing but water,' Ben said, sweeping his hands around him.

Emma gaped. 'You are right. How does the captain even know where he is? We could get lost.'

It was time for the Sunday church service, and the migrants began to swarm onto the deck.

The Reverend Mr Lionel William Stanton walked serenely to his pulpit, which was a Union Jack tied to the railing of the poop deck. The reverends were accustomed to large congregations. His father, also named the Reverend L W Stanton, had taught his son well over the years. The master of the ship knew he was lucky to have such a well-qualified man on the journey.

'The Lord hath spoken!' Stanton boomed, raising his fist. Now he raised both hands. 'Come ye and repent!' He turned to his left and his right. 'Let us pray.' He steepled his hands and the passengers knelt.

> Our Father which art in heaven,
> Hallowed be thy name ...
> Thy kingdom come ...

The passengers' voices rose in unison. Ben wondered what his family would think of them communing with Catholics and Presbyterians.

17

It was hard to believe it was only eight days since that unnerving day when they last saw their family and boarded the steam packet at Gweek.

The clergyman lifted his Bible from the deck, and opened the ribbon bookmark.

'Today's reading is from Proverbs, Chapter Twenty.'

> *Wine is a mocker, strong drink is raging:*
> *and whosoever is deceived is not wise …*

He closed the Bible and waved it. 'This is the word of God. There are those who say drink is not above the law. I don't give tuppence for the law; the evils of drink are clearly evident. We were sailing but one day, and ye succumbed.

'If we deny God by our own desire…we allow sin to destroy our faith…'

Ben frowned. For the first time in his life he did not accept the clerical criticism. He knew he wasn't perfect, but he wasn't a drinking man, and as far as he was concerned both the stout and gin were necessary for his health.

After the prayer, the migrants sang lustily, William Whiting's new hymn 'Travellers by the Sea.'

> *Eternal Father, strong to save…*
> *… O hear us when we cry to thee*
> *For those in peril on the sea.*

Emma, stirred by the powerful hymn and its lyrics, was comforted. God was listening; He knew of their fears. Australia was a destination as distant and unfathomable as the ocean. She must have faith. And the Christian thing to do would be to forgive Ben.

After the service, Emma recognised a friend from Constantine. She rushed toward her, a fair-haired woman who was just eighteen. They both squealed and hugged. Ben joined them.

'Grace Retallick, of Trenarth,' said Emma, teary-eyed. She held Grace at arms-length. 'I can't believe it is you.'

'I haven't seen you since you left Sabbath School,' Grace said, laughing.

'Oh, Grace, isn't this terrible – those storms. I wish I was back home. But what are you doing here?'

Grace took Emma's arm, and they sat on the deck.

Ben joined a group of Cornishmen gathered beside a lifeboat, wisps of smoke issuing from their pipes.

Mr Bice was speaking. 'I was eight years old when I first worked in my father's silver-lead mine. But we had to close it. It got too deep. However, God has been good to us. The mine managers are crying out for Cornish miners at this new mine at Moonta, in South Australia. At Moonta, the copper is just below the surface.'

Ben raised his eyebrows. A mine agent's son was emigrating? This new colony was promising the moon and stars to everyone.

'My brother Henry works there,' Samuel Bice continued. 'Captain Warmington sent for us.'

'I couldn't bear to be a miner,' Walter Sims interjected. He was a carter from Plymouth, and his remark brought a silence. Ben stared at Sims. No doubt the man thought he was above everyone else because he had a trade. Well, this time he was outnumbered; most of the Cornishmen were miners.

Mr Bice, frowning at Sims, turned to Ben. "By the way, are you related to Benjamin Bowden in Bodmin?'

'I'm not sure,' said Ben. 'Benjamin Bowdens are everywhere. I'm the sixth successive Benjamin in our line. And I've, what? Two uncles and six cousins, just in Constantine, all farmers.'

'Ever thought of mining to set you up?' asked Mr Bice.

'I've no experience,' Ben admitted.

'You can dig a hole I presume?' Danny Rowe said.

The men chuckled.

Ben explained about Emma's brother, William, and Ben's promised job, working on a fruit farm in Adelaide.

Mr Bice nodded. 'Knowing someone there makes all the difference. We wouldn't be going if Henry wasn't there. And Danny's father is also out there – and an uncle of Charlie Pryor.'

Ben was encouraged as he re-joined Emma. 'The men were talking about mining,' he told her. They say the mines in Moonta are much safer, and you have to admit, Mr Bice looks perfectly well after thirty-four years of mining. If farming doesn't work out, I might try it. Unlike farmers, miners can get rich overnight.'

Emma rolled her eyes. 'Mining is dangerous, Ben, everyone knows that.'

Emma repeated her mantra over breakfast the next day, Sarah Murley, who had until then kept to herself, began glaring at Emma. 'The Moonta mines have excellent safety records,' she said to Emma.

'My uncles are the mine managers.'

'Your uncles?' asked Mrs Bice. 'There are two managers?'

'Uncle William is at Moonta and Uncle Eneder at Wallaroo,' Mrs Murley preened.

The group went quiet. They hadn't known she was related to the mine managers and couldn't remember what they'd said in her presence. The miners withdrew, while their wives gathered around to question Mrs Murley.

Ben tuned out. He finished his cup of tea and took out a ship's biscuit. They were rock hard. 'Looks like bread baked a dozen times,' he said to Emma, tapping it on the table.

'Let me show you.' Emma drizzled the biscuit with a slick of molasses and dipped it into her tea. 'Perfect,' she mumbled.

The surgeon arrived, snapped his heels, and looked down at the migrants.

'I shouldn't have to remind you; you are supposed to be on deck in fine weather.' He waved his hands. 'Come on. Out, out!'

They hurried up the steps. Amelia, who was with child, and suffering from a serious case of seasickness, was weak and needed to be carried. The doctor was right, Emma thought, it did cheer Amelia, who smiled when she saw flying fish, small, slender, strange-winged creatures, landing on the deck.

When Matron appeared, Emma expected more trouble. But the woman gave them a linen bag full of fabrics.

'These have been donated by the British Women's Emigration Association,' she said. 'In the tin are needles, thread, and half a gross of thimbles. I'll leave it in your capable hands, Mrs Bice.'

'Free!' Susan, Mary Ann, Emma, and the others chorused as they swarmed around.

Emma dove into the fabrics and chose a soft white remnant for Amelia's expected baby, and they all set-to, stitching, mending, and embroidering. But when Amelia put a needle to the fabric, she started vomiting, and required assistance back to bed.

The following morning, Emma noticed James talking heatedly to his mother. 'That doctor's a monster,' he said. 'He agrees Amelia must rest, but I'm not allowed to sit with her for more than an hour.'

'That doesn't sound right dear,' said Mrs Vicary.

'He says I must be in the fresh air as much as possible, or I too could fall ill.' James ran a hand through his hair. 'I can't leave her all alone.'

'I'll sit with her for an hour,' said Susan.

'And me,' Emma said, as did Mary Ann.

'That's wonderful,' said Mrs Bice. 'Look, why don't I make a roster? We always cared for our own in Cornwall…'

James looked at them gratefully.

The surgeon refused at first, but faced by the staunch Cornishwomen, he acquiesced.

Emma, sitting with the sleeping Amelia, tried to copy words from the Bible:

In the beginning God created…

She wrote, but the constant movement of the ship sent her hand skidding across the page. She would never do it, she scolded herself, and began to feel nauseous.

When Mrs Vicary took over sitting with Amelia, Emma climbed onto her bunk and fell asleep.

At the next meal, Emma pushed her food around its plate. Ben was certain she was spending too much time with Amelia when she should be up in the fresh sea air. But with Amelia so unwell, Emma was still edgy, and he dared not suggest she abandon her friend.

3. Warmer Climes

The air was warm on 24 March as the ship passed the north of Africa. The emigrants had been eight long days at sea, and it was twelve days since Emma and Ben left home. They still had a long way to go, but at least the cold weather was behind them. The seamen told Ben it would become much hotter, but he couldn't imagine it.

Up on the deck early, Ben and Emma moved to the starboard side of the 165 foot sailing ship. They had seen some of the Cheshire weavers pointing out to sea. Ben saw the Marsden man, who was holding his toddler Agnes, indicating a large school of shiny fish, which were leaping gracefully in and out of the water.

'Porpoises,' Marsden said, smiling, as the little girl excitedly waved her hand.

'That's the weaver I was telling you about,' Ben said.

'He is so lovely with his little girl,' Emma said.

The crowd cheered, and Emma watched the leaping fish with glee. 'There are so many of them.' More porpoises broke the water, some exposing their white underbelly before diving again. And another school of fish further out continued the display.

Mary Ann Vicary joined Emma and said, 'We are so lucky to see them.'

After their midday meal, Emma's childhood friend, Grace, sought Emma out on deck.

'Did you hear the ruckus last night?' Grace said.

'The what?' Emma asked.

'The noise, in our cabin. The fights were something terrible.'

Emma shook her head. 'Our place is noisy; I didn't hear anything different.'

Grace leaned closer. 'The older girls started teasing the youngsters. Matron went at them with a brush, but there are so many – and some of those older girls are in their twenties – been on the street for years. Then the Irish started.

'...but those poor young girls. Some are only fourteen, and they're not allowed to see their mothers for more than fifteen minutes a week.'

'Fifteen minutes?' said Emma. 'That's not fair, and surely it's unnecessary.'

Grace threw up her hands. 'Who knows? The surgeon says they will get too used to seeing their family, and then they'll be even more upset. But that's not how I see it. The man obviously has no children.'

'My poor baby,' Mrs Temby said, 'would you keep an eye on Elizabeth, Grace? If she saw a friendly face…'

Grace smiled. 'Of course, I will. She's a sweet girl.'

With the calmer seas, and warmer air, Emma was encouraged with the cleaner, dryer cabin. At last, it was becoming bearable, she thought, apart from the almost permanently clogged water closets. If the ship stopped rocking altogether it might have been perfect.

Ben was pleased to see Emma looking better, and that she was out in the fresh air for most of the day. Surely, the seasickness would pass now.

However, Emma started retching again the following morning, and Ben snapped. 'The sea is calm, and you were on deck all day yesterday. Let's go see that surgeon. There must be something he can do.'

Dr Baker-Brown didn't take long and soon called Ben in. 'Your wife is with child, young man. Congratulations.'

Emma beamed at Ben. She felt warm inside. She had of course thought of the possibility, before the storms took over her life. She remembered her mother with her brothers and sisters. Each new baby had been a miracle. And she had dreamed of the day when she would have children of her own.

Ben shook the doctor's hand. He was going to be a father. His whole life would change. And the baby would bind him even more firmly to Emma.

Emma ran her hand over her belly. 'Keep well, little one,' she whispered.

'Don't forget the medical comforts, Mrs Bowden,' the doctor said.

'Comforts?' Ben asked.

'I can have extras,' said Emma as the two departed, 'such as scotch barley, sago, and one egg a day. He says I must eat every day, no matter what.'

Ben took Emma's arm, assisting her up the steps. He wasn't going to let her out of his sight.

When Emma tucked into a dish of steaming sago that evening, Susan Hore guessed its significance and whispered to Emma, 'Can I tell the others?'

Emma blushed.

'Tell us what?' said Mary Ann Vicary.

'Shush,' said Emma. But by lights out everyone knew, and Emma and Ben were thoroughly congratulated.

Ben lay with his hands clasped under his head. 'It was a difficult decision, leaving as we did,' he said. 'But I'm glad now, off to a new country where our child will have a better future. I'll earn a real wage, we will eat well, in a new country, where there is plenty of sunshine.'

Two days later, the ship's bell rang repeatedly. There was to be an immediate assembly.

On deck, the surgeon demanded quiet and made the announcement. 'We have a medical emergency. A nine-year-old boy from Cheshire, by the name of William Standring, has contracted Scarlatina. He is washed, his clothes destroyed, and he is isolated, but you must be vigilant, further outbreaks will occur.'

Ben grimaced as his eyes met Emma's. Several migrants began to whisper.

The surgeon raised his hands. 'Please listen carefully. It is of utmost importance that you wash yourselves, your bedding, and the deck as often as possible; the weekly wash will not suffice. I repeat. The weekly wash will not suffice. More buckets will be made available. You may go now. Matron Newberry and Constables Gale and Kimbly will answer your questions.'

'So much for a better future,' Emma cried. 'Ma says that scarlet thing is deadly. What about our baby?'

Ben's heart thumped. If anything happened to Emma, or their child, he would never forgive himself. Ben took Emma's hand, but she wrested it free and fled down the steps.

Susan Hore had been observing them. When Emma ran, she approached Ben and said, 'Motherhood makes us worry a lot. Sometimes we cry, and we just cannot be comforted.'

Ben looked out over the water.

She patted his shoulder. 'I hope you don't mind, me saying so.'

'No. No. Thank you. I'm very grateful. Will you... Would you talk to her – for me?'

Ben often wondered how he would have managed without Susan Hore.

Within a week there was another case of Scarlatina.

Emma worried about the Standring family, but she only saw Margaret Standring twice in the following weeks. And each time the woman was rushed and tearful.

'Don't get too close,' Margaret said as Emma reached out to her.

Emma stopped and let her arm drop. Was she about to deny the woman friendship as well?

'Is he any better?' Emma asked. Her heart ached as Margaret screwed up her face and blinked away the tears.

'His throat is so sore. He can barely swallow...'

Emma felt her eyes fill and turned away.

'Why am I crying?' Emma said to Elizabeth Bice. 'Ben will wonder what's wrong.'

'I was often teary when I was with child,' said Mrs Bice. 'Sam used to worry. My eyes just leaked every time someone sympathised. And you won't believe this, sometimes I even cried when I heard about a kindness! As far as the Scarletina is concerned, we are in good hands. The good news is – if there is any – is that the surgeon seems to be handling this outbreak quite well. Surgeons on ships have been keeping records for some years now, and each one documents in full, how sickness on ships can be better managed. I was impressed with his sensible instructions. I thought nothing could be done, until I heard him speak.'

'Will it really help if we wash everything more?'

'I believe so,' said Mrs Bice. 'The captain told us the number of sick people is surprisingly small so far.'

Emma's shoulders relaxed. Maybe, just maybe, everyone would be all right.

Ben was busied with the buckets and had winched up yet another of salt water. He began rubbing the clothes vigorously with soap.

'No, Ben,' Emma said. 'It's soap once, and rinse twice, not the other way round.'

'Two washes must be better than one,' he protested.

'You're probably right, but the truth is we'll run out of soap.' Emma kneeled beside him and took his hand. 'But you are a good man,' she added, seeing the hurt in his eyes.

John Vicary, senior, pushed his way around the lines full of sheets 'The deck is more like a gypsy camp these days,' he said, scowling.

Fully aware of the family's grief over Amelia's continued ill health, Emma simply nodded in agreement. She had been shocked when she last saw Amelia, so thin and helpless, her lips dried and cracked. Emma couldn't help but wonder if her baby should survive the illness.

Of course, it will, she chided herself, it was only seasickness.

On April 10, twenty-five days after departing Plymouth, the *Eastern Empire* slowed to a complete stop.

'Why aren't we moving?' Emma asked Ben, repeatedly mopping her brow, uncomfortable in her wool twill frock.

'There's no wind,' Ben said. 'They warned it would happen. Danny says it's called the Doldrums. Hopefully we won't be here long.'

'But if there's no wind, how will the ship move?'

'The wind just comes and goes,' Ben said, finishing his breakfast. Emma had only eaten a few mouthfuls. 'Are you finished?' he asked.

'The day is already too hot,' said Emma. 'And the smell of the water closets is vile. I don't know how you can stand it.' Emma found it almost impossible to eat a full meal. Would she become like Amelia?

She became light-headed. So often, she just wanted to lie on her bed. But she dared not. She knew the surgeon would oust her.

If only they would arrive in Australia. How little she had appreciated her modest life in Cornwall.

Ben and Emma attended the usual church service on Sunday. Emma thought it seemed extra-long in the extreme heat, and after the last prayer she stood, ready to go.

'Attention, please, stay where you are,' the surgeon said, replacing the clergyman at the makeshift pulpit. 'There is now an emergency muster. Quiet, please.'

Emma gazed at the loosely hanging sails. The lack of movement of the ship was unbearable.

The surgeon looked right and left, cleared his throat, and began by saying, 'It is my sad duty to report the death of young William Standring of Cheshire.'

Emma tasted bile at the back of her throat.

Ben supported Emma heavily, as she trembled and cried, on the crowded deck during the service. It was a funeral like no other. No one would visit the watery grave of this much-loved child.

It was an inhuman ask.

The Reverend Stanton read from Deuteronomy:

> *The eternal God is thy refuge, and underneath are the ever-lasting arms.*
> *He will drive out your enemies before you…*

After a hymn and the Benediction, the crowd milled back to their cabins.

Safely back in bed, Emma tried to talk away her sadness. 'That poor little body, splashing into the sea. I will never forget the shrieking of those poor women. How does one live on through such misery? Poor Margaret and Thomas, leaving their wee son thousands of miles from nowhere. Oh, when will this cursed ship *move*?'

Ben was forever regretting the voyage. What a fool he was to be risking their life and limb!

But he *had* thought about it, with great care, and for many months. He remembered sneaking off to emigration meetings. Determined to get it right, he had taken notes as Mr Jones read facts from his various books and letters. Ben even paid for a copy of *The Emigrants Friend*.

The emigration agent, Mr Jones, had been in no doubt when telling them that South Australia was far more promising than any other migrant destination. 'In Adelaide, unlike the convict states,' Jones had said, 'they have introduced a brilliant new plan. They take no convicts, and instead of giving land to ex-convicts or free settlers, they sell it to British investors. The money thus raised builds the new colony, and subsidises the fares of upstanding, diligent migrants. And jobs are waiting for us to work the land.'

Ben remembered reading William's letter.

'Thousands of migrants have made the journey safely,' he had written. 'Even convicts for New South Wales arrived safely. And, of course, so did me and Eliza.'

William had also assured Ben that the architect of this new colony, Mr Edward Gibbon Wakefield was a clever man with a vision. 'He has thought of everything, and most importantly, he wants us to succeed.'

William's words had stayed somewhere deep within him, and he needed to remember them now.

When Emma was rested, Ben encouraged her to return to the deck.

They looked out at the smooth sea that glittered in the sunshine. Angry voices broke their reverie.

Emma looked around. 'What's that noise?'

She clung to Ben's arm when she saw two men, with knees bent, circling each other. The taller blond male swung at the small ginger haired man and missed. Several of the onlookers jeered, others laughed, until they saw the surgeon, who was marching toward them.

Emma tensed. 'Let's go,' she whispered.

'Stay right where you are everybody!' the surgeon boomed. 'This behaviour will not be tolerated.'

The surgeon gestured toward the two men. 'Tie them up,' he said to two constables, 'and, lock them in the hold for a week. Any more infringements and you will be South Australia's first convicts.'

Emma watched as the surgeon perused his list.

'From now on, I will publicly announce all infringements,' the surgeon said, reading the notice with relish. 'For talking to women and playing cards on Sunday, Paddy Ryan and Mick Howe, your sugar and meat are stopped for a week.' There was a groan from the young men. The surgeon read out the names of several more offenders.

Ben sympathised. Many of the men were older than him, and there were dozens of lovely girls on display every Sunday – and at every muster. Three whole months! What was the harm in talking to them?

Charlie Bennett, from Cornwall, had passed notes through Ben and on to Elizabeth Bice. Elizabeth had agreed to marry Charlie.

Emma gritted her teeth when Ben told her about the note. 'The surgeon will have you in the hold, Ben. Then where will all our plans go? With you in prison, what would I do?' Emma began to cry.

'Not so loudly, dear,' Ben said, leading her away. 'Please, I won't do it again.'

'It might already be too late,' Emma protested. 'As if it's not bad enough on this floating piece of junk, with crazy people, fevers, and death.'

When Grace appeared on deck again, Emma hugged her. 'Grace, Gracie, where have you been?'

'We were locked up. The fighting's been terrible. I suppose the heat, and the fact that we're not moving, it's driving them mad.' Grace beckoned to a pretty Cornish girl with long auburn hair tied at the back of her neck. 'This is Mary Gartrell. I was telling Mr and Mrs Bowden about the trouble in the cabin.'

'I'm surprised you didn't hear us,' Mary said. 'Some of the Irish and English can't abide one another. Last week it was scratching and hair pulling, and one of the girls put the hose on them. Matron was raging. The place was soaked. And she reported them to the surgeon.'

'No one got pudding that weekend,' Grace added. 'But on Friday, poor little Betty was caught in a fight and got pushed against a bedpost. You should have seen the blood, all over her face, from a cut on her eyebrow. They were pretty heated by then, and I must say it looked terrible.'

'Mary and I took Betty up to see the surgeon, and we said we weren't taking any more nonsense; we wanted the matron to go.'

'Don't you need a matron?' Emma asked in disbelief.

'We do,' Grace said. 'But not her. He appointed new ones. He had to. A young English matron for us, and a young Irish one for them. But the surgeon is furious. I heard him tell the matron it never happened before, and now he has a discipline problem.'

'He has a problem all right,' Mary said.

'Mary shush,' Grace said, looking around.

'It's such a relief,' Mary said more quietly. 'We left home to get away from the likes of Matron Newberry. She reminds me of that harridan at Rose Manor who fed us potatoes and point.'

'Potatoes and what?' asked Ben.

'You know, point your potato at the herring and hope the potato tastes better.'

'You jest,' said Ben, gaping.

Grace shook her head. 'No, she's right.'

The ship remained motionless for several more days, and the clergyman arranged for the passengers' boxes to be winched from the hold.

The emigrants, excited at first, gasped at the sight of black and mouldy bread.

'Of course,' William Temby said to Ben. 'It got wet when the wave went over us.'

Ben, with his arm around Emma, waited for his box, silently praying the damage wasn't widespread.

As boxes were opened, Ben saw the dismay on several faces as they discovered a bottle of sauce or pickles had leaked onto their belongings. William had warned Ben and Emma about this in the only letter Ben received, seven months after William's departure.

'Here it is,' Ben said, moving toward the shiny chest his uncle had gifted them.

'The timing is perfect,' said Emma, kneeling beside the box. 'It feels like Christmas. New shirts for you, and print dresses...' Emma delved to the bottom of the chest, discovering small gifts: embroidered handkerchiefs, a table doily, and a pencil drawing by her youngest sister, Jane. She wondered how long the drawing would last; it had already faded, like Emma's memories.

Reluctantly, Emma relinquished her treasure trove, and the boxes were returned to the hold. But when she first slipped on one of her two new summer print frocks, she grinned, running her hand down the fabric. 'Compared to that heavy wool, it's like silk to touch.'

Emma was soon on deck beside Ben, fanning herself in the midday sun. 'When, oh when, will the breeze return?'

'A new breeze would set me right,' Ben agreed.

Emma smiled. 'But I'm happy watching the seamen fishing. Look at that fish, Ben, it's almost as tall as he is.'

'It will be tastier than our dried meat too,' Ben said. 'Pity the ham is finished.' He watched enviously as the seamen took lifeboats out and swam in the dark blue sea, sending ripples in their wake. It looked wonderfully cool out there. 'If only I could swim.'

They pulled a bucket of salt water and Emma swished her feet in it while Ben pulled another for himself. 'I think I'll sleep like this,' Emma said.

'There's no need,' Mrs Bice said, as she and Mary Ann Vicary settled nearer. 'I just heard. They are putting up a closeted saltwater shower for us.'

'About time,' said Mary Ann, 'the men have one. At last, they have noticed there are women on board.'

'Mary, you remind me of my sister, Elizabeth,' Emma said. 'She would have said that about women, too. She was clever. She went to Sunday School for many years. I only went for a bit over a year. It wasn't fair really. Don't tell anyone. People knowing is almost worse than being so, but I do feel stupid, not being able to read and write.'

Mary Ann knitted her eyebrows. 'You're not the only one on board – but why didn't you go to Sunday School?'

'Mama had twelve babies, some quite close together. I was in the middle. Too young for this, and too old for that.'

Mary Ann laughed. 'I know the feeling.'

'When I was nine,' Emma continued, 'Mary, Kitty and Elizabeth, my older sisters, had been to Sunday school, then they went to work in the big houses. William and John had also been to Sunday School, before they helped Da run the farm.'

'And you didn't go again?' Mary Ann asked.

'They said I had plenty of time.' Emma's bottom lip trembled. She counted on her fingers. 'Even Charles and George went; they were only six and seven. By then, Ma was nearly fifty, and she said I was a great help with the babies. And I did love them. Little Emily was gorgeous. She used to call me Mama.' Emma looked over at the Marsden baby.

'I went to work at Tyacke's when I was thirteen, and after that our Caroline and Henry went to the English School. And when Emily and Jane were old enough, they went too. But never me. Not after that one year.'

'You are right, that wasn't fair,' Mary Ann said. 'We won't do that, will we Emma? Have lots of children, and not educate them? Not in Australia.'

Emma's eyes shone. 'That's right. Everyone says dissenters are welcome in Australia. And they have chapels and Sunday Schools everywhere. And if I learn to read and write on the voyage, no one will know, will they? I'm only nineteen.'

'I'll help you if you like,' Mary Ann said.

Emma smiled gratefully and hummed her way back to the cabin for her book and pencil.

The following morning, Ben and James were on deck early. 'Maybe there'll be a breeze today,' Ben said, looking up, hopefully. But, although they had drifted southwards, there was no wind.

Ben was suddenly drenched with water. 'What...' he said. 'Is it raining?' He looked up and heard laughter from midway up the mainsail. He moved quickly as another bucket of water headed their way.

James wiped his face. 'So, this is what Sam meant. He said there would be a bizarre ceremony when we crossed the Equator.'

'William said something about that,' Ben said.

Ben watched as water cascaded onto countless other passengers.

'I'd better go and warn Emma,' Ben said. But he was too late, and the bevy of women squealed when the seamen continued with their fun.

After dinner, a red clad King Neptune arrived. 'Ahaarrgh!' he roared, brandishing a three-pronged fork.

Then he turned a hose on the crowd. 'Oh no,' cried Emma, burrowing closer to Ben.

But her squeals turned to laughter when she felt cool at last.

When they went below for supper, sitting in the crowded steamy space, perspiration again poured from their brows, Ben and Emma mopped their faces. They ate quickly.

'Let's go back up,' Ben said. 'This is stifling.'

Several passengers, including Ben and Emma returned to the cool of the deck each evening, and slept there. They watched the sunrises and sunsets, the blood red sun rising and sinking below the horizon.

Ben unbuttoned his waistcoat, sat up and removed it. 'You're taking that off, too?' Emma asked, eyebrows raised. Ben grinned, lay down, and pulled Emma closer.

By April 17, the ship had made little progress, as another day of unbearable heat dawned. An extra-large canvas shade was erected for the church service, and, although the men wore lighter pants and shirts, and the women light prints and muslin ducks, their clothes were stained with sweat, and their cheeks still glistened under their hats.

With no waves in the sea, the discarded sewage, food scraps, soiled diapers, and ruined clothing were visible to all, as it floated and festered beside them. Emma dry-retched when she saw the mess. She longed to return to her bed.

In his sermon, Rev Stanton told the weary passengers that the trials and hardships emigrants underwent on these journeys were similar to those of a Christian passing through life. Suddenly the surgeon-superintendent laughed out loud, startling the congregation.

Ben, mopping his face, asked John Vicary, 'Did he just laugh at the clergyman?'

'Appalling behaviour,' John said.

Ben splayed his hands when he caught Danny Rowe's stare of disapproval.

The Reverend Stanton glowered at the surgeon, realised he should continue, and gradually recovered his composure. But the migrants were provoked and restless. The clergyman led the migrants in another hymn and prayer and released them all early. Dispersed, the emigrants discussed the matter in every quarter of the ship.

'I'm befuddled,' Danny said to Mr Vicary. 'After him being so strict with everyone. What a nerve.'

Mr Vicary nodded. 'I think it's because our surgeon isn't a religious man, and he probably expected the clergyman to praise the officers, including himself – and to glorify our opportunities.'

'And there is the issue of drink,' Danny said. 'The Reverend Stanton is dead against it. But if the surgeon and the seamen are used to imbibing while at sea, well, it's a long time to be without it.'

'That's no excuse,' Mr Bice said. 'It's despicable behaviour for an officer.'

'So, why did the doctor laugh?' Emma asked.

'He was worried we would complain about the 'trials and hardships,'

Mr Vicary said. 'But I took the Reverend's words as sympathy. We'll never forget those storms, the doldrums, and the boy dying; it's been terrible.'

Unfortunately, there followed another long, still and miserable twenty-four hours. The migrants grumbled and argued about the time lost. Ben made use of the time by offering to help Emma with her writing.

Just before supper, Emma clapped her hands and closed the book. 'I did it!'

Ben asked to see the letter. 'Excellent,' he said. 'Now read it back to me.'

And our minister caught too of the biggest fish ever. Thay were albatros, and sum of the wimmen used the fethers to make children's hats for landin in.

That is all for now Mama. I feel better to tell you things, and send much love.

From your Emma.

Emma's small crowd of friends had crept closer and clapped when Emma finished.

'I can write,' Emma said gleefully. Suddenly, she didn't care who knew. She probably wouldn't see these people again.

Emma's entry into the world of literacy boosted her morale. When the wind returned after several days, and the ship began to move, she still couldn't eat a lot, but she was dizzy with excitement. Every day, Ben and Emma faced into the breeze with a smile, hands firmly entwined. In the evenings, they watched as many danced and sang.

'What's the matter, my dear?' Ben asked. 'You had such a good day yesterday.'

'I'm worried about Amelia. James says she's started seeing spiders now.' Emma's face was drawn. 'Sarah Ann has been appointed to nurse her in the hospital now. Sea sickness must be serious, Ben. I don't want to die.'

'You are keeping most of your meals down. Let's pray you both improve soon.'

However, Amelia's condition continued to deteriorate until she could not swallow either food or water.

It was just one week later, on 3 May, when the surgeon announced the shocking news of Amelia's death, he didn't mention the loss of her unborn child.

Emma, still nauseous in the mornings, was fraught with misery. 'The poor Vicary family,' she told Ben. 'It's terrible.'

Mr Breen, from Plymouth, also travelling with his family, was fearful. He knew well the loss of a grown-up child. 'They will rue the day they paid the princely sum of fifteen pounds, nine shillings, and three pence each,' Mr Breen said to Ben, 'to accompany their children on the saddest journey of their lives.'

As everyone gathered for Amelia's funeral, Emma steeled herself. She gulped uncontrollably and could not stop the tears flowing down her cheeks. 'Poor James. Poor family.'

The bell rang, the clergyman prayed, and the same two men who'd pushed the Standring boy now pushed Amelia's body over the side.

Emma clung to Ben's arm and squeezed her eyes shut.

Every day Emma stared with disbelief at the bunk space vacated by Amelia. And two days later, Emma's nervousness again heightened when she heard that Esther and George Measeday from Kent lost their little Clara from Scarlatina. 'She was only two years old, Ben,' said Emma. 'Poor Esther, she is afraid to let baby Henry out of her sight.'

The ship, as if unwilling to move from the burial sites, again made no progress. But in the evening as the ship stirred the water at the bow, the water glowed a magnificent blue. The colour spread for some distance. Emma was entranced. 'It sparkles like stars…' she said. 'What is it?'

'Phosphorous… phosphorescence,' Mrs Bice's husband answered. 'Something like that. I don't know where it comes from. We are lucky to see it.'

'It'll turn your eyes,' said a young man from Kerry.

Mr Bice frowned at the man. 'The captain said it is harmless. That much we do know.'

The crowd sighed as a dolphin stirred the water.

Emma tried to describe the iridescent blue water in her mother's letter.

Certainly, the glittering event had cheered Emma a little. The following day, the calm morning enabled her to eat breakfast. Later, when the ship began to roll, Emma was jubilant. 'Moving at last,' she cried, as the wind caressed her face. Excitement rippled through the crowd. But then the wind increased, and another storm blew up. This time Emma held on tightly and allowed her body to tilt with the movement of the ship, rather than against it. Susan had told her it might help. Emma thought it another old folk tale, but Susan was right, and Emma moved closer to Ben. 'It feels so good to be moving,' she said in Ben's ear, 'every day brings us closer to the end.'

With the increased speed, it was a particularly noisy night, the thudding of the seamen's boots above rarely ceasing.

As Seaman Prendergast explained to Ben the following day, the storm had blown several sails into shreds. 'They had to replace six of them,' Ben told Emma. 'But it is day 68, and we've just rounded the Cape of Good Hope. Two thirds of our journey is over.'

'Two thirds?' Emma exclaimed, twirling with Susan and Rachel. 'We really are getting there. At last.'

Ben thought it was a treat to see Emma so cheerful.

Whenever she could, Emma sat with a pencil and her notebook, with Ben, or Mary Ann beside her, pointing to some of the more complex words in the well-worn King James Bible. Her most fervent wish had come true. She really could read and write.

Near the end of May, Ben called Emma back up on deck. 'You must see these birds. You too, Mary Ann,' he said, heading up the steps. One of the sailors and the Rev Stanton had tall fishing lines out and they had snared several of the largest birds he had ever seen. 'They're albatross.' Ben told Emma. "That one is huge, nearly as tall as you Em.'

'So beautiful,' Emma replied.

'It's a tradition in these parts,' Mr Vicary said, 'they make good eating. Our meat has all but gone.'

One morning a week later, it was still dark as Ben yawned and slipped his clothes on. 'My last turn at being sweeper,' he whispered to Emma, 'you go back to sleep.'

He placed fresh sticks on the fire and blew on the coals. When the flames caught, he left to collect the water ration. Thereafter Ben visited the purser every hour, and he was elbowed and crammed every time by the other sweepers. His first visit was for tea, the second for oatmeal, and others for ship's biscuits, butter, salted-dried-meat, and potato powder. For dinner, he had no option but to boil Emma's currant pudding with the salt meat. And on he went, washing tinware, carrying away slops, and scraping and holystoning the deck.

Afterwards, Ben sat slouched, his head on his hands.

'Are you all right, love?' Emma said.

'I don't mind the work, it passes the day quickly, but the complaining: The butter is *off*. The meat is *inedible*. The water *smells*.'

'It's not your fault.' Emma put her arm across his shoulders.

Ben lifted his head. 'I told them, the water is filtered with Dr Normanby's latest machine, but they wouldn't listen.'

'The water does taste a bit off, dear,' Emma admitted.

'Not you, too.' Ben shook off her arm and began to pace.

Emma went to him. 'I'm sorry, I didn't mean—'

'No, you are right,' he said. 'The water is sour. I just wish – we were there.'

'Only another fortnight, old chap,' Danny quipped, winking at Emma.

'Less of the old, Mr Rowe,' Ben growled, 'and, surely, it's not another fortnight?'

'Not quite,' agreed Danny. 'Prendergast says, once we get into those Forties, we'll fly along. He says it's the best part of the journey.'

And it was true. The Roaring Forties brought high winds, rain, even snow, and Ben had never felt so joyful. A week later, Emma and Ben were again encouraged when they saw the seamen scrub and paint the ship and lifeboats.

Grace watched with them, too, and hugged Emma. 'I'll not regret seeing the back of this place. I've made many friends, but I'll happily never see them again if I could just walk on sound dry earth.'

'Except me, I hope,' Emma pretended to chide her.

'Of course. I wonder how we'll keep in touch?'

'Ben will give you William's address. Make sure you write and tell us where you are.'

There was another commotion on deck in the early morning of June 20. Kimbly announced that the land they could see was only Kangaroo Island.

'Are we there?' Emma asked, rubbing her eyes.

'We've another seventy miles,' Ben replied. 'But by the time we have breakfast and pack up...' He grinned, being more relaxed since James Vicary had left for the deck. The young man's devastation had worried him deeply.

Some two hours later, when the mate called 'Land ahoy', the emigrants sighed with relief. Ben stood on the lower bunk and looked into the space between the bunk and the partition. 'I think we have it all.'

As Ben and Emma waited for the hatchway, Emma covered her mouth with her hands. 'We're there,' she squeaked.

Ben laughed. 'Settle down, my dear, you'll lose your voice.'

They waited and waited, every moment made sweeter by the delay.

'Praise the Lord.' Ben said, as they left the third cabin – for the last time – and set foot on the deck.

Emma's shining eyes darted to the tall overhanging cliffs and serrated bluffs. 'Pinch me,' she cried, shading her eyes with her hand.

The *Eastern Empire* entered a wide waterway and followed the eastern coast of the gulf.

Emma snuggled into Ben's shoulder. 'It's lovely, white beaches like Loe.'

The rolling foam gave way to more rugged cliffs covered by groves of unfamiliar grey-green trees. Now there were open plains, backed by lofty hills.

'Look!' said Ben. 'Huts. Surely, we can build one of those.' He could smell the place, too: the dry, heady scent of eucalypts.

The ship slowed and entered the river. The seamen swarmed from the ratlines to the deck, securing the ropes and sails. They continued their shouting, and marching around the capstan, readying the anchor. The clump of the seamen's boots on the well-worn deck continued. After bearing the noise for so long, Ben longed for it to stop.

From the deck, the migrants' view was of a large harbour with its criss-crossed masts and yardarms, and unfamiliar flags flapping in the breeze. There were over fifty ships moored in the Port of Adelaide.

'Sometimes we get stuck on the bar,' seaman Williams said, 'but today the tide is with us.'

A tugboat towed the ship over the shallows and moored her in the stream. The seamen released the heavy chain and anchor until it embedded in the sand.

Ben strained to see the Port Creek Settlement. There was a proper wharf, and a large warehouse near the railway station. 'Feel the warmth, Em,' he said. 'And it's only winter.'

'Do you suppose William knows we've arrived?' she asked.

Ben shrugged and pointed at the concourse as a train arrived at Port Dock Station. 'There's a big crowd down there.'

A little steamboat pulled up beside the ship, its ripples making slapping sounds at the *Empire's* hull. Seamen assisted the spritely and bewhiskered Dr Duncan of the Emigration Commission aboard. He,

Dr Baker-Brown, and Captain Jury disappeared into the first-class mess. When they re-appeared, the crowd heard the magic words. 'Congratulations. You have managed to contain the fever. You are all cleared to leave the ship.'

The single women made a show of themselves by crying out 'Hooray'. The other passengers knew better than to show their feelings.

Emma hugged her friends, wondering if they would ever meet again.

When the lighters approached, Ben and Emma gathered their belongings and happily joined the queue.

Ships at Port Adelaide, c. 1860s, courtesy, State Library of South Australia (SLSA), PRG 1373/38/11

4. Arrived

Emma, on solid ground at last that day, wanted to skip with joy, but people swarmed everywhere around them. Emma could barely believe it when she saw her brother William pushing his way through the crowd. She put her hands to her wet face as he raced toward her. He swung her off her feet.

'Such a long time!' said Emma, ecstatic. She searched William's freckled and suntanned face. 'You look so well!'

William held her at arm's length. 'I can't say the same for you; didn't they feed you?'

'It's a long story,' she said.

More questions flowed. Had William heard from home? Was there truly a job waiting for Ben? What was it really like, this new country? Soon, they fell into their old ways, William jesting, Ben wondering how much to believe, and the women, heads together, deep in conversation.

Eliza shrieked with delight. 'A baby,' she tugged at William's arm. 'Emma is with child. Isn't that the best news?'

'It is indeed, my dear,' he beamed, hugging his sister yet again.

Ben moved to where the assortment of trunks, chests, and boxes were winched from the hold. He was relieved to see his uncle's chest still intact. He and William lifted it onto the horse-drawn cart of William's employer. All four of them climbed aboard and joined the long line of carts attempting to pass through the settlement.

Ben and Emma constantly swiped at swarms of small black flies, but they stuck to their mouths, crawled into their eyes and noses. William handed Emma and Ben small branches of Mallee to swirl from side to side.

'That's better,' Emma said.

Ben squinted at the landscape. 'I never saw land so flat. Those houses, apart from those in the port, are mostly huts.'

'But they belong to the migrants, Ben,' William said. 'Think about that.'

'You mean we could build our own house – just like that?' Ben asked.

William tilted his head. 'Well, it's not *quite* that simple. Land is expensive. But, yes, in time, I think so.'

Ben rubbed his hands together. 'I can't wait. Those huts look cosy, with their gardens and goats, barefoot children, running and laughing. And heaps of dry timber to burn. No more wet logs and smoking chimneys.'

The Davenport conveyance continued towards the city. There were small villages, and further on, a town called Bowden. Here, many of the houses were more substantial, and there were at least two inns – and a Bible Christian chapel. William said the town was named Bowden, in Ben's honour.

Ben grinned. 'Right. Well, you haven't changed.'

Another mile on, William slowed the horses. 'There she is; the city of Adelaide.' He nodded at the fine buildings and several steeples. 'They say the city is a square mile. This is North Terrace. A mile down *that* way is East Terrace, and parallel to this one is South Terrace, and so on.'

'Quite impressive,' Ben said.

Emma looked at the width of North Terrace. 'There's not a narrow winding laneway to be seen,' she exclaimed. 'How do you get across without being trampled?'

William grinned. 'You run – and pray. They planned the city with the future in mind. The planner was another genius called William. William Light. These streets are so wide, they'll never fill them to capacity.'

William steered the cart right, into an equally wide thoroughfare. 'And this is King William Street, the centre of the city. As you will see, all the other streets cross it in an impressive grid.'

Rundle Street, Adelaide, c. 1863, courtesy, Lawton, C., SLSA B2858

'Well, I'm glad I'm not on foot,' Emma said, 'these roads are fair cluttered with rubbish.' Tins, papers and horse-dung floated everywhere, and slushed against the cartwheels.

Suddenly, Emma put her hand to her head. 'Ooh,' she said, 'the world keeps rocking from side to side.'

'That'll happen for a few days,' Eliza said, 'getting your land legs.'

Further on, Ben and Emma leaned back to look at the taller buildings, with their fine Victorian edifices. 'Just like Truro,' Ben said, but his words were lost in the cacophony of traffic. Hundreds of iron-rimmed wheels of cabs, carriages, and drays crunched on the macadamised surface. Dogs barked in their wake, and sellers and cab men shouted above it all.

William pointed to a building called The Beehive, which displayed all modes of clothing. 'And this is *Holden's*, the saddlers. They sell only the best new leather goods. Over there is WC Rigby. Full of shiny new books.'

'And there are gleaming pianos in Platt's,' Eliza said, 'and marvellous watches in Wendt's.'

Further on William pulled over in front of a new, elaborately adorned building, with a balcony straddling the footpath. 'This is the new town hall. As cities go, Adelaide must be one of the finest, and it's not yet thirty years old. However, progress has its downside. Sellers have ways of parting people from their money.' William pointed to a billboard with a picture of bubbles and a smiling housewife, espousing the wonders of Twelvetrees glycerine soap powder. The seller, brandishing a penny packet in each hand, smiled into every cart, singing his jingle:

Twelvetrees soap is the best, easiest, cheapest and safest.
With scarcely a rub,
Clothes are out of the tub, and on the line before breakfast.

Ben frowned. Emma and Eliza were already discussing the new soap. William was right; they'd always made their soap from ashes and cooking grease. Why would they change?

The Pirie Street Methodist Church, the dissenter's pride and joy, with its single spire and twin turrets came into view.

William leaned back and pulled on the reins. 'Whoa,' he said. The horses tossed their heads, eager to return home.

'This – is our wonderful Wesleyan chapel,' William said. 'Pirie Street, seats 1200 people.'

Pirie Street Methodist Church, c. 1851, demolished in the 1970s,
courtesy, SLSA, B345000

'They really do welcome dissenters here?' asked Ben.

'They do. Now we must go; Beaumont is still several miles away.'
William flicked the reins and the horses stretched into a trot. The
noise of the city faded and in the peace of the bush, kangaroos loped
and disappeared behind trees.

'I thought you said Adelaide was dry,' Ben remarked. 'This is very
green.'

'We often get rain in June, specially up here. In a few months,
everything will dry up. But Mr Davenport has its measure; he doesn't
depend on wheat and barley; he has groves of vines and fruit trees.'

'What is he like, this Mr Davenport?'

'He's most pleasant, in his forties, looks like an English squire, but
he's very fair. He lets the cottages on reasonable terms and is genuinely
concerned for our welfare.'

Ben looked for the hint of a smile. Was William serious?

'It's true. I'll show you his book. It's about new industries we can
try. Like growing olives and silk. He says the whole family can be
gainfully employed.'

Ben tilted his head and turned to William. 'Making silk? How on
earth?'

'We pick the leaves, and the women feed the silkworms.'

Steadily climbing into the hills, William regularly rested the
horses, and Ben took this opportunity to walk. 'Silkworms,' he
mumbled, striding, feeling the benefit of stretching his legs. How he'd
looked forward to this day. The group continued along the Stringy
Bark Forest Road, and a full moon glimmered between the trees.

William pulled into a clearing. 'This is a favourite picnic spot. People rest here on their way to Mt Lofty. And we live not far up that road.'

The trees backing the clearing were unfamiliar to Ben and Emma; pristine ghost gums, almost luminous in the moonlight, taller stringy-barks, and spotted straight, white gums.

'This is lovely, William,' said Emma. 'The trees still have their leaves.'

The weary travellers soon pulled up in front of a small stone dwelling, which was one of two set back-to-back, about a hundred yards from Mr Davenport's Italianate, *Beaumont House*.

The little cottage was perfect. When William and Eliza left, Emma began sniffing, trying to hold back tears.

'They'll be back, love,' Ben said, hugging her.

'No, these are happy tears. I love the quiet and comfort, after that awful journey!' She sank joyfully onto the soft, clean bed.

'Breakfast is ready.'

Long after morning birdsong, Emma had heard William's voice at the door. 'Coming!' she answered, forcing her eyes open.

She pulled back the curtain and the sun beamed in. She grinned at Ben. 'Look: sunshine. And everywhere is so clean.'

Eliza handed them plates of eggs, ham, and freshly baked bread.

'Mm. Real food,' Emma said as she rubbed her tummy and laughed. 'I won't need any more for a week.'

After breakfast, William showed Ben and Emma the little town of Beaumont, a group of smart houses facing onto a central green. Emma twirled around in awe. 'Who would have thought a new country would look like this.'

'Mr Davenport planned it to look like a proper English village,' William replied.

Emma wondered about this Mr Davenport. Was he responsible for the change in attitude of her brother?

As William walked them back to their cottages, he almost swaggered, plucking at the roadside grass, sliding the seed-heads up the stalks, then tossing them. 'Mr Davenport owns all this land,' he said, sweeping his hand around him. 'And more, I believe, in the country.'

Emma gaped. 'They are beautiful houses.'

'They belong to very important men: doctors, judges, Parliamentarians. They live on the best of land, deep rich loam, fanned by cool gulley breezes. We landed on our feet, beloved sister, being paid to live up here.'

She knitted her eyebrows and said, 'What I don't understand is why a rich man would buy land in Australia, of all places?'

'Burke says that Mr Davenport's father in England bought it,' William said. 'His father is a banker, and one of the many moneyed Wesleyans, who want to "help the poor help themselves".'

Emma leaned on the wooden gate and looked up at her brother.

'Think about it, Em. It's cheaper than putting people in the poor house. And, if the poor earn good money, they buy more produce and pay more tax.'

'It's a pity they didn't think of that back home,' Emma said.

Samuel Davenport, MP, personally interviewed all new employees. He met Ben the following Monday in his expansive gardens. When Ben arrived, Mr Davenport stopped dragging the hoe between rows of well-pruned rose bushes. This surprised Ben, this important, busy man, in his fine wool shirt and riding breeches, working in his own garden. Davenport took him on a tour of the estate. As they walked, he asked Ben about the journey.

'It was long. A few storms...' Ben didn't want to complain.

'It is twenty years since my wife and I arrived – under sail,' the older man said. 'The journey took us six months. We'll never forget it.'

Ben was again reassured. The man had no airs and graces, and he seemed genuinely interested in their welfare. Ben remembered his galling encounter with the Trelowarren gardener in Cornwall.

They entered a large grove. 'These are five-year-old olive trees,' Mr Davenport said, running his fingers over the dusky leaves. 'We picked olives a couple of months ago. Our second most productive crop is almonds. And here are the mulberry trees.'

Ben saw tidy, small trees with almost symmetrical branches. 'Mulberries?' he queried, remembering the knotted old tree back home.

'We prune them to grow like that. By keeping them in a small standard shape, the leaves are low down, easy to pick. We feed hundreds of pounds of leaves to our silkworms every season. That's when your wives can help too. Burke will show you our pruning stages. There is a lot to learn. This wonderful climate is much like the South of France. I feel it is my duty to get the best from the land. But new colonies abound with traps and tricks for fresh-comers, and we've had our problems. I lost over a thousand sheep at Rivoli Bay...'

44

'A thousand?' Ben was surprised that the man talked to him about his failures.

Mr Davenport nodded dolefully. 'But my father generously subsidises my experiments, and we now farm three or four lines of business every year. If one fails, we have the others to keep us afloat.' Just like Uncle William, Ben thought. Now, hopefully, he, Ben Bowden, would learn to be a successful farmer, rotating his crops. 'If you are as energetic and skilled as your brother-in-law, you will do well here.'

'I sure hope to,' Ben said.

'Here we are, Harry,' Mr Davenport said to a younger workman approaching them. 'This is Ben Bowden. I'll leave you to show him the grapes.'

Harry Burke nodded and pointed to a pile of baskets. 'You've farmed grapes before?' He was curt. When Ben shook his head, Bourke tutted impatiently. 'Immigrants,' he muttered.

'But I never said—'

'No matter,' Burke said, 'just make sure they're ripe, and fill the baskets as fast as you can.'

'How will I know...?'

Burke was stripping great bunches off the vines. Ben wasn't going to let the young man intimidate him. He studied the bunches. Some were almost white. But those which had fallen to the ground were nearly yellow. He tasted several.

'Are you going to just stand there and eat them?' Burke asked. 'They have to be in by dusk.' He pushed his full basket to one side. 'Tomorrow, we start on the citrus.'

Ben put his hand up. 'I'll be twice as quick if you show me how. I've never seen grapes before.'

Burke scowled. 'Honestly. Do you know anything?'

Ben wasn't tall, but he was nuggetty. He put his hands on his hips. 'I've heard just about enough from you. Now show me ripe, and not ripe.' Ben looked surreptitiously around, hoping Mr Davenport wasn't listening.

Burke picked three small bunches and pointed at them. 'Ripe. Nearly ripe. Not ripe.' Ben tested the ripe fruit and licked his lips. He had never tasted anything as delicious. He reached in front of Burke and quickly ripped the ripe bunches from in front of him. 'Careful, Mr Bowden.'

'There's plenty for both of us,' Ben said.

45

Burke was civil thereafter, even notifying Ben of his midday break. But it was a long day, and Ben wished he was working with William, who'd gone into Adelaide to buy more olive trees.

Just before his working day ended, Ben found there were no more baskets. He smiled. He hadn't been too slow after all. It was a small victory, and he knew Burke would probably find another opportunity to take him down. Ben hurried back to Emma.

Emma gave Ben a hug as he came through the door. 'What is it, my love?' she asked. 'William said it is a good place to work.'

Ben hesitated. It was embarrassing, talking about failure. But he had to tell someone. Emma wouldn't belittle him.

'I was so encouraged by Mr Davenport, a fine and kind man. Then his farm manager gives me gip for the rest of the day.'

'Harry Burke?' Emma said. 'What did Eliza say? That's right. He'd lost his son a few years ago. The boy was only four or five.'

Ben sat down beside Emma and unclenched his hands. 'What a difference it makes when I know why.'

Adelaide was dark by five-thirty during winter, and both couples enjoyed the freedom of the evenings, reminiscing, chattering, and reading. Ben continued to help Emma with her writing by firelight. The men also read from the daily newspaper, although it was always a few days old. Ben was thrilled when William told him about the newspapers; Ben cherished the written word, but his family hadn't bought newspapers since they left Trengilly. William told him the papers were discards from the master.

'It was Mrs Davenport who first told us we could have them,' William said.

'I am sure she did, Will,' Ben said, grinning.

'No. Seriously. They buy several newspapers. Afterwards they use some for the fires and throw the rest away. Soon after we arrived, Mrs Davenport gave Eliza our first one.'

William reached to the top of the dresser. 'Here it is. I don't keep many, but this is about the arrival of our ship, and it had a list of the passengers. She said we might like it for a souvenir.'

'You should have seen William,' Eliza said, 'he took up that paper and never let it down till he finished.'

'It was an eye-opener,' William admitted, 'the nonsense they go on with. The editors have their bias of course.'

Editors' bias? Ben would have to think about that.

William showed Ben an article about their employer from the *South Australian Advertiser* of 23 July.

'So, our esteemed employer is a member of Parliament, on what council?' Ben asked.

'The Legislative Council.' William clarified. 'It's like our House of Lords. Only we don't have many lords. And the House of Assembly is the same as the House of Commons.'

Ben was puzzled. 'Burke said Mr Davenport is in a serious debate over something.'

William poured himself another cup of tea. 'It's the *Wastelands Bill*. Mr Davenport is a squatter, and they don't want the squatters to vote on it.'

Ben thought for a minute. 'But if he's a squatter, and doesn't pay for the land, I suppose he shouldn't vote on it.'

'But he does pay,' William said, 'and good money too, to lease some pretty poor land up north. It's dry country. They say he shouldn't vote because he has an "interest" in the land. But what parliamentarian out here doesn't have an interest in anything they vote on? Whether it be water, land, or produce.'

Ben yawned. 'Parliamentarians. Lords. Who knows? If I had to trust any of them, it would be Mr Davenport.'

Early in September, the leaves on the mulberry trees proliferated, and, when the silkworms began to hatch, Ben and Emma joined others caring for, eventually, over ten thousand silkworms. Emma's homesickness diminished as she worked in the enclosed sheds with her sister-in-law Eliza, and a young girl named Jenny Walters.

The men picked the leaves, and the women fed them to the silkworms.

'So, this is just one of many of Mr Davenport's *New Industries*,' Ben said. 'Why new? Isn't that always a risk?'

'He is preparing us for the future,' William said. 'Later, when we have a family of youngsters – in a country with no light industry – the whole family can be employed, from an early age.'

'Provided I have a grove of four-year-old, standard, white, mulberry trees, and a few thousand healthy worms,' Ben argued. 'Where will I get that sort of money?'

William grinned and ducked. 'We earn it.'

'Seriously, William, sheep, beef, and barley will be my preference – out in the fresh air. If I get to choose…'

Emma brushed crumbs off the table into her hand. 'It's interesting though,' she said. 'I'd love to learn how to spin silk. Where do they do that?'

'I have no idea,' Ben said, patting her knee. 'But you, my love, will have to rest up. You've not long to go.'

'I know,' she said, rubbing her swollen ankles. She had been glad to see the end of the evening political discussions; she was nearly always asleep by eight o'clock.

When Emma showed her swollen ankles to Mrs Walters, the midwife advised her to terminate her employment.

Emma was relieved; she was feeling tired. But she felt spoiled too, knowing her mother wouldn't have been so lucky. She spent many afternoons sitting with her feet on a chair, while she stitched tiny clothes cut from well-worn garments. She stored the baby clothes in their chest, along with the layettes from church families whose babies had outgrown them.

Emma brought out the collection to show Eliza and William. 'I wish my sisters were here, but they wouldn't like the heat. And we have you both. The new baby will be our new family.'

Ben agreed. Life in South Australia had lived up to his dreams.

Emma woke, bathed in sweat, a crushing tightness gripping her whole body. 'I think it's coming, Ben.'

Ben's head whirled. The bed was saturated. The sky was still dark outside, and Ben dressed quickly. 'I'll fetch Eliza and Mrs Walters.'

Eliza was there in minutes. By the time the kettles were filled, and Mrs Walters installed, it was daylight, and Eliza, yawning, set off for the first round of silkworm feeding.

The September batch had almost all cocooned, but Mr Davenport had received another ten thousand silkworm eggs in October.

Ben kissed Emma and said, 'I will be thinking of you, my love.'

Time moved slowly for Emma. She didn't know whether to sit, stand, or lie when the strength of her contractions increased. Near the end, she bit on a towel to suppress her screams, thinking she wouldn't mind if she never had another child.

On November 27, not long after her last almighty push, Emma heard the plaintive cry of her baby. It was glorious, filling Emma with joy and wonder.

It was just three days before her twentieth birthday.

'Your first little Australian is a bonny boy,' Mrs Walters said, wiping the baby's face. She severed and tied his cord and wrapped him in swaddling.

Emma took in the wonder of him, his eyes closing and his tiny arms reaching out. How helpless he was.

Burke sent Ben home early because many of the silkworms had cocooned, and, fortuitously, Eliza also worked less shifts until the summer crops were ready.

Ben rushed into the cottage and kissed Emma's forehead. She cradled the baby in her arms. 'He's so – little, Ben,' she said. 'What if anything—'

Ben put his finger to her mouth. 'Don't worry yourself, love. You need to rest, my dear.'

Emma lay back and smiled at Ben. 'It's like he's still a part of me. I had no idea. Poor Mama. She went through this twelve times – and William and I just walked away. And you, too.'

The baby stirred and yawned. Ben closed his eyes. The child was a miracle.

In the evening, William and Eliza arrived and fawned over the baby.

Emma took Eliza's arm. 'How will I manage? I didn't dream I'd be so tired – and sore.'

'Don't worry. Mrs Davenport suggested I work a shorter day to help you.'

Emma relaxed her neck. 'Such a kind woman – and you. Thank you. I will, of course, return the favour.'

In the early days, Eliza and William brought Emma and Ben their dinners, and briefly checked on mother and child.

William gazed at the sleeping child. 'Here, take him if you like,' Emma offered. William carefully lifted the baby and soon the little boy's nightshirt was around his neck. 'It's alright,' Emma said. 'He'll hardly freeze to death in this weather.' She sighed and smiled. 'It's going to be a good Christmas. So much to celebrate.'

After William and Eliza left, Emma and the baby were soon asleep. In the quiet of the evening Ben wrote to their families about the baby's arrival. He only had one regret, he said, he wouldn't see their faces when they received the news.

Although dizzy with tiredness, and wondering when baby William would sleep through the night, Emma felt her love and attachment to him knew no bounds.

5. Baby William

The weather was, of course, hot in December, 1864, and Emma rocked the baby in her arms as the midwife, Mrs Walters, closed the door behind her. Emma caught a hint of dry eucalypts wafting into the small room as she drew a deep breath, trying to settle her stomach.

'We don't believe her, do we?' Emma crooned. 'Look at you, chubby little cheeks, how can you be sick?' The baby locked his deep brown eyes on her. 'That's Mama's little angel.' Emma rocked the radiata pine crib, lovingly crafted by Ben; William had said it looked more like a manger, but she loved its smallness, made up with tiny soft white sheets.

The baby finally closed his eyes. 'Now, will you sleep for me?' she whispered, as she tucked the sheet around him. She leaned back in the chair, her eyes heavy.

Just as Emma relaxed into sleep, the baby began to whimper. He'll settle soon, she told herself, using all her willpower not to comfort him. But his crying soon turned to wailing, and his face reddened as he kicked furiously at the sheets. 'You're insatiable.' Emma unbuttoned her frock and lifted him to her breast. He was wet, but she wasn't surprised. He was drinking more nowadays. She looked at his perfect fingers and toes. It was still hard to believe he was hers. She thought about her mother in Cornwall. If only she could see him, she would know what to do.

When the baby's suckling slowed, Emma put him to her shoulder.

Now he drew his legs up and cried. Emma felt another headache clawing up her neck as she walked around the room, shushing him. Ben said he was just crying because he was awake more. Emma wasn't so sure.

The heat of the fire was stifling. Glancing at the unrelenting blue sky through the small cottage window, she knew it would be even hotter outside. It looked cooler under the shade of the tree, and Emma wished she had one of those baby carriages. She had seen them in Helston. It would sooth the baby, but only the gentry could afford perambulators.

Yards from the cottages, Ben and his brother-in-law raked up their piles of weeds under the peach trees and hurried down the slopes.

They had picked the fruit early in the morning. Deep in conversation, the two men ducked into the stone walled hut, where it was mercifully cooler.

Ben poured them both a cup of water from the pitcher and wiped his forehead on his sleeve. 'Verdi-what?' he asked, frowning as he opened his small calico lunch bag.

'I'm serious,' William said. 'Verdigris is... You know, that green stuff on my lucky penny. Only mine's a dull green. What he's talking about is a brilliant colour. Let me see what Mr Davenport says about it.' William sat at the old desk, and opened the copy of *Some New Industries for South Australia*. He continued, 'Rigby has published this, but it's really just a copy of Mr Davenport's letters to the editor of the *South Australian Register*.

'But what possible use can this Verdigris be? You can hardly eat it. And how on earth do you make it? Worms and witch's spells?'

William grinned. 'Almost.' He turned the pages. 'Here: lay thin plates of copper on beds of marc... Marc, that's winery waste.'

'If you had a winery,' Ben said.

William read the passage. 'Verdigris is extensively used by painters, and in dyeing; it is also used to some extent in medicine.' He looked up at Ben. 'And presto. Green crystals appear within days.'

'Marc? Verdi? Silkworms. Honestly William, what's wrong with potatoes and barley?'

'Nothing, I'd say,' William said. 'But listen to this. Here's how it started: Ten years ago, the colony of South Australia spent £8,826 in the maintenance of female immigrants.' William showed the book to Ben. 'This was because, unlike Europe and Britain, South Australia had no industrial pursuits for women. Eight thousand pounds: a new colony couldn't really afford it. As you know, if the women had jobs they would be spending money, not expecting it from handouts. Our clever Mr Davenport visited various countries and looked at agricultural industries that employed women. It is those occupations that are listed in his book.'

'But I don't want to work for someone else forever – raising silkworms!' Ben lamented. 'We want our own farms. And Emma and Eliza will be busy raising our children.'

'I agree.' William collected their cups. 'We should get back out there.'

Ben grabbed his hat. Outside, the heat enveloped him again. He was in no hurry to climb back up the slopes, his legs suddenly feeling heavy. 'Everywhere is uphill in this place.'

'You're a bit grumpy, old chap. What's up?'

'You didn't hear? Emma and the baby were awake for hours.'

'I heard him early on,' William said. 'A bit of wool in the ears is a marvellous thing.'

'Your turn will come,' Ben said.

He found his weeding spot under the trees. William went further on. Ben sank to his knees in the lush brown soil. As he started ripping weeds from the dry ground, ignoring the prickles puncturing his raw hands, Ben's mind turned to Cornwall. The cool days. The evergreen pastures. Why had he been so hasty to leave? It was much easier to work in a cooler climate.

The workers' bell sounded as the sun drifted westwards. Ben forked the weeds onto the barrow and began the precarious descent.

Safely on the flat, he dumped the weeds and brushed his hands together.

William joined him. 'Ready?'

They tipped their hats to Burke and walked back to the cottages.

As Ben thought of his baby, his face softened. 'I want to send the little fellow to Reverend Moody's school for boys. Moody cares about everyone – not just the big penny droppers in church. A good education will be the making of my boy. He will be beholden to no one.'

William raised his eyebrows. 'He's only three weeks old – but don't let me stop you.'

They approached the south-facing wall of the cottage, which was well-shaded by large eucalypts. Ben waited as William fought off a myriad of flies and fled through the door.

For a moment, Ben pretended he was back in Cornwall, outside the Trethowan cottage, longing to see Emma. She always had little stories to tell him about her work, and about people who came to the house. Their future had seemed so full of potential. It still was, he told himself. It had to be.

He continued to the far side of the building, warding off flies. Inside, everything was in its place.

'You're looking better,' he said, putting his arms around Emma.

Although Eliza continued cooking for them, Ben didn't enjoy cleaning the pots and pans, or trying to put the cottage to rights before he retired. Before the baby, Emma had kept it immaculate, stowing everything out of sight while dampening and stamping the earthen floor.

Emma handed him a cob of bread to put in the oven. He joined Emma watching the sleeping infant. The baby stirred and raised his fist. Ben's heart warmed. Emma was right, the little mite was worth more than his own life. Contentment crept over Ben.

Eliza and William looked in briefly after supper, and all of them watched the baby as he kicked his legs and waved his arms. Emma smiled. She could already feel the memory of the midwife's visit fading away. They were going to be all right.

William said to Emma, 'Did you know Mr Davenport is giving us three free days over Christmas!'

'Three days?' Emma said. 'I only had two at Tyackes.'

'There's an extra holiday on the twenty-eighth of December.' Ben said. 'What's it called?'

'Proclamation Day,' William answered. Emma gave him a puzzled look. 'It's to celebrate the day South Australia became part of Britain. Mr Davenport is providing food on the Green and entertainment. You know, three legged races, and the greasy pole with a leg of lamb – and catch the greasy pig.'

Emma scowled. 'William, Ben is not going near any greasy pig. I can never get that smell out of his clothes.'

'I know,' William said, chuckling. 'I'm glad you came, sis. It was so dull without you.'

Emma sighed. 'Anyway, thank God for Mr Davenport. It won't be like at home, but at least the four of us can share our little fellow around.'

Emma stared at the heat radiating from the oven. 'We should have Christmas in June or July, with our coats on, like at home.'

'If only,' Ben said.

When William and Eliza had gone, Ben continued to gaze at his son. 'Hello, little one,' he hummed, and the baby looked into his eyes. 'Look, Em. He knows me.'

'Of course, he does.'

The baby pursed his lips.

'Now he's trying to talk,' Ben said.

'I doubt that, love. It's food he wants. It's always food.' The baby began to cry, and Emma put him to her breast, wondering if she was doing it right. Her sister Mary had said there was a special knack, but Emma didn't understand it at the time. Now her sisters were so far away. She frowned and tried to swallow the lump in her throat.

When Emma finished feeding the baby, Ben took him. 'I'll put him on my shoulder while you fix his bed.' But then he added, 'He's hot, Emma.'

'Aren't we all?' Emma replied, taking the child and covering him with a sheet.

A piercing scream woke them in the night.

'I hope he didn't wake William and Eliza,' Emma cried, rolling out of bed. 'Oh baby,' she murmured, cuddling him, and opening her nightshirt. But the infant strained and filled his diaper. Emma tried again, but he pummelled her breast and her heart quickened. 'All right, I'll change you.'

Emma unwrapped him. 'Any wonder,' she said. 'Ben, his bottom is red raw – bring me a bowl of cold water. As Emma changed his diaper, she whispered to the baby, 'What am I going to do with you?'

Ben scooped him in his arms. 'Shush,' he crooned. Ben could feel Emma watching him. But he was going to do it this time. How hard could it be, to settle a baby? He rocked the baby ever more vigorously and paced up and down. Each time the baby stirred, Ben walked faster, even stepped outside, and soon the baby stopped crying.

'Bless you,' Emma said, leaning her head on Ben's arm.

An hour later, the baby cried again, his legs and fists fighting their way out of the wrap.

Emma changed and fed him and handed him to Ben. She was exhausted. She sighed and climbed into bed. She slept until the baby screamed again.

It was nearly daylight. William and Eliza knocked on their door soon afterwards. 'Thank God you're here,' Emma cried.

Eliza lifted the crying baby, and William hugged Emma. 'I'll fetch a doctor,' he said. Eliza continued to rock the baby while Emma dressed. Emma hurried back into the kitchen as Ben stoked the fire. Eliza put the kettle on, and they waited for the sound of beating hooves.

'Will he ever come?' Emma said, pacing the room, the baby on her shoulder.

Finally, the doctor strode in and opened his black bag. He checked the baby's eyes, mouth, and stomach, and asked Emma to unpin the baby's diaper. 'My, my,' he said, then asked for tepid water and baking soda. Eliza did the doctor's bidding, and the baby stopped crying. But it wasn't long until he screamed again, as blood and mucus soaked the clean diaper. 'It is a nasty infection,' the doctor said, removing a small bottle from his bag. He dropped a little medicine on the baby's tongue. 'Laudanum relieves pain and helps slow diarrhoea. But he must only have one drop on his tongue, twice a day, twelve hours apart. No more.'

Emma breathed easier as the baby became drowsy. 'Mrs Walters will be along shortly,' the doctor said. Emma barely heard him promise to return the following day.

Mrs Walters arrived several hours later. 'I won't lie,' she said. 'Dysentery is serious, my dear. But you must rest. If he does recover, he will need your milk, an abundance of it. Now help me cut up more towels for diapers, and I'll make up a bottle of water and soda for cleaning him.'

When the midwife left, Emma reached for her cup of tea. She drank it, poured another, and swallowed it quickly. Still, her mouth was dry. Her hands shook as she processed the words: *If he does recover.* She kept those terrible words to herself. It was not going to happen.

The room was quiet at last, and Emma prayed. Comforted momentarily, she leaned over the cradle and sang:

Gentle Jesus, meek and mild. Look upon a little child.
Pity my simplicity, Suffer me to come to thee

When William began to cry again, Emma picked him up and rocked him. Exhausted, she fell asleep with him on her lap.

Eliza tried to lift the child. 'No,' cried Emma, snatching the baby back. 'I know him best. Leave him with me.'

Eliza quietly said, 'I could watch him while you rest.'

'Eliza,' Emma said through gritted teeth, 'he knows my voice. I can't desert him.'

'You need to rest,' Ben said.

'You think I can't manage, too?' Emma cried, glaring at Ben.

'No, Em. That's not true.' Ben's voice was hoarse.

Emma lay on the bed with the baby. 'Mamma will mind you, darling.' But baby William did not suckle.

When the doctor returned, he lifted the baby from his mother's arms. 'He has no energy, Mrs Bowden. Try to give him a little of your milk on a spoon. Mrs Walters will come every day.' The doctor then took Ben aside and said softly, 'Mr Bowden, I'm sorry to tell you that it is most serious. You should fetch a clergyman.'

When Ben told Emma, she was stricken. 'You think he's going to die? You're giving up on him?'

'Of course not, it's just what we must do. Only the Lord can help us now.'

'If I was a proper mother, he would get better.'

'Em, that's not—'

'Who else can we blame?' she snapped back at him. 'I gave birth to him. It is *my* milk which feeds him. I am with him all day, *every* day.'

'Emma, some things are out of our control. Blaming yourself doesn't help.'

'No,' she shrieked. 'Leave me alone!'

Mrs Walters arrived with a baptismal gown for the baby. She slowly undressed him and slipped the long lace-edged gown over his head. Still, he did not stir. 'I'll watch baby while you change,' Mrs Walters said. 'Emma?'

But Emma's mind was far away.

Eliza took Emma by the hand and selected her Sunday frock. 'Put this on, dear, for the Christening.'

Emma shook herself into action. 'Of course.' She could smell the stale milk on herself and longed for a bath. But she could see, now, that they were all waiting for her. She dressed and slipped on her shoes.

Finally, the two families were ready, and they lined up in the small hot front room of the cottage.

The Reverend Moody, the Glen Osmond preacher, led Emma and Ben, Eliza and William, and Mrs Walters to recite The Lord's Prayer. Then he took the baby into his arms. Under heavy sedation, it slept soundly. 'How do you name this child?'

'William,' Emma heard Ben say, as though he was in another world.

'William,' Moody intoned, 'I baptise thee in the Name of the Father, and of the Son, and of the Holy Ghost. Amen.'

After the service, Mrs Walters and Eliza made tea, and served saffron buns, provided by Mrs Walters.

The following morning, Eliza and William tapped on Emma and Ben's door. Ben looked quizzically at William.

'Is there anything we can – do?' William asked.

'Will you stay?'

'Of course.'

Eliza rushed to hug Emma, who looked down at her baby. His cheeks were hollow, his little hands no longer puffy. But he was asleep, and Emma resisted picking him up.

William began to sing his favourite hymn, and Eliza and Ben joined him. Emma tried to sing with them, but no sound came out.

As the days passed, William and Eliza watched over Emma, Ben, and baby William. Emma wanted to believe her son would recover, but he was fading before her eyes. Ben tried to be strong for Emma, but a sob escaped as he covered his face with his hands. Soon all four of them were crying.

It was easier not having to worry about the tears.

Both families watched, waited, and wrung their hands. The three free holidays came and went, until baby William Bowden, unrecognisable now, with his skin stretched tight over his little bones, took his last breath on 30 December. It had been just thirty-three days since he was born.

The doctor, the clergyman, and all their friends came and went, and two days later Baby William was laid to rest in an unmarked plot, beside so many others, on the outer edges of St Saviour's Anglican Church Yard, Glen Osmond.

Emma kneeled on the sloping site with Ben's arms tightly around her. When they stood, she vowed to visit the grave every week. 'I can't bear to just leave him here.'

They looked up at the eucalypts, cypress and olive trees above them, where two Sulphur-crested Cockatoos had been stripping the tips off a branch. The large white birds screeched and flew away.

Emma cowed. 'What was that?' she cried, clutching Ben's hand.

'Just cockatoos, dear. They sound like I feel. Very sad.'

Back in the cottage, Emma's body shook as she tightly gripped the empty crib. It was very hot, the fire burning twenty-four hours a day.

Ben tried to put his arms around Emma, but she turned away. Her belly was soft, her breasts ached, and she smelled of stale milk. 'Ben, we have to go back. No one can live in this heat. Is it any wonder he died… My poor baby… I need Mama.' She sat and leaned her forehead on her hands.

'It's forty pounds each to go back,' Ben said.

Emma sat up. 'That much?'

Ben pulled away, feeling his father's past jibes; Mr Trethowan's misgivings. Why ever did I leave home, he thought, without a penny in my pocket?

He ran outside and leaned his head against the tree trunk.

His father had been right; he wouldn't be happy anywhere.

6. Constantine

Constantine cottage

Ben's father made the announcement over breakfast of 25 March, 1860, avoiding his son's eyes.

'You lost the lease for Trengilly Wartha?' asked Ben. The nineteen-year-old was stirring his steaming oatmeal disconsolately. 'How did that happen?'

'The twenty years is up in April and our rainy-day money is gone. We can't even afford the penalty.'

'Penalty?'

'Yes.' His father breathed deeply. 'The place is worth more because of the improvements.'

'But it was us who improved it.'

'I don't make the rules, son. And the plain truth is your uncle has more than enough money, and we don't. He is going to lease both farms.'

'Uncle Will? Of the Wollas? He wouldn't do that to us.'

'It's not that simple. He married money, and he knew how to use it. In the bad years he didn't just depend on barley and potatoes, he sowed mangold wurzels and bought breeding cattle. Now he can knock down some walls, and with his fine big machine, reap his crops in a few days.'

'Lucky him,' muttered Ben.

'And you might remember it was your uncle who fetched and paid for dressing the fields last year, a hundred bushels for every acre. I can never pay him back.'

Ben slowly shook his head. 'But, what will we do?'

'Worry not, son. The Lord will provide.' He tapped his pipe against the fireplace, emptying it out before feeding it with what little tobacco was left in his pocket packet. 'The trials of life are sent to test us for the great hereafter.'

Ben picked at his fingers. Could his father not see? The Lord had not provided. Maybe Emma's brother, William, was right about moving to the colonies.

On a Saturday two weeks later, after Ben's father had been to the markets, he returned looking triumphant as he hung his hat and dragged a teacup toward him. 'There's a place for lease in Polwheveral,' he told Ben. 'Twenty acres. Owner says it's been a good solid little farm.'

Ben sat and stared at his father. It was only half the size of Trengilly, half the miserable profits. 'Polwheveral?' His father nodded. 'But those awful tin stamps,' said Ben, 'they're so – so noisy and they foul the water.' When his father simply lit his pipe, Ben left the room in a fury.

Outside, he took up the slash hook and swiped at the weeds like never before. The thistles were in full flower, and once they were cut Ben kicked them into the air.

The Trengilly lease had been for three lives, and his father had promised Trengilly would be Ben's one day. Now, his cousins would be all over it. As if they didn't have everything they wanted already, a pony for Ben-Thomas, and one for his younger brother too.

Ben spent a restless night.

In the morning, his father was eager to go. 'Come on, Ben' he said, rubbing his hands together, and donning his coat. 'Let's go see this place.'

Ben's mother patted the boy's arm and said, 'Go with him.'

Ben followed his father along the muddy narrow laneway. As they neared Polwheveral, his shoulders tensed as the frames of the tin stamps rose up, stark in the rural setting. The farm was small, and the cottage dark. And it was mostly covered in brambles. His father caught his gaze.

'We can soon tidy it.' his father said. 'Cut back the weeds, let in a bit of light.'

Ben held his tongue. The two men approached the front door, which was swinging open, and when they stepped inside the small parlour, pigeons scattered, flying into the walls and a broken window. There were more in the kitchen, perched on a shredded drying-rope above the hearth.

Ben grabbed an old besom sweeping brush. 'Out,' he shouted, waving at the birds. He looked at the fireplace. 'That chimney is blocked with jackdaws' nests. It's – awful, Da. We can't.'

'It's too late. I've signed the lease. There's nothing else… It's only for ten years. Something else will come up.'

They moved to the Polwheveral farm in 1861, and Ben, his parents, and his sister Elizabeth worked every daylight hour to make it liveable.

Ben sowed any seeds he had, including their sprouting potatoes, cutting some in halves, even quarters, to fill the drills he had prepared. Wet clay seeped into his cracked boots, which rubbed his skin raw. He threw the shovel down. He would get a new pair of boots, if he had to steal them.

What was he thinking? Stealing? He could be transported for that. He retrieved his shovel and faced his father.

'I'll have to get more work; I need boots.'

'I'll see your uncle tonight. He'll have an old pair.'

'But I'll have to earn more, Da. I want to marry Emma. How will I ever lease a place of my own?'

'You probably won't. You can't afford to be choosey. Not these days.'

Ben felt like shouting at his father. But he had a better plan.

The following Monday, Ben woke before dawn. He did his chores and slipped away. He would try Trelowarren, the home of a Baronet and politician named Vyvyan. It was possible the hallowed, thousand-acre estate would have work for him. The Trengilly lads told him they employed dozens of footmen, gardeners, and stableboys.

It was a grey day, but there was no rain, and with a softer pair of boots and salve on his sores, Ben enjoyed the walk to Mawgan-in-Meneage. Approaching the gates, he was apprehensive.

A surly gate man greeted Ben and sent a boy to escort him to the head gardener. Ben, following the boy through the splendid estate, gawped at the huge castellated dwelling house, the private Gothic chapel, the symmetrically splayed flowerbeds, which bordered the central fountain. He then looked down at his own threadbare clothes, his boots tied up with string.

'You're too old,' the head gardener said. 'We'd have to train you. I employ nine-year-olds. Sir Richard employs hundreds of lads on his many estates. And we have twelve acres of the finest rococo gardens in Cornwall. Do you even know what that means, Mister Bowden? Go back and tend your bit of barley.'

'But I do herbs and vegetables, and flowers...' Ben said, as the man pushed past him.

The previous year, the Trethowan family also lost their lease to the Mellingey Farm, moving on to the nearby nine-acre farm at Nancenoy. Ben met one of the many Trethowan girls, Emma, who enchanted him with her easy chatter and mass of black unruly curls. But Emma was only 16, and Mr Trethowan turned the ragged Ben away at the gate.

Emma was drawn to the quiet young man and asked William to arrange outings with William and Eliza to Loe Bar. As they frolicked along the half mile of shingle, which cuts Loe Lake from the ocean, Emma felt a love for the sea.

William and his beloved, Eliza, planned to marry, and William said they would emigrate to the promising, new, convict-free colony of South Australia. Emma was aghast and asked Ben to stop her brother, but William had a copy of *The Emigrants' Friend*, and Ben read it greedily.

> Good wages, and every possibility of a little freehold...and good health, no agues, asthma, and no dysentery.

Ben couldn't believe his eyes.

> His family will be well provided for while young, and not growing up to be a burden, to toil through life without profit.

Exactly, Ben thought. These people knew what they were talking about. Here was no living.

William also showed Ben copies of letters written by earlier immigrants. 'Listen to this,' he said, smoothing a puckered piece of paper.

> You're mad staying home a day longer. We feed our dogs more meat than we ever had back there. This is a splendid country, plenty of sunshine, and there's mines worth all Cornwall...
>
> And when times are hard, I can shoot all the birds and ducks I like.

'He's right,' Ben said, 'Here a man doesn't dare kill a hare for his starving family.'

William and Eliza married, sailing from Constantine on January 10, 1863. It was heart-wrenching for their families.

Ben and Emma argued. Emma said she was not going anywhere. But Emma's work as a servant, and the incessant summer rain, separated them. Emma was often drenched when walking the five miles from work to see her family on a Sunday. After they'd missed two Sundays, there was another particularly stormy day, and Ben borrowed his uncle's horse to rescue Emma.

There had been a letter from William, who had offered to sponsor them. With William leaving a hole in their lives, Emma did not want to be parted from Ben again, so she agreed to marry him. With nowhere to call their own in Cornwall, they applied for passages to South Australia, to set sail March 16, 1864.

7. The Aftermath

Emma was still accusatory, unable to move on after her baby son's death.

'It was William's grand idea to emigrate,' Emma said. 'He should pay our fare to go home. And God, and the preachers, too, they should take some responsibility. And why did that Mr Jones say Australia was a healthy place for children?'

'It was the Wakefield man who said that,' Ben said. 'He blamed the loss of his first child on the cold, wet climate of England.'

'Well, now we know it takes more than sunshine. We should have known it was all lies, just to get us here.'

Ben thought Emma was right. That emigration agent, Mr Jones, had misled them. Why had he not seen that? 'I am sorry, Em, so very sorry.'

'It's a bit late for sorry,' she flung at him. 'Six months here, and… Life will never be the same.'

But Ben dwelled on the fact that it really had been William's idea to leave their families and settle thousands of miles from home. The same, clever, courageous William Trethowan who lived in the other side of the cottage. If Ben had made a terrible mistake, then so had William.

Ben was wakeful in bed. The loss of his little boy and Emma's rejections were unbearable.

Every evening, when Ben returned from work, he found the table as he had left it in the morning, the oatmeal still hard in the pan, the cups unwashed. He quickly tidied it away, knowing Eliza would soon be in with their meal.

The following Saturday after breakfast, there was a polite knock at the door, and Ben flashed a nervous smile. 'Reverend Moody,' he said, 'how good to see you!' Ben removed newspapers and his coat from the chair. 'Emma is – indisposed.'

The clergyman put up his hand. 'Don't apologise. Shall I say a prayer with you both?'

'Please.'

Ben knocked on the bedroom door and peeped in.

'Go away,' Emma cried.

'I'm sorry,' Moody said, as Ben backed away. 'It is a – a terrible time.'

'I didn't know how terrible, until now,' Ben said. 'When I see that look on Emma's face, it reminds me of my own mother.'

Moody nodded and asked, 'Your mother lost a child?'

'Not just one.' It suddenly hit Ben, the magnitude of it all. 'I had no idea, what my parents went through. You'd think I'd have known—'

'We had enough to deal with when we were children,' the clergyman said.

'I was only three when our first little Richard died. He was nine months old. It was my fault. I rolled the ball to him, and Mama fell, spilling the broth.'

'It was hardly your fault. As you say, you were only three.'

'After the funeral, I wanted Mama, but she stayed in her room. Aunt Sarah came to live with us.'

Moody breathed through his teeth. 'You said more babies died?'

'You hardly want to hear any more?'

'You have a lot to think about at the moment... Maybe it would help you clear your mind.'

Ben made tea for three and, after taking a cup to Emma, he pushed his chair closer to the clergyman. It would agitate Emma if she heard him talking for too long. 'Another Richard was born when I was about – five. He followed me everywhere. It was such fun having a brother. We loved playing in the creek – we tried to dam it up with stones. Elizabeth wouldn't play outside.' Ben stared into the distance. 'When Richard was three, he was big enough to climb the apple trees with me. We took the apples in for Mama. When he got catarrh... I remember hearing him breathe – that sharp, wheezing, crackling sound – until one night I couldn't anymore. I remember thinking he was better. But he wasn't... Aunt Sarah moved back in with us again. She was lovely in her white pinny, I wanted to marry her!' Ben turned red, then squeezed his eyes. 'Sorry,' he said, blowing his nose loudly. 'There isn't much to know about the other two. I was thirteen, and twin baby boys died when they were born. It's only now I realise why my parents were so cross.' Ben looked at his feet. 'Papa would shout and rage, and I'd run to my grandmother. I feel bad about that, but I didn't know.'

'You were only a child,' Moody assured him.

'I was... And look at me now. I have lost one child, and I'm falling apart. When my mother encouraged me to emigrate, I really thought she didn't like me.'

'So, now you know,' Moody intoned, 'she loves you very much. It is the ultimate sacrifice, to let our loved ones go.'

Every morning, Ben made tea and oatmeal. But Emma only picked at it. With a heavy heart, Ben left for work. By midday the heat was unbearable. Ben could almost see it, shimmering like water. Even the leaves on the great gum tree drooped. He poured another bucketful of water on the young olive tree, and wiping the sweat with his sleeve, he sheltered under the generous heart-shaped leaves of the adjacent mulberry trees. He gulped more water from his hessian bag. Renewed, he weeded and watered vigorously. The more he worked, the better he felt. Was doing something the answer? He wondered; if Emma had a job, to take her mind off it all, would she too feel better?

But, when he later asked Emma, she only glared at him. 'Don't you think it'd be a good idea, Em?'

'Surely you can manage without my wages for a little while,' she said, retreating to the bedroom. 'I'd never thought of you as a selfish man, until now.'

She was so, very angry – all the time. Ben wondered if she would ever recover from the loss.

Ben hadn't seen much of his brother-in-law of late, now that he was working on a new olive plantation. Ben rattled William's front door. When Eliza answered, Ben said, 'Send him out.' When Ben finally saw William emerge, his rage had boiled over. 'You realise that it's all your fault! You have no idea how difficult...' He couldn't say any more. He retreated, turning to leave, but William caught his arm.

'Wait a minute, Ben Bowden, nobody forced you to emigrate. I was out here at the time. Remember? And – we do know something of what it's like,' he whispered. 'We lost – our first baby – on the voyage.' His face twisted.

Ben groaned with guilt. 'You didn't say...'

'The baby,' said William softly, 'he came early, far too early. Never took a breath. The dreams we had...'

'I'm so sorry,' Ben said. What had he done? He was mortified by the minute just gone.

'You weren't to know,' William said. 'And you are right; I am to blame.'

'No, hold on, Will,' Ben said, but William had already closed the door. Ben just stared at it. As he backed away, he almost fell over a fallen branch. He went for his axe and cut it into sections, stacking the sticks beside William's door.

Emma continued to withdraw, and it was when Ben found her rocking to and fro in a corner, sucking her thumb, that he realised Emma's grief had gone too far.

He knocked on William's door again. 'Please help me. Emma's not right, and I don't know what to do!'

William offered to fetch the doctor.

The doctor prescribed Laudanum, and Ben prayed she would soon settle into the sleep she so badly needed.

During the day, Eliza fed Emma broths, and Emma began to sleep more, though she remained lethargic and spoke very little. Then, as if some heavenly switch had been flipped, Emma woke early one Sunday morning, dressing herself prettily before walking about the house in search of Ben. 'Where is everyone?' she called out. 'Isn't it Sunday?' Ben was standing carefully still in their back yard, hardly believing his own ears. Emma stopped and stared at him from the back door. 'There you are, darling,' she said, in that much beloved voice from home. Her smile looked just the same as all those years ago.

He ran to her, awash with tears.

8. Recovery

Emma remained unable to face work and felt agitated when left alone.

'I'll go mad here by myself,' she cried, when Ben returned from work. 'I miss him so much.'

It was nearly sunset as Ben walked Emma toward the forest.

She lifted her face into the gulley breeze that dried the sweat on her brow. 'You are a good man... Will I ever forget him?'

'I don't know, my love.' He put his arm around her.

Back at the cottage, the heat engulfed Ben. He left the door open.

Emma put away their supper plates and cups. 'William doesn't visit anymore. Was I that bad?'

'Not – too bad,' Ben said.

'So, I was?'

Ben sighed. 'Emma, don't do this.'

'So, it *is* my fault.'

'Em...'

Sometime after the February heat had given way to cooler evenings in March, 1865, Emma was somewhat delighted to find William and Eliza chattering near her front door. The sound of their footsteps provided Emma the opportunity to open the door before they'd even knocked.

'You were expecting us?' William asked.

'Don't flatter yourself, William Trethowan,' Emma said as she moved to put the kettle on. 'We were just enjoying the breeze.'

Eliza put up her hand. 'No tea for us, thank you.' She smiled up at William. 'We've come with news.'

'What kind of news?' Emma asked.

'I, *we*, are expecting a baby.'

Emma's heart leaped; how would she bear it, another baby in the house, but not her own? She hoped Eliza didn't sense her disquiet as she put her arms around them. 'That's wonderful news,' Emma said.

Ben also had mixed feelings. But surely a new baby would help, he thought. 'Congratulations old fellow.'

Only then did Emma see the rounding of Eliza's tummy. 'I can't believe I didn't notice. When is the—'

'Sometime late in June,' Eliza said.

'And you.' Emma turned to her brother, kissing his cheek. 'I am so happy for you.'

Emma returned to work at the end of the month, and minutes, sometimes even an hour, went by without her thinking about baby William.

When Emma missed her monthly curse twice, she realised that she, too, was expecting. She rushed to meet Ben after work.

Eliza and William followed them home. 'Are you squealing for any particular reason, Sis?' William said, catching Emma by the arm. Emma beamed and nodded. William and Eliza hugged her.

As the months went on, Emma worried. She presumed Eliza would be worried too. Emma knew she had to help Eliza. At twenty-seven, Eliza wasn't young anymore, though Emma repeatedly told her she looked well. 'And lucky you, having a winter baby.'

'Thanks, Em. Keep telling me that.'

'I will,' Emma said, 'after all you did for me.'

Emily Catherine Trethowan was born on a wet June day in the middle of their second Australian winter.

Emma happily cooked and cared for Eliza, before and after work, and took every opportunity to gaze at the silky haired infant. When the baby stretched her tiny hands, arched her back and whimpered, Emma was unable to resist lifting her. 'Come to Aunty Emma,' she crooned, breathing in the sweet smell of baby, and the sun-dried swaddling. She turned to offer the baby back to Eliza.

'It's all right,' Eliza said, 'you hold her for a bit. My nipples are dry and sore.'

For several weeks, Emma was often at her brother's house when he came in from work. On this occasion, he walked in and looked at her with mock severity. 'That child has two mothers; she'll be ruined.'

Ben was delighted to see Emma smiling as she crooned to little Emily.

However, Emma continued to worry about her next baby. She could not be reassured.

When summer had well and truly arrived, Emma's temper began to fray again.

'It's too hot for this,' she said to Ben, rubbing her swollen belly and removing her apron.

Ben backed away. He was relieved to see Eliza, and he stepped outside.

He heard Emma say, 'I wish we had one of those hoses, like on the ship.'

'I can soon fix that,' Eliza said.

Ben peeped in to see Eliza pour a cup of water on Emma's head.

Emma put up her hand, then gave in to it, as the cold water trickled down her neck.

Their laughter was a tonic for them all.

In August, Ben kept the letter hidden. He didn't want to spoil Emma's mood. His grandmother Grace had passed away in April, but surely it was too late to make much of it. Ben had loved her dearly, and it gave him a jolt when he realised he would never see any of his family again. And the news was always months old – if they heard at all.

Emma, aided by Mrs Walters, gave birth to her first daughter on December 6. They named her Elizabeth Anne, after their mothers.

From the outset, Emma couldn't take her eyes off the little girl. At the back of her mind was always the worry, and she panicked with every cough and sneeze. Secretly she didn't dare hope, in case hope itself cursed her. Emma celebrated the festive season with caution, but little Annie, as Emma called her, was a delight, growing steadily, mushing her heart.

Ben was also content. Scrubbing clothes and washing dishes were no longer chores to him, as long as Emma and their baby remained healthy.

William suggested that Ben join him to read the newspapers.

Ben stifled a yawn. 'I won't,' he said. 'My eyes are glazed by eight o'clock.'

'I know,' William said, 'only too well. That child of ours has a healthy set of lungs.'

'Glad to hear it,' Ben said. 'A little wool in the ears…'

'Ha ha…' William said, shoving Ben's shoulder gently.

It was a surprise to Ben and William when Burke told them that Samuel Davenport had resigned from parliament, and that he, Burke, was leaving Glen Osmond to work the northern runs. The two Cornishmen were now required to work longer hours, and with little Emily and Annie learning to crawl and walk, both families were busy.

Twenty months after Annie was born, Emma gave birth to another girl, Eliza Jane, on August 30, 1867. With Annie already taking up most of Emma's day, she wondered how she would manage now.

'I'm still tired and in a muddle,' Emma said to Eliza, lightly patting her newborn on the shoulder. 'But a sleeping child is a gift. I was convinced I was a hopeless mother; Annie never slept like this.'

The spring weather was perfect, and when little Lizey, as Annie called her, slept, Annie and Emily played with sticks and small round stones. They dressed the sticks as people, and pretended stones were anything they wanted, from a seat, to a house, to a horse. Their thankful mothers sat nearby and knitted, darned socks, and patched elbows and knees. Emma loved to watch the little girls as their imaginations played out.

As the weather warmed, Lizey became more wakeful and took more of her mother's time. Annie whined, and Emma gritted her teeth.

When Ben arrived home, Emma closed her dress and handed Lizey to Ben. 'Bless you. Do you think you can put her to bed while I put your meal on the table?'

When the girls were asleep, Ben pulled two letters from his pocket. 'Here's one from your father Emma.'

'I hope Grandma Philley is alright,' Emma lamented. 'Let me see.' Emma let the page go as her eyes misted. 'When it starts with *I'm sorry to have to tell you...* it can't be anything good. You read it to me.'

'Yes, your gran has passed,' Ben said. 'She was eighty-four. At least it was quick.' He pulled Emma to him. 'I'm sorry, love; it was hard enough leaving them.'

Ben prised the second letter open. 'This one's from Danny Rowe at Moonta Mines. He's heard from the Vicary family.' Then he paled and sat down.

'What?'

'It's John Vicary, James's brother,' Ben whispered. 'He has died, in an accident. He was twenty-five, Emma, the same as me. I can't believe it.' He stared into the fire.

'Mr and Mrs Vicary must hate this country,' Emma said. 'And poor James. First Amelia and the baby, and now his brother.'

'Hopefully there's some good news...' Ben read on. 'Aha,' he said. 'Danny says the government is making land more affordable. William and I had best comb through those newspapers again.'

On Saturday, William hauled in the latest pile of newspapers.

Ben quickly leafed through the pages. 'Ah. *Proceedings in Parliament.* Nothing there.'

Then William found the amended *Wastelands Act, January 1869.* 'Here it is,' he said. 'Of course, we have a new Attorney-General, and he's our premier too. Henry-Bull-Templar-Strangways: what a mouthful, and he's not waiting around either. The act will allow for smaller parcels of land to be sold for agriculture. At the moment, there are mostly huge pastoral runs for sheep and cattle. The amendment will be law in two months!'

'We can afford to buy land?' Ben asked.

William showed him the page. 'Well, they are introducing a system of credit. Credit! Now that's good news. But we're not there yet. It's only for land over 320 acres. And it could be costly. Selling it to the highest bidder.' William took out a pencil and checked the numbers.

'At £2 an acre and a down-payment of 20%, that's a minimum of, let me see. £128. We don't have anything like that. And at £3 or £4 an acre – forget it.'

9. Moonta Mines

Emma stared at a cluster of magpies nattering on the grass outside the small kitchen window. It was another hot and clear day. The two girls were asleep, so Emma snatched a few minutes to write to her family. She poised her pen; should she tell them about Ben and William's latest idea of moving to the ever-dangerous mines?

She put the letter on the dresser for posting. There was no point worrying them just yet; they knew she was happy at Beaumont, with her little group of friends. And the thought of leaving baby William's grave worried Emma. But she had to concede that William's four-year term was well up, and Ben's was heading that way. She suspected their leaving was inevitable.

In another letter, Danny Rowe told Ben that many had made fortunes in the booming mines.

> This new man at the helm was appointed when he was only twenty-eight. Young fellow, called Henry Richard Hancock. I wondered at first, but he is a clever man. And he wants a lot more Cornishmen here.

> The mines are shallow, and well ventilated. There are new ladders, and man-skips – cages to pull us up and down the mine. And Captain Hancock is very fair, if we work hard. We're earning three pounds a week, and more if we're lucky.

> And we don't pay much for the cottages, neither do we walk miles to work, like we used to at home. We actually live on the mining lease.

> There is a medical club, for one shilling and sixpence 1/6d a week. They're opening up land here soon. Come to Moonta, make your money and that little freehold could be yours.

Ben was as excited as Emma was not. 'You know what I think.' Emma cried, rocking a child on each hip. She put the girls down and took his hands. 'Explosions, cave-ins, and even a bit of hammer-and-tap could maim you.'

74

'William says Moonta is much safer,' argued Ben. 'The copper isn't far underground. Can't you see that has to be safer?'

'They'll still use explosives. And living at the mines will be horrible, dirty, and dangerous. I won't be able to take my eyes off the children.'

'Surely, such a brilliant man has all of that covered.'

'I doubt it,' Emma said, glaring. 'Maybe you should go to Moonta. Leave us here until you make your money.'

'I couldn't. Not without you – and the girls.'

'Why not? Go now and make your "fortune" faster. You'll be back in no time.'

'Em, you know I couldn't do that.'

Ben tried to take Emma in his arms that night, but she pushed him away and said, 'If you're going off to the wilds of Australia, I don't need another child to care for.'

However, it wasn't long before Emma became nauseous in the mornings again. 'What are we going to do?' she asked Eliza. 'You're due in June, and me in September. How will we manage without the men?'

Eliza gave a cynical laugh. 'Probably very well. At least there won't be any more babies for a while. Two will do me.'

Ben worked harder at helping Emma and the girls. He took Annie and Lizey to see the birds flocking to the woods in the evenings, while Emma prepared their supper. On Sunday, Ben told Emma that she and Eliza deserved a break.

'You and Eliza take the morning off,' Ben said. 'We'll watch the children and cook dinner.'

'You can't cook,' Emma said.

'William can. I'm going to play knucklebones with the girls.' He displayed the five little bones, saved after five expensive roast-leg-of-lamb dinners. 'From the big house. Burke had them for his girls.'

'You've been complaining to Burke?'

'We were only talking about how difficult it was for you—'

'Bah,' Emma said.

Ben received another missive from Danny Rowe at the end of March.

There are thousands of Cornish people living at Moonta. It's like being at home, only the weather is better. There are plenty of Cornish midwives, and the children will have friends all around them. Best of all, the captain runs the biggest Sabbath School in Australia. It is most promising for their education...

'Education?' Emma said.

'We're going to the markets today to collect some fig trees,' Ben announced. 'We'll get some Rigby books for the girls while we are there.'

'Aren't they expensive?' Emma asked.

'Nothing is too dear to educate our children,' William countered, ushering Ben out the door.

When their fathers returned, the girls were enraptured with the books. 'What does it say, Da?' Annie asked, taking the proffered book.

'Little Dora Playfair'.

Annie held the book close and sniffed the cover. 'It smells nice.' She studied the picture. 'Why is the preacher cross with the girl?'

Ben turned the pages. 'Dora doesn't want to go to school. She is vain and wilful.'

Annie turned to Emily. 'What's in your book?' Emily looked to her father for help.

'What Trying May Do,' William read from the cover over Emily's shoulder.

The two girls sat with their books while Emma watched and worried about the future. 'If we must go,' she sighed, 'it should be soon. We don't want our babies born on a long road in the middle of nowhere.'

The two families planned to leave for Moonta in April. The men sent the bulk of their belongings ahead to Port Wallaroo by sea, and on Thursday, April 15, 1869, Emma tearfully closed the cottage door and left Beaumont. 'We might come back,' she whispered. Eliza nodded.

Mr Walters drove them into the city in his buggy while the children, Emily Trethowan, Annie Bowden, and Lizey Bowden, aged almost four, three, and two respectively, bobbed happily in the back, searching their surroundings for birds and kangaroos.

The two families stayed overnight at an inn near the Adelaide Railway Station. Early next morning, they pulled the children from their beds, and were glad to leave the yellow stained walls of their musty room. They walked to the railway and found the steam train to Salisbury waiting on its irons.

Emma tried to calm Ben when he paid for the tickets. 'Three shillings!' he complained. 'To Salisbury. And children half price. That isn't cheap, given that Moonta is another 90 miles from there.'

The giant locomotive hissed, and Emily, Annie and Lizey jumped.

But, once seated in the shiny wooden carriage, they giggled as they looked out the window.

Ben looked at his daughters – gorgeous in their new dresses, and curls peeping under their bonnets. He took Emma's hand. They were blessed.

Amid clouds of black smoke and white steam, the train set off. The land was flat and dry, but there were enough sightings of villages, farmers, and dogs to keep the girls amused. This was the Gawler train, the ticket man announced. 'It stops at North Adelaide, Grand Junction, Dry Creek, and Salisbury.'

The journey took forty minutes.

Salisbury, not far from the city, was a sparse settlement, and its functional, dreary architecture told of the heat of its summers and the dryness of its river. Ben hoped it wasn't a foretaste of northern living. Moonta didn't even have a river.

They walked to the coach stop in front of the Railway Hotel and, after an hour or so, Ben could hear the six-horse coach rattle around the corner. The coachman looked capable, a strong, middle-aged man with a voluminous beard and a broad brimmed hat.

'All aboard for Yorke's Peninsula,' he shouted, jumping down.

Annie looked at him gravely. 'Where's York, Mummy?'

'It's a long way, missy,' the coachman replied, lifting her into the coach. 'A long, long way.'

The two families and four other men climbed aboard. The driver cracked his whip, and soon they were bumping along through more flat plains. As they travelled further north, the traffic threw up clouds of dust, and the girls coughed and complained.

Emma was surprised to see so many other vehicles. Where were they going? All she could see were flat, treeless plains and white grass. She remembered leaving Cornwall on the train. The countryside had been so green, with its rolling hills and flowering trees. And Brunel's magnificent lacy bridges, which seemed to be around every corner, spanning massive gullies.

Emma looked at Eliza, her tummy tight, trying to find comfort in the jolting carriage. It was a relief each time the coach stopped so the coachman could fling mailbags from the trunk.

The girls pointed to two ostlers who untethered the tired horses and replaced them with a fresh clopping six. 'How many stops will it take?' Emma whispered to Ben. Two of the other passengers reeked of liquor.

Ben shook his head. 'I've no idea. Not too many, I hope.'

Emma lost count of the number of stops, and, each time the door opened, more flies droned in.

Ben folded his splurged newspaper and tried to swat them. The girls had long ago closed their books, and constantly waved at the flies, until they cried themselves to sleep.

The next stop was Port Wakefield. 'Halfway House,' the coachman announced. 'Everybody out. But don't go far, we leave in forty-five minutes.'

'Halfway?' Eliza moaned as she lowered herself to sit on the grass.

The children leaped around and pointed at the boats on the Wakefield River. Emma loosened the string from their second food parcel, and they all ate.

Bullock wagons, with chains rattling, trundled by. They stared at the drivers who cracked their whips and pitied the slathering beasts.

When the families re-boarded the coach, it continued through the town.

'Look, there's a post office, courthouse, and an institute!' Ben said to William. 'Maybe Moonta will have some too.' Ben relaxed a little.

They continued to the base of the Hummocks, where the driver stopped. 'Everyone out. The horses need help up this hill.'

They walked up the hill, swiping at the flies, then gratefully re-boarded the carriage. There were three more changes of horses, and the leaping and lurching of the coach increased after sunset. By then the girls were heavy, asleep in their parents' arms. Finally, the silhouettes of the Moonta Mines chimney stacks appeared on the horizon. Emma thought the place looked snug with its tiny twinkling candle lights. Danny Rowe was waiting for them. He hugged them and led them to their cottages, brightly lit with candles.

'The cottages are a bit sparse,' Danny apologised. 'Built by the miners, they were supposed to be temporary. But the men liked living close to work. And the boss is happy we are miles from a tippling house.'

There were no shelves, and the floor of the two rooms was stamped earth. At one end was a broad stone chimney venting the camp-oven.

Danny pointed to the lavatory, a few yards away, a shadow in the dark. 'Best use the chamber-pot overnight,' he whispered.

In the morning, the sky was blue, and the air was blessedly cool. Emma was pleased to see the walls were whitewashed. At the back was a washroom, under a skillion roof. But then she stepped outside. 'Oh Ben, it's filthy.' She stepped back from the muck which seeped into her shoe. 'These so-called cottages are, what? Mud huts? So smelly and – close together. Not even in a straight line.' A goat nibbled at her other shoe. 'Go away,' she shouted.

Ben pulled at a sagging fence, its uprights as uneven as an old crone's teeth. He tried to wedge one post beside another, but it sank back into the muck. He pointed to a cluster of freshly painted huts up along the hill, one looking smart with a wooden veranda. 'There are a few nice cottages up there. We will smarten this one up. I'll get a garden started with our slips and seeds.'

Emma bit her tongue, thinking she should give him a chance.

After Ben left to find the employment office, Elizabeth Bennett and Rachel Rowe were at her door.

'Welcome to Little Cornwall,' Rachel said.

'And this is little Mary-Ann?' Emma said, of the five-year-old.

The little girl showed them her doll, a wonderful creation with two blue eyes and a wide smile embroidered on its face. Annie and Lizey were delighted.

Elizabeth, obviously with child, handed Emma a tray of pasties.

'You must have been up early,' Emma declared 'But you should take it easy.'

'It stops me from worrying,' Elizabeth said with a thin smile.

Emma wondered if Elizabeth had lost a baby, too.

Emma, flustered, looked at the muddle of her belongings. 'There are no cupboards,' she complained.

'It's not easy at first,' Rachel replied. 'Some places are better than others. Danny will bring some gravel for your path. And we can give you boxes for shelves.'

Elizabeth added. 'We have an underground tank to catch the rainwater. It's great for washing clothes, but don't drink it. There is proper condensed water available from the still, for tuppence a bucket.'

Emma unfolded her arms. They were almost like family.

Superintendent Henry Richard Hancock, from Devon, known as HRH, handsome, bearded and frock-coated, was only thirty-three, yet he swished around like royalty. With his superior knowledge and careful planning, he had turned the Moonta mines into one of the richest in the world, employing twelve hundred men.

At his interview, Ben cricked his neck to look up at the man.

Although he was six-foot-two and towered over the nuggetty Cornishman, Hancock clutched the paperwork to his chest and mounted a pulpit for all interviews. No man except Hancock would see any important documents. Hancock said to Ben, 'Drinking, fighting, or laziness will not be tolerated. Work hard and you have a job for life.'

Ben liked his straightforward attitude. Hard and sober work was the least of Ben's worries.

Afterwards, Superintendent Hancock blew a whistle into his speaking-tube and asked that Captain Bice show Mr Bowden around. Ben recognised the man immediately.

'So, you made it?' Samuel Bice said. Ben leaned in, it was difficult to hear, amid a sea of workshops, foundries, and head frames. Men everywhere were digging, sawing, trenching, and hammering.

When Ben and Samuel left the workshops area, Samuel happened to glance back at the superintendent, who had appeared on his rooftop. Ben shaded his eyes. 'What is he doing up there?'

'From there, he can see the whole lease,' Samuel explained,' but you've nothing to fear. He watches over everything. I've worked in less congenial surroundings. Drunkenness and riots were rife on the goldfields. Convicts too. You won't see any of that here. And sorry is the man who doesn't go t' chapel every Sunday.'

Ben stared briefly at four black workers digging a trench.

Samuel said, 'Captain Hancock shows the natives great kindness. They are a bit irregular, but he says it is better that they earn an honest living. He gives them clothes and food parcels, and he had a big tea for them lately, in the Institute. What a day it was with their lubras and piccaninnies.'

Ben smiled weakly and nodded; he knew nothing about natives.

Ben was up early the following morning, and at dawn, Danny Rowe knocked to introduce Ben to Charlie Pryor. 'Charlie was on the ship with us,' Danny said. 'You're assigned to his team. They're bidding for a pitch today.'

Ben waited for someone to explain the procedure as he and Charlie headed into the central workshop area. Near the counting house, Charlie stopped and said, 'There are ten of us on the team, and we're bidding for a pitch today. This being your first, leave the bidding to us.'

Ben took a deep breath. 'You'll get no interference from me.'

Dozens of bantering men crowded around the Count House window quickly quietened themselves as the auction began. 'There are three teams of tut-workers bidding,' Danny whispered.

Ben nodded, though he didn't even know what they were bidding on.

'Sold!' the auctioneer cried.

'We lost that one,' Charlie explained. 'Now, we try for another.'

The auctioneer began again, 'Work on the Prince Alfred shaft; eighty fathoms long; three foot wide; six foot deep; to be completed in four weeks. What am I bid?'

'One hundred and twenty pounds,' said Danny.

'One hundred and ten,' said another.

'Ninety-five pounds,' Charlie shouted.

The auctioneer threw a pebble into the air. 'Sold,' he shouted.

'What was that about?' Ben asked.

'They always throw a pebble – makes it fair. If someone bids less before the pebble drops, they win.'

Ben scratched his head and replaced his cap. 'So, we won?'

'Yes, lowest bidder wins. All up, we'll be paid about nine pounds and fifty shillings each. We could hit a hard spot, or a wet one, and not finish on time, but I thought it best we get you working straight away. You have your own candles and sharp new picks, so there'll be no deductions on that.'

The two men started work that day and found the autumn days ideal for working out in the open.

Ben told Emma, 'Tunnelling is back-breaking work, but it's good steady money.'

William was behind Ben. 'Where's your sense of adventure? I can't wait to be a Tributer, paid for quality, not quantity.'

'Not me,' Ben said. 'This is safer. At least there's a fair chance we'll meet the deadline. What if you work a whole month and find no copper?'

'It's a rich mine. Surely that's unlikely.'

Timber men, Moonta Mines, c. 1910, courtesy, SLSA, B24094

Ben soon felt at home amongst his jovial countrymen, being plied with a constant barrage of leg-pulling jokes. Tales of HR Hancock's supposed bungles and dalliances were legion at Moonta Mines.

'Why do they say those things about him and other women?' Ben asked Charlie. 'Mr Bice said that Captain Hancock is a fine upstanding Wesleyan.'

'It's not as though the man can sneak around unseen,' Charlie replied. 'But he is a handsome bloke, swishing around, tipping his top hat to the ladies on a Sunday.'

Leg pulling already being second nature to him, William quickly joined in. His first trick was to send Charlie to the counting house for a new assignment.

Charlie came back, raging that William had made a fool of him, and had sent him for nothing. 'Right, Trethowan,' he added. 'I thought we were friends. I'll sort you out later.'

'Come on, Ben,' Charlie said, 'let me show you around a bit more, I've a few more tips for you. If your friend is so smart, he can work them out for himself.'

'There's more to see?' Ben asked, when they moved away.

'More to *know*,' Charlie said. 'Men will tease you at every opportunity. They sent me on a long errand, looking for the superintendent's white cow. They misdirected me, sent me in circles. Of course, there is no such beast. Captain Hancock's *white cow* is his mines, the world's most productive bovine.'

'Thanks for the warning.'

'But you are lucky to be here. The superintendent has a genius for investment. With the copper so rich near the surface, he convinced the shareholders to put aside some of the profit for leaner days.'

'Like farmers,' Ben said.

'That's right. He spent the surplus by going deeper than they needed at the time. He also built larger pumps and crushers. So that when the price of copper falls, he will be ready to shift the men to unsorted heaps of diggings. That way, the profits and dividends will continue – more or less seamlessly.'

That evening Ben told Emma about the astute superintendent. Emma relaxed a little as she put Ben's supper on the table. 'Let's hope the mines are safer with such a smart man in charge,' she said.

There were many children in the adjoining cottages for Annie and Lizey to play with, and, surrounded by the achingly familiar brogue of home, Emma began to warm to Moonta Mines. Just as they might in the real Cornwall, Moonta Mines' ovens issued forth the most gorgeous smell of pasties, pastry baking in the juices of meat and vegetables.

Emma and Eliza asked Elizabeth Bennett about a midwife.

'Look no further,' Elizabeth replied, 'Mama says you'll not find better than Mrs Nancarrow.'

Mrs Nancarrow delivered Eliza a soft downy-haired son, William John Trethowan, on June 4, 1869. Four-year-old Emily rushed to tell Annie about her new baby. After Emily's bragging for some hours, Annie began pestering her mother.

'When we getting our baby?' Annie whined.

'When we getting our baby?' repeated Lizey.

Emma was soon sorry she had told them.

Mrs Nancarrow and Emma cared for Eliza for the first weeks. Emma gave Annie and Emily strict instructions to look after two-year-old Lizey, who was likely to wander from the house.

'But she can't play hide and seek, Mama,' protested Annie.

'Well, think of some games she can play. Come on now, you're a clever girl.'

Annie pouted and, taking Lizey by the hand outside, Emma heard her tell Emily the bad news.

On September 24, Ben and Emma's third daughter, Mary, was born.

Emma wrote to her mother to tell of the arrival of Mary, that Lizey had turned two, and Annie could write her name. The news filled a page, but there was so much more to say. Would she try to explain the superintendent's white cow?

If only I could see you all, just to catch up. Everything is so different here. Yet I can only imagine you all to be as you were, on that awful day we left.

It's hard to believe George and John are stonemasons – and that John is married to Esther. I wish I could see Kitty's new baby. That's what I really miss, the weddings and babies. And Mary – do you ever hear from her? Is she still in Dorset?

There are thousands of Cornish here, so it sounds like home.

Write soon, your letters mean everything to me.

Emma wanted to ask more important questions, too. Face-to-face questions she could only ask of people she knew and trusted. Was it all right to buy the new soap powders instead of making their own? Was it normal to not want more children? She would want to see their faces when she broached those subjects.

When baby Mary became more wakeful, and Emma was wondering if she would retain her sanity, her friend Grace Retallick knocked on the cottage door.

'Grace – is it really you?' Emma said, hugging her friend. 'However did you find us?'

'Where do I start?' Grace said. 'I met a man, Christopher Medlin. We worked in the fish market in Adelaide. He hated it there, so he applied to work at Wallaroo Mines. I sort of followed him here.' She blushed.

'Grace!'

'I surprised myself,' Grace said. 'But now, I have a good position as a shopgirl, and I have one free afternoon every fortnight. Christopher works with Joseph Hore. Remember Susan from the ship? They told us you were here. And there's a bus between the two mines, three times a week.'

Emma sat back and relaxed. Even Mary lay quietly against her mother's chest, and Annie and Lizey sat cross-legged, listening to their mother and Grace. After a pleasant afternoon, with promises to return regularly, Grace left for the last omnibus.

When Ben came in from work, Emma was bursting with the news. 'It's a miracle. Grace is at Wallaroo Mines; she caught the bus here. I was so longing to talk to someone from home.'

Ben washed the last of the grime from his face. 'Slow down, Em, you've lost me. Grace is where?'

'She came here on the mines' bus. Susan Hore told her we were here. She said she'd bring something for the girls the next time she's visiting.'

The following fortnight, the girls welcomed their Aunty Grace with huge hugs around her knees. 'And how are my girls?' she said, bending down to kiss their rosy cheeks. When Grace sat back, she noticed Emma's dark rings under her eyes. 'How are you?'

'Mary – didn't give me much sleep this week.'

Grace swooped on the clothes basket. 'I'll take this up to the mangle room. Come on, girls.'

'You can't do that,' Emma protested, 'Look at you, dressed like

Sundays.'

'Piffle. It will wash, and don't worry. Some nice young man will carry the basket for me and put the clothes through the mangle.'

10. Roundabouts and Swings

Gusts of wind and rain blew the kitchen door open, and Emma's three children howled. Emma ran and slammed the door.

'Why the door oping, Mamma?' Lizey cried.

Little Mary cried, too, as they both clung to Emma.

'It's the wind, sweetheart.'

When rain blew under the door, Emma blocked it with a towel and asked Annie and Lizey to help cover the floor with newspaper. Mary wailed again. Emma thought of the rain in Cornwall and was surprised how quickly she tired of rain here. She had seen more sunshine in six years in South Australia than in her entire life back home. Eliza knocked and tried to open the door. Emma pulled the wet cloth back and welcomed in Eliza and her children.

'Let's do this turn-about,' Emma said. 'I feel better already.'

Eliza agreed. 'One of us can watch the children while the other bakes or mends. We can even bring washing to the mangle room.'

The rain continued, and, in mid-June, 1870, Emma, on her way to Eliza's cottage, saw Mrs Nancarrow. The flushed midwife rushed right past.

Emma sat Mary on the floor beside William-John.

Eliza looked pensive, staring after Mrs Nancarrow through the window.

'What is it?' Emma whispered, removing her wet bonnet.

'Seven children have died of typhoid,' Eliza said. 'Some living not far from here.'

Emma blanched. 'Typhoid?' she whispered. 'They said it wasn't. You can't believe those medical men for a minute.'

While they were sipping tea, Emma bit at a fingernail. 'We won't allow the children outside until the dying stops. I don't know what else to do. Where does it come from?'

'Where does what come from, Mamma?' said Annie, arms around her waist.

Emma hugged her and smoothed her curls. 'The rain, darling,' she said. 'The rain.'

Later, Emma buried her tears in Ben's shoulder. 'I can't bear it,' she whispered. 'Look.'

They stared through the small window. The mining lease was quite flat, and, with the rain sheeting down, the muck swirled outside the houses, and vermin swam in it.

'Look at those rats,' said Emma. 'I couldn't go on if anything happened to the girls. There isn't a day I don't think about little William.'

Ben's heart also ached. The girls were fighting. But Lizey was no match for Annie. 'Hey,' their father growled. Lizey began to cry. Ben picked her up. 'Now, now,' he said. He tickled under her chin until she smiled. 'That's better. Now, you be good to your sister.' He put more logs on the fire, sending sparks onto the hearth.

Lizey's eyes twinkled. 'More sparks, Dada,' she said, clapping her hands.

'No more just now, or I'll – tickle you again,' he said, spreading his fingers toward her.

'No!' she squealed.

Emma smiled.

When the children were in bed, Ben again tried to reassure Emma. 'Most of the children affected lived in Cemetery Flats, it's awfully low there. The water is knee deep.'

'That's not so far from us, Ben,' she said, 'there are muckheaps everywhere. And everyone knows that infections grow around the smell of muck heaps.'

Each time the bell tolled, heralding another funeral, Emma's fears increased. She knew it was only a matter of time. With the continuing rain, she refused to take the children to chapel. She wondered if the Lord would punish her, but every Sunday she went to one service, and Ben to the other.

As the number of deaths grew, the 750 seats in the chapel were full to overflowing. During the services, Emma watched many men and women rush to the pulpit and offer themselves to God.

In the midst of the tragedies and religious zeal, a traveling circus had arrived.

'They've parked their yellow caravans on a high spot, about halfway to the chapel,' Danny quipped to Ben. 'I must say we have more than circuses to think about.'

That evening, Ben and William saw the ringmaster outside of his tent, under a large umbrella.

'Roll up! Roll up!' the ringmaster cried. 'See the world's largest circus! We have gorillas, clowns, acrobats, and much, much more.'

William looked back. 'I thought as much. Everyone is just walking past. There's no one in there.'

Later, Ben saw the ringmaster standing at the back of the packed chapel. In the morning, the circus was gone.

The mine bell tolled loudly on June 27. Emma stepped outside and looked at Marianne, her nearest neighbour.

'Must be a cave-in,' Marianne said.

Soon a stream of black-faced miners had returned early. Emma looked anxiously for Ben.

'Praise the Lord,' she said when she saw him, closely followed by William.

'It's not the mines,' Ben told Emma. 'You won't believe it, but the wife of the superintendent, Mrs Hancock, and the wife of Captain Cowling, have both died of typhoid. The superintendent has closed the mines. Everyone is shocked.

Ben hugged Emma. 'You were right, my dear – it knows no bounds. But we must have faith. You and Eliza have managed so well. Little Mary, and William-John, not twelve months old, and Mrs Nancarrow says they are two of the bonniest babies on the lease.'

'They are now, but those ladies had the best of everything, living in the woods with their servants, water closets and grand stone houses.' Emma blew her nose loudly. 'Captain Hancock might be the best mining superintendent in the world, but he knows nothing about sickness.'

The Moonta Mines Wesleyan Chapel overflowed with mourners at the two large funerals, and prayer meetings.

Emma was almost dizzy with worry as she waited for her children to fall ill. When Lizey woke one morning with a rash and vomited, Emma, with a devastating sinking feeling, picked up Mary, told the girls to be good, and ran white-faced to Eliza. 'Don't come near us – Lizey is sick,' Emma cried.

Eliza sent for Mrs Nancarrow, but, by then, Lizey had brightened and was asking for food. Mrs Nancarrow put her hand to the child's brow. 'Just a little tummy upset,' she said. 'Try not to worry.'

Try not to worry! Emma thought, gritting her teeth.

Although the deaths continued, remarkably, the Bowden and Trethowan children remained safe.

When the rain ceased in July, relief flooded through Emma, and her headaches eased.

'More bad news,' Ben told Emma when he returned from the mine, 'the superintendent's mother in Devon has died. They say he has a plan to appease the Lord. We don't know what it is, but he's called a public meeting. Some say he's leaving Australia. Others say we'll all be sent to Moonta to live.'

Emma's eyes brightened. 'To Moonta? In the town?'

The miners filled the church, and Superintendent Hancock addressed them from the pulpit. 'Let it be heard. I will expand the seating of this chapel, by building an internal gallery on the upper level. As with the church, we will build it ourselves. You will work some shifts in the mines and spend the rest of your time working here. See your captains for details.'

Emma squealed when Ben brought the news. 'You are actually going to work above the ground?'

'Until the gallery is finished.'

'Let's hope it never is,' Emma said.

The project began almost immediately. The captains, along with a carpenter from Moonta, supervised the workers. Ben warmed to the work. If only he was a tradesman, he thought, again, admiring the shiny turned cedar rails. He would earn respect – and a lot more money. He found it enormously rewarding, working with his hands.

When the new gallery opened three months later, the spruced-up Bowden family made their way to the chapel, pushing under the modest bunting that fluttered from its tent.

Annie jumped with excitement. 'Do you hear it, Mamma? The band?'

Emma smiled. How could she not hear the trumpets and trombones of the Moonta Brass Band?

With the 1250 seats of the Moonta Mines Wesleyan Chapel filled, Superintendent Hancock congratulated the congregation, saying they now had the biggest church in South Australia.

Ben's work on the Chapel would always be there, for his life, and his children's lives. He wasn't just digging holes anymore.

With the arrival of spring, the weather continued to improve. Emma was charmed by the magpies warbling and picking in the gardens. The rain, which caused so much terror, had quite a beneficial effect on the soil. Seedlings of every kind appeared in their gardens.

Ben removed the weeds and discovered a bountiful crop of swede-turnips, which just grew and grew. And Emma felt stronger, eating every day the green turnip tops for salads, and the tender thinned turnips with her dinner. Those tubers that took root some distance from the main crop grew even bigger.

Neighbours stopped to comment on Ben's garden, and both families feasted off the vegetables for weeks. Emma boiled and baked the yellow flesh, made turnip cakes, turnip soup, and the children had raw turnip snacks. As a special treat, Emma added a little sugar and made pasties.

'It tastes like apple,' Annie said. 'Tapple pie!'

Emily giggled.

Such was the talk of the turnips that the preacher congratulated Ben from the pulpit one Sunday.

After church, Charlie Pryor hailed Ben. 'The turnip expert, I believe,' he said, waving a page from the local newspaper. 'Look. You are quite famous.'

Ben blushed. 'They're only turnips,' he said.

William stepped in and took the newspaper from Charlie. 'May I?' He found the column and began to read.

> *The Wallaroo Times,* October 8, 1870:
> A considerable peculiarity of the soil in the neighbourhood, although it is mostly sand, it is amazingly fertile…A few enormous turnips which came under our notice lately…

'Here we are,' William said,

> they were grown by Mr Ben Bowden, of Moonta Mine, and the largest of them measured no less than 33 inches in circumference.

William gave Charlie his page and laughed. 'Thirty-three inches? Is he sure? And let's not forget you're an expert cabbage man. I'd say you can give up mining now, Ben.' William referred to a time in Cornwall, when Ben, defying his father, thinned the cabbage plants too far apart. To his father's chagrin, the cabbage crop was the best ever.

Ben couldn't wait to be a farmer, earning the respect of his fellow men. And his family would never go hungry.

After Emma gave birth to a son on 31 May 1871, continuing with the family tradition, they named him Ben. He was the seventh and last successive Bowden baby to be named thus.

Emma was exhausted, but Mary, not yet two, still demanded Mamma's milk.

'Let me take her for a few days,' Eliza offered. 'Emily will enjoy looking after her, won't you love? She's like a little doll, with those gorgeous blue eyes.'

'Do you want to come and stay with us, Mary?' asked Emily.

Mary smiled and ran to Emily, little legs flying. 'Bye, Mamma,' she said.

Emma laughed. 'Not just yet,' she said to Mary.

'Annie,' Eliza said, 'pack her a little bundle will you, love?'

Six months later, William, Eliza, and their two children filed into the Bowden-family mining hut to wish Emma a happy birthday. She was twenty-six.

Eliza presented Emma with a cake covered with cream and flowers. The children gathered around the cake, the two-year-olds reaching in with their fingers. 'No!' said Annie and Emily both, moving the cake away. Emma was pleased Eliza and William remembered. She was exhausted and looked forward to any distraction. Baby Ben was six months old, and Annie, Lizey and Mary were six, five, and two. Emma wasn't the only woman on the lease with four children, but she hoped little Ben was her last.

The baby gurgled as his uncle tipped him under the chin. 'Hey, sis, don't forget that Annie and Emily are going to Sunday school in December,' William said.

'Absolutely,' Emma said. 'The Sunday school anniversary last year was wonderful. I was just sorry they didn't get to sing or march.'

'You have to admit,' William said, 'with four hundred children and sixty teachers, our esteemed superintendent is a good man. We must educate our children in these modern times.'

'He is bent on educating us all,' Ben said. 'Every boy who works here has to attend night school. And that new reading room of ours has nearly forty books. Each book must have cost him a week's wages.'

'And we can play chess in the library too,' William said, his eyes twinkling.

'In your spare time, you mean?' Emma said, as William side-stepped his sister.

'You have to admit, though,' William countered, 'that man does look after us. You didn't complain when he encouraged cricket and foot racing over wrestling.'

William was right, but Emma wasn't about to say so.

In December, 1872, William and Eliza's third child was due. Sweat rolled off Eliza's face while she waited for the midwife. But Mrs Nancarrow was birthing twins elsewhere.

Eliza wailed. 'Don't leave me, Em. You've had five babies. Couldn't you...?'

Emma paled. 'All right,' she said.

Her nearest neighbour, Marianne, agreed to look after both Emma and Eliza's children. Emma sat with Eliza, and when she finally heard Eliza's guttural groan, she agreed Eliza should push her baby into the world.

Rosina Jane slipped into Emma's waiting hands and wailed a lusty cry. Emma breathed a sigh of relief. They had been lucky there were no complications.

Soon after little Rosina arrived, William's opportunity to join a tribute team came up. William told Ben, 'Manny Martin is injured, and they're letting me replace him. I must have been in the right place at the right time.'

Ben shook William's hand. 'Congratulations.'

'I could be rich by Christmas.'

'It might take time, Will, but I'll help you carry it to the bank.'

After another hot night in January, 1873, Emma woke to a thunderclap explosion that shook the ground. Emma pulled the bedsheet to her face and suppressed a scream, 'Ben! What was that?'

The children woke, crying. Ben dressed and rushed to the door.

It was just after five in the morning, and people oozed from their cottages in various states of dress. Women clutched babies and children trailed their mother's skirts. When the bell rang continuously, it confirmed what Emma had feared. The explosion was not planned. It was an accident.

After breakfast, Ben pulled on his boots. 'I have to go. If the area is closed, I'll be back.'

When Ben arrived back home, Emma asked what had happened. 'Some say three men died. Tell me it's not true.'

'I'm afraid one man died,' Ben said. 'James Williams. But the

Purling boy is all right.' He didn't tell her that the stoker at Ryan's engine house had seen Williams, and the roof of the hut, blown into the air.

'Poor Williams is one too many.'

'I know, love, but, according to Turner, the engine driver, Williams and Purling went into the hut to rest, taking a lighted candle. Before they went to sleep, Williams stuck the candle onto the side of a box to keep it from falling over. Unfortunately, the box contained dynamite and detonators.'

'He what?' Emma said.

'And, apparently, it was Williams himself who put the boxes in there, just the day before!'

'I told you we're not safe,' Emma cried. 'What if there were more boxes?'

'If the rules are followed, everyone will be safe,' Ben countered.

'But they don't always follow the rules, do they? Working nights in this heat, I can see how they might forget.'

'They are paid well not to forget!' Ben shouted.

Emma cowed; Ben rarely raised his voice.

When there were two more accidental deaths within the month, Emma raged at him. '*Now* do you see?' she said.

'The lad shouldn't have been near the shaft,' Ben said.

'What if one of our children wandered in the night, and we went looking for them, in the dark. We could fall down a shaft too. How many more have to die before you admit it's not safe here?' She rubbed her tummy, as yet another baby kicked and twisted inside her.

'Of course,' Ben said. 'I'm sorry. The problem is, I can't see a way out. Maybe we can build a house further away from the mines – if the superintendent agrees. The only problem is it will cost us time and money. That will delay our leaving here. Which sort of defeats the purpose. But let me talk to William.'

William was secretive. 'Something has come up. Don't breathe a word, but my luck might be about to change.'

'How is that?'

'It's, ah, complicated. Just trust me. You'll know soon enough.'

And, a week later Ben did know, but then so did everyone else. It was a memorable day, when the men returning from the early shift at Prince Alfred Shaft sang an achingly familiar tune. They weren't usually as vocal, and Ben wondered what had happened. Then he saw William, hailed by a small crowd singing:

And shall Trelawny live
And shall Trelawny die
Here's twenty thousand Cornishmen
Will know the reason why

William grinned as the men clapped one another on the back. Eliza and Emma joined Ben, and William sauntered over. 'We found a good lode,' he said, hugging his wife and sister. 'Danny guesses we'll get about two hundred pounds each. We won't know until they smelt it, but it will be enough for a deposit. I can finally buy my farm.'

'So, what was the big secret?' Ben said quietly.

'Nothing really,' William said, turning back to Eliza.

When the ore bonanza was assayed, William told Ben it was time to move. 'I've seen a land agent, and he says farmland has opened up nearby. With only a twenty percent deposit required. With the balance not due for four years, I can, at last, afford it!'

'Lucky you,' Ben said, thinking of the explosions, and endless choking tunnels. 'If only...'

'Maybe I can pay you to help me clear it, Ben.'

Ben sighed. 'It won't be too soon for Emma.'

'Mind you, at two pounds an acre, equal to the best in the hundred, he said it's not great value for unimproved mallee country. And, if it was unsold, I could buy it a week later for a pound an acre. I'm tempted to wait. That money was hard earned.'

'Difficult decision,' Ben said. 'But it is only a week.'

'You are right. I think I'll wait.'

On 4 February, another emergency bell rang at the mines.

Emma was expecting her sixth baby any day. She felt enormous, was sweating profusely, and again overwhelmed by her tetchy children in the February heat. She was glad Elizabeth Bennett was visiting with her four-year-old. She missed her dear friend Grace, who had just given birth to a daughter, Mary Grace.

Elizabeth and Emma were setting out teacups when the bell rang. When it continued to ring, Elizabeth raised her eyebrows. 'Now we wait.'

Emma put her hand to her back. 'Please God, no mine manager

comes our way.' After thirty minutes, Emma relaxed, no one had arrived, Ben is all right, she reassured herself.

Soon afterwards a dog barked endlessly, and, looking out the door again, Emma saw two captains approaching. One was Captain Bice, who looked her in the eyes. She put her hand to her belly and took a short breath. Elizabeth turned to her. But the managers walked past Emma and fixed their gaze on Eliza.

They spoke quietly to her.

'No! No!' Eliza cried. Mr Bice took Eliza's arm and looked for Emma. Although Emma had prayed it wasn't Ben, she couldn't bear anything to happen to her brother, either. Her heart began to pound.

Mr Bice put a hand on both their shoulders. 'The mine wall collapsed, and William is trapped,' he told them. 'It is taking time, but we will bring him up.' He lowered his voice. 'Unfortunately, we don't know whether he has survived or not.'

When the two men left, Emma clung to a dazed Eliza, and women surrounded them. Emma hated the inactivity, the waiting. She had to do something. 'Elizabeth, can you help?'

'Of course.'

'We need to get the children out of William's house.'

Elizabeth Bennett marshalled the small tribe into the Bowden cottage. 'Now, who wants tea?'

'I'll help too, Emma,' said Marianne.

Her heart still racing, Emma looked around Eliza's kitchen. 'Marianne, they'll put William on the table. Will you ask those young men to bring some boiling kettles, and more wood for the fire? And we'll need some clean towels and rags.'

Ben arrived. He was pale, and near tears.

'They sent me to tell you they are working as fast as they can,' he said. 'What can I do?'

'Tell me why we are here,' Emma said. 'Ah – don't bother. Just help clear the kitchen.'

Ben helped remove the bench and chairs and pulled the table into the centre of the room.

'Where are they, Emma?' Eliza began to cry again. 'I can't...'

It took them an hour to free an unconscious William from his prison of mud and rock. Emma watched Eliza run out to meet the procession of men carrying him on a stretcher, before she had the bravery to do so herself. Once she was at William's side, Emma willed her brother to wake up.

'He's still breathing, Mrs,' said the first man.

'Jim, watch that leg while we get him on the table.'

'The doctor is on his way,' the underground-captain told Eliza.

With mine dirt caked blood at several points on his body, William looked horrific. Seeing his twisted, bleeding leg, Emma quickly looked away. Eliza retched.

Emma thought that they might both feel better helping, so she filled two bowls with water and handed one to Eliza. 'Help me wash him a little, so the doctor can see what is broken.'

The *Yorke's Peninsula Advertiser*, Saturday, February 8, 1873:
A miner, William Trethowan … at the Moonta Mines met
with a serious accident. He was working at the 45 fm. Level, Prince Alfred Shaft, when a quantity of ground from the
hanging wall fell on him. From his appearance and evident
suffering, it was first feared that his injuries were of a fatal
character, but Doctor Goss found that his hurts only consisted
of a broken leg and various bruises from which it is believed
he will recover in due time.

'Various bruises!' Ben said. 'The man is broken in a dozen places!'

Doctor Goss had set William's leg as best he could, and William roused two days later. He gripped Emma's hands, crying out for every breath made through his broken ribs.

Eliza clutched her hands together. 'Please, Dr Goss, can he have more pain medicine?'

Emma added her pleas to Eliza's, but the doctor was firm. 'Too risky,' he said. 'It may affect his breathing, and we can't chance a case of pneumonia.'

Emma and Eliza sobbed. If they persisted, they were afraid the doctor would send William to the Wallaroo Hospital, and they might never see him again. When the doctor *did* mention the hospital, the tall and kindly Mrs Woods quickly defeated it. 'We prefer to keep family members at home,' she said.

After the doctor had left, Mrs Woods explained, 'He's a good man, but I hear there's a new doctor in Kadina, fresh from England. They say he is excellent with mine injuries. He would have to travel, of course.'

Eliza said she didn't care what it cost. Soon enough, one shiny black buggy owned by one of England's finest doctors was rolling into town.

'You wouldn't believe how nice that man is,' Eliza told Emma.

'And he's worth every penny.'

'He talked to me as though I was important,' William said. 'Imagine that.'

'I can't really, William,' Emma said.

'He told us of a new way of thinking about illness,' William added. 'What's the word? Antisepsis...'

'You should have seen him,' Eliza said. 'He put a new cleansing dressing on and said, when the wound is under control, he's going to teach me.' Her face was full of hope.

Three weeks after William's accident in March, 1873, Emma gave birth to her sixth baby, John.

Emma missed Eliza's support, and baby John did not sleep well. Ben watched as Emma seemed to have several pairs of hands. What a woman, he thought. They were so lucky to have her.

When the skies turned grey, and talk of measles and typhoid spread, Ben saw the heaviness around Emma's eyes. She leaned her head on Ben's shoulder before he left for work. 'I don't know who to worry about most,' she said, 'baby John, the older children playing in the rain, or poor William...'

'I know, my love,' Ben said. 'Let me take baby John while you get comfortable. Don't worry about dinner tonight. Marianne has brought a stew, and Annie will heat it in the oven. I know Mrs Nancarrow is sending us down a perambulator. It is a marvel for rocking babies to sleep.'

'Bless Mrs Nancarrow,' Emma said, with a weary smile.

'And the Moonta Sanitary Inspector is sending farmers here to the mines,' Ben said, 'to move the muck from around the cottages. The north-west corner is finished; it looks so good. But Captain Hancock is furious at the interference.'

'Well, poor him. His Royal Highness will just have to accept he doesn't know everything.'

Five months after William's accident, Emma heard a knock at the door. The three girls rushed to open it, knocking Benjy to the floor. He wailed.

'Girls, be careful,' Emma shrieked.

Emma, pushing her hair back from her face, opened the door and was staggered to see her brother standing there, aided by Danny and Charlie.

William grinned wickedly at his dishevelled sister. 'No need to roll out the red carpet, sis, it's only me.'

Emma flushed. 'Children!' she said, handing the baby to Annie as she lifted Benjy onto her hip. 'Oh, Will, you are such a welcome sight. Here, sit down.'

William wavered a little and groaned. 'No, you don't,' he growled, addressing his injured leg. 'Do as I tell you!' Beads of sweat broke across William's face as he lowered onto a chair. He smiled at it all. 'I really thought I'd never walk again,' he said. 'Some are calling it quackery, but that doctor and his newer treatments are really making a difference. The edges of the wound are pink now. It feels so much better.'

William continued to shuffle and struggle, leaning heavily on sound shoulders, until he could walk unaided. And, a year later, with the aid of his father's blackthorn stick, he walked alongside Ben to the mangle room. Ben, hearing a few somethings shuffling behind, looked back and laughed.

'What is it?' William asked.

'You're like the Pied Piper,' Ben said. 'The boys of the lease are out in force behind you.'

When the two arrived at the washroom, William eased himself onto a bench, and the curious boys crowded around, plying him with questions about the incident.

'Did the mine really fall on yer, mister?'

'What was it like?'

'Can I see yer leg?'

Ben wondered what his brother-in-law would say. William had said he remembered nothing. But there was no shortage of detail today. William's fertile imagination took over, and stories abounded for the lads to tell over the picky tables. Ben realised how much the Trethowan family meant to him. They were his family. He couldn't have been prouder of them.

Praise the Lord for the cooler mornings of March, Emma thought. And, with a spring in her stride, she set out for the Moonta Mines Chapel. With Annie and Lizey helping with the babies, Emma didn't feel as overwhelmed. Ben carried one-year-old Jack, and Benjy ran with the girls.

Annie, Lizey, and Mary split off for the Sabbath School, while Ben and Emma made their way inside. They took their pew beside Eliza and little Rosina.

The minister's voice rose as the room quietened. 'Let us pray.'

Emma sank to her knees in prayer. When she stood for the hymns, the united voices of a thousand Cornishmen and women soared sweetly around her. She leaned closer to Ben and sang in smiling unison.

The Lord's my shepherd, I'll not want…

After the service, the children ran to meet Emma outside. 'It's only four weeks to our anniversary. And there's going to be tea treats,' Annie said, tugging at her mother. 'There is singing practice on Saturdays. Can we go – please?'

Emma teased them by humming over it. Lizey and Mary jumped up and down. Her children had escaped the shame of illiteracy. Now, they would enjoy the special days of the chapel anniversary, the parade, and the tea treats. 'Of course, my darlings.'

Eliza eased over to Emma. 'William says he will attend the anniversary. Mr Bice is organising the mines' chaise for him.'

Later that evening, Emma took three dresses from the nail, which hung hidden behind one of her pinnies. She continued stitching. Ben peered over her shoulder.

'What are you doing now?'

'It's the girls' frocks for the anniversary. I don't know if we can do it, but wouldn't it be nice if they had a new dress every year, or at least a hand-me-down?'

'How on earth…?' he said, in wonderment.

'Elizabeth Bice gave me an old dress and some ribbons. And I cut down one of my old prints. Elizabeth helped me start them and Annie and I stitched the rest.'

Ben smiled widely as she leaned her head on his shoulder.

Five-year-old Mary, up early for the Sabbath School anniversary on Easter Sunday, 1874, reached up for her frilled, beribboned frock. 'Wait until after breakfast,' Emma said. 'Your little brothers might have sticky hands.'

'Aw,' said Mary.

Annie was up, too, and she took Mary by the hand, steering her toward the breakfast table. After the meal, Emma changed little Jack, while Ben helped the other children scramble for their best clothes and find four pairs of matching shoes and socks.

The Moonta Mines Wesleyan Chapel entrance was crowded, and when the chaise with William pulled up, people stood back and clapped as he walked in. Tears sprang to Emma's eyes. When the shuffling ceased, and everyone was seated, Emma heard the sweet sound of the children, singing while they marched in:

Jesus bids us shine, with a pure clear light,
Like a little candle, burning in the night,
In this world of darkness, we must shine,
You in your small corner,
And I in mine.

After this, the children sat on the temporary stage behind the lectern, and the minister prayed. Benjy wriggled and pointed. 'See Annie...'

'Hush darling,' Emma whispered. She smoothed his hair as the children sang another favourite:

Gentle Jesus, meek and mild,
Look upon a little child,
Pity my simplicity,
Suffer me to come to thee.

Emma's heart was full. It was all more than she had dreamed possible. Mary gave a little wave from the platform.

Through the long homily and prayers, Emma and Ben wrestled with the two little boys. As the service finished, the tired children met on the lawns for saffron buns, and soon left for home with their parents.

Part two of the annual celebrations was a parade by the children on the following day. They would march from the chapel to Cross Roads and back again. It was about three miles, and Emma wondered if her children could manage another long day. They were already bickering. 'They're too tired, Ben.'

'Don't you worry,' said Ben. 'I'll watch Mary. I'll bring Benjy too.' He kissed her. 'You take it easy.'

Ben praised the Lord as he watched the children's band assemble behind the Moonta Brass Band. Superintendent Hancock gave the word, and the march began. Ben hadn't realised that both bands were commissioned by Hancock; there was no doubt in his mind now, that the man had invested greatly in the welfare of his employees.

As the march proceeded, the children's tasselled hats bobbed up and down to the music of their accordions, tambourines, drums, and concertinas. Ben hoped they could afford tambourines for the two older girls next year.

'Captain Hancock knows how to put on a show,' Charlie Bennett said to Ben as a train swished by, the open carriages packed with handkerchief-waving well-wishers.

Afterwards the children sat on the grass and eagerly partook of the tea-treats, platefuls of cakes and lollies.

In the great hall, the men lit fires under the boilers and set up tables, while the ladies prepared a public tea. The event had become enormously popular, and Ben worried that Emma might overdo it. 'Anyone who ever lived here comes back for the event,' he told William.

Afterwards, the men dismantled the trestle tables for a public meeting. As Emma tried to calm her restless children, she heard her name called.

'Sarah-Ann Vicary?' Emma said, amazed. 'Is it really you?'

Sarah-Ann was heavy with child. Emma remembered the woman's large brown eyes, similar to those of her brother, James.

'Emma, this is Tom, my husband. He is a miner. We married a year ago. And Mary-Ann will be thrilled to know you're here. She and Mama are visiting soon.'

'They are coming to Moonta?' Emma asked. 'That's wonderful, Sarah-Ann.'

The crowd pushed on and the congregation shuffled to their seats.

The reverend, Mr Warner, opened with a prayer, then handed over to Superintendent Hancock, who, impeccable as always, acknowledged the preacher and swung into his speech. He had no notes.

'There are over six hundred children educated at the Sabbath School, by 110 officers, and that doesn't include our boys' evening classes...'

Ben nodded his head as the superintendent continued at length about the importance of a good Christian education.

Following this, Mr Warner called Mr Stephens, the secretary, to read his long report; the treasurer's report was equally lengthy. As the hours passed on the balmy March evening, Ben lost concentration, while Emma stifled yawns. All around them children wriggled, cried, and fell asleep. Emma was right, Ben thought, it was a long day, but the sense of belonging, the sheer pride of witnessing his children's participation in such a meaningful service, was worth the effort.

In October, Annie answered the door and ran to her mother, jiggling with excitement. 'Mama, Mama, there's three ladies at the door.'

Emma, washing clothes in the back room, followed the girls. When she saw the three Vicary women, tears sprang to her eyes. 'Come in, come in,' Emma cried. 'It's been so long.'

'Nine years,' Mrs Vicary replied, hugging Emma. 'I hope you don't mind, but I'm meeting Mrs Bice afterwards.'

'Of course not. How are you?' Emma asked softly, leading her to a chair.

'Losing John was – terrible, but the family keep me busy. Not as busy as you, I see.'

Emma's five children had assembled. 'Benjy and Jack, look at you,' Emma said, plunging their hands into a basin. 'You little monkeys, playing in mud again.' She turned to her other children and said, 'Annie, Lizey, do you remember Mrs Orsmond from the anniversary? These ladies were on the same ship as Mama and Dada.'

Annie and Mary smiled shyly, ducking their heads. Lizey stayed beside her mother. But soon they relaxed, drawn by the baby's bubbling coos. The girls edged closer to Sarah-Ann.

'What's her name?' Annie asked.

'Mary,' Sarah-Ann said, sitting the infant up and spreading her long snowy white smock.

'We have a Mary, too,' Lizey said.

Annie and Lizey leaned in and spoke to the baby who again cooed and waved her arms up and down.

'We must visit more often,' said Sarah-Ann.

Mary-Ann's nine-year-old daughter, Mary-Annie, was frocked in blue, with a long sash at her back. She asked Emma's children if they wanted to play. They moved outside, clamouring around her.

'Ah, the peace,' Emma said, pushing her curls behind her ears. She put the kettle on and set out Mrs Vicary's freshly baked saffron buns.

'Ben will be sorry he missed you, Mary-Ann.'

'Oh, I am sure we will meet again,' the 36-year-old said, coy now. 'I am going to marry Tom Warn.'

'From the shop?' Emma said. 'You said "never" Mary-Ann, but that *is* wonderful news. You'll like Moonta. It has everything. With the road metalled, and a free horse-omnibus to the town, we have great choice in there.'

When tea was finished, Mrs Vicary departed.

Emma heard the children laughing; Mary-Annie was telling a story. If only her Annie was as confident, Emma thought.

'What a wonderful girl you have there,' Emma said.

'She is rather special. Well, I would say that, wouldn't I?'

Mary-Ann leaned forward. 'How do you manage so many children, Emma? Even one child is a handful.'

'And for me,' added Sarah-Ann, laughing.

A smile spread over Emma's face. 'That's a relief,' she said. 'I thought it was just me. It's not that I don't love them, but even feeding them is like walking up hill backwards. I cook all day, then start again the next morning.' Emma put her hands to her face. 'But what am I saying? I'd rather have a dozen than lose another one.'

They talked more about the trials of the new country, and Emma sank back, renewed. When the visitors rose to go, Emma sighed. 'I hope we meet again soon,' she said.

Afterwards everyone was happier, Emma thought. Even Jack and Benjy weren't fighting, and Emma hummed as she heated their meal.

On March 3, 1875, Eliza gave birth to her fourth child, George. It was also time to rehearse for the next Sabbath School anniversary.

On March 15, a young mine manager, Hugh Datson, a devout Christian, died in a mine rock fall. He was highly thought of in the church, and his death sparked another religious revival. The Wesleyan church again overflowed, and Emma, heavily pregnant with her seventh child, felt obliged to bake for the anniversary celebrations. But she couldn't face waiting on the tables, which seated over a thousand this year. She said a prayer and sat back to watch over her offspring. She felt a great relief in her weary feet.

The ladies poured tea, and everyone partook of the food. The room quieted. Suddenly, a girl screamed, and, to Emma's horror, young Jenny Martin's muslin frock was on fire. Jenny had collected hot water from the fire-burning copper. The crowd erupted, what were they to do?

Superintendent Hancock, the quickest thinker in the room, ran toward the girl in flames. Emma watched, her hands pressed into her cheeks, as Hancock clasped the girl in his arms, smothering the fire.

Children wailed, and Emma and Ben, with most of the congregation, stood. Captain Deeble called for calm, but it was too late. Everyone was leaving.

Outside, Emma and Eliza agreed; Captain Hancock had saved the girl's life.

Emma said, 'He left the room pretty quickly afterwards. Underneath that costume of his, your Captain Hancock is truly a good man.'

11. A Little Freehold

On April 1, Emma and Ben and their five children crammed into the Trethowan hut to hear the news.

'I have been declared fit for work,' William said.

'Wait a minute, Mr Trethowan,' Ben said, with a grin. 'You caught me out last year, but not this time. I know what day it is.'

'You wouldn't dare, William,' Emma said, hands on her hips.

'You are right, my dear, I wouldn't.' He handed her the letter from the doctor.

'Say what you like,' said Emma, 'but you are not going near a mine again. Ever.'

William copied her stance. 'I totally agree. I have other plans.'

'Such as?'

'I'll bid on some land, and I think Ben might also.'

Emma looked at Ben. 'We can afford it?'

'They've changed the *Wastelands Act* again. The deposit is now 10%, with five years to pay. And land has fallen to £1 an acre.'

So it was, after eleven years, Ben Bowden and William Trethowan waited in the queue at the South Australian Bank.

The assistant manager checked Ben's statement and agreed he had sufficient funds for a modest loan. Tears threatened Ben, and he couldn't meet William's eyes.

'Get a hold of yourself,' William said. 'Don't set me off. People are watching.'

As Ben picked his way through the horse muck on George Street, he realised that, once penniless, he was going to be a landowner.

It was the blithe Cornishman, Walter Sims, who greeted them at the land office.

'This is a surprise,' said Ben.' Last I heard you were a cab man in Adelaide.'

'I was. But the miners recommended Moonta.'

The miners? Ben thought, remembering Sims's patronising attitude toward the miners on the ship.

'I was town crier here for a while,' Sims said.

Ben almost laughed. He could just see the man in a shiny red and gold costume, looking a bit like Cornwall's Mock Mayor on Furry Day, ringing his bell, and shouting:

'I bought my first land and married five years ago,' Sims continued. 'I've just taken out another credit agreement for more land. This one is nearly 400 acres. It has a slab hut on it, so we moved right in.'

'You're farming?' Ben queried.

Sims nodded. 'Some of the land was cleared, so we mullenised a bit, that's the easy way – just break up the ground with a big spikey log.'

A spikey log? Ben thought. Whatever was he talking about?

'It's better for the children living out here,' Sims continued, twiddling his thumbs. 'We have a few horses, ducks, and fowls, and we're next door to Sarah's parents.'

As the crowd pushed, Ben and William eased closer to the noticeboard. 'How is that man always a step ahead of us?' Ben whispered. 'A ready-made hut, ducks, and horses – his wife's family.'

William laughed.

'Hey, look at this,' William said, pointing to the handbill.

> The following portions of Crown Lands will be open for se-
> lection Tuesday, May 11, 1875, for one pound per acre. What
> ever is best.

'That's a month away,' Ben said. 'There are two hundreds listed: Tiparra and Kadina.'

William pointed to the map. 'As I see it, the closest is Tiparra, about ten miles from Moonta Mines.'

'They say this is in the newspaper,' Ben said. 'Why don't we splurge threepence and show it to Emma and Eliza in writing?'

Later that evening, William and Eliza arrived at their cottage. It was a tight squeeze with four adults, eight children, and baby George.

Ben nodded. 'You tell them, William, while I finish my supper.'

'Oyez, oyez...' William said, brandishing a three-cornered hat, borrowed from Sims.

> The *Yorke Peninsula Advertiser*, and *Miners' and Farmers'*
> *Journal*, Friday April 2, 1875:
> Peninsula Land Sales: Newly opened country lands
> Hundred of Tiparra: Northerly and westerly of Agery, from 8
> to 10 miles south-easterly of the Township of Moonta.'

Section/ Acres
315   406
316   441
317   327
319   276
395   290
Signed, G. W. Goyder, Surveyor-General.

'Sections 395, and 319, have about three hundred acres, which is all we can afford,' William said to Emma and Eliza. 'We have to apply by the eleventh of May.'

While Emma slept, Ben sorted through the forms and applied for Section 319.

Wallaroo Mines, 1901, courtesy, SLSA, B28701

When Ben returned to work, reinforcing tunnels in the dark mine, he prayed he would soon be out of there.

On May 19, Emma gave birth to their seventh child, and fourth son, Richard Rawling, named in honour of Ben's two baby brothers.

Emma was again plunged into the ever-challenging chaos of managing her family, and a new baby, in the small mining cottage.

On 1 July, Ben gathered Emma and the children together in the warm kitchen.

'Listen up children,' he said, winking at Emma. 'I have bought us a farm that is 276 acres, in a place called Agery. And we have our very own lake.' He bowed as they clapped.

Benjy leaned closer to Jack. 'We going to get a farm.'

Jack's eyes widened. 'Aminals?'

'Yeh. And a lake.'

'So,' Ben told Emma, 'they say we must live on the land, pay another 10% in three years, and the balance within five years. We also have to cultivate – or clear – one-fifth of the land annually. I think we can manage that.'

Ben reported the news to his employer and was pleasantly surprised. HRH said they could live at the mines for three months while they built their new house.'

'That is generous,' Emma said. 'It would be awful with eight of us living in a tent way down there.'

'So,' Ben said, 'William and I will ride down every day, maybe sleep over occasionally.'

Emma reminded him, 'You'll have to buy a horse first.'

'I have my eye on Rattler, an old mine horse. Was a bit of a goer in his day, but he's quieter now.'

On that first day, Rattler pranced as Ben packed his spade, axe-head, and a saw into a saddlebag across his lap. 'You said he'd mellowed,' William said.

Ben rolled his eyes. 'That's what they told me.'

William held Rattler's bridle while Ben climbed into the saddle. The horse stepped back nervously, as Emma pulled their two youngest boys back from behind.

As the two men set out, their families waved, and walked a little way after them.

Breaking into a trot, the two men headed in a south-easterly direction. 'I asked the men about materials,' William said. 'Bricks are expensive, timber rots. I doubt there are enough stones, and they are heavy. The mud has served us at the mines, and with your lake, it will be ideal.'

Riding off into the bush, they looked for the land parcel numbers pinned on various stakes.

'Well, there's 303 East, 304, and 305,' Ben said, pointing, 'but somebody is busy working on them.'

'Aha,' William said, slowing down. 'Sims is on 307, isn't he? Now that's a real farm, and that hut has a paling roof too.'

'Best keep on, I suppose,' William said. 'Here are 312 and 317, on the right.'

And not minutes after, almost reverentially, Ben said, 'Here I am. Three hundred and nineteen.'

William shook Ben's hand. 'Congratulations, old chap.'

'Never thought it would happen,' Ben said, blinking his wet eyes. 'Well, let's have a quick look around here, and go on to find yours.'

They led their horses around the perimeter. 'Peaceful, isn't it,' Ben said. 'Emma's right, the mines is no place to live.'

'There's a good, elevated area over there,' William said.

'True,' Ben said. 'A house can't be too high if it rains a lot.'

'Now, where's 395?' Ben said. 'Only a mile or two? Is that right?'

There were no more numbered plots until they found the lone stake numbered 395. William grinned. Ben shook his hand vigorously. They jumped down and tied their horses, walking at a leisurely pace, not wanting the magic to stop.

'There are a couple of flat areas for the house,' William said. 'And some sand over there. Perfect. I'll call the place Silver Hill, like the place back home.'

Ben said, 'Wonder what I'll call ours?'

'Anyway,' William said, 'I'll potter here for a couple of hours, and I'll see you back at yours, then.'

Ben rode back to Section 319 and wandered around. He sang quietly to himself, kicking at tree stumps and noting any large rocks. He stood back and measured with his eye. The flat elevated section was about two hundred yards from the track. Most of his land was dense Mallee scrub, with a few gumtrees.

Ben cut footholds in a large gum tree and lopped some of the lower branches. He dragged them to the western border, trimmed and divided them into kindling and logs. He repeated the process on another tree, jumped down, and cleaned the site with a large leafy branch. He hadn't enjoyed a day so much since they worked on the chapel.

When the sun was in the west, he climbed back up the tree and waited for William. From that vantage point, he could see a few more of his neighbours' huts dotted among the thick foliage. Then he spotted William trotting toward him.

The two men continued their daily sojourns from Moonta Mines on Hamley Hill to their farms at Agery. They cut red gum beams and posts, and wattle saplings for the walls.

Ben was glad of his little lake for the daub filler. The house would be small at first, but it would be theirs. He dug a deep hole for a privy, smoothing the surface of the two seats with a knife and some sandstone, and attaching it to six boxed-in legs. At last, an amenity they could keep clean, he thought. Next, he put in four posts for a screen.

Some weeks later, Ben confessed to Emma that the house was taking longer than he'd expected. 'Are you up to bringing the children down for a few days?'

Emma raised her eyebrows. 'Well, they are begging to see the place.'

Early the following Monday, Ben and Emma packed the dray with equipment, and food boxes, and Ben called the children to jump up. 'What about the two boys?' Emma said. 'I can't see them sitting still for a couple of hours. And if they fell under the cart wheels…'

'Wait here, all of you, I'll be back in a few minutes.' Ben returned with a plank and cut it to the width of the cart. 'I needed this for windowsills, but this is more important.' He anchored the timber with several nails. 'Now sit on the rug, children, and Mary, Benjy, Jack, hold onto that bar.'

It was a different journey with a cart full of children; the road being deeply scored. They couldn't avoid the gutters and holes as they had on horseback. But the spring weather was perfect, the children excited, and it was the furthest most of them had travelled.

'Marmy, Marmy look,' fair-haired Mary cried, pointing to the animals hopping away.

'Doggy,' said Jack. Everyone laughed.

'They're kangaroos,' Annie corrected.

On their arrival, Ben announced, spreading his hands around him. 'All this land is ours. I think I'll call it Wakefield Farm.'

'Why?' said Annie. Benjy and Mary, also fond of the word 'why', echoed the question.

'Because if it hadn't been for a man called Wakefield,' Emma said, 'there would be no farm.'

'Why?' repeated Mary.

'Now, never mind *why*, Miss Mary,' Ben said, picking her up. 'Let's have our pasties.'

After every crumb was devoured, Ben showed Emma how to interweave saplings for the walls and showed the children how to spread the daub mixture over the woven sticks. They loved sploshing and patting the daub.

By the day's end, the children were covered with mud, and Ben and Emma took them to the lake.

Freshly clothed and warm, lying on top of, and under a blanket, all of them but Annie were asleep when they arrived back at the mines.

Ben and William only rested on the Sabbath when they attended the Wesleyan Chapel. After the service the two families walked home. The children were usually full of energy, and William often lagged behind.

One Sunday in October, William was even slower. When an hour passed and he still hadn't arrived home, Ben told Eliza he would go look for him.

Not far away, Ben found a large crowd gathered around Grey's cottage, and William standing anxiously near the door. 'What are you doing?' he whispered to William. 'Eliza is worried.'

Dr Elphick arrived, examined the man lying on the floor, then announced to the crowd. 'Poor Sol is dead. You can go home now.'

'Let's go,' said William.

'What happened?' Ben asked as they trudged down the road. William limped heavily.

'I heard a man cry out. Then I saw Mr Grey with a lantern, looking into his own water tank.'

'He said he couldn't find Sol.'

'Sol Knuckey?' Ben asked.

William nodded. 'Grey then looked into his neighbour's tank, and said he saw a man. He gave an awful cry; that's when I heard him. Then he yelled for a rope and ladder.'

'Poor Knuckey,' Ben said.

'Tom Warn was there and he dove straight in. When he brought Sol to the surface, several men carried him into the house. They laid him on his back on the floor. Mrs Knuckey and Mrs Grey were wailing, and they began to rub Sol with salt and towels to draw the water out. But nothing worked.'

'What was Knucky doing near the tanks, at night?'

'Mr Grey invited the Knuckeys in for a cup of tea after chapel. Sol was in a hurry to leave, so Mrs Grey asked him if he would help. He could get the water, she suggested, while she milked the cow.

'She had no water, or milk?' Ben asked. 'On a Sunday?'

William nodded. 'Apparently.'

The following morning, William appeared agitated. 'I feel terrible,' he said to Emma and Eliza, 'I should have saved him. All for a pitcher of water.'

'You didn't see him. Not even Mr Grey saw him. Just ride down and finish your house and stop worrying.' Emma said.

The two men planned to work on the roofing joists at Ben's site. But when William stepped on the ladder, he winced, leaned over, and with his hands, moved his leg off the ladder.

'I can't, Ben. That thing jiggers my leg. I'm sorry.'

'William. It's about time you stopped being so – strong about everything. You are still healing.'

'Nonsense,' William groaned. 'It's nearly three years…'

Ben stared at William's tears. What was he to do? 'A mine wall fell on you, William Trethowan.'

'I was lucky, very lucky,' William said, looking around him. 'But I brought this upon myself.'

'Don't be silly.'

'I'm paying for my sins. It's the secret I never told you. We should have reported that big lode of copper when we found it. But our manager didn't come near us. He didn't care if we were safe or not. And our lease was almost up. The price would have been prohibitive if we reported it, and then we'd have had to bid at the next auction. It was so far down; we could barely breathe down there; our candles kept going out… We were so fed up.'

'Phew… Will, Hancock could throw you out.'

'Or put me in jail. You won't say a word?'

'Of course not. You're right. You've paid for your – sins. And you *are* mending. That's the main thing.'

'But you'll not finish in time, Ben, without my help.'

'Forget it, Will, I'm just glad you are alive. There's a builder at the mines, Dick Shuggs. They say he is worth two men on a building site.'

'It'll cost you…'

Ben puffed out his chest. It felt good, taking control. If only his father could see him now.

Dick Shuggs was appointed by the next day. He even helped Ben's family onto the cart. 'I know the roads, Ben,' Dick said. 'I'll drive, while you watch your little ones.'

When Dick set the horse at a cracking pace, they flew over a large rut in the road and the cart jolted. Emma lurched with it, and baby Richard woke, screaming. Rattler took the bit between his teeth and bolted. Ben and Dick heaved on the reins. 'Whoa, boy,' Ben said, tense, and tugged again. But the horse barely slowed, and when they hit another bump, the baby squalled louder.

Rattler continued in this fashion until they arrived at Section 319, in record time.

'That was fun, Da,' Benjy and Jack said as they jumped down and ran off.

'Fun? Ha,' said Ben, shaking his head. 'Small boys.'

Emma looked at the two men who sat on logs, too exhausted to move.

In November, six months after they began, Ben's house was finally finished. They were finally going to live on their own little freehold.

'Tomorrow?' Benjy asked.

'Yes, Benjy, tomorrow, we are moving to Wakefield farm.'

Benjy hooted. 'For forever, Da?'

'Forever,' his father said, tears glinting.

William helped Ben load the bench, meat safe, bed frames and roughly hewn table-top, onto William's cart. 'Those rails will hold them,' William said, pushing the meat safe safely into a corner. Then they turned their attention to Ben's wagon, with its borrowed hood.

To load the wagon, Ben lined his children up, and they passed the parcels along and up to Annie and their mother. All tucked up, the children waved to the mines' families, and they were on their way. Emma couldn't have been happier. The horse was, as Ben hoped, much more docile with the heavy load. The children chattered and argued all the way. They were full of plans to best one another at running, riding horses, and climbing trees.

As they arrived, Annie and Lizey were ecstatic. 'Look,' Annie said, pointing to the little house with its stone chimney and front awning.

'It's a weal house,' said Mary.

'Whoa,' Ben said to the horse. But he didn't have to pull hard; Rattler was tired – and he'd seen the plentiful grass. When the children climbed down, their fathers again lined them up, to ferry everything inside the house.

The children were extremely tired and not easy to settle. 'Are we really going to sleep in one room?' four-year-old Benjy whined.

'Baby Richard and Jack will sleep with us,' Emma said. 'You and the three girls will be head to toe in the other bed.'

'Aww,' Benjy yowled. 'Girls.'

William returned to Moonta Mines, knowing Ben would return the favour the following Monday. After supper, Ben drew water for the morning. When he returned his family was asleep. Emma had her arms around the two little boys. Ben wriggled in beside them.

Birdsong woke them.

Emma sighed. 'I love it here already,' she whispered to Ben. 'It's so quiet. And surely that's the freshest smell in the whole world.'

Emma was glad of the shady trees as the children played happily outside. Ben carted sand from the lakeside, and, with improvised shovels and broken spades, the children were happily occupied, building sandcastles. It was messy work, and Emma despaired of ever keeping the house and its beds clean.

Within weeks, Ben had dug and lined the new water tank with mutton fat and sand and had put a strong fence around it. He also purchased a goat for fresh milk and began work on the mallee. He was a happy man. 'Some say this is poor country,' he told Emma. 'But if trees grow, so will crops.'

However, when the time came, after two hours of digging, he returned to the house, red-faced and, wet with sweat, downed several cups of cold tea. 'You won't believe it, Em, that mallee. It looks so harmless on top. Just a few saplings, I thought. But some of them have enormous roots *under* the ground, buried in hard-packed soil, and rocks. Lots of rocks.'

'Surely not everywhere, Ben.'

'The axe just bounces off them. The shovel makes no impression, and of course I can't get near them with a saw. I wonder if William's land is any easier.'

'He hasn't been here in days.'

Realising this was true, Ben decided to take Rattler on a trot to William's farm.

Seeing him, William put his shovel down, his face dejected.

Ben peered into the hole. 'Those roots are glued to the ground.'

'That trunk is over a foot thick,' William said. 'Those taproots are the size of my arm. I'll never get it out.'

'How is it you always do better than me, Will?'

'Guess I'm just lucky 'cousin'. But hey, there's only a few thousand,' William said, straight faced. They both started laughing nervously at each other, breaking further into fits. Ben hoped no one heard their heehawing and snorting. But Eliza had seen Ben arrive and brought her children out to welcome him over.

'What's so funny?' she asked. 'William said it is terrible, heavy work.'

Ben straightened up. 'It is,' he said, looking back at William. They doubled over again.

Eliza put the back of her hand to William's forehead. 'Come in out of the heat; both of you.'

The men drank thirstily, and William said he was ready to tackle it again.

'Wait,' Ben said. 'Remember the day we saw Sims? He said something about 'the easy way – mullenising the ground first, with a spiky log.'

'I – we need to investigate that,' William said. 'I'd say Sims knows all of the shortcuts.'

'Now that I think of it,' Ben said, 'Henry Howlett has heavy logs too, gigantic things, pulled by his oxen. He dragged it over the ground soon after we arrived. I see a bit of wheat growing there. Do you suppose…?'

William nodded, 'Let's go see your neighbour.'

Henry Howlett was about the same age as Ben and, although he had only been in Agery since February, he knew the land well; he was South Australian born.

Ben and William climbed under the fence, as Henry walked up to greet them.

'Sorry to intrude,' said Ben. 'But we were wondering about the mallee. I see you have a nice crop of wheat there, nearly ready for a Ridley.'

'If I had a Ridley.' Henry wiped his eyes with his sleeve. 'That *nice crop* is hiding a multitude of mallee stumps, thanks to my Mullenisers.'

'Mullenisers?' Ben asked, still mystified.

'A chap by the name of Mullen thought it up. We use heavy logs. First, we cut down the tall mallee tops, and dig out as many roots as possible, but that's a slow business. In time, with the roots still there, the mallee will reshoot, again and again. So, we roll a big log over and smash the new growth. When it's dry, we burn it all off.'

'How do you sow the wheat?' William asked.

'We hitch up a bullock, and rough the surface up with a spiked roller. Then we scatter the seed.'

'With the stumps still there?' Ben said.

Henry walked over to the crop, and squatting on one knee, parting the wheat. 'There are plenty of stumps under there. After we harvest the wheat, we roll the stubble – and any new mallee shoots as well. Then we burn it all off and start again.'

Ben's brow creased. 'You don't plough it?'

Henry shook his head. 'Not everyone agrees, but I have to feed my family. And the regular rolling and burning, year in, year out, weakens the stumps. In the end, it gets easier.'

'Now you're talking,' William said.

Ben inspected the log. 'Whew, it's heavy.'

'You can borrow it when you're ready.'

'I wouldn't…' Ben didn't want to intrude.

'Don't worry; you'll hardly break it,' Henry grinned. 'Out here, we have to pull together. That scrub is dense. That's why they call the town Moonta, it means impenetrable scrub.'

'Well, they got that right,' Ben agreed, examining the blisters on his hands.

'The peppermint and black mallee are the worst,' Henry warned. 'The pink and red are easier; just burn them.'

'Our Mr Wakefield, did he lure us here under false pretences?'

'They say he farmed in Sydney,' Henry said. 'Some of the land was covered in Mallee. No, his plan was excellent.'

Several weeks later, Ben's other neighbour, George Matters, saw him digging. 'Heavy work?' he asked.

'You could say that,' Ben replied, glad of an excuse to stop the bone-shattering spade-work.

'The secret is to find and cut the tap roots first,' said George. 'Here, I'll show you. You've made a good start. I'll keep clearing around this root.' He dug with great vigour, the spade rasping and clunking as small rocks flew out. 'See that root now? It's nearly ready for the axe. When you've cut all the main roots, it's possible to move the stump with a fulcrum. I have a lever with a nice cutting tip, about fourteen feet long.'

'That makes sense,' Ben said. He'd seen George and his neighbours using the lever and fulcrum. 'But it's huge work for a bunch of small trees, isn't it?'

'It is. But we get paid for the stumps. They're good slow burners for the mines.'

'Glad they're good for something.'

'Before I go, Ben…' George straightened up and stretched out his back. 'There is no church around here, so we have a Wesleyan service at our house every Sunday. You are, of course, welcome. Ten o'clock. And afterwards there will be no shortage of men willing to discuss our various land issues.' George gave a half salute and left.

Ben told Emma over dinner about Mr Matters.

'That's wonderful about the service,' Emma said. 'It has been a worry, us not going. Not that it stopped us praying. But it's not the same – without a church.'

Emma spent a few days adapting and mending clothes to dress up her six children, and the family joined the Agery parishioners on Sundays, in Matters's spacious front room.

Ben, with William's help, applied the new methods to the stump removal. They both acquired a lever and fulcrum, and alternately worked between their two farms.

When Ben's first stump was ready, George put the lever under the stump and over the fulcrum.

Ben, William, and George pulled the lever downwards, grunting and growling. When the stump shifted a little, George shouted, 'more', 'more,' and with a final heave, the massive stump rose up and turned on its side.

'There are still two roots attached, but they are easy to cut,' George said.

After several months, the two brothers-in-law were exhausted by the work. 'It's not exactly what I had in mind.' William said to Ben. 'As you know, we have to cultivate a portion of our land every year. It sounded easy…'

'I agree,' Ben said. 'I might have known they wouldn't let us have real farming country. This is nothing like the farms in the foothills of Adelaide. That land must have cost them a fortune. Even at £1 an acre, this is hard work.'

'Yes,' William said. 'I am going to have to take it easy. I'll pay a man. George says there's an itinerant woodcutter in town.'

The lumberman, Tobias Moon, was a hard worker, and several of the farmers had employed him, before he left to try his hand in Maitland, further south.

'Moon saved my life,' William told Ben. 'Got me through the summer. Now let's buy a bullock and haul the stumps onto the cart.'

Managing bullocks wasn't new to the two men, but it took patience and energy harnessing and teaching the beasts the commands to go left, right, forwards, and backwards. But it reaped its rewards when Ben and William finally sold their stumps to the mines.

'Now,' William announced, to the gathered families, patting his bag of money, 'it's about time we all went into the town and celebrated Christmas.'

Emma was delighted. She hadn't been near a store in months. It was still a long bumpy ride, but worth it when she and the children arrived and joined the throng.

William mopped his face. 'They say twelve thousand people live in Moonta.'

'And they are surely all here tonight,' Ben said, bumping into several lads who jammed into nearby retail premises. The town hummed under the glow of Chinese lanterns and sparkling flashing lights.

'Listen, Mama, carols,' Annie said, dragging on her mother's arm as they moved towards the top of the town.

'Daddy, those lights are flashing on and off,' said Mary, her eyes wide.

'And there's a star in Drew's – and I see circles,' said Benjy, pointing all around him. 'It's magic.'

The sparkling, flashing lights were formed into patterns by jets of gas, all piped from the new gas company plant in Ellen Street.

When the family reached the town hall, a large brass band was playing. Emma moved closer to Ben. 'Remember Helston?' she said, smiling and tearful. 'This is fun for our children, too.'

12. Progress

Ben took a short break from cutting the mallee to dig a kitchen garden. He dug in several patches, and although he found some softer ground, he noted there were a lot of stones. He hoped it was just an isolated patch.

Several weeks later, Ben stayed on after Sunday service, hoping the other farmers would tell him the stones were not really a problem. But he was to be disappointed. George Matters and William Gluyas were in fits of laughter, proposing to make stone soup 'with the devils'.

Henry Howlett said the Smith brothers would do well to invent a stone picking machine. More laughter.

'Well, the larger stones will be good for building,' Ben added. 'And now that it's a bit cooler the children can help. I might even make them a billy goat cart to collect stones in.'

'Now, there's an idea, Henry,' Ben heard Gluyas say, 'a billy goat cart for the children?'

'You're not missing an opportunity these days, Ben,' William said.

'It's this lot,' Ben said gesturing toward Gluyas, George, and Mullen, 'ready for anything they are.'

'However,' William said quietly, 'we've promised Emma and Eliza the children will go to school.'

Ben sighed. William was right.

However, although the *Education Act of 1875* made school compulsory for children between ages seven and thirteen, the minimum number was to be sixteen pupils.

George said to Ben, 'There are only seven school aged children in Agery: John, Thomas, and Richard Gluyas, aged nine to sixteen, Emily Trethowan, and your Annie, Lizey, and Mary. 'They won't build a school and pay a teacher for just seven children,' he said.

It was to be five years before there were sixteen school-aged children in Agery.

In summer, 1876, the newspapers reported a thermometrical reading of 148° Fahrenheit in the sun, on two consecutive days. As the soil dried out, Ben coughed fitfully and retired early in the day. He wiped his eyes and took sips of water. 'It's only been a year and that dust is killing me.'

'The mine dust didn't do you any good either,' Emma said tersely.

'You are right, love,' Ben said. 'And I will have to keep on with it. On the hottest days, the children and I can pick stones in the mornings, and I'll take them to the lake in the evenings.'

Emma hugged him. 'I'll join you at the lake when I can.'

When the weather cooled, George Matters helped Ben hitch the heavy roller to the bullock. It was time to roll the new Mallee shoots.

As the shoots withered and died, Ben was anxious to burn them, but a new fire regulation forbade outside burning until April 15 each year. He returned to digging stumps, and he also cut a firebreak around the rolled site.

To Ben's delight, the burn-off was successful, after which he applied the spiked roller and with his children helping, scattered the wheat.

As months passed, the wheat grew and grew. Ben thought it a miracle, wheat growing in no apparent depth of soil. Maybe the land *was* worth what he paid for it.

Standing in the shade outside Matters's house, a group of farmers talked about the upcoming Moonta Agricultural, Horticultural, and Floricultural Society's Show. Ben heard a man named Owens say it was a long way to travel, to pay good money just to see a few flowers.

'You obviously haven't been to one,' William Matters retorted. 'I never saw finer exhibits anywhere –magnificent flowers and vegetables. And every manner of farm machinery.'

Henry Howlett agreed. 'Last year they had a chaff cutter with a reversing gear! And as you know, our Kalkaberry neighbours, the Smiths, are exhibiting their new wonder plough.'

Ben had heard about the newly invented plough, but he was cautious.

'Can't imagine what sort of plough would work here,' he said to William. 'For a plough to get through, even the smaller roots, it would be too heavy for bullocks.'

William suggested they go to the show and see for themselves. 'I don't think the women will mind. The babies are nearly a year old now.'

'I'll bring Benjy. He's five. And your William-John would love it.'

William agreed. 'We could show the little blighters the new plough.'

119

The cool of the morning had long gone, by the time Ben and William reached the showgrounds. The two boys, long since tetchy on the endless drive, eagerly jumped down from the cart.

Ben tethered the horse. 'It's a big crowd.'

'I suppose it's the miners; it's a holiday for them,' William said. They joined the crowds, Benjy pitched high on Ben's shoulders as he inched them forward to gain a view. 'That farm machinery is popular.'

William whistled. 'Would you look at that?'

Un-enumerated.
Triple plough. RB Smith. First prize.
Vixen Single plough. RB Smith. First prize.

'First prize! Wonder how they work?' Ben said.

'They won't,' said an irate Kadina farmer. 'Never saw such rubbish. A man needs a good deep plough to get any sort of crop.'

Ben saw Sims eyeing the two ploughs. 'Let's see what the master thinks,' he said. He placed Benjy down and said to him, 'This is Mr Sims.'

Sims patted the boy's head. 'My little Mary is nearly as big as you. Well, Ben, what do you think?'

'I was going to ask you.'

'I just saw Richard and Clarence Smith,' Sims said, 'rightly pleased they were, until the men started heckling. Richard said they invented the plough after an accident. He had broken a tine and noticed it flipped over the stumps and stones.'

'Genius,' William said. 'So, he... hinged all the tines?'

'He did,' Sims said. 'And see that iron weight hanging above the tines? It's fifty-six pounds. That ensures the tines will re-embed. It could be great, but at nineteen pounds five pence, I'd want to see it in action first.'

The three men walked in the direction of the tented exhibits. Ben had heard about Sims's winning entries with ducks and fowls the previous year. 'How many prizes did you carry off this year?'

'I didn't enter any,' Sims said. 'It's been far too hot.'

Ben and William took the boys to sit under the shade of a tree, where they ate their pasties. 'It's a pity about the plough,' Ben said, biting his lip. 'There are those who could well afford to buy one. I only wish I had the money. I'd need a new-age plough to bring on some crops to pay for it.'

In May, 1877, Eliza's last child, Emma, was born. Emily was twelve,

William-John, Rosina, and George, eight, five, and two.

And Emma gave birth to her seventh child and fourth son on August 17, 1877.

'We've run out of names,' Emma said to Ben. 'There've been too many Bens.'

The baby was still unnamed when William and his family visited Constantine Farm the day before Ben's thirty-sixth birthday at the end of August.

'Congratulations, old chap,' said William, clapping Ben on the back as the two peered into the bundle of soft bedding and baby.

Eliza and Annie set out tea plates. Lizey squealed as the boys taunted her.

'Stop it, all of you,' Emma shouted. Silence followed. Emma turned to Ben and William. 'I'm sorry. I'm exhausted. If only we'd built another room. Benjy and Jack – I swear Annie will kill one of them soon.'

William looked at Ben. 'Maybe I could give you a hand? We could cover in the lean-to and provide you another room, and maybe put up another lean-to before harvest. There's some nice pine nearby.'

'I can't take your time like that,' Ben argued.

'Nonsense,' William said, 'I owe you.'

Ben almost laughed. 'You do not.'

'I insist.' William clapped him on the shoulder. 'It's done.'

Emma, after listening, admiring, and appreciating every word passed, leaned forward, and whispered into her husband's ear.

'Of course,' said Ben, smiling. He looked up and announced to everyone, 'Our baby is going to be named William Trethowan Bowden. Your uncle William is our greatest friend.'

When the next annual show came around, Ben reluctantly admitted to William that he couldn't attend, as baby William Trethowan Bowden was still only three months old.

'I'll go,' William said, grinning widely. 'I can update you and you won't miss out on a thing.'

Ben frowned.

Upon his return, William told Ben about the latest machinery at the show. 'The Smith brothers didn't even enter their ploughs this time,' he said. 'They say they can't sell them. Richard Smith was one of the judges this year. He said it was pitiful that plough design hadn't changed in twelve years.'

'It's true,' Ben said. 'The diehards want a good, deep English plough. But I think Henry is right. We have to take a different approach out here.'

In January 1878, Ben kicked at the dusty dead stems that littered his carefully prepared field of wheat. 'A total disaster!' he said. 'Not a drop of rain.'

'It's a joke,' William said. 'We've moved from one foot-shaped peninsula to another. One too wet, the other too dry.'

'That Wakefield man really got it wrong,' Ben said. 'I'm going to change the name of the farm, something like yours, to remind me of home. Let me see... How does *Constantine Farm* sound?'

'I like it,' William said. 'I feel cooler already.'

'Ha, ha. But what do you really think?'

'No, it's good,' William said. 'And it's where you were born.'

'Now let's get back into the Mallee again,' Ben said. 'I'm not looking forward to it. But I'm not giving up. Poor William Gluyas is leaving. His six hundred acres... Well, that's too much land, too many brutal stumps. He's not getting anywhere. Says he's applied to the railways.'

'A few others are selling too,' William said. 'You have to wonder who will take over the farms. They're not an attractive proposition right now.'

Early one cold morning that May, Emma sadly watched the Gluyas family leave Section 312 for Port Augusta. Their horse-and-dray was piled high with rudimentary furniture. After a flurry of dust, they were gone. Anne Gluyas had been expecting her eighth child in December and told Emma she looked forward to living closer to at least one general store.

Their farm was taken over by James Oxenberry Tiddy, the Moonta draper who now had a large general store in Maitland as well.

'We'll have nothing in common with them, their servants and marvellous clothes,' Emma complained to William and Eliza. 'And they hardly need all that land.'

'It's a well-known fact, my dear,' William said, 'people with money always need more land.'

It was another lean year, but the stumps were loosening now, and Ben moved several, and in doing so, had cleared a significant portion of Section 319.

'Progress at last,' he said to Emma. But Emma was teary. 'It's all right, love,' Ben assured her. 'We're getting by. I trapped another half-dozen rabbits today.'

'It's not that, Ben. These last three years... I felt so free without another baby. I was hoping little William was the last.'

Ben looked at her waistline.

Emma nodded. 'We'll have eight by June next year.'

Ben put his arms around her. 'You're wonderful.'

'I'm just so tired.'

'At least, you have Annie and Lizey.' Ben said.

'I'd be lost without them,' Emma agreed.

The following year, when the cooler days of autumn arrived, William Matters's front room was crowded for the Wesleyan meeting. As the service closed, George Matters announced that the Education Department had finally accepted their deposition for a school.

'Agery now has sixteen children of school age,' George said. 'They will despatch a teacher when school opens in June.'

The crowd clapped and cheered.

'There'll be no delay, because the church room here can double as the school,' George said.

Henry Howlett spoke up. 'Once again, we are indebted to the Matters family for their unstinting generosity.'

Annie complained to her mother. 'It's too late for me. I'm fifteen. I can't go to school with seven-year-olds. They'll know more than me.'

'Nonsense.' her mother said. 'You've learned to read, write, and count in Sabbath School, and you cook and sew. You know a whole lot more than I did at fifteen.'

'It's not the same as school learning.'

'Annie, love, the department is depending on the fifteen-year-olds for the numbers.'

Annie's stare was icy. 'I'll never be able to stay ahead of Lizey. It's not fair. Even Jack will be there, waiting for me to make a mistake.' Tearful, she ran off.

Emma told Eliza. 'I don't particularly want to part with Annie, either. The baby will probably arrive the day the school opens.'

'Don't worry. I'll take your small boys for a few days.'

Emma gripped Eliza's arm in appreciation. But she was tired of stumbling from one crying child to another. Staying in Cornwall had seemed impossible at the time, but at least over there her family was within walking distance.

In May 1880, Emma, aged thirty-five, was in labour again. Nothing else mattered but to push her baby out into the world. Mrs Matters attended, and Charles Henry was born.

Emma slept fitfully, and was crying the following day when Eliza looked in.

'I'm tired beyond belief, and I'm wetting the bed,' she whispered.

'There, there,' soothed Eliza.

'He was such a big baby, I had to push forever. It's so embarrassing. Who's going to wash the towels?'

'Give them to me, I'll send some clean ones over with William in the morning.'

'I can't, Eliza. You know what they're like.'

'Emma! I'm going to do it.'

'Do you think the teacher will let Annie stay home for a few days? Richard listens to me, but William. A three-year-old can wander for miles.' Emma put her head back against the wall.

'Emma, I'm taking the two boys with me. They're the same ages as George and little Emmy. It'll be a luxury for me, having them entertained.'

'It's a blessing the school is on our doorstep,' Emma said, feeling less brittle. 'At least your children can wait here until William arrives. And if it's raining, well, they can shelter here.'

Two weeks later, Emma felt more energetic and pulled herself from her bed. Annie needed to be at school. After the exodus of her five children, Emma spent her days in a hopeless round of cooking, washing, keeping an eye on Richard and William, and tending to the baby. She was more miserable than she thought possible. And her three daughters added to her pain by complaining about the cooking, cleaning, and mending waiting for them after school. The boys teased the girls, and they always seemed to be arguing, especially when it was feeding time for the baby.

Ben brought out his belt.

Emma trembled. 'No, Ben.'

'They are unmanageable, Em. It's for their own good.'

'You heard that, children,' Emma said, her eyes mutinous. 'One more fight – and it will be the strap.'

Agery School was Elisha Williams's first teaching post, and Annie was quick to complain.

'He spends most of the day teaching the little ones. He says we are old enough to learn by ourselves. We have to write stories, and then he asks us about history, stuff he never told us. And now we have to learn the "Song of Australia". What's *witching harmonies?*

'I don't know,' her mother said. 'But give the man time. It can't be easy teaching all ages in the same room, at the same time. Some children are clever, others have no learning. I'd say we'll be lucky to keep him.'

A year after the Gluyas family departed, John Eden and his wife and family arrived from Moonta Mines and took up Section 423, which was beside Tiddy's 312, and not far across the road from Constantine Farm.

'There's six children, Mama,' Annie said. 'But the oldest are boys.' Annie pretended disinterest.

Emma met Caroline Eden at the school door and liked her immediately. Caroline was soon telling Emma about the loss of two of her babies at Moonta Mines from typhoid. Memories of the terrible epidemic quickly came back to Emma. 'I can't imagine your pain,' she said, although her grief for her own baby William had carried on forever.

'I couldn't go through it again,' Caroline said, tears springing to her eyes.

Emma also felt the urge to cry. 'It's my worst fear,' she solemnly admitted. 'But I must go.' Emma left, taking the hand of her unwilling one-year-old, Charles Henry.

Richard and William, now six and four, bored when their brothers were at school, caused less havoc now that they deigned to play with girls, Emily and Florrie Eden, who were the same ages.

The Bowden and Eden children migrated across the road almost daily, and Emma was surprised when Caroline called to see her early one sunny morning.

'I won't come in, Emma,' Caroline said, as she hoisted baby Lilly higher onto her hip. Six-year-old Emily was by her side. 'Have you seen Florrie?'

'Neither of them have been here today, Caroline.'

'I can't find her, and I've searched everywhere.'

'What about Howletts?' Emma said, 'or the school?'

'No, I went there first.' Caroline turned to her daughter. 'Think, Emily, Florrie was sitting beside me when I was feeding Lilly. Where did she go?'

'She just ran off; I thought she was going to Howletts'.'

'I must get John,' Caroline said. 'Florrie's only three, and barefoot; she can't have gone far. But if she gets into that scrub…'

'Let me keep Lilly and Emily while you fetch John,' Emma offered.

John Eden wasn't long returning home, and, after a quick search, he and Ben notified the neighbouring families. When it was accepted the child really was missing, the men organised a search party.

The news spread rapidly, and women arrived at Eden's laden with sandwiches, pasties and soup. The men ate quickly, and, forming two parties, they set out to search in opposite directions, constantly calling for Florrie.

When night fell at six o'clock, and there was no sign of the child, Ben was baffled.

'How could she have travelled so far out of earshot?' Ben said. 'John doesn't want to stop the search, and I'm inclined to agree. She can't be far now.'

It was then that a large carriage pulled up at Eden's house. It was Henry Richard Hancock.

The mine superintendent jumped down and shook John Eden's hand. 'I'm sorry about your little girl. All available miners will join the search in the morning. We'll keep a few to work the pumps. The rest are yours, until she is found.'

John's voice was husky as he thanked his former employer. Caroline looked at the ground, crying quietly.

In the morning, hundreds thronged to Eden's farm. Mrs Matters, Mrs Tiddy, and Emma got to making pasties. It was an enormous task and Emma started early. She made the pastry before breakfast and covered it with a damp cloth. Before the children left for school, they washed and cut a small bucketful of potatoes, swede turnips, and onions.

As the children filed out for school, Emma insisted Richard stay in with William and little Charles-Henry. 'William's the same age as Florrie,' Emma said. 'He'll be lost next.'

Only minutes later, young William stood up on his toes to reach and open the door. 'William! I will tie both of you to the bedpost if you don't do as I say. Do not go outside at all today.'

'But I wanna,' William cried.

'William!' Emma gritted her teeth. 'Here, you sprinkle the salt on those vegetables, while I cut up the meat. No, one spoon is enough,' Emma said, taking the spoon from him.

'But I want to help,' said Richard, who was six.

Emma searched for the old knucklebones and wooden blocks, and, while the children played, she stole time to roll and cut the pastry into large rounds. She filled the rounds with meat and vegetables and folded the pastry over. Lastly, she dipped her fingers in water and crimped the edges together. The boys began to fight again, and Emma hollered, hoping no one heard her.

Emma preferred to bake the pasties slowly, to mingle the flavours, but she hadn't watched the fire, and when she opened the lid of the oven, a whoosh of heat told her it was too hot.

The search for Florrie Eden continued into a third day and, after darkness fell, Ben was dispirited. 'Where can the child have gone?' he said to Emma. 'The police are flummoxed, too. They have sent to Adelaide for black trackers and dogs.'

At dawn, John Eden continued to head his group. Walking with the western arm of the group, Ben saw another party of men, headed by a farmer and the Moonta Constable.

'Cooee!' the Moonta party shouted. 'Are you looking for this wee one?' They held Florrie Eden aloft.

'It's her!' John said, running toward them. 'Florrie, my baby,' he cried, taking her into his arms. Three cheers resounded across the bush, while Florrie and her father wept.

That evening, in the crowded Matters' sitting room, a thanksgiving service was held. Ben and Emma learned that the three-year-old had been found twenty miles from home, without bonnet or shoes. And that the farmer who found her brought her to the police the following morning.

Soon after Florrie's return, two more Matters families moved in with George Matters. They were George's father and brother, both named William. When they heard about Emma and her eight boisterous children, they brought her bread and casseroles.

And so Emma gradually regained her strength and restored order. She soon learned that the two new families had given up mining.

'And that house is big enough to accommodate them all,' Caroline had told her.

'They are so kind,' Emma said. 'I'm glad they've escaped the mines.'

Emma noticed a change in the tiny community. The Matters family had twelve children, and now grown up, they visited regularly.

'It's more like a village over there,' Emma told Eliza. 'Imagine, Eliza, twelve children. I've only eight, and I swear I can't manage one more.'

After the Sunday services, with dozens standing every Sunday now, Ben listened thoughtfully as his neighbours suggested it was time to build a church.

'Henry and George will talk to the Reverend Warner of Moonta,' Ben told Emma.

'So, they're serious?' she said, rocking Charles Henry, hoping he would sleep. 'Will you take Richard and William to pick stones with you?'

The following Sunday, Warner announced that they should call a public meeting. 'If you want to build a church, you will have pay for it – and build it yourselves.'

Ben worried. They had no money to spare. But he attended anyway.

After a prayer, Warner opened the meeting. 'Have we suggestions on how to proceed?'

Mr Matters, Senior stood. 'On behalf of my family, I will donate an acre of land from our new Section 317.'

When he sat, Henry Howlett stood. He also offered to give an acre. 'Section 19,' he said to George Matters, who was taking notes.

Ben, longing to serve the Lord in such a grand manner, quickly raised his hand and stood. 'I will also give an acre. 319.' Ben couldn't believe he had done it. Could he really afford to give land away? But it was only one acre, and it might not happen; they hardly needed three acres for a church.

'This is exceedingly generous, gentlemen,' the Rev Warner said. 'Let's form a committee to manage the project.'

Mr Matters Senior was declared chairman unopposed. He asked for votes for the committee members. Ben watched as nominees Thomas Matters, Henry Howlett, and John Eden accepted. When he heard his name put forward, Ben flushed from his neck. He wasn't expecting to be on any committee. But John Eden nodded his encouragement, so Ben accepted.

William Matters Senior thanked everyone and called for suggestions to fund the project.

'Henry and I saw an architect and builder this week,' Young Thomas Matters responded. 'They said a stone church for 150 people costs about £300.'

He totted with a pencil. 'I suggest each family give two pounds

128

over three years, and we will fix a donations box inside the door.' There was a hum in the room. 'If the ladies support our fund-raising activities with their usual vigour,' he went on, 'we could well raise the money in three years.'

The chairman spoke again. 'It has also been suggested we address the immediate problem of overcrowding, by buying the iron and timber building, which is for sale at Moonta Bay. 'Those in favour?'

Ben joined in the unanimous 'Ay'.

As he told Emma later, the committee planned to bring a temporary building to Agery in sections, put it together, then paint it. 'And when we don't need it, we can sell it again. More seats now, means more money in the collection plates.'

'Thank goodness for that,' Emma said. 'We are so crowded these days.'

'And not only am I on the church committee, I gave an acre of land to build the church on,' he stuttered.

Emma hugged him, and he relaxed in her arms. Emma was so dependable. Her support had been paramount for them to survive the rigors of their chosen way.

13. Suffer Little Children

The schoolroom was crowded, and the parents angry.

'The school has only been open for two years,' Ben heard John Eden say, amid shoe shuffling and whispering. 'You can't close it.'

'You tell him, John,' said a voice from the back of the room.

Adjusting his cravat, Elisha Williams called for order. 'Provisional schools always depend on numbers, and we are not closing, just transferring to Penang. There's a fine Bible-Christian chapel on Section 5. A sturdy and cool building, built with stone from Donaldson's quarry.'

'That's three miles from here, a long walk on a hot day for young children,' William protested.

'Some children walk a lot further,' Elisha said. 'It will toughen them up.'

The room grew noisy again. 'Let's go,' William said, taking Eliza's arm. 'We had better start toughening up our children!' Ben followed them out.

Back at Constantine Farm, Emma was also incensed. 'They can't,' she cried. 'What's wrong with here?'

'It's numbers again,' Ben said, defeated. 'Come on, let's get some sleep.'

The new school opened in January, 1883, and William and Eliza's children often walked the entire four miles, the Bowden children joining them for the last three.

Within weeks, Richard Bowden, and his cousin George, were caught in a heavy rainstorm. They became unwell, with a sore throat and wheezing cough.

'It is just catarrh,' the doctor said.

Although Richard recovered quickly, the prescribed liniment and cough mixture wasn't helping young George.

'Get the doctor back, Will,' Emma said.

'If I can; he didn't seem very concerned.'

On 5 February, none of William's children arrived at Constantine Farm for school. Ben said he would ride over, but, before he left, the doctor, looking grave, called to see Ben and Emma and asked them to visit William and Eliza immediately.

Their little boy had developed pneumonia and had died overnight. Emma gasped.

'Unbelievable... Such a robust little boy,' Ben declared. 'I'll get Annie from school. She can watch Charlie and Billy.'

They hurried to Silver Hill with Emma, tears streaming.

'What have we gotten ourselves into?' William cried. 'Toughen them up!'

Ben and Emma stayed with Eliza and William while the clergyman and undertaker made their arrangements. It was a long tearful morning. At half past two, Ben and Emma left to collect their children from school and to break the news to them.

After the harrowing funeral, Benjy, Jack and Richard, now ten, eight and seven, pale and fractious, refused to go to school. Ben wanted to insist, but Emma caught his eye and said they could stay home for a week.

'We have to go back,' Lizey said. 'Mary and I want to be teachers. Can we go on Wednesday?'

'Of course, dear.' Emma tried to control her tears in front of the children.

In the following weeks, the children fought frequently.

'It's going to be a long winter,' Emma said, as Ben warned his children again.

In April, fourteen-year-old Lizey burst through the door after school, eyes shining. 'Mama. The teacher wants me to be a pupil-teacher. All the girls have to do needlework now, you know, sewing, mending, and knitting. And I am to teach them. Can I? Please? He said they will call me Miss Bowden.'

'Of course, you can, dear,' Emma said. 'Let's tell your father; it will cheer him up.'

'What about me?' cried Annie, leaving the room. Emma followed her. 'Everyone hates me.' Annie said.

'Annie, dear, they do not.'

'I do nothing but work, and everybody just complains. I'll never be good enough. Why didn't he pick me?'

'It's just that Lizey is at school, and you are not.'

'He has a short memory; I was there last year.'

'I wish I could help, love, but I can't, much as I'd like to.'

Emma's sixth baby boy, Lloyd Herbert was born on September 11.

Emma and Annie continued to struggle.

When Emma's voice became particularly shrill, Ben intervened. 'Right,' he said, appearing at the door. 'Benjy, Jack, Richard. Outside. Now! You will work on the stones while I bring in the vegetables and help your mother. I have marked an area over there.' He pointed. 'And don't let me find one stone there when I return.'

'They have so much energy,' Emma said. 'And I have none. It feels like they are sapping the life out of me.' She put her hands to her mouth. 'I'm a terrible mother.'

'Of course you're not,' Ben leaned in. 'Aren't they a fine bunch? Growing and learning?'

'And driving everybody mad,' Emma said.

Emma was to rue the day she complained about her energetic, healthy children. For thirteen years, they had avoided all epidemics that had constantly circled the district.

Early that year, there was another bout of dysentery. At first, it was only in Kalkabury and Wallaroo Mines. Some said thirteen children had died, others said thirty. Soon, it spread to Moonta and Moonta Mines.

Emma wasn't as worried this time; they were living in fresh farm air, growing their own vegetables, and baby Bert and little Charles-Henry were strong and healthy.

When thirteen-year-old Mary showed signs of dysentery, they were concerned, but mostly because of the risk to the babies. However, age did not protect Mary, and the diarrhoea soon exhausted her. When it turned bloody, she cried out and fouled her bed. The smell filled the tiny bedroom, and Mary's hollow eyes saw the revulsion on her siblings' faces.

Emma fashioned large nappies from old towels, and Annie gave her sister her prized lavender water. Emma would never forget her pitiful smile that day, thanking Annie, not a week before she died in June.

Emma sat clutching the girl's hand, unable to believe she would breathe no more. Her dear, dear girl; so full of plans to be a teacher like her sister. And she had failed her. Why had they come to this hot miserable country?

Ben watched helplessly as Emma staggered under the weight of her guilt. During the day, she put on a brave face, but it made no difference; the small boys still wet their beds and were even more quarrelsome. Mary had been such a presence, and Emma's pain showed no signs of abating.

Emma still expected the girl to run through the door with wildflowers, or with a funny tale to tell.

Ten months after Mary's death, Emma, still wondering when the pain would ease, woke to hear three-year-old Charles Henry struggling for breath. Trembling, she shook Ben. They leaned over the boy who whimpered between rasping breaths. Emma gathered him in her arms and sat rocking him by the fire. His face was burning hot, his lips a faint blue. 'Ben, you should fetch the doctor, but I don't want you to leave us.'

Emma barely knew what she was doing over the next few days, insisting the child would be all right. But his fever increased, and he, too, died on April 17, 1884.

When the doctor left, Emma's head pounded, and her eyes hurt as she tried to stifle her sobbing.

'Why does God not heed our prayers?' she cried to Ben. 'What have I done to anger Him so? I have failed miserably...'

'Don't do this to yourself, my love,' Ben said.

'It's not fair; I can't do this,' Emma raged. 'At no age are they safe. Why ever did we leave Cornwall?'

'They've had their losses, too, Em,' Ben said gently. 'Look at Uncle William of Trengilly, died at fifty-two, and poor Ben-Thomas lost two little girls in a year.'

'At least we'd be together in our losses,' Emma retorted. 'We could help poor Kitty, with Richard dead, leaving seven children without a father.'

Ben agreed that it would be easier, with their family around them. But it was just far too late. 'Nine passages to Britain. It's unthinkable, Em. Even Tiddy couldn't afford that.'

Emma wept continually. Ben worked on the stumps and stones vigorously to help take his mind off his pain. After the first rain in May, he borrowed an old stump-jump plough from George Matters and was delighted with its efficiency. He sowed twenty acres of wheat that year and watched with amazement as it grew and grew. But it was a hollow victory, without his two children. And when he stopped working, the pain formed a tight knot in his chest.

'Everywhere I look, I see Mary and little Charles,' Ben told Emma. 'I can't bear it any longer. I'm going to build a new house.'

Their savings, no longer a *rainy-day* fund, was now their *bad-years* fund. 'If these aren't bad years, I don't know what are,' Ben said.

Emma brimmed with tears again. 'It's true, Ben. The walls are so thin, it gets quite cold in here. Why didn't I see it before? No wonder our children died.'

Once it was in their minds, Ben and Emma couldn't wait to move out of the ten-year-old wattle-and-daub. The whole family became engrossed in planning the new home. It was going to be a real house, like Trengilly, with proper stone walls.

Ben said, 'At last I have a use for that interminable limestone.'

Ben's neighbours helped when they could, embedding the larger stones in walls with mortar made of powdered limestone and ashes. A nearby forest provided the pine, and a carpenter installed proper windows and doors. And the new fire regulations mandated they use galvanised iron roofing.

'The house will be so much bigger,' Ben told the children. 'We'll have three bedrooms, a proper kitchen with an oven and skillet. And a big dining room – thirty feet by twelve.'

'Look here,' Emma said, pointing to the drawing, 'we're going to have a covered cellar to keep the meat, milk, and butter cool. It has a little window to catch the draft.'

'An underground cellar?' William said, enthralled. 'Will I fit?' At six, he was an imaginative child.

'When I send you to fetch milk or butter, you will,' said his mother, patting him on the head. 'You'll fit just fine.'

Second house, 1884, drawing courtesy, Mark Browning

When the new house was completed and the rubble dumped in the rock field, William helped Ben rake the surrounding area. Annie and Emily drew lines in the soil, and the children placed rows of white stones to define a path. Ben planted Emma's pelargoniums and dianthus, which were brilliant against the white wall.

The new dwelling had four windows and a proper door opening onto the front. Painted a gleaming white, with its large stone chimney, it was just like Trengilly.

'And with rain running directly off the roof into the new tank,' Ben announced, 'we will, at last, have drinkable water.'

For safety, half the tank was above ground, being contained within a high wall. And to minimise seepage, Ben lined it with limestone and mortar, just like the house. The rainwater was not only clean, its volume proved invaluable.

The children were entranced when they moved in. 'It's so sparkling white, Mamma,' Annie said. 'It only took a few minutes to clean yesterday.'

'You sound like one of those soap ladies in the town, *your clothes will be clean in minutes*,' Benjy mimicked.

'I look forward to the day when you clean anything, Ben grot,' she retorted.

William and Richard ran into the dining room followed by Bertie.

Ben was unusually patient with them. 'There you are, boys,' Ben said. 'Now bring me the two chairs from the sitting room. With the two new benches we can all sit and eat together. Even the parson will fit.'

It was another bumper crop that year and, early in 1885, the farmers talked about a new land offer in the area.

Ben was more cheerful than Emma had seen him for a long time. 'There's more land available. And its upset price is only one pound an acre. The wheat is all in. I think I will take out two more credit agreements. See here, 242 is just the other side of our swamp, and 246E is next to it.' He showed her a map he had drawn.

'That will bring us up to 1,033 acres.'

The boys gathered around their father. 'Where?' Benjy said. 'Show me, Da.'

'One thousand acres!' Benjy and Jack said. 'How many did you have in Cornwall, Da?'

'Well, forty-five in Trengilly. Twenty in Polwheveral.'

The boys laughed.

'But it is much richer soil over there,' Ben said, 'and it costs a lot, lot more.'

'And there was none for sale,' Emma added.

With the help of his three boys, Ben tilled and sowed the new sections with wheat. The boys were proud of their handiwork and experienced their own anxious wait for rain.

There was none in April or May.

One June day, Jack raced inside and said to Benjy, 'There's clouds everywhere, come and look.'

'They're only white, Jack.'

'Well, what's that if it's not grey?'

'Oh.'

When the rain fell, it was sparse, but the boys danced in it, and a week later green shoots appeared here and there. But it soon became dry everywhere, even in Adelaide. Ben believed it did not bode well. 'We'd best get into the Mallee,' he said to the disappointed boys.

Fourteen-year-old Benjy was quick. 'Sorry, Da, we have school.'

'You and Jack can do an hour before you go – and afterwards too.'

'Aww...' Benjy saw Richard grinning. 'And Richard, too? And Willie?'

'They can water the vegetables and feed the pigs.'

'So, it wasn't enough rain?' Emma said, putting in a tray of pasties. She and two-year-old Bert were covered with flour.

'It's sparse,' said Ben. 'I see Tiddy is waiting for rain before he sows. I'll try to catch more eagle hawks. I wasn't keen at first, but they're a menace with the lambs. And that bounty of ten shillings will add up nicely.'

In August, Emma's eleventh pregnancy bore them their eighth son.

'He has fair hair like Mary,' Ben said, leaning over to kiss him.

'Such a little angel,' Emma said. 'Let's name him Charles Wesley, after the hymnist.' She also wanted to remember little Charles Henry.

Again, Emma hoped this would be her last child. She was forty now, and Ben forty-four.

The church committee announced they had reached their target for the new church.

Ben, looking less harried, told Emma, 'everyone agrees, we might as well build it now. Mr Prisk, the builder from Moonta is surveying the area on Monday. The church could be ready to christen little Charles Wesley.'

Thomas Prisk tied up his horse in front of Matters's house, greeting Ben, Thomas Matters and Henry Howlett. As they had tea, they pored over the map of all three sites.

'You see, in here is Section 19, and over here are 317 and 319,' Henry said, pointing with his knife.

'Let's walk the sites,' said Prisk, picking up the map. They began with Howlett's section and continued on. Prisk squatted here and there to judge the lay of the land. 'They are all sufficiently flat, with access to the road. But bear with me. Isn't there a corner site down there? With a bit of wasteland beside it?' Prisk pointed to the lower border of Ben's Section 319.

'There is,' Ben said, so they continued in that direction.

Prisk folded his arms and stared out at the lake, the wildflowers and trees. 'It has an attractive outlook. And that wasteland beyond – a church seating 150 people requires a large reception area for horses and buggies. I like it.'

The three men weren't going to disagree with him; not over the House of God.

Mr Breaker, Agery's regular Wesleyan lay preacher, asked for helpers to build the new church. Most of the farmers, including Ben and William, offered to help.

After just four weeks, in September, it was time to lay the foundation stones.

Carriages and carts arrived early on the day, and over 500 people gathered around the site. Just before the ceremony began, the Reverend Mr Lane announced that Mrs Hancock, who was to lay one of the foundation stones, was ill and unable to attend, so Mrs Lane would take her place.

After presenting the ladies with splendidly engraved silver trowels, Lane read the document to be placed under the stones.

> The Memorial Stones of this Church, were laid by Mesdames Hancock, Roach, Wearne and Miss Holman. On this day, Wednesday, September 23, 1885, in the 48th Year of the reign of Her Most Gracious Majesty, Queen Victoria. The Governor of the Colony, Sir William Cleaver Francis Robinson, K.C.M.G, &c; in the presence of the President of the Conference, Rev. C.T. Newman; Chairman of the Yorke's Peninsula District and Superintendent of the Moonta Circuit, Rev C. Lane; Trustees of the Church, Rev C. Lane, W.B. Wearne,

Thomas Matters, William Matters, Benjamin Bowden, H.R. Hancock, J. Butterfield and H. Howlett.

Also laid under the stones were a copy of the Architect's Plan, a plan of Local Preachers, and copies of the current *South Australian Advertiser*, the Yorke's *Peninsula Advertiser* and the *Wallaroo Times*.

Agery Church, built 1885, photo by Rosie Bowden

After the ceremony, the crowd jostled their way to the little wooden chapel for tea.

'There's just no room; it's a regular tea fight today.' Ben declared, eyeing the backs of the anxious crowd. 'And the tea and donations are already at fifty pounds!' He rubbed his hands together.

The Yorke's *Peninsula Advertiser*, and the *Wallaroo Times*, Friday, September 25, 1885:

A half-holiday was declared in the Moonta area, and from noon vehicles of every description, from handsome four wheelers to farmers' humble market carts were wending their way through the picturesque scrub to the scene of action, which was thronged long before the time specified...

As was the custom, the Reverend Mr Lane compared the doctrines of the Methodist Church, with those of the Church of England, Congregationalism and Presbyterianism...

14. The Moonta Show

The chapel – built in record time – was opened in November, 1885, by the Reverend Mr Lane.

Still in awe, Ben looked over the grand entrance again. As he had said more than once to his son, he was not so much proud that he had given the land, for pride was a sin. He was instead thankful, satisfied, that God had brought him to this great country, and had enabled him to serve the Lord in this manner.

And the preacher said. 'The fine stone building, with its neat brick trims at the corners, doorway, and windows, was not only a lasting monument to the Lord, it would also be an important centre from which the close-knit community would continue to grow.'

Ben, Emma, and their children took their seats and looked up at the sunshine streaming through the three long eastern windows. It was pleasantly cool inside, and soon all 150 seats were full. Emma held Ben's hand, and they immersed themselves in the prayers, homilies, and hymns ringing out in the new Agery Wesleyan Chapel.

Superintendent Hancock attended the service, and afterwards congratulated the committee and parishioners on their splendid achievement.

William, Eliza, and their family walked back with the Bowdens to Constantine Farm for tea. On their way, William inspected Ben's vegetable garden and plucked out a pod of peas. 'Sweet,' he said, savouring the flavour. 'I'm impressed. But I suppose why not, with blue skies and a good water tank.'

'It's not that easy,' Ben said.

'Your carrots and parsnips are huge, too,' William said. 'And we all remember your famous turnips. You want to know what I think?'

'Do I?'

'Ha-ha. I think you should enter them in the Moonta Show,' William said.

'I never know when you are serious.' Ben's eyes shifted from the vegetables to William's face. 'They're hardly that good.'

'Have faith, my friend. There might be better, but I'd swear those peas can't be beat.' He tilted his head back and popped another pod into his mouth.

139

'I'll show them if you agree to stop eating them, and only if you enter your beans too.'

William barely hesitated. 'Done,' he said, shaking Ben's hand.

The Moonta Horticultural, Agricultural, and Flower Society's Show, on November 9, had become the greatest non-denominational event of the year in the area, and Ben's family were up early for it.

'Come on, boys. The vegetables have to arrive crisp. And Uncle William is waiting.'

The children climbed aboard, and Emma kissed three-year-old Bert. Fourteen-year-old Benjy took Bert's hand. Annie, twenty, and Lizey, eighteen, were pretty in their new frocks and bonnets, stitched from Mrs Tiddy's discards. So clever, Emma thought, the way they had banished the bustles and added crocheted collars.

Emma waved and waited until the clip clopping of the horse faded. Back inside, she sank into the unusual quiet. It was part of the plan, to give her a much-needed rest. But two-month-old Charles Wesley was sleeping. She stoked the fire and prepared pans; just a little baking first.

The Agery-Moonta Road was badly guttered and crammed with traffic. Ben coughed with the dust, and his bones pained him. After he paid at the gate and secured the horses, the boys ran off to join their school friends. Ben's girls and Emily merged with the crowds.

Annie had a firm grip of Bert's hand.

'Leave Bert with me,' Ben said, eyes twinkling, 'you'll be busy looking for husbands.'

'Bah,' Lizey blushed.

'Come on, little fellow,' Ben said, swinging Bert onto his shoulders and bringing him firstly to the selection of farm machinery. He set him down beside a wide variety of winnowers, mullenising ploughs and scarifiers.

'Richard Smith didn't renew his patent,' William told Ben. 'And it seems every ironmonger is making his own stump-jump plough now. I just saw Henry. He said the judges had trouble placing them.'

'Not surprised,' said Ben, retrieving Bert, who was about to remove a prize card. 'Come on, son. Let's look at the big reapers.'

Just before lunch, Ben and William inspected their exhibits.

William walked ahead. 'I told you, Ben. Look, your peas, they got a first. And your French beans.' He thumped Ben on the back.

'Careful,' said Ben, cringing. 'And what did I tell you? Your broad beans have a red ribbon.'

'Pretty good,' young Benjy chipped in, 'but neither of you are a patch on William-John. Only sixteen, he got three firsts: green fodder, truss of hay, and fifty pounds of chaffed hay! William-John, come over here and show your face.'

'This calls for a celebration,' William said. 'Let's go to the tea tent.'

After their meal, Ben noticed that Annie, Lizey, and Emily had met up with Mary-Annie Vicary. Emma would be pleased.

Lizey pointed to a bright painting on the makeshift wall. 'Look, Da, Mary-Anne exhibited a painting. If only I was half as good.'

'I like your drawings,' Ben said, but Lizey scoffed; she didn't believe him.

Ben and William met Tom Warn, and together they mourned the drought, and the downturn in Tom's drapery. Ben tapped and refilled his pipe. 'I see you are still judging, Tom.'

'They twisted my arm. You should join us, Ben.'

'Farmers exhibit,' Ben, said, 'and judges value.'

'A good farmer,' Tom said, 'is the mainstay of the country. Only farmers know the true value of grain and machinery.'

'I suppose so,' Ben said, but he didn't know what to think.

Home later in the evening, Ben repeated the conversation to Emma, 'Farmers – not this one anyway – aren't really qualified to judge.'

'Well,' she said, putting the baby to her shoulder. 'You are in the Agery Mutual Improvement Society, and on the church and school committees. And you're not poor; you own one thousand acres. And you live in a smart new house.'

'I suppose that is all true,' Ben conceded.

'Who else won prizes?' Emma asked, just as the boys were straggling in from their chores.

'Mr Matters got best ploughing pair,' Benjy said, 'and, of course, Captain Hancock's draught horses won.'

'Don't forget Mr Sims's yearling draught-filly,' Ben said, 'his two-year-old blood-colt, *and* his pen of six sheep. He's judging poultry too. He's an expert in every field, that man.'

'You could be a judge, too, Da,' Jack said.

'We'll see, son.'

The crops, at first promising, failed miserably when no rain fell.

'I'm going to have to sell that land again,' Ben said to William in December. 'John Denyer wants a bit to graze his sheep on.'

141

'You're not alone,' William said. 'King and Triplett are selling, and Peter Lomman.'

In January, 1886, several South Australians died of sunstroke. Farmers were warned to stay inside during the middle of the day when there was excessive heat.

It was certainly good advice, Ben thought. But if there was work to be done, animals to shelter and water to be carted, he couldn't just sit and watch them die. It reminded Ben of that night in 1861, which was excessively cold, when they hadn't enough blankets, and his mother almost succumbed to pneumonia. There had never been a cold week like it. And he'd never been so afraid. How naive he had been, thinking that moving to Australia would cure all their ills.

And it wasn't just the weather which sallied the year. A disastrous financial panic also swept across the country's south in February when the Commercial Bank of Australia closed its doors.

Ben had heard that all of the banks had closed, and Emma hadn't seen him as worried since the early mining days. 'I don't understand. What happened?' she asked.

'I've no idea, love,' Ben said. 'News travels slowly to the Peninsula.'

There were long queues in Moonta, the speculation being as wild as the collapse was sudden. Ben waited patiently to discover his fate and was relieved to see Henry Freeman nearby. Henry was a modern farmer, who ran stables, and traded in farm implements. He would know.

'Is it true?' Ben asked Henry. 'Have all the banks closed?'

'No. It's only the Commercial. But, with the drought, the terrible wheat crops, and prices bottoming for wool and copper, there is hardly any ready money anywhere. So, of course, no one can buy what they need, and businesses will close. We are not selling many farm implements – or anything much at all. We could lose everything.'

'I had hoped to be more secure,' Ben said. 'We have our own land – and the vote. And we can kill a pig. And I could turn it all around if I bought a few more sheep, and fenced those new fields, but prices have rocketed, even for a bit of fencing wire, never mind sheep. And flour has gone through the roof.'

'Maybe come back to the AMIS,' Henry said. 'Talk about it with other farmers. You haven't been for a while?'

'After losing the children,' Ben said with a catch in his throat, 'I didn't have the heart.'

'There's a meeting Thursday week. Make a comeback, Ben. You won't be sorry. At the Blacksmith's shop. Seven-thirty.'

Ben had to admit he had missed the meetings, and, on March 4, he was hopeful as twenty-five men filed in for the AMIS meeting.

The secretary, Walter Sims, read the minutes, after which Mr Breaker proposed they agitate for a school in Agery.

'We need a school right here on your own doorstep, not three miles away in Penang,' he said. 'It wastes so much time. We're busy enough trying to make a living.'

Ben raised his hand. 'I'll second that.'

Mr James Oxenberry Tiddy stood. 'And I propose we have a post office at Agery. Business cannot be conducted with any haste under the present system.'

'Seconded,' said Mr Butterfield.

At the conclusion, Henry Freeman proposed they call a public meeting regarding the two matters.

'Mr Bowden to the chair,' William said.

'Agreed,' said Henry.

Ben glared at William. 'You'll be writing my speech, William Trethowan. I've not run a meeting in my life.'

Over the weeks, Ben, cursing William's tomfoolery, rehearsed his speech a dozen times.

On March 17, William was the second to arrive at the blacksmith's shop. 'I'm a bit early.'

'So you should be,' Ben said. 'Now help me with these benches. You'll pay for this, Mister Trethowan.'

The evening was crisp, and the furnace pleasantly warm. Soon afterwards, Henry Freeman arrived, and a crowd followed. They packed into the small room, some sitting on anvils, others leaning against benches littered with horseshoes.

Ben took a deep breath after reading a short prayer and glanced at his notes. 'Agery has seen amazing growth in the last ten years,' he began, 'but there has been a significant downturn in prices for our wool and wheat. We propose that the Postmaster General establish a post office in Agery. And, secondly, that the Education Department open a day school here.

'The defective postal arrangements for the Hundred of Tiparra are a great inconvenience, obliging us to travel to Moonta for our mail.

With the drought, we are fully employed carting water and digging stumps. We can ill afford the best part of a day to post a letter.'

'Here, here,' said the crowd.

'As for the school,' Ben continued, 'it is a serious drawback to the rising generation, which, owing to the fruitfulness of the neighbourhood, is becoming numerous.' He stumbled over the big words when he realised his family was one of the most fruitful in the area. 'Our children deserve a proper education, but they need to be closer to home, so that after school, they can learn about farming too.'

The crowd clapped and cheered.

'Ben for Premier,' William said. And the crowd cheered again.

Henry called for quiet and proposed that Mr Butterfield and Mr Bowden wait upon the district inspector regarding the school. James Tiddy offered to inform the post-master-general that, for a trifling cost, the mail cart from Maitland to Moonta could pass through Agery on the return journey, giving them three mails per week.

It took several weeks to hear back from the two departments, but both proposals were successful, and Ben was elated.

He said to Emma, 'It really is up to us. And you won't believe, the Education Department is paying five shillings a week to hire the church. Henry suggests we hire it out for concerts, fairs, and public meetings as well. That'll more than pay for the upkeep of the building.'

Emma hugged him. 'And the school just there, where we can see it.'

At the end of the week, Billy and Richard arrived home late from school and complaining.

'What is it this time, boys?' Emma said.

'Well, on Mondays and Fridays,' Richard said, exasperated, nearly twisting a loose button off his shirt, 'we have to move the benches, desks, and blackboards to change it from a church to a school and back again. We never did that at Penang.'

'And who else would do it?' said Emma. 'Your father? The teacher? Big strong lads of eleven and nine – now that you're not walking six miles every day – I'd have thought you'd have plenty of energy.'

'Aww.'

'Don't let your father hear you complain. A fine warm school at your back door. Whatever next?'

The sound of rumbling carts, and whip cracking bullockies permeated the air, as the timber carters arrived at the nearby government dam. Emma's sons' smiles returned as they ran out to watch the action.

Several carts were piled high with timber for the mines.

'Can we go down, Ma?' Richard cried.

'Remember what your father said. Those beasts can land a heavy kick.'

Benjy and Richard, followed by Jack, raced across the field.

Afterwards, when the bullockies left, the boys were full of tales they had heard. With impish grins, they repeated some of the driver's commands: 'Come hither; Redmond, gee up Strawberry; Jacob, you lousy, good for drone; I'll cut the hide off you; too tired to chew your own cud.' Ben thought they were rough words for young boy's ears, but he supposed he couldn't protect them forever.

At supper, the boys talked again about the beasts and their drivers. 'Da, Da. The bullocks know their names, and whether to turn left or right,' Billy said, his eyes wide.

Richard joined in. 'A man called Arthur said his cart turned all the way over on a sharp corner.'

'And the inspector makes them pay,' Jack said, 'if their load is too heavy. I'm not going to be a bullocky.'

Emma was at last enjoying country life. And the children's persistent colds and coughs had almost disappeared since the school was so near.

Eliza agreed. 'That old tale about sitting in wet clothes being bad for children must be true.'

It was at the next meeting of the AMIS that Henry Freeman suggested Ben attend the annual Show Committee meeting in May. 'It's in the council chambers. Are you ready to become a judge?'

'I suppose so…' Ben said.

'Tom Warn and I will nominate you,' he told Ben.

Ben told Emma, 'I might become a judge, after all. I suppose I can thank your brother for pushing me at that meeting.'

Emma tried to picture Ben in the council offices. Memories surfaced of the important men back home, in the town of Constantine. 'You need to look the part, Ben. Get yourself a good black coat. I know, you hate spending money, but that coat is over twenty years old.'

Ben was glad of his new coat and hat – the Moonta Town Hall chambers with its ornate plasterwork and plush chairs lent itself to tidy black coats.

At the meeting, while speaking from behind his hand to Ben, Henry said, 'There's only twenty here.'

The meeting began with several apologies, including that of Chairman Hancock. After a lengthy recap by the president, secretary and treasurer of the previous year's event, they discussed the date for future shows.

'Back in 1871,' Dr Archer said, 'it was only a flower show, and the Prince of Wales's birthday was ideal. However, November is too late for vegetables, and it interferes with haymaking. October is preferable, and Superintendent Hancock agrees. He has granted the miners an additional holiday.'

Ben joined the men in a cheerful: 'Here-here!'

When nominations began, Henry Freeman said he would judge the farm implements, and that Ben would assist him. Ben was relieved; he had seen a good few farm implements made by several local ironmongers, and he would hopefully learn the rest from Henry.

He listened with interest when the men discussed the eligibility of entries. He had to agree, that it wasn't fair to show sheep raised on the Peninsula, beside those from the plusher pastures of Adelaide. There followed an intense debate on the subject between Sims and several others.

'Surely the purpose of the exposition is to improve our stock, raising standards for export,' said Henry.

'Here, here,' said Sims, 'I propose that six months grazing on the Peninsula is reasonable.'

Much to Ben's surprise, the motion passed.

A few weeks before the Moonta Show, Henry and Ben attended the Kadina Show. Leading the way, Henry said, 'Let's see what we are up against; these men have been judging for years.' They looked over the scarifiers, ploughs, and harvesters. Ben went back to the winning stump-jump ploughs again.

'I'm probably showing my ignorance,' he said, 'but I'm not sure I agree with their winning entry.'

'No, you're right,' Henry said. 'May's automatic plough is pure engineering genius. But it's delicate; it will probably break at the first stone.'

Thus armed, Ben set out early on October 13, for the Moonta Showgrounds. He headed for the roped areas enclosing the farm machinery. Henry arrived soon afterwards, and they examined the many ploughs while taking notes.

When Henry compared their notes, he was pleased. 'That's good, Ben,' he said. 'We agree. Smith's and Phelps's are definitely the winners.

Again, May's Triple Furrow is a brilliant piece of machinery, but it's fragile. It's like choosing a wife: you have to look beyond a pretty face.'

They attached cards to winning entries and, in recognition of the Triple Furrow's magnificent craftsmanship, awarded May a special prize.

As Henry said later, it was nonsense to say that they had chosen Smith's plough over May's just because Smith was their neighbour. However, neither farmers nor townsfolk were impressed, and Ben was glad Henry was there when the Kadina committee descended upon them.

'Our decision is final,' Henry said. 'In fact, we are so sure, we are willing to test them all on a typical local farm, a heavy ground with stumps and stones embedded. With so many new ploughs on the market, it's time we had another ploughing match.'

The contestants quietened and agreed. Henry proposed the competition would be open to all manufacturers, and, if each entrant paid five pounds, the prize money would be substantial.

'Five pounds is costly,' he spoke over the muttering crowd. 'But it is cheap advertising for the sponsors.'

Now all of the contestants were interested, and the match was fixed for November 3.

It was a glorious sunny day, and a large crowd gathered in the Staples' field ready to pin their faith to one of the five contestants: William May, Clarence Smith, Jim Phelps, Messrs Horwood and Co, and Henry Pearson.

Having both the Kadina and Moonta judges there meant there were more judges than entrants. Several remarked on this.

'It's the only fair way to do it,' Henry told them.

When the ploughmen were ready, Mr Wilkinson, proprietor of the Moonta newspaper, stepped forward and read the rules: 'In four hours, you must plough one acre, four-and-a-half inches deep. No assistance is permitted after the first round. The full depth of ploughing is to be reached on the second round. A true Stump-Jumping Plough jumps over large stumps, breaks up hard ground and rips out smaller stumps.

'Good luck – and begin!' he shouted.

Only seconds passed before Mr Horwood's plough caught a share in a stump. It twisted and broke. Mr Horwood approached Mr Wilkinson, who allowed Horwood to visit the Agery smithy. The other contestants waited and grumbled noisily as they tried to control their fresh horses. Ben thought the delay was unfair, but what could he do? When Horwood finally returned, the contestants lined up again.

Ben was enthralled by May's marvellous plough. For two rounds, it was an exhibition of precision and invention. Then a united groan greeted the snapping noise – the automatic gears of the plough-of-the-future had broken in half.

May's team eventually employed a length of number eight fencing wire, and the plough limped back into action. However, more breakages required an assistant for every round. Ben put a line through the name 'May' and wrote 'Disqualified'.

Horwood had finished in record time, but there was no depth to his ploughing. Henry suggested Phelps might have won if he had employed a practical ploughman to control his six fresh horses. In the ploughs entered by Smith, Phelps, and Pearson, there were no breaks or hitches, although Pearson's plough did not jump at all.

'Phew!' said Ben. 'We were right.'

He and Henry handed their slips in. But when Mr Wilkinson read out the winning names some thirty minutes later, awarding first prize to Henry Pearson, with seventy points out of a possible eighty-five, Ben was nonplussed. 'But his plough didn't jump,' he whispered to Henry, glowering.

'Clarence Smith,' called Mr Wilkinson, 'second place, with a total of sixty-five points.' Undoubtedly, Smith was the winner; Ben and Henry had given him 73 points. 'William May, third place, with a total of forty-five points.'

Ben was astounded. 'May was surely disqualified,' he said.

'And not a mention of James Phelps, who deserved second,' Henry said.

Henry stood to object, but the secretary cried out, 'Three cheers for the judges!'

Suddenly, it was all over, and the contestants were shaking the judges' hands.

'Thank you,' William May said to Ben, 'I am absolutely certain I can perfect it now.'

Clarence Smith was also gracious, 'May has a marvellous machine.'

'So,' Henry said, turning to Ben, 'what do you think of that little fiasco?'

'How did...?'

'They were determined to prove us wrong.'

William and the boys surrounded Ben. 'Bit rough,' said William. 'Pearson's plough didn't jump at all.'

The 1886 ploughing match wasn't the first to have its results contested, and this one kept the community arguing for weeks. When it seemed there would be no end to the criticisms, Henry approached Ben about writing a letter to The *Yorke's Peninsula Advertiser*, to dissociate themselves from the results. 'A good ploughing man is the backbone of the peninsula,' he said.

'You're right,' Ben said. 'We don't want people thinking we agreed with that nonsense.'

Henry drafted a letter, listed the scale of points, and showed it to Ben:

> Being two of the judges we want the public to understand
> that we do not consider the results to be fair or just. The very
> principles we set out to test, the depth of ploughing and the
> sturdiness and freedom of the stump jumping mechanism,
> were not considered...

The letter was published, and Ben and Henry were applauded by their community.

'Look at you,' Emma said proudly, as another farmer shook Ben's hand. 'Everyone asking for your advice.'

'Not everyone,' he said. 'But there are quite a few.'

Emma beamed. 'If only it was as simple to be a good mother.'

'Nonsense. You're a wonderful mother.'

'I can't do anything right according to Annie.'

'Where is she...?'

'Don't, Ben, she's lonely. Emily was her closest friend until John Roberts came along. Now Emily is getting married. At twenty-two, Annie's an old maid.'

'That's ridiculous.'

'I was nineteen when we married. And two of Annie's friends are married.'

Ben couldn't see the problem. 'She'll see how lucky she is,' he said, 'not to be burdened by a houseful of children too early in life.'

Emma again took the brunt of Annie's discontent after a dust storm on a hot December evening. Mercifully it was short, but Annie, caught outside, came in choking, her hair and eyes caked with grit.

The following morning, she was in a dreadful rage. 'South Australia is the worst place on earth. Why ever did you come here?' Her face was matted with sweat and dust as she tried to clean the table. She gritted her teeth. 'I hate it here. There's no shops, in fact, we're ten miles from almost anywhere. Nothing is ten miles away in Constantine. And over there they have festivals all the time.'

'We have all the same feast days here,' Ben pointed out. 'We have sunshine – and our very own farm.'

'Too much sunshine; it turns the place to dust. Ba!' she said as her scarf fell from her mouth.

'Mind your manners, Annie,' Emma said.

'Ma, you must admit, Midwinter is hardly Helston Furry Day. Aunt Emily and Jane say nothing compares. The whole of Cornwall is there, dancing through the streets. There are sideshows with hoopla, acrobats, and gorillas. And they have travelling circuses.'

'Australia has travelling circuses too,' Ben said.

'We've never seen one,' Annie said. She stopped dusting.

'You were young, and we had no money. We thought it more important to save for the farm. Maybe I was wrong.'

With his admission of possible fault, Annie's face softened a little, and she quietly said, 'It's just… Farming is so boring for girls. I think I will explode if I hear about one more ploughing match.'

Fifteen-year-old Jack saw a foothold. 'You should watch the ploughing instead of looking at the fashions. 'You can't get more exciting than that last match.'

'See what I mean?' she said to her mother. 'Boys! It's all ploughing, cricket, and football.'

Emma wondered if she was going to feel her children's pain forever.

Emma's last son and twelfth child, Arnold Henry, was born in October, 1887. Emma, at forty-two, wondered when the Lord would stop blessing her with children. Of late, she became so muddled, sometimes she forgot what day it was.

Fortunately, agricultural prices stabilized that year, and Ben and his boys joyfully reaped twelve bushels of wheat to the acre.

Ben said to Emma, as she nursed little Arnold, 'You, my love, are due for a break. We are going to mill all the flour you want. Kimber's Mill does as fine a job as any I've seen.'

Emma sat and beamed. She had craved white bread – and the pastry for the pasties was just not the same without proper flour.

At last, Benjy felt it was reasonable to ask that his father replace Rattler, who had died at an old age.

'Another horse, Da,' Benjy said, 'would mean we could watch the sheep better.'

Ben was delighted with his sons' efforts; they almost ran the farm for him now. 'We might just do that,' he said. 'Let's go see Henry

Freeman.'

'Nothing fancy,' Ben said to Henry, just a good willing horse. He likes to go, don't you Benjy?'

'This one might suit,' Henry said, hitching a rope to the halter of a roman-nosed chestnut. 'You want to try him? He's called Cent, sired by Centurion.'

Benjy put the rope bridle on and swung onto the horse. 'No,' Benjy said quietly to the fussing horse. 'Now, walk.' When the horse settled, Benjy trotted him to the far end of the field and cantered back.

'May I gallop him?' he asked.

'If you can hold him,' said Henry.

Benjy galloped off, the horse's hooves beating into the distance. Ben was glad Emma wasn't there. She would worry. But Benjy was safe as he slowly turned the horse in ever tighter circles until the horse stopped. Benjy jumped down and grinned. 'Henry, I think we have ourselves a deal,' Ben said.

The sixteen-year-old was up at first light every morning to train the horse. Ben often watched as he trotted, then cantered him left, and then right, around the circumference of the field, morning and night.

About three months later, Benjy approached his father. 'Da, I think he is a racehorse. Some of our neighbours have been over and we had little races. He's streets ahead of them. Can I – will you let me, well, take him to the races? Only as a novice, of course.'

Ben turned on him. 'I am extremely disappointed, son. You know the evils of gambling.'

'I wouldn't bet on him, Da, just race him. Foot racing isn't a sin, or ploughing matches. Why should horse racing be?' In the silence that followed, Benjy searched for more reasons. 'And if we don't gamble it would be a good example to others. People look up to you. Why don't you ask Mr Breaker?'

Ben relaxed. The lay preacher would sort the boy out. 'That's probably not a good idea, son. Why don't you ask him.'

When the lay preacher next dined with them after the Agery church service, Ben was unusually tense, ready for the man to rain fire and brimstone on them. Benjy asked his question and the preacher pulled in his chair.

'Let me think about that,' said Breaker. 'Now, Ben, ask the blessing, I am dying to get into that roast and a bit of your wonderful, clotted cream.' Ben smiled at Emma; Breaker loved eating their clotted cream.

The boys were particularly quiet during the meal, and, when Mr Breaker finished, he dabbed his lips. 'I think Benjy is right, Ben,' he decided at last. 'Setting a good example is also God's work.'

15. A Racehorse

On March 31, 1888, Cent was entered in the Hack's Race at the Moonta Spring Meeting.

'Look at that sky,' Ben said to Emma. 'Pure blue. I was hoping for a downpour.'

Emma grinned. 'Off you go. And smile, you are having a day out. I don't even know what that means.'

'Oh, dear.'

'Go on. Arnold's a lot easier now he's walking, and Charles-Wesley will sleep.'

So, Ben and his four oldest sons set out for the East Moonta racecourse.

The racecourse was crowded. Having secured the horse and cart, Ben straightened his coat and pulled down his hat. He wondered if he could get through the day unnoticed. But Henry Freeman joined him for the first race, the Maiden Plate, and W Sims was also there talking to Hollingsworth, the ironmonger, and Nankervis, the carriage builder. The air was thick with excitement as the commentator called the race.

Watching the next four races, Ben relaxed; not everyone was betting, and Nankervis's enthusiasm was contagious; his horse, Lightning, previously unheard of, won three races.

The Hack's race was next, and Ben went out to the boys. Benjy was saddling Cent. The other three argued about who would hold the horse's reins.

'Stop it, boys,' their father said, pulling Jack by the ear.

'It was Richard—' Jack began, but his father was quick to be firm.

'I said stop it.' Ben held the small boys back and said to Benjy, 'Off you go, son. We'll be watching from the fence.'

The race began and the horses were neck and neck until Cent came up on the outside and was set to win. Ben's boys wriggled with excitement.

'It's a three-horse race,' Jack said. 'Benjy'll win easy.'

But, at the post, Mr Nankervis's Lightfoot inched past and won by half a length.

'Aww,' sighed the boys.

Benjy slowed the horse and Mr Nankervis went to meet him. 'You almost beat us,' he said, patting the horse. 'If you ever think of selling him, let me know.'

'Thank you, sir. But we'll keep him for now.'

After the race, Ben had relaxed a little on the matter of horse-racing. Certainly, no harm was done, and his sons were thrilled, and the chatter of horses had brought them all closer together.

Soon it was time for ploughing and seeding again. After a light shower in May, the boys scattered the seeds and raked them in. But there was no rain.

'Not a drop,' Ben lamented. 'The rainwater tank is quite empty.'

Emma put her hands to her head. 'What about the washing?'

'We'll get into the never-ending run with the barrels to Tiddy Widdy Wells again,' Ben scowled. 'I'll tell the boys. A sixty-mile round trip for water is all we need to spice up our day. Look at that lake, it's parched.'

The edges were dried and cracked like old leather.

'Da, come and see this,' Jack said, after Benjy had left for Tiddy-Widdy Wells. 'It's rabbits, they're eating everything. Even the roots have gone.'

Ben threw his hat to the ground and began to cough. 'Lord, bless us and keep us, we'll never get them under control. And the inspector will fine me.'

Jack frowned and retrieved his father's hat. 'Don't worry, Da,' he said. 'We'll make more traps, and there'll be no shortage of meat.'

'And that bounty of ten shillings on eagle hawks will add up nicely,' Ben said.

As the months passed, Ben prayed for rain. He remembered his prayers for sunshine in Cornwall. Now it seemed there would be nothing else.

Benjy returned late in the day from Tiddy Widdy Wells. 'That track is gouged everywhere. I must have lost a third of the water.'

'Benjy...' Ben looked anxious. 'I'm afraid – we're going to have to sell Cent.' Benjy was beyond tired, and Ben watched him wrestle with his anger. 'I know, son. I know how much he means to you, but it's a one hundred percent profit. And he said we can buy him back later. You can't get fairer than that.'

'When will we be able to afford that?'

'Doesn't Mr Hollingsworth want you to ride his trotters at Kadina?' his father asked. 'With a few wins, and a good crop, we might well have enough.'

Amid the desperate drought came a welcome letter:

February 27, 1889

Dear Aunt Emma,

As you know, after Ma died, Dad remarried. I like her a lot, but I miss Ma... I want to come and see you all. Now that I'm a stonemason, I can afford the fare to Australia.

The first available ship is to Melbourne, and I am on that. But being Melbourne, I'm not sure when I will arrive in Agery.

Your loving nephew

John Trethowan.

'Look.' Emma waved the letter at Ben. 'John, the boy, from Cornwall. It's dated three months ago.'

Although Emma knew her nephew would arrive any day, he still caught her by surprise. Wes and Arnold were at her feet, and she was baking when she heard the knock. She put another batch of saffron buns in the camp-oven, brushed her apron, and opened the door, expecting to see one of her neighbours.

She gasped. 'You are the image of your father, and a welcome sight, lad.' She hugged her nephew tightly.

William and Eliza, who had driven John over, came in, and Ben, who saw the buggy arrive, wasn't far behind. Last were Annie and Lizey, who had been milking. The girls stared at John, who hugged them both.

'Don't tell me. You are Annie, and you must be Lizey. I'm John.'

Emma's mind buzzed merrily as she filled the kettle. When tea was ready Eliza and Annie helped serve it.

John bit into the warm bun. 'Mmm,' he mumbled. 'Home cooking. The food on the *Oroya*...' He rolled his eyes.

They sat around the table for hours, John answering the many questions about home.

'Grandpapa fell off the ladder just before I left. Dad was annoyed; Grandpapa knows he should ask for help.'

'Of course, we're a bit scattered now, with the girls moving away.'

As he explained, Emma was surprised. She still imagined them all close together.

'Grandma Trethowan is not sprightly anymore. And she misses her gardening. Wait a minute.' John opened his carry bag. 'Grandma wants you to have these.' He gave his aunt two bundles of letters. 'They're all the letters you'd sent to her. She thought you might like to keep them.'

'Thank you,' Emma said, clasping them to her, wondering what she had written all those years ago.

John resumed answering their questions, while the younger children fell asleep at their feet. His Cornish twang was music to Ben and Emma's ears.

It was late when William stood. 'We should go.'

Emma looked at John. 'You are welcome to stay here.'

'If it's all right, I'd like to spend a fortnight with both you and Uncle William, while I look for work.'

'Of course, any time,' Emma said.

'I hear there's a drought, so any work will be fine. My things are at Silver Hill. I'll stay there tonight.'

Locally, only Sims had work, and with his abundance of land, John was employed to clear trees and stumps.

After a solid week of the heaviest work he'd ever done, John visited Ben and his family on Sunday. When he saw his uncle alone, John

Benjamin Bowden, c. 1880

said. 'Are you all right, Uncle Ben?'

Ben sat, rubbing his legs. 'I'm plagued with rheumatism. And with the drought, I'm forced to grub stumps. But I'm not able anymore. Your Aunt Emma says I should apply for the position as postmaster at Agery.'

'Sounds grand, Uncle Ben.'

'I suppose I can always help the boys before and after post office hours. It would be good if I can get the job.'

Ben was pleasantly surprised when appointed. The sitting room was ideal for the post office. And the new house extension meant there were two entrances. Ben locked the communicating door between the two.

Weeks later, the office looked and smelled as it should, with its red gum bench, paper, pencils, parcels, sealing wax, and letters in the boxes which lined the back wall.

The children inspected the new post office.

'Is Papa really going to be the postman,' twelve-year-old Billie said, eyes sparkling, as Bert and Charles-Wesley jumped up and down. 'Wait till I tell them in school.'

Ben enjoyed his new job immensely, and his general health responded well to the easier life. When an election was announced, Ben overheard a group of men complaining about travelling to Moonta to vote.

When a confidant young candidate visited Agery, Ben told him that he could possibly acquire a lot more votes if he arranged for a polling booth at the Agery Post Office. 'Farmers can't afford to waste a whole day going to Moonta just to vote,' he told him.

To Ben's surprise, a polling booth was installed. And it being a popular arrangement, his neighbours suggested Ben become a councillor.

'Slowly but surely things might change around here,' George Matters said. 'Look at these roads. They'll never be metalled in our time. We need a voice in there for us.'

But Ben resisted. Emma was with child again.

After their thirteenth child, Vera Mary Emma, was born April 18, 1890, Emma, forty-five, surfaced from her haze. Ben told her he had refused to put himself forward for the council. 'I'm not ready for that.'

'You could learn,' Emma said.

'But you and the baby... I couldn't.'

'It is bedlam sometimes, and I did wonder... But Annie and Lizey are twenty-five and twenty-three, and they are quite marvellous in the house. What George said is right. Keeping an eye on Agery's needs is important too. Hopefully we will all benefit.'

When Ben's customers promised him votes, he finally agreed to apply. But waiting for his reply became a worry too. And, as time progressed, Ben's heart gave little flutters at the thought of winning – or losing. Everyone knew he had put his name forward.

'I've no idea what to expect,' he told Henry Freeman.

'Ben, you're almost on more committees than I am. Think of your triumphs with the school, the church, the AMIS, and we can't forget the Show Committee.'

'It doesn't sound easy, though,' Ben said. 'All of those by-laws…'

Ben was finally elected. And he was right; it wasn't an easy job. In the hallowed council chambers, they were responsible for approving tenders, building roads, and policing local by-laws. The budget was always tight. And the councillors regularly disagreed.

During the meetings, Ben was quiet, afraid of looking foolish.

Walter Sims, on the other hand, who had been a councillor for many years, spoke up at every meeting. As the inspector for the *Width of Tyres Act*, Sims fined endless drivers who, he said, overloaded their carts on their way to the mines.

'They are cutting the roads to pieces,' Sims said. 'And they are grubbing roadside timber. Stealing timber is one thing, but they don't even repair the road afterwards. We need more inspectors. The council loses seventy to one hundred pounds per year through the misappropriation of timber. I caught four offenders recently, and I believe there are twenty more out there, living off council timber.'

Councillor Crosby was prepared for Sims's tirade and began to question him. 'Is it true you had personal disputes with the offenders?'

'No.'

'And that while you rigorously enforced the law in this instance, another was breaking the same law with your knowledge?'

'No.'

'Isn't it true, you allowed some persons to grub stumps on the roads?'

'No.'

The councillor waited for quiet and proposed the offenders pay half the value of the timber. Sims began to protest, before he sunk back, realising he should let the matter rest.

Ben learned a lot about Sims over the next few months and told Emma and William about the proceedings, swearing them to secrecy. 'At another meeting,' Ben said, 'Sims arrived late. They told him it wasn't good enough. But his horse had run off. I felt sorry for him. Then he got into trouble again at the last meeting. He asked that leased lands not be taxed as "improved land", and Chairman Hawkes ruled him out of order, saying he should have raised the matter at the previous meeting.'

'That fellow doesn't know when to give in,' William said.

'He doesn't,' Ben said. 'And he just doesn't realise how much he annoys them. I supported him about metalling the Moonta Road, and he really appreciated that.'

At the next Moonta Cup, Sims sought Ben's company. 'Thanks for bailing me out,' he said. 'They are quick to criticize, but I am no fool. I had a proper education.' He jutted out his chin. 'My mother took in washing to send us all to school.'

Ben could see now that Sims had been poor, too, and he had also worked hard to be where he was. He and Sims walked to the fence to watch the race. Mr Nankervis was racing Cent, and Sims now owned Lightning. Ben noticed Sims wince when Cent beat Lightning by a head.

Cent also won the Flying Handicap. Sims was victorious in the Publican's Purse; Lightning beating Cent at the post. Ben had enjoyed those few days at the races. It took his mind off the ongoing drought. All around him were farmers who faced bankruptcy.

A crowd gathered at the post office that week, and they told Ben they had called for a general meeting about the high cost they'd paid for marginal land.

Henry Howlett was the spokesman. He moved nearer to the counter. 'They're serious about this,' Henry said. 'And they want Henry Hancock to chair it. Hancock has large holdings around here, and he's no fool.'

'I won't argue with that,' Ben muttered to William.

The Agery church was full on the evening nominated, and the crowd were abuzz.

Henry R Hancock called for quiet and opened with a prayer. 'You may begin gentlemen,' he said to the pre-arranged speakers.

'The situation here is outrageous,' William Matters said. 'Many have already left the district. It's a long way to Victoria, but land is only a quarter the price over there, and the terms quite generous. We were definitely duped.'

'Australia is a dry country,' Hancock said, 'but some parts are drier than others. Mr Goyder tried to warn the government, and it seems his drought line of twenty years ago was clearly correct.'

William Trethowan asked Hancock the question on their lips. 'Why did they not listen to Goyder?'

'Those were years of extraordinary rainfall,' he said. 'People were hungry for land, so they ridiculed Goyder. Now we are paying the price.'

'The government needs to back down,' Sims said. 'Two pounds per acre was exorbitant, even one pound is too much for Mallee country.'

When the meeting was over, Sims stood at the door and handed out letters. 'Write your own or copy this and post it to your Member of Parliament.'

On their way home, Ben said to William, folding the piece of paper carefully, 'You must admit that was a good move by Sims.'

Early in December, 1890, Ben received a reply from the government.

'It's the best Christmas news ever,' he told Emma. 'The *Land Act* is amended, and we can now choose twenty-one-year leases, or right-to-purchase leases.'

'Leases?' Emma said. 'We won't lose them?'

'No, we just pay whenever we can. It sounded easy, paying off a percentage every year, but we didn't reckon on so many problems.'

As word spread, farmers flocked to the post office. The noise was deafening.

'It's really true, then?' said John Eden.

The men shook hands all around and cheers rang out.

'However,' William said, 'There is a process. We must show receipts for buying land, the cost of clearing it, and crop yields.'

'But…' Ben said. 'I have no idea how much it cost to clear. As you know, no one was paid; we just worked till we could do no more.'

William agreed. 'We're going to be judged by a jury of bookkeepers who never cleared a stump in their lives. All the same, let's be prepared. When did we arrive?'

'You are right,' said Ben. 'We'd better go in with something written down.'

The Land Board interviewed everyone late in December, and Ben and the other Tiparra farmers waited nervously. Ben remembered the government's treatment of the pastoralists, and he wondered if they'd be treated as unfairly. But many small farmers, including Ben, were pleasantly surprised. They were granted their new leases.

Emma hugged Ben tightly. 'You did well, love. It's been difficult – and me bogged down with babies for so much of it.'

Nineteen-year-old Benjy rushed in and patted his father on the back. 'Well done, Da.'

Ben looked at the new glow on his son's face. He remembered days when his sons had almost pushed him aside, thinking he was too old. Now he was content. His land problem was settled; it boded well for his large family of boys.

The following day at morning tea, Emma noticed Ben frowning again. 'I just saw Mr Matters,' he said. 'He's going to lose the farm and the lot. The man is over seventy, for goodness sake.'

Emma was aghast. 'They can't leave.'

'They've no choice. That man worked his fingers to the bone over that place. Fourteen years…'

'But where will they go?'

'Broken Hill. There's work at the mines.'

'Mining? That's not fair.' Emma said, angrily.

Ben didn't know what to say to George, the man who had so generously given him his time, all those years ago, when Ben was a complete stranger.

ITEMS FOR SALE:

21 good horses	Stump-jump harrows
Trotter *Lady Calcutta*	Winnower
19 cattle	Seed sower
40 pigs	2 elevators
200 fowls	Chaff cutter
9 turkeys	Land roller
150 tons hay	Horse rake
3 reapers	2 mowers
3x3 furrow stump-jump ploughs	Weighing machine
Double plough	Wagon
Single plough	Heavy dray
Spring dray	Spring cart
Wagonette	Blacksmith's anvils
Vice, copper	Bellows
Sack truck	Water troughs
3 saddles, 6 harnesses	Wheelbarrows

At the auction, Matters's belongings were sold well below their value.

'They over borrowed,' Sims said. 'But they weren't to know it would come to this.'

Ben nodded. 'This whole business calls for – a fitting farewell.'

'Let me manage that,' Sims said.

'Really?' Ben asked.

'Sarah is upset too. And she hasn't as many little ones as you. It would be an honour. Such a fine family. But you must chair the event.'

And so, a tea and social was held on February 25, 1891, at the Agery Church.

As arranged, Ben addressed the gathering. 'On behalf of everyone here, we sincerely regret your removal.' Ben coughed. 'We cannot thank you enough for your neighbourliness, hospitality, and your many services to the church and local institutions... Without you, Agery would not be the fine community it is today. We wish you the very best for the future.'

Walter Sims followed with another address, and a presentation of artwork. Sims also hailed Matters's unstinting aid to the church. 'In particular, opening your house to all of God's messengers.' Here the crowd stood, clapped, and cheered.

The Bowdens and Trethowans alternated hosting Sunday tea, with the cousins continuing their hilarity and leg-pulling.

Late in May, William's daughter, Emily Roberts, and her husband, John, and two-year-old, Albert, had left early, and, just before dusk, everyone else walked the visitors to their horse and buggy.

'What the—?' John Roberts said, looking around the yard. His spring cart had been moved. The horse was hitched on one side of the fence, to the buggy on the other side. William-John, and John Trethowan backed away.

But Roberts went after them and brought them both to the ground, saying, in a menacing tone. 'Right, you two, you are for it.'

'I surrender,' said John of Cornwall.

What happened next horrified them all. Instead of jumping up and continuing the fracas, William-John started to twitch. As they watched, the boy frothed at the mouth.

'His face is blue,' his mother shouted. 'Get a doctor someone! She tried to steady the boy's jerking limbs.

Thankfully, William-John's spasms decreased slowly.

When the doctor arrived Ben and William lifted the boy inside, and the doctor gave him a sedative.

'The boy has a fever,' the doctor said. 'You must apply cold compresses to his head continuously, or he could fit again.'

Emma and Eliza tore and applied wet cloths to the boy's head. Eliza cried softly, unable to take her eyes off her only surviving son.

Emma and Ben went home late and returned to Silver Hill farm in the morning.

'He hasn't woken…' Nineteen-year-old Rosina said. 'We're waiting for the doctor.'

But William-John didn't wake from his stupor.

When the doctor arrived, he cleared his throat. 'I am almost certain your boy has consumption of the brain, and I'm afraid it is fatal.'

Eliza gasped, and William and Ben supported her as she almost fell.

'No, no… NO!' Eliza cried.

'But he's just twenty-two,' William said, trying to catch his breath. 'Strong young farmers don't just suddenly die.'

'I'm afraid they sometimes do,' the doctor said. 'I am so sorry.'

In the early hours of May 31, the boy's fever increased, and he began to shake violently.

Before Ben had the horse ready to fetch the doctor, William called out to him, 'He's gone, Ben!'

After the funeral, Eliza and William looked hollow and winded.

'We're returning to Cornwall,' William told Ben and Emma.

Emma went cold. 'But you can't!'

'I'm no use to anyone,' William said, crumpling onto the bench.

Eliza, now fifty-three, seemed to fade before Emma's eyes. She lost weight rapidly and her hair suddenly greyed.

'I'm worried about William,' she told Emma. 'As you know, he is vehemently opposed to *the demon drink*. But he regularly medicates himself with brandy.'

Benjy now worked Silver Hill farm for his uncle, and Ben and Emma spent as much time as they could there. Sometimes, William and Eliza wanted to talk about their son, and sometimes they didn't.

William showed Ben William-John's schoolbook from the Moonta Mines Model School. It was leather-bound with a small brass clasp. Ben marvelled at the extent of the boy's learning and his neat handwriting.

'The kings of France… Maps of rivers and mountains in Europe,' Ben read, pointing with his pipe. 'Look at this Emma. A hand drawn map of England – and he has named London and several principal towns. I couldn't do that.'

'Me neither,' said William.

Eliza began weeping again. 'Why would the Lord…?'

Four months later, Charles Wesley Bowden, still a much-cosseted child, asked to go to school.

163

He was six-years old and overconfident, but Emma agreed he was probably ready.

Ben remarked, 'Ever since William-John passed, Annie and those boys have attended to Charles Wesley's every need. He's quite spoiled.'

Emma nodded. 'And we did too. Let's face it: Wes's a sunny little chap.'

'He is,' Ben said, pulling the boy onto his knee.

The first day of school, Emma combed Wes's fine sandy hair, straightened his shirt, and kissed him. He pulled away and ran to catch up to Bert. Wes returned from school still quite confident. 'I mostly listen with the older boys. My lessons are too easy.' But soon, the teacher, Miss Birt, had complained that Wes was too easily distracted.

'Just like his brothers,' Emma said. 'The minute those timber carts rumble up the road…'

Ben said, 'The boys can't resist a run down to hear about the men's latest escapades. Wes talks of little else than Mr Allen. Tom Allen has been driving so long that his sons are taking over now.'

Still, at the end of the year, Wes passed all of his tests.

'Now, can I please see the bullockies?' Wes asked. 'You said if I passed…'

By Christmas, William Trethowan was still miserable. 'I can't face Christmas without my boy,' he said to Emma, as they sought solace in the shade of the gum trees.

'Why don't we go to the sea?' Emma said. 'Just the four of us. We can leave the children at home. Vera is nearly two, and Annie can organise Christmas the way she prefers, with her salads and fresh fruit.'

William liked the idea, and Eliza too was delighted. 'I don't seem to be able to drag myself anywhere these days,' she said. 'Let's do it.'

They set out early on Christmas Day and were quiet on the journey. As they neared Moonta, Emma smelled roasting meat from the hotels. 'Why don't we have a proper Christmas dinner at the Royal Hotel?' she asked everyone. 'Just this once?'

When William nodded, Ben pulled over and tied the horses to the Royal rail.

Sitting in the dining room, Emma occasionally looked behind her.

'What is it, Em?' Ben whispered.

'I feel I'm missing something – but it is the children. I always have

164

at least one at my heels.'

'Should we go back?'

'Oh, no – I'm getting used to it!' she said, tucking into a meal cooked by someone else.

At Moonta Bay the men took off their shoes and walked in the water.

'Cool at last,' William said, sitting on the sand. 'This heat could drive a man mad.'

Emma turned her face into the cool breeze. 'If only we could stay here for a while longer,' she said. 'After two or three days here, we would have to feel better. Look at that lovely hotel up there. Is that what they call Cliff House?'

'It is,' William said, 'but you can forget about that, sis, it's far too expensive.'

'I know. We will always be the "have-nots".

16. Cousins

Ben cupped twenty-one-year-old Benjy's shoulder as the lad sat on the bench. 'You did well with the harvest, boy, all of you. A record I'd say.'

'I'm fair done,' said nineteen-year-old Jack. 'Move along Benjy.'

'The good news is Mr Nankervis is coming over,' said Ben. 'We're getting Cent back.'

'Richard – Bill, did you hear that?' Benjy said. 'We'll have a horse again.'

When they heard the wheels of Mr Nankervis's spring cart on the driveway, the boys raced out.

Benjy flung his arms around the animal. 'How are you, fellow?' he said, patting his neck.

Benjy worked hard to increase the horse's speed, however, though he entered Cent in several races, he had little success.

'Winning isn't everything,' his father said, after another day of no placings for Cent.

'I know,' Benjy said.

As time passed, William and Eliza didn't talk so much about returning to Cornwall.

'The girls are settled here now,' Eliza told Emma. 'And we love Emily's little Bert so much.'

Ben, fifty-one, and Emma, forty-seven, relaxed. Emma had finally emerged from her milky haze, and Ben had more time for the younger boys, Bert (ten), Wes (seven) and Arnold (five). Ben loved their curiosity, their ability to grasp language, and realised how much he had missed with his older boys.

After the harvests, the young men from Agery and Arthurton worked together, grubbing loads of stumps and timber, and, when their carts were full, carting them to the mines. It was a healthy, sensible way to make a living on scrubland, Ben thought, and the boys would make good, hard-working friends for life.

However, with so many young men unsupervised, tricks and pranks abounded. Emma first became concerned when, in the middle of winter, her boys arrived home soaked to their skin – and laughing loudly.

'Benjy?' Emma called. 'What... Where have you been?'

Benjy's teeth were chattering. 'As you, you know, when we leave the mines, we have to p-pay Iron Grey Dick royally for his hogshead of water. But, after that, we can relax. We tie the six drays together and trail the other five horses from the back. Then we all ride home together on the lead dray. It's hilarious.'

Emma could picture them, tired, with loose horses, and playing the fool after a hard day's work. She handed them each a towel.

'But this time,' Benjy said, rubbing his arms vigorously, 'after about thirty minutes, Bill pulled into the old quarry, saying his horse hadn't drunk enough at Dick's trough. So, we waited, and waited. Suddenly, the dray separated from the horse, and we were all thrown into the water! It was freezing.' He laughed again. 'It was so funny.'

'Anyone of you could have drowned, or been trampled on,' Emma said, frowning.

'But we weren't, were we?'

Emma gave an exasperated sigh. 'You have to admit, you could have been. Just be a bit more careful, will you?'

'We'll be all right, Ma,' Benjy said.

But a few weeks later Emma was nervous when she saw four of her sons and two neighbours' boys out in the field, as an empty dray rolled down a slope. The boys walked slowly, watching. Emma saw young William swinging around with the wheel, hanging onto a spoke, with his legs flailing. He let go of the wheel, rolled away, and jumped up. 'I did it!' he shouted.

'You did what?' Emma hollered. 'Grow up. The wheel could have rolled right over you – with your little brothers watching!'

When Emma told Ben, he put his hands up. 'We probably can't stop them, Em.'

Emma rolled her eyes and went back to the kitchen. What was it about men and danger? 'Listen to me, boys,' she said as her sons came in. 'We have lost three children already, and there will be no more dying, not on my watch, not in the name of fun! Do you hear me?'

'Sorry, Ma,' Benjy and William muttered.

In the months that followed, the older boys went out of their way to help and heed their mother, and Emma relaxed a little.

Ben was concerned about the latest government proposals about a United Australia. 'It sounds serious. No-one can know how that will work out. Do we want to be tied to the wishes and whims of the other colonies?'

'Eliza says it will never happen,' Emma said.

William stopped and stared at the two women.

'Look at the latest banking crisis,' Eliza said, 'they say it started in Victoria this time, but banks here are affected too, and jobs. There are thousands out of work, begging on every street corner.'

'You were never interested in this stuff before,' William said.

'That's because we've been busy, Will,' Eliza said. 'Emma's been housebound for nearly twenty-eight years. Now that we don't have to rush home with babies after church, we can talk to some of the other women. They told us about the suffragettes...'

'So, now you want to vote?' William said.

'Why not?' Emma replied. 'We at least need to support the women trying to change things. Some women have it pretty rough, thrown out of their homes, penniless, by bullying husbands... And their children taken from them... It's dreadful. Women like that have NO rights!'

Ben was stunned. What had happened to them?

Young John Trethowan from Cornwall often dined with his cousins at Constantine Farm on a Sunday, but this was going to be a special Sunday, and he fidgeted with his cravat and suit buttons. He wanted to talk to Ben alone first, but his uncle was on his knees, stoking their first autumn fire.

'Uncle Ben, I want to...'

'Yes, son?

'I want to ask your permission to marry Lizey.'

'You what?' Ben cried. John and Lizey had always been good friends, but they were first cousins.

'Can this wait a bit?' Ben said. 'Emma is just about to serve dinner.'

'Of course, sir,' said John. 'I'll call Lizey.'

Ben quietly told Emma of John's proposal before he picked up the dishes of potatoes and cabbage and put them on the table.

'Marry?' Emma said. 'They are cousins.'

'They wouldn't be the first or last.' He put his finger to his lips. Annie had fetched milk and was heading toward them.

Emma worried that her girls were still single. Annie at 28 was undoubtedly an old-maid, and at 26 Lizey wasn't far behind. But she hadn't dreamed the cousins would want to marry.

When the younger children left the table, Emma told Lizey and John she was concerned about the children that would come of such a marriage.

'I would rather die than live without John,' Lizey said, almost hidden behind him. 'And there's no law says we can't marry.'

Emma had to admit she hadn't seen two people more suited, walking the countryside together, identifying birds and trees, and they were forever laughing. Most importantly, neither missed a Sunday at church. Lizey, enthralled by her mother's tales of moving from the other side of the world, said she longed to travel. And John's work, now that he was building houses and churches, was going to take him all over Australia.

'I saved money from my schoolwork and John has put away a tidy sum,' Lizey said.

'That won't help if you have a blind or deaf child, Lizey,' her mother said.

Lizey gasped and ran from the room, followed by John.

Emma smarted. 'What am I supposed to do? Not care?'

But they talked about it again later and, not wanting to alienate Lizey, agreed to give their blessing to the union. But Lizey was still seething and refused to talk about it.

Having anticipated a bumper harvest, Ben shaded his eyes and stared in disbelief at his tall waving fields of wheat. It looked different. He turned to William. 'Is it going red?'

'You don't suppose it's rust?'

'Rust?' Ben's hands became sweaty. He had heard Matters talking about it.

The news spread as quickly, and discontent with Northern Yorke's Peninsula land again grew. The rust crumbled the wheat crop, and Benjy and Richard, more outspoken than Jack, challenged their father.

'There have been too many poor crops,' Benjy grumbled. 'Is this really farming country?'

'We'll get nothing this year,' Richard declared. 'I'm going mining. I hear they are still making good money.'

'You can't,' Ben said, 'your mother won't... We've told you enough times about the dangers, and your Uncle William's accident. You don't need it; you have your timber money.'

'That's a pittance compared to a real wage,' Richard cried.

'It's safer, though,' said Emma. 'An injury will put you back more than any mining salary.'

But Richard wasn't convinced. 'Ma, I'm going to be careful – like Da was. I'll be fine.'

When John Eden knocked, Richard left the room. 'Rotten luck, this rust,' John said. 'Pa says Mr Hancock is calling another meeting. He has been in touch with Roseworthy, a college for farmers near Adelaide.'

At the meeting, the church was overflowing, with the local farmers hoping for a miracle from the Mines Superintendent. It was pleasantly cool in the stone church – a perfect venue for angry farmers.

HRH, still a regal figure in his long coat and bell-topper, told them about the model farm, and about the students who were taught the science behind farming methods.

Ben leaned a little. 'John Eden was right,' he whispered to Benjy, 'A school for farmers does make sense.' Benjy glanced at his father, wondering.

Henry Hancock continued. 'Rust appears in wheat sporadically, and so they identified several strains which are rust resistant,' Hancock said, producing the letter. 'These strains are Steinwedel, Defiance, and Rattling Jack; the consensus being you should try Steinwedel. I suggest you use what you can of this crop and put in your order for Steinwedel for next year.'

'It won't be cheap,' William muttered, 'but I'll go along with it.'

Ben agreed. 'He's got a good mind. He made those mines pay. Then there were the libraries – and the AMIS.'

'I think his best effort was sending the mine boys to school.' William said.

Ben procured the recommended grain, and the following year it rained soon after sowing. With rain falling at the right times, it became one of his best harvests ever.

'But it's too late,' Emma said, still lamenting Richard's departure to Moonta Mines.

Lizey's wedding was now going to be everything Emma had dreamed of. Annie, Emily, and Lizey talked about nothing else, and stitched several evenings a week under the lamp light.

Annie organised her brothers to put the house to rights and decorate it with greenery the day before. Four-year-old Vera chattered happily and was a great comfort to her mother.

On a chilly morning in May, 1894, Annie restarted the fire early. After breakfast, the girls disappeared into the bedroom to help Lizey dress. When they finally emerged, Lizey was breathtaking in her long white satin gown and frothy veil.

'Darling,' Emma said. She hugged Lizey gently, afraid of dislodging her headpiece.

Ben hugged Lizey, too. She looked so much like her mother had when they wed. Annie was also a picture in palest pink, with a wide black hat and shiny black high-heeled shoes. When it was time, they walked the short distance to the Agery Wesleyan Chapel. The boys were almost unrecognisable in their Sunday best, shining boots, and new bow ties.

John waited at the front of the church, and Ben and Lizey waited at the door.

Eliza and John Trethowan's wedding (1890)

Emma, both sad and happy, pulled Vera onto her knees to stem her tears. But Lizey and John were obviously overjoyed, and Emma knew she could ask no more.

Afterwards, a giggling Vera and Arnold ran ahead of Lizey and John and led family and friends to the farmhouse for entertainment, speeches, and a grand repast. Emma had said she didn't want any help, but when her neighbours put their pinnies on in the kitchen, she didn't stop them.

Next morning, it was still dark when Emma, tears threatening, laid out their breakfasts, and helped Lizey pack the last of her belongings. When Lizey and John were ready to leave, Emma handed them a packed lunch. The newlyweds hugged her, and Lizey caught her mother's eye. 'I'm sorry, Mama,' Lizey said. 'Fremantle *is* a long way.'

'It's about as far away as you can go,' Annie said sharply.

Lizey glared at her sister and said, 'But John fully intends to work in Adelaide, too, don't you dear?'

Lizey didn't return to Constantine Farm until May the following year, when she and John introduced their first grandchild, Christobel Florine Trethowan.

It was a memorable day, when they arrived, the baby snug in a snowy white shawl, with a woollen bonnet and mittens. 'At last, we meet, little one,' Emma said, her heart swelling as she carefully took her from Lizey.

Emma and Vera spent as much time with the new baby as Lizey would allow. 'It's been like having my little Lizey back,' Emma said, holding the baby's hands and bouncing her on her knee. 'I'm going to miss you.'

All too soon, the visit was over. 'It's so far away, almost as far as Cornwall,' Emma said to Ben, tears gushing.

In September, 1895, Ben's crop was again stunted.

'What now?' he complained to William. 'We've had plenty of rain, there's no rust – and it's still only six inches high.'

It was a widespread problem. After Superintendent Hancock contacted the college again, he promised another meeting.

Ben was agitated. They needed an answer straight away to save their crops.

The church was crowded, and the men stood and clapped HRH when he arrived.

'Thank you,' Hancock said. 'The problem this time is a peculiar one. They want us to send soil samples.' He raised his hands to stay the crowd. 'Yes, it will take time, but it could save years of hardship. They suspect that, after twenty years of continuous cropping, there is a lack of phosphorous in the soil. They have successfully treated several areas around Adelaide. It will cost money of course.'

This wasn't what the farmers wanted to hear, and the meeting was followed by a hot discussion. Ben talked to Sims afterwards. William joined them.

'It's called Superphosphate,' Sims said. 'Some are buying it, anyway, but they're not sure…so I'll wait. Seeding 1200 acres has cost me enough.'

'This college – who runs it?' Ben said.

'An English professor from a big agricultural university back home,' Sims said.

'A university for farmers?'

'Sort of. Only the rich can afford it.'

'Of course,' Ben said 'A pity. Knowing about the best seeds is a definite advantage. And I suppose they learn how to make wine – and Verdigris too?' Ben's face lit up. 'Remember Will?'

'How could I forget?' William said.

'You learned how to make Verdigris?' Sims said.

'Not really…' Ben said. 'But we might have. It's a long story.'

Benjy lined up the last of the bags and approached his father. 'We can't keep this up, can we?'

'The bad years are coming too often,' Ben replied. 'I won't borrow any more money. I'll sell some land. Maybe 424 West; that's 190 acres. Henry Freeman says he and Matthew Lomman will give me a fair price.'

Benjy was relieved – his savings were becoming meagre.

While selling a small section of land was common in the district, the neighbourhood was astonished when Walter Sims put nearly all of his land up for sale.

'Did you see this, William?' said Ben, leaning heavily on the post office bench, his ankles paining him. 'He's selling 307, 25E, 25W, 392, 311, 53 and 23. That's over 2000 acres.

'I heard a rumour,' William said.

'The talk around here says he won't sell at today's prices,' Ben said. 'Others say he's going into butchering.'

'Clever,' said William. 'Raising your own animals and selling directly to the public. He can't lose.'

Emma hugged her chirpy little Vera, and the five-year-old ran after the boys to the school. Emma, after four wonderful baby-free years, could sit back.

'I hope she likes it,' Annie said. 'Did you hear that Miss Maloney is leaving?'

'At least she stayed four years,' Emma said. 'Remember poor Miss Birt? Gone after just three months.'

Annie chuckled. 'Didn't harm Charles Wesley's schooling. Little prig was so confident, he passed everything. Where did he get that from?'

'I don't know,' Emma said.

The young men of Agery were agog when the new teacher arrived in October, 1895. Even her name was exotic, they said: Miss Isabella Bond.

Annie said to her mother, 'The boys have their eyes out on stalks. Benjy is already smitten.'

'Benjy?' Emma said. 'He's a bit young.'

'And Jack and Richard.'

'That can only end badly,' Emma said. 'Is she really that pretty?'

'She is,' said Richard, who travelled back to Agery every Sunday now. Benjy followed Richard into the kitchen.

'You haven't a hope,' Richard said to Benjy.

Emma looked at Richard's aquiline features and broad shoulders. He was certainly popular with the girls.

'You should have come to the mines with me,' Richard said. 'I have twice as much in the bank as you.'

'But I live here. And I'll see her morning, noon, and after school.'

'Hah,' said Richard, 'we'll see.'

Surprisingly, within weeks, Benjy told his parents he and Bella were courting.

Ben smiled, watching the mutinous looks on the other boys' faces.

'Courting's not marrying,' Jack said, disdainfully. 'She'll see through you soon enough.'

But three weeks later, Benjy and Bella arrived hand in hand at church, and barely a month passed before he announced that they were to be married in July. When Benjy finally brought Isabella home for tea, the boys' faces were a picture. Isabella charmed them all.

'And I'm not going back teaching after the wedding, Mrs Bowden,' she said. 'The Education Department are dispatching Miss Laura Starrs for you. I'm sorry for the disruption, but Vera is managing nicely, aren't you dear?' Vera beamed. 'But the best news,' Bella added, 'is that Benjy has taken out a credit agreement for section 25-West. We'll have our own farm. It's opposite Sims's on the Moonta Road.'

It was good news, indeed, Ben thought. His son had a down-payment on a farm, and he was only twenty-five-years old.

On July 21, 1896, the Bowden family travelled to Gumeracha for the marriage of Benjy and Isabella. Emma was in good health, but Ben found the day long. Emma worried, watching him hobble.

Benjy and Bella made a handsome couple, he with his brown eyes, square jaw, and dark hair parted in the middle, and wide-eyed Bella, with her rippling hair pinned on top and flowing down the back of her glorious cream lace gown.

Some months later, Benjy and Isabella presented Emma and Ben with their first grandson, and the new parents proudly brought him to Constantine farm.

As Emma looked in at the little boy in the basket, her love of the tiny infant kindled; all the wonder of a small baby, without the

174

sleepless nights.

'You can lift him if you like,' Bella said. 'He won't break.'

Emma leaned over and took the little boy into her arms.

Ben moved closer. 'So, little Sydney, you are the image of your father.'

The baby began to cry. 'Don't annoy him, Da,' Benjy said.

But when Emma put the baby to her shoulder, he stopped crying almost immediately.

'You can visit anytime,' Bella said to Emma, continuing with her needlework.

'What do you think about this Federation, then?' Ben said to his son.

'It looks like it might go ahead. I suppose it makes sense, having one government to sort out trade, immigration and the like.'

'It will be the only continent-nation in the world,' Isabella said. Benjy looked at her. She splayed her hands. 'Just geography.'

Lizey's two-year-old Christobel died that year, before they saw her again. Emma was bereft and longed to comfort Lizey. But they lived in Fremantle. When Lizey and John finally made the long trek home Emma asked Lizey what had happened, but Lizey wouldn't talk about it.

At a family dinner, Emma heard Lizey talking to Bella 'The doctor said…'

When Lizey caught her mother's eye, she lowered her voice and Emma heard no more. Emma turned to her sister-in-law, Eliza. 'When is she going to tell me? Or is she going to hold a grudge forever?'

'I don't think it's that. Emily is the same. She doesn't tell me much. They know we love them and that we'll want to help.'

'Of course, we do,' Emma cried.

'But there's nothing we can say to help them, not really. And so, they imagine that anything we say will be criticism. Lizey is probably blaming herself.'

'But she happily pours her heart out to the girls.'

'That's because she doesn't care what they say,' Eliza said.

Emma nodded sagely. So that was it?

After dinner, when the others had gone, Lizey's attitude softened. She told Emma that Christobel had died of pneumonia.

Tearful, Emma hugged Lizey. 'I'm so sorry, dear.'

'I know, Mammy.'

Lizey pulled away. 'Now, let's clear the table, I must pack.'

Emma grieved for all of her lost babies, and now she would grieve for Christobel. She would always worry about her children, and their children. She broached the subject with Caroline.

'I can't forget them, either.' Caroline said. 'The only way I manage is to truly believe they are safely in heaven.'

'It is so difficult.' Emma said. 'Sometimes, just sometimes, I don't know what to believe.'

Six months after they returned to Western Australia, Lizey wrote that she was with child again. Emma prayed this baby would remain well. And her prayers were answered: John Cyril Carlyle Trethowan was a lusty, healthy child.

'It's a battle, getting Australia to agree,' Ben said, handing the newspaper to William. 'There are so many issues. A navy and army will cost a fortune, and there'll be more politicians to pay for. A Federal government won't come cheap, and Henry says small businesses will suffer. They'll face some stiff competition.'

'But it's good for our wheat,' William said. 'Getting rid of the border tariffs?'

'Of course,' Ben said. 'And this convention in Adelaide should sort them out, with Mr Kingston at the helm. He's a formidable man.'

Annie, tired of all the talk, said, 'Everyone has a different opinion. I can't be bothered with them. It'll make no difference to me, I'll still be an old maid.'

Emma tried to cheer her. 'With the vote, at least you have more say over your life, and being single has its advantages. I had my first child when I was nineteen, and, by the time I was your age, I had buried one and given birth to six more. Look at you. You wake up at a reasonable hour, eat your meals without too much interruption – and make a few pence helping out at the school. You are out more evenings than you are in, with all of the Band of Hope and musical evenings.'

'But boys can do so much more.' Annie counted on her fingers: 'The Arthurton Catholic Sports Meeting has foot racing, hammer throwing, putting the shot, they go horse racing, kangaroo and rabbit shooting – and play football and cricket.'

'Cricket is a day out for you, too, helping with the teas and luncheons – and you get to watch the match. Like today.'

'Cricket is more boring than a ploughing match. And serving tea's not fun.'

Emma closed her eyes. What could she say?

However, there was one cricket match that Annie did enjoy, a match between Agery and their neighbours, Arthurton.

Ben, Emma, Annie, and Vera watched the Bowden players line up. Jack was captain, and Richard and Bill were on the team. Although Charles-Wesley wasn't old enough for the team, he was dressed in his whites, agreeing to be their 12th man.

Ben patted Wes on the shoulder. 'When we left Cornwall, I couldn't imagine being a landowner. Now look at you. You take part in almost everything, cricket, football, and tennis. And you live way out here on a farm. It's a miracle.'

Wes tried to imagine what it was like. His father was well respected in Agery and Moonta. Surely, he would be as well back in Cornwall.

As the captains tossed a coin, Annie grimaced. 'Oh, no,' she said, 'Richard has the ball. Arthurton has won the toss again.' She deduced this when Richard was bowling. Batting first was an advantage as the pitch, a rough country one, was always cut up after an innings.

Two hours later, Annie stood, aching and bored, as Pat Murnane smashed another ball to the boundary. 'We've only taken two wickets! And Murnane is on ninety-nine. Now they are breaking for lunch. 'Murnane'll get a second wind.'

Ben agreed. 'They'll need a bowling miracle to shift him.'

Richard came limping over. 'My ankle,' he said. 'I'm going to sit this one out. And Wes is going to take my place.'

When the players returned to the pitch, Wes had the ball. He took a long run up and hurled the ball wildly.

'Did he just close his eyes?' asked Richard.

A shout rang out from the Agery side as two stumps upended, and the umpire cried, 'Out!'

Pat Murnane scowled, tapped the uneven surface with the bat in his left hand, and walked off the pitch.

'Look at Wes,' Annie said. 'He has no idea how he did that.'

The team crowded around Wes, patting him on the back.

'Now he'll be unbearable,' Richard said.

Grinning, Wes was clapped off the field. It was the beginning of the end for Arthurton, and Agery won the match by two wickets.

Ben rubbed his legs. Sitting for so long pained him. But he recovered after supper as they talked about the game again. After the women had scattered, Wes confided to his father, 'Don't tell them, but my legs were shaking so much, I could hardly run up the crease. And I was expecting the ball to be hit to Wallaroo.'

That night, Ben told Emma about Wes's admission, and they both laughed again. Suddenly, Ben couldn't get his breath and his face was grey. He clutched his left shoulder.

'What is it, Ben?' Emma asked, as Ben was finding it difficult to breath. Emma trembled, as she clambered into the passageway.

She knocked on Jack's door. 'Wake up!' she cried.

'What is it, Ma?'

'It's your father. Fetch the doctor…'

When she rushed back to the bedroom. Ben's skin was clammy, and he was breathing loudly.

By the time the doctor arrived, Ben had improved a little. The doctor listened to Ben's chest with his wooden stethoscope and took his pulse, then administered laudanum. Ben's colour returned, and the doctor told him to rest.

Ben stayed in bed the next morning, for the first time in his life. 'No more cricket for you,' Emma said, sitting on the edge of the bed. But Ben was ready to work in the Post Office again on Monday morning, and she said no more about it.

As the new century arrived, plans for Federation steamed ahead.

Wes was obsessed by it. 'Australia will be like America,' he said.

'Not exactly, Wes,' Jack said, 'there are two nations on that continent.'

'Well, maybe we'll be better than them.'

'Maybe. If Western Australia agrees.'

'The queen has already signed the constitution,' Wes said. 'It can't be stopped.'

'I suppose it can't,' Jack replied.

All but Bert and Jack travelled into Moonta early on January 1, 1901, for the celebration. Bunting fluttered everywhere, and flags and souvenirs were available for purchase.

Ben couldn't help but be moved as they joined the thousands gathering there. Two brass bands were in full swing, and strains of the *Song of Australia* rang out at regular intervals.

> There is a land where summer skies,
> Are gleaming with a thousand dyes,
> Blending in witching harmonies,
>   … in harmonies;
> And grassy knoll and forest height,
> Are flushing in the rosy light,

And all above is azure bright –
Australia, Australia! Australia!

Arnold and Vera were hoarse, hungry, and tired by the day's end, and Ben and Emma were glad to return home.

Ben's feet were severely paining him. 'Cursed rheumatism,' he groaned.

Emma worried more about William and Eliza than Ben. Her brother was now sixty-three and his hair quite grey, and Eliza, thinner than ever, had a permanent pallor. Would they ever recover from the death of their sons?

When Emma asked Eliza about her health, Eliza smiled and said she would soon be with her boys in heaven.

'What did you say?' Emma asked.

'I'm not afraid, Em,' Eliza said.

'What about your girls?'

'They have husbands and children. They'll be all right.'

'Please... Don't leave us, Eliza. These are the good years we worked so hard for.'

Weeks later, Eliza told Emma that she had cancer, and was glad of it. Emma ached with the terrible news.

When Eliza was confined to bed, she and William moved in with Emily and John.

Ben and Emma saw Eliza weekly until she died July 24, 1901, thirty-six years after she arrived in Australia.

'She was only sixty-three,' Emma cried.

After the funeral, William was adamant. 'I'm selling up. I mean it this time.'

Eliza's demise heightened Ben's nervousness about his own health. After another small episode of chest pain and breathlessness, he insisted the boys take him into town to make a will.

'You're tempting fate,' Emma told him. 'Please don't talk about dying.'

'It's just a will, Em.'

In August, William put his farm up for sale.

'You didn't deserve this, Will, this whole...' Ben waved his hand, unable to go on. Both men stared out the window.

William promised to give Ben first option on his farming equipment.

'I want none of it…sorry,' Ben replied. 'I couldn't possibly benefit…'

William gave him William-John's school notebook, opened to the page where he had jotted down his assets. 'If your boys could arrange the sale of these for me, I'd be grateful. And I'd like that book returned to me.'

Ben copied out the list and gave it to Jack and William.

'We have to sell these for your uncle. And let's be quite clear, we will not profit from his misfortune.'

6 draught horses	Hay tools
190 sheep	1 stump-jump scarifier
35 fat wethers	1 damp weather reaper
1 reaper	1 winnower
1 tip dray	1 horse rake
1 grubber	1 hand seed sower
1 hand chaff cutter	1 grubbing machine
2 heavy saddles	harness and winkers
1 English and wood wagon	1 four-furrow paring
1 three-furrow stump-jump plough	plough

'I'd like this wet-weather reaper,' said young William. 'I wonder if Da…'

Jack narrowed his eyes. 'You heard what he said.'

'I know, but we'd pay a fair price.'

'Bert's the banker. Let's ask him.'

There was an auction for Silver Hill farm in March, 1902.

Ben's sons attended and reported to their father. 'There was no final bidder that we could see,' Jack said, 'But there were a few bids. They might make an arrangement when the pressure is off. Uncle William was pretty annoyed.'

17. Intense Sorrow and Widespread Regret

Ben had been tolerating the summers better as the years went by, but the hot summer of 1902 was particularly tiring. Autumn brought him relief, although his rheumatism continued to cause him great annoyance, and he was more breathless.

Emma was glad of the distraction for him when their neighbour, John Eden, came by. John had long since expanded his farm by purchasing Tiddy's section 312.

'These house plans, Ben,' John said, 'you said you'd look at them for me.'

'Show me,' Ben said, leading John to the dining room table. But Ben had only walked a short distance when he suddenly dropped to the floor gasping. John called for the boys. They carried Ben back to his bed.

When the doctor arrived and examined him, he said, 'It's not just rheumatism; you have dropsy. Your heart is weak.' He gave Ben a linctus. 'This will ease your pain.'

'Dropsy?' Emma said, when the doctor left. 'You'll be fine.'

'Don't let them take me to the hospital,' Ben begged.

Emma put her arms around him. 'We'll just stay here and talk about the good days,' she said, reminding him of his turnips at Moonta Mines, the ploughing match debacle, and going to the sea.

Ben smiled. 'Don't forget to keep up the donations for the poor.'

'Of course, my love,' she said.

Emma encouraged her family to bring their children for short visits. Benjy and Bella visited with Sydney, now six, and his baby brother, Claude. Lizey and John, now living in Adelaide, arrived with John, five, and Dorothy, a charming two-year-old.

So it was, surrounded by his large family, that Ben Bowden, of Constantine Cornwall, aged sixty years, collapsed for a third and final time, and died almost immediately on May 24, 1902.

'Sixty isn't old,' Emma said to the doctor, as she sat, red eyed, willing Ben's chest to rise. 'His father lived to seventy-five!'

'The dust from the mines didn't help,' the doctor said.

'But my brother worked there,' Emma said, 'and he's hale and hearty.'

'Everyone is different, my dear.'

After the clergyman said his prayers, he tried to lead Emma away, but she wouldn't move from Ben's bedside.

'I've been with him for thirty-eight years, and I never needed him more than now,' she cried. 'Annie, what will I do? I don't want to be a widow...'

The funeral was the following day, and, as Jack and Bill assisted Emma into the vehicle, she suddenly felt important. It was only a flash, and she whimpered, mortified. She was nothing without Ben.

The *Yorke's Peninsula Advertiser*, Friday June 13, 1902:
Agery, May 31
Intense sorrow and widespread regret were expressed on every hand when it became known that Mr B Bowden, a well-known and highly respected resident of this place, had passed away on the morning of the 24th. Deceased had been suffering from rheumatism for many years, but about six months ago, he was overtaken by asthma and dropsy, and from that time up to his death he had suffered great pain until near the end he gradually got weaker, and at last passed quietly and peacefully away. The funeral took place next day, when his remains were interred in the Moonta Cemetery. The respect and esteem in which deceased was held was manifested by the long line of vehicles...and the large crowd around the graveside. Deceased was born in Cornwall in the year, 1841, and about twenty two years later, after taking himself a partner, sailed for Australia, arriving in Adelaide in the year 1864. He worked in the suburbs for some time, subsequently wending his way to the Moonta Mines, where he resided for a number of years. Having a desire to engage in agricultural pursuits, he selected a block of land here (on which the Methodist Church stands) on which he resided for about 27 years, and up to the time of his death. It is due to his efforts we have a post office here. He also held the position of Postmaster. It was also due to his instrumentality we had a polling booth at the last elections. He was a counsellor, and worked hard in various public matters for the good of the community. He was treasurer and trustee of the Methodist Church, a position he held since a place of worship was erected here. Deceased was always of a kindly disposition and endeared himself to all with whom he came in contact. Many poor people in Moonta will have cause to remember him for his charitable acts; many were his acts of

kindness which never saw the light. Deceased leaves a widow, seven sons, three daughters and four grandchildren – everyone of whom was present at his death.

Emma put the paper aside; it had taken so long to read, with her tears brimming at every sentence. His mother would be so proud by the tribute; she would get Annie to buy another newspaper and send her the page.

Not long after the newspaper cutting arrived in Cornwall, Ben's mother, Elizabeth Rowling Bowden died, aged eighty-one.

Emma then wondered what their poor parents might have suffered, knowing they would never see her, Ben, William or Eliza again. So innocent they had been, running off to the other side of the world.

In the winter of 1904, after a church service, Annie introduced her mother to Richard Mahar, a widower, whose wife had died eight years previously. It only occurred to Emma that there was anything between the two, when she saw Annie's eyes smiling directly into his.

The man was at least fifteen years Annie's senior, but Annie was blooming.

Emma was torn and said to her, 'He seems like a nice man dear, but he – has several children.'

'Why do you always have to state the obvious?' Annie snapped. 'Most of his children are married. Ethel is fourteen, and little Freddie is nine… We're just stepping out, Ma.'

Annie was happier than she had ever been. And when they announced their intention to marry, Emma cried with joy. If only Ben had lived to see the day.

It was, of course, the talk of the district, and when Emma suggested a nice wedding in spring, she was swiftly rebuffed.

'Richard wants a quiet wedding, and he wants it now,' Annie said. 'So, we will arrange it.'

Annie was thirty-nine, and Richard fifty-two, when they married on August 25, and moved to East Moonta.

By year's end, they presented Emma with a bonny fair-haired grandson, Colin. Most of Emma's grandchildren didn't follow the old family names, and Emma wasn't sorry. She had tripped over far too many Bens, Johns, Elizabeths, and Mary-Anns over her lifetime.

Now almost sixty, and still missing Ben, Emma was lost without Annie, who had ruled over them all, and had carried a large workload. How would she manage? For most of her day, she and Vera were washing clothes, or in the hot kitchen, straining milk, making butter, and the never-ending preparation of bread, vegetables, tray-loads of pasties, and saffron buns, which disappeared almost as soon as they were baked.

If only more of the boys had married, Emma thought. But six of them, aged from seventeen to thirty, were still single. They seemed to manage the farm well enough when Ben was alive, but Emma worried that they would get up to their usual pranks, or even worse.

She remembered William hanging on to the cartwheels, rolling down the hill. She had screamed then, 'What on earth are you doing? Trying to kill one another!' Why did they have to live so dangerously?

Will explained on the afternoon he nearly drowned that it wasn't all deliberate. 'It was hot out there, as you know. We went to the lake.'

The first Emma had heard was the boys shouting in the yard. She looked out and saw Bert and Wes half-carrying Bill, who was dragging his feet and quite pale. Emma put her hand to her mouth. What now? Was Bill alive?

Bert and Wes dragged Bill inside, and Wes asked for towels.

They wrapped the towels around Bill and rubbed his face and arms.

'Oh, my heavens,' Emma said. 'What happened?'

'We were swimming in the lake,' Bert said.

'And we were stuck up by a huge kangaroo,' Wes added.

'Your father always told you not to mess with kangaroos,' Emma said, hands on hips.

'There weren't any there when we arrived at the lake,' said Bert. 'Then this big one came down to drink. I wasn't afraid; we had Kaiser with us. But Bill was closer to the roo, and when he grabbed hold of a branch, it broke – shattered more like it, and suddenly the roo grabbed Bill and pinned him under the water. Can you believe that?'

'He what?' Emma said, gasping.

'Tried to drown him. But, quick as a flash, Kaiser leapt at the roo's throat and killed him. Just like that,' Bert said clicking his fingers. 'Then I grabbed Bill and dragged him out.'

The steady hand of their father was sorely missed.

Emma recounted the tale to Grace on her next visit. 'Kaiser sleeps inside now, with Bill never far away. You are lucky you have no boys.'

'I don't know,' said Grace. 'Mary-Grace was pretty reckless, climbing trees she couldn't get down from, and yes, chasing kangaroos. Christopher couldn't believe that one small girl could get into so much trouble. But she's settled now. Benny Hand and three babies have seen to that.'

The boys' next adventure was also an accident. It was about half past ten on a cold night in June. The loud voices woke Emma. She got up and heard nineteen-year-old Wes say that a horse with a trap had galloped down the road.

'I tell you, there was no driver,' Wes said to Jack and Bill. 'He's probably fallen.'

'Ghost carriages, eh, Wes?'

'Listen to the lad,' Emma said.

'I saw an empty carriage go past. It was going fast,' Wes said. 'They don't believe me, but the driver must have fallen off. And I'm going to find him. He could be injured.'

'Whoa, you'd best wait for us, Shorty,' Bill said, grabbing his hat. 'You'll get lost out there in the dark.'

'You have cat's eyes, I suppose?' Wes said.

'All right, you two,' Jack said, 'if Wes is right, we need to go.'

Bill lit two lanterns.

'The cart went that way,' Wes pointed toward Maitland.

Emma wanted to stop them. It was dark, and they too could fall or get lost. But they rushed past her. Emma slept fitfully until they'd returned at dawn.

'It took us an hour to find him,' Bill said. 'He was slumped like a shadow at the side of the road.'

'When we lifted him,' Wes said, 'his hat fell off. It was full of blood. I was nearly sick… You tell them Bert.'

'We took the man into town to find a doctor, but everywhere was closed – except the police station. The sergeant sent his constable for the doctor.'

'How is he – the man?' Emma asked.

'Captain Smith?' Wes replied. 'He's going to be all right. The doctor said he was lucky. The cold could have killed him.'

The *People's Weekly*, Saturday, August 5, 1905:
Captain M Smith desires to thank his many friends in Moon-
ta for the kindness and attention shown in connection with
his serious accident, especially Messers Jack, Bill and Wes
Bowden who brought him to Moonta and Sergeant Deane and
Dr James.

Emma was impressed. Dangerous, yes, but Ben would have been proud of them, especially Wes.

Captain Smith later visited the boys and presented them each with a gold medal, engraved with their names and the date. Wes showed his mother. She was wide-eyed.

'I can't read it, son, what does it say?'

With thanks for saving the life of Captain Smith.

18. A Musical Evening, and a New Barn

Emma was excited as she made up the beds in the third bedroom. She was only just in time, hearing the unmistakable grind of a horse-drawn carriage on the driveway. She rushed outside.

'You made great time,' Emma said to John, and patted five-year-old Dorothy's hand.

Young John jumped down.

'We were up early with missy here,' Lizey said, nodding toward three-year-old Nellie.

'Where's Aunty Vera?' said Dorothy.

'Vera,' called Emma. The three children rushed to their aunt, who led them to see the new puppy.

'It's a long one hundred miles,' Lizey said to Emma, rubbing her temples.

'I'll never forget that first trip we made from Adelaide to Moonta,' Emma said. 'Was it really thirty years ago?'

'Still,' Lizey said. 'It's not near as far as Fremantle. But I don't regret our time over there. Western Australia was good for John. He built five houses, and a church. More than we'd dreamed of.'

John, Elaine and Dorothy Trethowan, Colin Maher's cousins, c. 1905

Bill and Wes, having dusted the powder from their overalls, ambled in. 'The iron for the roof is here,' Bill told John.

'Then we're sure to finish the barn this trip,' John said, looking puzzled. 'Your faces are white, what have you been up to?'

'You should see Jack and Bert; it's superphosphate,' Wes said. 'We're nearly done. Then we can help with the roof.'

John's eight-year-old son, Johnny, dragged on his father's arm. 'Can we go now?'

'After you,' Bill said, nodding to the boy's father as they left for the yard.

After their midday meal the following day, Lizey suggested Emma have a rest. 'I have made saffron buns for your supper,' she said. 'If you are going to sit up with the children, you'll be tired by the time we get home.'

To her surprise, Emma slept that afternoon, waking to the strains of Wes and Lizey practicing their duet.

That evening, they supped around the dining room table, catching up on the news, before leaving for the annual Christian Endeavour Meeting.

'So, you are ready to lift their hats tonight, Lizey?' Jack asked.

'If the Reverend Daddow's *short* address allows,' Lizey said wryly. 'And there's lots performing: Harry Cadd, Tom Howlett, Misses Eden and Daddow. I do enjoy the recitations.'

Emma didn't hear them return that night, and the small children didn't stir.

Next morning, Lizey yawned, and the children giggled when their mother appeared in an old, frilled gown and bonnet.

'Why are you dressed funny?' Dorothy asked.

'We're going to have a ceremony,' Lizey said. 'Grandma is going to open the new stables and cow-barn that Daddy helped build.'

Lizey turned to her mother. 'Mama, where's that lovely merino dress of yours?'

Emma was amazed Lizey remembered. And she was surprised the dress was still in one piece. Her sisters had obviously paid dearly for the fabric.

When the men appeared in black, with top hats and painted moustaches, their wives pealed with laughter.

Emma, having donned her old frock and hat, re-appeared, and Lizey handed her a bottle of cider.

'Right, let's get this done,' Lizey said.

John escorted Emma around the new building. 'These steps lead to the hayloft. Hay is fed up there, and the lads just throw a bundle down to the cows each morning.'

It sounded so easy, so sensible, Emma thought.

'Now, Ma,' John said. 'It's your turn.'

'I declare this cow barn – open,' Emma said uncertainly, pouring the cider over the manger.

There were giggles, and Emma's heart warmed. What fun her

family were.

In June, 1905, Emma was again looking after her three grandchildren while John and Lizey joined their brothers and sisters at a musical evening at Wattle Farm.

Lizey told Emma about it the next day. 'There were flaming candles lighting the whole driveway.'

'I thought we were going to be early,' Wes said. 'But it was already crowded when we arrived.'

'The room looked huge,' Lizey said. 'Of course, they'd moved the furniture out, but it looked gorgeously festive with greenery.'

'Show Ma the program, Wes.'

'Recitations, dialogues, the Misses Butler,' Emma read.

'And Wes and Benjy sang beautifully,' Eliza said.

'But Hartley Cadd stole the show with his recitation,' Wes said.

'He's only a child,' Emma said.

'And those Christy Minstrels,' Wes said, laughing. 'They came all the way from Adelaide – with boot black on their faces. Harry has contacts in the right places.'

Emma Bowden, c. 1909

Emma was delighted that out-of-the-way Agery provided, at least what sounded to be, an excellent night's entertainment.

'You would have loved it, Ma.' Eliza said. 'When I think of all of that time you spent, sitting in, year after year; bad roads, sick children, and not a musical evening in sight. Maybe next time you should go too.'

Emma had presumed she was too old. But maybe, just maybe, she thought, she would go as she took her daily stroll around the church field.

Constantine Farm saw more changes in the next year. First to move was Jack, who was thirty-two. His news surprised them all. He hadn't even told his mother about his trip into Moonta.

'You're doing what?' Bill said, stopping mid-air with a bowl of potatoes.

'I'm buying a farm. This place can't support us all. No disrespect to Da, but Richard was right to go to the mines; he's making good money.'

'But how can you farm without a wife?'

'I can cook a rasher – and wash a few clothes – thanks to Mama. I can manage.'

Ever fearful of the mines, Emma said, 'Jack is right. Why should he risk life and limb when he has a deposit for a farm?'

'But Section 252?' Wes said. 'Daniel Phillips's farm? You'll be paying it off forever.'

'Wes, it's the same size as this place, and most of it is cleared.'

Emma had always worried about Jack. Overshadowed by his rowdy brothers, he rarely had a girlfriend. But now a fine young man and superintendent of the Sunday School, he would make some girl a lovely husband.

'That still leaves four of you here,' Jack said. 'Arny is nineteen now. You'll manage.'

Near the end of the year, William, now seventy-one, called to Constantine Farm.

Emma hugged him. 'You're looking well.'

'I feel well… And I have a new friend, Em. Her name is Grace. Grace Welsh.'

Emma beamed. 'That's wonderful.' She hugged him again.

'She's about your age. I know Eliza would approve.'

'Of course.'

'I want to marry her, but I have to tell the girls first.'

Emma sighed sympathetically. 'Surely, they'll understand.'

'I hope so.' He gave her a knowing smile and asked, 'How are you going?'

'Not that I have much time to dwell, but I still miss Ben dreadfully. He would so have welcomed your news!'

William nodded. 'And then you remember he's not there? I know. I do that all the time.'

Emma handed him a cup of tea. 'But now you have Grace, and I'm so glad.'

After a sip of tea, William said, 'So, you're on the school committee now?'

'And with the same old problems; trying to keep teachers here. We've had another four in four years.'

'Aren't they supposed to stay two years?'

'They are, but those inspectors don't help. Isabella said they are vicious. I doubt they give anyone a good report. They write stuff like "lacks vigour", or "wanting stimulus" ...'

'That is a bit vague,' William agreed.

'Exactly. Poor girls. It's their first job, and so far from home. However, we are pinning our hopes on another new one. Miss Tunkin. Agery is her second school.'

It was in July, 1906, when Emma first saw Miss Tunkin sitting in church beside Mr and Mrs Cadd. She noticed the young men too, some openly staring at the young and pretty woman. She had bright blue eyes and a flawless skin. She was immaculate in a white high-necked blouse, and a black skirt and knitted shawl..

As the families mingled afterwards, Wes, confident after taking five wickets for twenty-five runs at the recent cricket match, told his mother the new teacher smiled at him.

Eleanor Tunkin, c. 1906

'Are you serious?' Bill said. 'She'll want a real man. What are you, twenty-one? And where's your farm?'

Emma watched as Wes gritted his teeth. But she supposed they were right. Richard and William were years older and had money in the bank.

A few weeks later, Wes confided to his mother, 'I just took Miss Tunkin home.'

'You what?'

'After school, she was standing beside her carriage, quite dejected. So, I went over. There was a crack in the rim of her wheel.'

'You couldn't have fixed it for her,' Emma said.

Wes nodded. 'I said I'd take her carriage to the blacksmith and then drove her home. She was ever so grateful. You should have seen the boys' faces when I drove past them. Mr Cadd will bring her to school every day until the carriage is fixed. And...'

'Yes?' Emma raised her eyebrows.

'Ma, she said she would attend the next musical evening with me.'

Emma smiled. Wes's confidence hadn't waned. Was it because of, or in spite of, the teasing by his brothers?

A week later, Wes told her, 'Miss Tunkin has a bereavement. Her sister died, at only twenty-seven. So, the school is closing for three days.'

'That's terrible, dear.' Emma patted Wes's hand.

When Miss Tunkin returned from the funeral, Wes told Emma she had walked straight past him. 'She stared straight through me, Ma. I'll have to start all over again.'

'Give her time, son.' Emma thought it was best. Wes couldn't offer the woman a home as yet.

But Wes was not deterred, and soon he and Miss Tunkin resumed their friendship.

Meanwhile, his older brothers were still unmarried, although Richard was courting Eva Lodge. After Richard announced his betrothal to the vivacious Eva, Wes declared that he had invited Eleanor to the wedding. Emma wondered what the older boys would say. But only Bill was there, and he clapped Wes on the shoulder.

'Well done, Wes. She's quite a catch.'

Emma sat quietly in the church as Eva Lodge walked up the aisle on her father's arm. Emma was both joyful and sad, still missing Ben so much. As the bride passed by, Emma saw Eva's heavily embroidered frock. It was gorgeous, and Vera had told her it was pure silk. Emma remembered the silkworms at Beaumont House. Untold hours of work for one garment.

Emma watched Richard as he faced Eva. They were so much in love, and indeed a handsome pair. Richard was clean shaven with his hair in a fashionable central part. Lastly came the bridesmaids, Vera, Minnie, and Winnie Lodge, in cream and pink.

After the wedding feast, Emma sat beside Bella. 'No expense has been spared for Eva,' Emma said. 'And Richard looks so happy.'

A hushed wail interrupted their conversation.

'What is it, child?' Bella said to little Ross.

'Here, sit on my knee Ross,' Emma said to the three-year-old.

'Bless you,' said Bella. 'I'd asked Sydney to mind him, but he's forgotten again. Eleven is a curious age, but he does work hard on the farm. How did you manage, Ma? Baby after baby.' She looked down at baby Gerald who was waking.

Emma smiled and admitted, 'It was – dare I say, frightful at times.'

'That's a relief. My friends say their babies are perfect. They supposedly sleep all night…'

'Probably not *all* night,' Emma said.

After the honeymoon, Richard and Eva moved onto a farm on the Agery-Kadina Road.

They showed Emma through the house, with its new furniture, new kitchen, shiny pans. It was perfect. 'All the peace of the countryside,' Emma said, 'with Kadina not a mile away. Your hard work has paid off, Richy. No long drives to the town, and not another day down those mines.'

Richard beamed. 'I must admit, I'm happy to leave mining behind me.'

Wes took a towel and began to wipe the plates after his mother washed them. 'Err…Ma,' he said, blushing. 'I want to marry Eleanor, but I can't afford a farm. My work is here. Can we – live here?'

'On Constantine Farm? It is owned by you all, so I'd have to ask your brothers. And do you really want to live with them? You know what they're like.'

'Eleanor's parents are from Cornwall,' Wes pointed out. 'She is one of eleven leg-pullers. We'll manage.'

'But it won't be easy. And what if Bill or Bert want to bring their wives here?'

'They don't have girlfriends yet, and they've already saved a bit. They'll want their own farms.'

'We could ask them,' Emma whispered. 'I would love some help in the house. But you had better ask Eleanor first.'

The next musical event was at Cadd's. Wes looked dashing in a new shirt, bowtie, and waistcoat, and Emma suspected Wes was planning to propose to Eleanor. Emma hoped it went well for him. He was only twenty-three. She wished him good luck.

Wes declared his successful engagement the following day.

'Well done, brother,' said Bert.

'Yes, great,' said Bill, again without a hint of sarcasm.

'I hope you're not expecting to take ownership of the farm?' Bert said.

'Of course not, I just want somewhere to live until I can afford my own place.'

'Eleanor will be most welcome,' Emma said. 'And your father and I worked it out years ago; everyone will get their fair share of the farm.'

'How does that work?' Bill said.

'Well, the portions won't be exactly the same...'

Arnold tilted his head. 'Wait a minute.'

'It will depend on how many years each of you have invested in the farm. Now, you, Wes and Bert, have worked full time here, bringing the farm on. You will be due more than Benjy and Lizey, who moved out much earlier.'

The boys' faces were a picture. A smile played at Emma's lips. 'Don't worry, I'll work it out fairly.'

Emma Bowden, c. 1915

Bert and Wes drove Emma into town to make a will.

'You are quite right, Mrs Bowden, your investment has grown, and it is never too soon to make a will,' said the land agent, Leslie Bennett, who ushered her in to the office. 'You are a wealthy woman.'

'Do you think so, Mr Bennett?' Emma said. 'Ben always said it was poor land. Look at Mr Sims. He had over 2000 acres and couldn't sell it.'

'It's different now. Those were hard times. Too many sold at once. But since superphosphate, farmers haven't looked back.'

Emma raised her eyebrows.

'Well, mostly,' he said. 'There's always the drought.'

Back home again, Emma told them of her conversation.

'But it's true,' said Wes, 'you are wealthy. Land around here is expensive. Look what Jack paid for Phillips's farm. That was a lot of money.'

19. Quarantined, 1909

After their midday meal, Bill and Bert left the house to bring in and saddle the horses. But both boys were back soon. Bert was pale. Wes, now ready to join them, stood back as they pushed their way in.

'There's several days of ploughing out there,' Wes said. 'You hardly even found the horses in that time.'

'We did find them,' Bill said, looking at his feet. 'The mare... She's dead.'

'Dead?'

'She was ten years old.' Bill said.

'That's not old,' Wes said. 'What happened?'

Bill shrugged. 'Come and see for yourself.'

It was hours before the boys returned, exhausted after digging and filling the deep grave.

'Just as well you weren't there, Ma,' Wes said. 'The smell. The flies...'

'How did she die?' Emma asked.

'Could have been poisonous weeds,' said Wes. 'We'll probably never know for sure.'

'We'll have to tighten our belts,' Bill said. 'She'll have to be replaced. And we still have that ploughing to do.'

Five days later, Wes limped into the house.

'What is it, son?' Emma asked.

'My horse just crumpled under me. My foot was trapped under her.'

Bill rubbed his head. 'It's not right. A young horse like that. Sims is a veterinarian now. You'd best pay him a visit.'

When they returned from the vet, Wes looked ready to explode.

'We sat in that waiting room for an hour,' Bert explained.

'But that wasn't the worst,' Wes said. 'He yelled at us. Said we weren't half the farmers our father was.'

'Why?' Emma asked.

'He asked us if we'd changed our boots. He said we probably infected the whole Peninsula. With *Anthrax*. How were we to know? We could lose everything.'

Emma's heart skipped a beat.

'He says there's anthrax at Queale's, not fifteen miles away. And that anyone within miles of here with cattle, or sheep, and of course horses, could be ruined.'

'We didn't bring it into the area,' Wes insisted, pacing up and down. 'And where did Queale get it from? How did Da tolerate that Sims man?'

'Anyway,' Bert said, 'Sims contacted the chief inspector of stock on his new speaking machine. He and the inspector will be here as soon as they can. Apparently, they can tell immediately, by looking at the horse's blood under one of those new magnifying machines.'

Sims and Williams arrived in a shiny new horseless carriage and soon made their diagnosis.

When they returned to the house, Wes was near to tears. 'We have to burn the horse, the bedding, everything,' he said.

'That's not going to be easy,' Emma said, glad the boys were in charge.

'We won't know for about a month if the outbreak is contained,' Bert said. 'And we're quarantined for three months. No animal or vehicle leaves or visits the farm until then.'

Tension rose within the family over the following weeks. Wes was particularly impatient because, again, he saw less of Eleanor.

'We are all affected, Wes,' his mother said gently.

'I only see her after school now. The pupils whistle and giggle every time I go near her.'

'Well, we know who our friends are now,' Bert said, after several weeks of seeing only one neighbour. 'We've only had one offer to fetch supplies from the town. If it weren't for Benjy, and Annie's Richard, we'd starve.'

Another month of making do with what supplies they had passed slowly. Emma hated to hear the boys so angry with one another.

Finally, the quarantine was lifted.

Wes raced to the school that very afternoon. But his streak of bad luck was only beginning. Early in June, a week after he bought a new horse, he dragged himself inside, his trousers soaked with blood.

'What happened?' Emma cried, hand to her mouth.

'That new gelding is frisky. He took fright when a bird flew out of the mallee and dragged me into a barbed-wire fence.'

Wes clutched his right calf but put his other hand up. 'I'll be all right, Ma,' he said, sinking onto the nearest chair.

'You're hardly that son,' she said. 'There's blood everywhere. Show me.'

Wes eased up his trouser leg.

'What did she do to you, Shorty?' Bill said, backing out of Wes's reach.

Emma glared at him. 'Behave, son, for five minutes.'

'It's a deep cut, Wes,' Emma said. 'You'll have to see a doctor.'

'Not tonight, Ma. I'm a bit sore. And we won't find a doctor open now.'

'Dr Clayton is open all hours,' she countered.

'And there's always Sims,' Bill said. 'He'll stitch anything that moves.'

Emma gave Bill another withering look.

Bill said, 'Sims went from farmer to butcher, selling his own meat. Now he's carved enough beasts to call himself a veterinarian?'

'There's no end to that man's ambitions,' said Wes.

Bill gave a placatory smile to Wes. 'Come on, old chap, I'll drive you to the doctor.'

'Not likely,' said Wes.

Doctor Clayton inserted seventeen stitches in Wes's leg. 'You have torn a muscle. You must stay in bed for a month.'

After only a week, Wes grumbled, 'If I have to stay in bed for a month… Well, I can't see Eleanor Ma. What will I do?'

'Bill is going to arrange it for you,' Emma said.

'Why should I trust him?'

'Tell him, Bill,' Emma said.

Bill looked embarrassed. 'I just spoke to John Eden. He's going to loan you his settle-bed. Bert and I will bring it over.'

Wes gaped. 'Ma, did you hold a gun to his head?'

Emma laughed. 'Almost. No, Bill has apologised.'

Bill smiled. 'Ma was always singing your praises, Wes. I was sick of hearing it. But without your help, Bert and I have never been busier. We are way behind with the superphosphate.'

Wes sighed. 'Just don't forget that.'

After two weeks, Wes, still frustrated, complained to the doctor. 'You were right, my leg is too sore to put to the floor. You don't have any magic potions, I suppose.'

'I could try a splint on it,' the doctor offered, 'You seem pretty determined to get up, and that's good. But the muscle must have rest and support.'

Emma remembered William's struggle with his damaged leg. Wes would get there too.

Once Wes gained some movement, he asked Benjy to book the church for his marriage. 'I've waited long enough, and you can call a meeting to form a football club. We have three Pedlars, three Bowdens, and two Nankivells. And that's just our immediate neighbours.'

By the time the new football club met, Wes sat at the head of the table and was elected chairman.

Also pleased with the lifting of the quarantine, young Vera-Mary-Emma Bowden had gone ahead with plans for her wedding, to Stephen Edwards, a painter and decorator.

Emma hummed to herself while her daughters-in-law baked and tidied. It was now, 1910, and Vera was just twenty years old, and radiant in white silk organza.

The young couple were moving to Adelaide. 'The city is where the big money is, Mrs Bowden,' Stephen explained. Emma would miss Vera's endless chatter.

Wes also looked forward to the end of his tortuous wait to marry Eleanor. However, his long list of obstacles seemed to forever extend, as Eleanor explained, 'I sent my notification to the department, of my intention to marry you in June, a… So, they are sending me to Sunny Hills for my last two months.'

'How could they?' Emma said.

'They have arranged a replacement for Agery from April,' Eleanor added.

'But you've been here four years. It's almost a record. Why not send the new teacher to Sunny Hills?'

'I dare not argue,' Eleanor said. 'Not after that last inspector's report.'

'Those inspectors,' Emma said. 'They don't know what a good report looks like. The parents and children are going to miss you dreadfully.'

'I should like to resign, but I want to put a bit of money aside. I don't want to have to ask Wes for everything.'

Emma understood.

It was an emotional day when Eleanor Tunkin left Agery School for Sunny Hills. The schoolchildren, some in tears, waved and chorused their goodbyes. Wes followed her carriage up the road. He wasn't going to farewell Eleanor in front of everyone.

'What do you mean you can't spare a horse?' Wes said to Bill. 'How am I supposed to visit her. Or are you suggesting I just don't see her for eight weeks?'

'Times are hard,' said Bill. 'The horses are needed here. Someone will give you a lift.'

'Thanks,' Wes said, 'for nothing.'

Wes's neighbour Jim Eden was more helpful. He said to Wes, 'Why don't you purchase a bicycle?'

'Surely you are jesting?'

But Jim was not. 'And I have a plan. I have a cousin over that way. His daughter needs a bit of extra tuition. If Len could do that, my cousin says you can have a bed on Saturday nights. And think how fit you'll be for football, after all that exercise.'

'Jim. You're a marvel. Wait until I tell Len.'

When Wes first wobbled his way up the road on his bicycle, his brothers jeered and laughed.

'Leave him alone,' said Emma. 'That road is terrible. They'll never surface it.'

As the sun set that Saturday night, the boys looked up the road for Wes.

Emma let them wait a while. 'You don't seriously expect him to return today?' she said. 'Be off – you've work to do. He'll be home Sunday evening.'

Wes didn't see the time passing, arranging his life around seeing Eleanor every weekend.

As the day of his marriage approached, Wes confided to his mother. 'I've been praying for rain for most of my life,'

'But for the last week of June, you want a few fine days?' Emma said.

'Exactly.'

'Best of luck,' Bill said, 'It is the middle of winter you know.'

'You'll get wet as well,' Wes said.

'Right, boys, give it a rest,' said Annie. 'We have to plan your groom's party.'

Annie, Bill, and Benjy's Isabella began to make a list with Wes.

'There's so much local talent,' Wes said, 'but we can't have everyone.'

'It will be costly to bring Misses Carter and Metherall,' Lizey said.

But Wes was in love. 'I'm tired of settling for second best,' he said. 'I'll take out another small mortgage, so that we can honeymoon in

Adelaide, and I can buy those fox furs for Eleanor as well.'

Emma let the others organise the groom's party.

Wes said, 'Ma, do you think we could have dancing between the entertainments? Everyone is having them now.'

A true Wesleyan, Emma doubted that. Still, it was Wes's special day, and she wouldn't deny him.

On the day of the groom's party, Emma baked pasties, and Lizey, Annie and Bella arrived with their trays of assorted sweet and savoury cakes and pastries. The boys cleared the large dining room of all but the table and chairs, and Annie and six-year-old Colin decorated the windows, doorways, and fireplace with shrubbery. As the sun went down, neighbours carried benches and extra chairs to line the room, and Wes and Eleanor's many excited friends converged on Constantine Farm. A full moon beamed through the windows onto the happy couple, and Eleanor's hair gleamed like spun gold.

Emma was thrilled but felt all of her sixty-five years amongst the young people. There were amusing recitations, and Misses Carter and Metherall delighted everyone with their songs, as did Richard and Wes with their duets.

Lizey was right, Emma thought. It was about time she had a night out.

Everyone rose early. The wedding, to be held in Balaklava, was sixty miles away.

Charles Wesley Bowden and Eleanor Beatrice Tunkin, 1910

Emma pulled her cape and knee rug tightly around her as the horses clip-clopped toward Port Wakefield. There were few towns along the way, but the only landmarks Emma recognised were at Wakefield itself. Here they rested the horses and watched a steam train pull in.

'On our honeymoon,' Wes said, 'the train will take us from here to Adelaide in just over two hours. A bit different to forty years ago, eh Ma?'

Nearing Balaklava, the countryside became lush, and the town was a picture with its gardens and handsome sandstone buildings – all overlooking the Wakefield River.

They pulled in beside the large, newly built Church of Christ where Eleanor's brothers William and Frank welcomed them.

'Those windows are beautiful,' Emma whispered to Annie, as she sat back against the shiny new pews. There were small posies of flowers tied to each pew, and on either side of the pulpit, stood two magnificent urns of pink and white fringe-myrtle. Emma was content, surrounded by her family. Her ten grandchildren chirped quietly while Richard and Eva's baby, Melva, slept.

The organ music soared as Eleanor, gloriously frothy in white, entered the church on her father's arm.

Emma loved the familiar words of the service.

After the service, Eleanor introduced her parents to Emma, who liked them at once. Samuel Tunkin with his kindly face and heavy grey beard was about her age. Mary Grace, thirteen years younger, had wide smiling brown eyes.

'Wes said you were at Moonta Mines?' Emma asked Mary Grace.

'In 1862, but not for long. I was six. It was a terrible time. My father and sister died of Scarlatina. Mama married again, and we moved to Gumeracha in the Adelaide Hills. It was lovely there, so green and quiet, with farms all around us.'

'And my good fortune,' said Samuel, taking Mary Grace's hand.

'But Eleanor was born in Mintaro, not Gumeracha?' Emma asked.

'Most of our children were. Sam is a blacksmith and coachbuilder. Mintaro is halfway between Burra and Port Wakefield. It's a busy road. Ideal spot for a blacksmith.'

Ben would have liked Sam, Emma thought. Although a successful tradesman, he was modest about it.

As soon as the newly-weds left the venue, the Bowdens set out for home, on the short midwinter eve. There would be no moon until midnight. They lit lanterns after Port Wakefield and progress was slow, giving the boys ample time to comment on the attractive Tunkin girls, three of whom were single. Bill, having been paired with Emily in the bridal party, warned his brothers to keep their distance from her. He was already smitten.

The People's Weekly described the ceremony as a pretty wedding. It was their stock phrase, Emma thought, but all was not lost; they did mention the fox furs.

The newlyweds returned to Constantine Farm after a week away.

'They're here,' yelled Bill, carrying Eleanor's bag inside.

Eleanor and Wes followed him, Bert not far behind with Wes's bags. Emma smoothed her curls and removed her apron.

'Mm,' Eleanor said. 'Pasties?'

Emma nodded and hugged them both. 'You made good time.'

'We caught the early train, and a coach was waiting at Port Wakefield,' Wes said, his eyes full of love for Eleanor.

'How was Adelaide?' Bert asked.

'Cold,' they both said, laughing together.

'You'll need some help collecting Eleanor's belongings from Balaklava,' said Bill.

'As if you care,' Wes said. 'Don't forget, it's sixty miles away. And you'd better hope she's home when you get there.'

After they had eaten, Emma began to gather the empty plates.

'Let me do that,' said Eleanor, leaning across and taking the plates from her.

'Aren't you tired after travelling so far?'

'I'm only tired after a long day with fifteen or twenty children at several different levels, in one classroom.' She smiled. 'This is easy.'

Emma felt a weight lift from her shoulders. It was the same with the washing. 'I'll do it,' Eleanor said on that first Monday morning, taking the four men's winter work trousers. 'And one of the boys will hang them outside for me.'

Eleanor, Wes, and Bill made the trip to Balaklava to bring Eleanor's trinkets, a modest trunk of clothes and a large box of books, to her new abode.

'Well, was she there?' Bert asked.

Bill was smug. 'She was, and as beautiful as ever.

Although Eleanor was quiet in the house, Emma was glad of her company. After the midday meal on the colder days, Eleanor often pulled a chair close to the open oven door. This time, she gave a conspiratorial smile to Emma and said, 'I always get more done if I have a little rest after dinner. Why don't you join me?' She pulled over another chair.

Emma sat, pulled her knee rug up, and nodded off. When she woke, Eleanor was reading. It became a regular arrangement, the two of them sitting together, and sometimes Eleanor would crochet or knit. She was quiet, but she was rarely idle.

In July, Arnold announced, 'The Kitto boys say land is really cheap in New South Wales.'

'New South Wales?' his mother said, her heart sinking. 'That's a long way.'

'It can't hurt to have a look, and Tom Pedlar says he'll come, too.'

'Where?' asked Bill and Bert, who were followed in by Wes.

Arnold drew himself up and told them.

'It's probably in the middle of nowhere, Arny,' Bill said. 'And full of convicts and bushrangers.'

'Nowhere could be more isolated than here,' said Arnold, 'and they don't have convicts anymore.'

Wes opened his mouth to speak but Emma quickly put her hand up. 'Stop it, Wes,' she warned. 'He'll go anyway, just to prove you wrong.'

Several weeks later, Arny packed his bag. 'We've a lift to Pt Wakefield, Ma, and we'll get a bus from there. Not sure after that, but Allan has some ideas.'

Emma hugged him goodbye.

Eleanor, now showing signs of pregnancy, accompanied Emma back inside. 'I just hope he will be all right,' Emma said, her face lined with worry. 'He's only twenty-three. Look at the others, still up to nonsense.'

'He has a good head on his shoulders, Ma. And don't forget, you and Da were much younger when you left home.'

Eleanor was right.

It was a long few weeks before Emma heard from Arny. Tom wants to return, he wrote, so I will come back with him. But I'm hoping to go back; Allan Forrest says he'll give it a go.

Arnold's visit was short, and Emma waved another tearful goodbye as he and Allan Forrest left for New South Wales. Emma doubted she would see much of Arnold again. He was really taken with share-farming and had made some good friends.

Constantine Farm had never been so quiet as Emma nodded off to sleep beside the oven. Alicia Doris Bowden, Eleanor and Wes's first child, born on April 3, 1911, seemed to be sleeping day and night. When Eleanor woke, Emma pushed the kettle on.

Alicia Doris Bowden, c. 1912

'I don't remember any of my babies sleeping so well,' she said.

'I was up twice last night,' Eleanor said, suppressing a yawn. 'But you're right, she settles quickly. Long may it last.'

'It's such a luxury seeing her every day,' Emma said. Without having to ask, she thought, a real luxury.

Several months later, Grace visited, and she and Emma watched as little Doris grasped a wooden block and put it to her mouth.

'Aren't grandchildren wonderful?' Emma said.

'Indeed. Our wee Annie has saved my life, now that Christopher has gone.'

'And did you ever hear the like?' Emma said. 'As you know, we Cornish never had a ken for hospitals of any sort. Nursed at home, by our own, is our way. But Eleanor believes it's safer to give birth in nursing homes for mothers. She dotes on Mrs Elliot, who's in William Street. Not only does she birth babies; she mends broken bones, and she wants to remove two of my back teeth. I'm not so sure about that.'

When Doris was nearly two years old, Eleanor's second daughter was born. Emma, although now sixty-eight, was confident she could care for little Doris while Eleanor was in Mrs Elliot's Nursing Home.

It was a hot week in January, and Emma kept the child indoors until the cool of the evenings. On the third day, Doris took her grandmother's hand.

'Ous side,' she said, tugging Emma toward the door. 'Ous side.'

'You want to go out?'

'Es.'

The sun was in the west. She looked at the child's red, wispy curls and porcelain skin. 'I suppose we can go out now.'

Emma reached for the child's bonnet.

'No, no, no,' Doris protested. 'No bonney.'

'I am afraid so, young lady. No bonney, no outside.'

To Emma's surprise, Doris acquiesced. Were her own children as easy to manage, she wondered.

However, Clarice Mary Bowden, born January 2, 1913, was a polar opposite to Doris.

'I can't believe it,' Eleanor said, dark rings under her eyes. 'Do you suppose we have the right baby?' she asked Emma.

'She's the image of Wes.'

'You're right. I'm so tired. I hope she is my last… How did you ever manage?'

Emma smiled. 'I didn't always. Some of it was nightmarish stuff, particularly when we were all sick at once.'

Eleanor looked at her curiously. 'That's a relief,' she said. 'I wondered what I was doing wrong.'

Eleanor's sister, Emily, visited Constantine Farm supposedly to see the new baby. But when Bill stood with his arm around Emily, Emma soon guessed there was another reason for her visit.

'We're getting married,' Emily announced.

Eleanor squealed and hugged her sister.

'And Bill is buying Howlett's 215, on the Arthurton Road,' Emily added. 'Not far away at all.'

The two sisters were going to be neighbours; Emma was thrilled for them. It would make all the difference. Now to marry off Jack and Bert, Emma thought, knowing full well, of course, they would only marry when they were ready.

'So,' Wes said to Bert, 'soon it'll be just you and me, when once we were seven.'

In March, 1914, Emma set out with Wes and Eleanor, for the second Tunkin-Bowden wedding.

The horses were young and trotted at a good pace, whinnying as they passed through the towns. Eleanor's Mary yowled as she fought with her sister, Doris.

Wes rolled his eyes. 'Heed me, gentlemen,' he said, 'no more

Balaklava brides. It's too far for my babies.'

'Learn to control them, Wes,' Bert grinned. 'They're a disgrace.'

'You try,' Wes said. 'She's two.'

When they arrived, the little girls ran to Lizey's girls, Dorothy and Nellie. Suddenly tired, Emma heaved a sigh of relief.

After the ceremony Mary-Grace and Sam Tunkin greeted Emma warmly. 'I believe,' Samuel said, 'that you have more single boys. We still have Mabel, Annie, and Louisa,' Sam's eyes twinkled.

'Sam!' said Mary-Grace.

Emma received another letter from Arnold and handed it to Annie.

Dear Mama,

I feel guilty about the war, but they need us here too – to grow food for the troops. We are working hard, and the money is good, so I've sent money to the Patriotic fund.

Did I tell you about Bell Cummins? She lives on Yogalgrin Station – it's not far from us. She's really lovely.

And Allan has just married her sister, Edda.

'That sounds ominous,' Annie said.

Annie, Emma, Lizey, with Vera at back

20. World War I, 1914-1916

Emma's small worries about her boys, and keeping the peace between her children, paled into insignificance, when war broke out in Europe.

At first, Emma knew little about it. It was a long way from Australia. However, with Britain involved, the boys soon talked of nothing else. As a British colony, they said, surely, they must defend Britain. When Emma heard that Jack and Bert were going to enlist, her heart thumped.

'Farmers are exempt,' she pleaded.

'But it's the manly thing to do, Ma,' Bert said.

'Manly! Getting yourselves killed! And how will Wes manage without you?'

Emma concealed her relief when both Jack and Bert were rejected on medical grounds. Bert's feet were too flat. More worrying was the report on Jack. His health was poor, they said, and he was only forty-one.

Emma was busy helping with her grandchildren and was grateful for her own good health. Approaching seventy, felt no different to being sixty, even fifty, she thought. Little Mary continued to confound both her mother and her grandmother. Only that morning, the eighteen-month-old had grabbed Len's skirt and pulled herself up beside the chair, smiling beatifically. Then she swiped the knitting from her mother's hands and sat, the work unravelling as she landed.

'You little minx,' Eleanor cried. 'What is it with this child? It's because of your father; he laughs at everything you do. He thinks the sun shines out of you.'

'Dad, dad,' Mary said.

Emma lifted the child and handed Eleanor her knitting.

Mary settled on her grandmother's knee. 'Once upon a time, there was a little girl who lived in Cornwall...' Emma began.

'Me, too,' said Doris, leaving her blocks, 'tell me, too.'

Emma put her arm around Doris too. Eleanor smiled. 'Thanks, I'm so tired,' she said, rubbing her midriff, 'and in a few months there'll be another.'

Soon, Mary wriggled down and headed for the camp oven.

'Noo!' said both women.

Mary screamed, holding out her sore hand.

'It's hot, Mary…' Eleanor said, exasperated. 'Will she ever learn?' Eleanor shook her head. 'I can't complain,' she said to Emma. 'At least I have Wes here. This war is terrible. With two Agery boys gone to fight… I want to help Eva and Isabella open an Agery branch of the Moonta Comforts Fund.'

'You are pushing yourself already, Len, with the school Patriotic Fund,' Emma said.

'I'll just knit faster and make double the quantity of biscuits, if you'll watch the two ladies.'

'Of course, I will,' Emma said. 'Well, hopefully I'll manage that mini tornado of yours. I'll bring out Lizey's knitted dolls. Ha-ha. Maybe we'll both find time to bake.'

The Agery women sent countless parcels of biscuits, dried meat, fruit, knitted socks, scarves, and gloves overseas for the troops. When Eleanor's time came, she reminded Emma, 'No heroics while I'm in there, Ma, please. No more baking for the troops.'

Wes and Eleanor's third child was born October 30, 1915, and was christened Lionel Frank, to be always known as Jim.

It was a busy year, but Eleanor was determined they would have a celebration for Emma's seventieth birthday. Emma asked that, in view of the times, it be a modest celebration, with no new frocks or finery, or gifts. The women duly arrived in serviceable satins and neck pins. The men also wore their Sunday best, replete with waistcoats and watch chains. Annie introduced a surprise guest, a studio photographer. Emma protested about the cost, but her family put their hands on their ears.

'Ma!' Annie said. 'We have no family likenesses so far. And I think it's about time.'

Emma put her hand to her mouth. 'It does. Everything is changing. My old bones don't like change.'

Eleanor joined them. 'Some change is good, though, Ma. Have you heard about the machine that carries voices down a wire?'

'Down a wire?' Emma looked at her. 'But how? And whose voices?'

'I have no idea, but when Eva and Richard get one, and we have ours, we will show you. I believe Eva will send a signal to us, and when it comes, we put our hearing piece to our ear and talk to them – through a speaking tube. Does that make sense?'

'Not really. But you are right, it would be wonderful, talking to them when they're not here.'

It was some time before the telephone engineer called to Constantine Farm, a young man with a large tool kit, and cables over his shoulders.

'He's making a hole in the passage wall,' Emma reported to Len.

Wes had been watching the man as well. 'He'll probably make more than one,' he said.

Emma watched and wondered about the new machine.

There were more visits by the engineer before the machine was ready.

'Now Ma,' Wes said. 'See those numbers? Len is going to dial it to two, and then to three, for twenty-three; that's Richard and Eva's number.' Wes waited and listened. 'Eva? It's Wes. Pardon? No, it's Wes. Can you hear me? Yes, Eva, it's wonderful. I want to show Ma how it works, have you a minute?'

Wes handed Emma the earpiece.

'Talk into the speaker, Ma,' he said. 'No, keep the earpiece up, too.'

The voice didn't sound exactly like Eva, but Wes was nodding, and Emma said a faint, 'Hello.'

When Eva finished talking, Emma bundled the earpiece into Wes's hand.

'Thank goodness that's over,' she said, and they laughed.

Emma was determined to make it work, and months later, after several telephone calls, she was more confident. But when another letter arrived from Arnold, Emma lamented.

'It's a pity Arnold hasn't a telephone,' she said, tearing open his letter. She read it and sighed. 'Oh, dear, he is getting married – over there – in a few weeks,' Emma said, her heart falling.

I am the happiest man on earth, Mama. We will be married soon.

Here is the poem I wrote for her. Don't show my brothers, will you?

The Bible says thou shalt not covet your neighbour's wife.
His ox thou shalt not slaughter.
But thank the Lord it does not say
Thou shalt not covet his daughter.

Emma wondered if her own mother had been as sad when she couldn't see the weddings, the babies, and all those precious moments that constituted Emma's life? Of course, she thought.

Hopefully, her letters to her mother back then had somewhat filled the void. Certainly, her mother's letters had been the light of her day, every time they arrived, for weeks, even months.

When Emma wiped her eyes, she saw the end of Arnold's letter. 'Len, Wes, listen to this,' she called. 'Arnold and Annabell are travelling by train to Adelaide and Moonta, to be with us for their honeymoon.'

The whole family pitched in to ready the farm for their arrival. A touch of paint here and there, the garden was given a makeover, and beds were made up.

Wes took the horses and buggy to meet Arnold and Eliza Annabell Cummins at the Moonta Railway Station.

Moonta Railway Station, built 1909, now an historic premises

Several hours later, Eleanor heard horses approaching. She knew the sound of each family's conveyance and immediately alerted the others that Arnold and Annabell had arrived. They all rushed out to greet them, just so Emma could usher them back inside.

When Emma was seated, Bell called to Arnold, 'Joe, will you bring me my brown bag?'

'Joe?' repeated Emma.

'Oops,' Bell said. 'Sorry, and he reminded me all the way here. You see, no one over there has heard of the name Arnold. So, they call him Joe.'

'And some call me Ray,' Arnold added.

'They what?' Emma said.

211

'It's all right, Ma, I can still be Arnold here.' He took his mother's arm. 'Let me see the place.' He went from room to room like an eager child, and, after tea, he walked the fields with Wes.

'It's great to be here again,' Arnold said.

'Sorry you left?' Wes asked.

'Well, not really, because I wouldn't have met Bell. And I would never have had my farm. What Jack paid for Daniels's is outrageous, nearly three pounds an acre. It's much cheaper over there.'

'How cheap?'

'Five shillings.'

Wes looked sceptical. 'Five shillings? Must be poor land. With the convicts and all. Good luck!'

21. A Holiday by the Sea

The war raged on, but Emma still didn't want to know about it. She had seen enough dying, she told the boys. They gave conciliatory smiles and retreated from earshot.

Emma was otherwise busy with her grandchildren, their numbers ever increasing, and those on Constantine Farm growing up fast. Doris was almost six and had started school in January, 1917.

Wes praised Doris for every book she read and her every mathematical achievement, but her younger sister, Mary, was not too pleased for missing out and demanded to go to school as well.

'You are barely four, Mary,' her father said. 'Wait your turn.' But one day, when nobody might take notice, Mary had set off across the field and filed into school with the other children. As Miss Barbary read out their names, she noticed Mary sinking under her bench.

'Your name, child?' she called.

'Clarice Mary Bowden,' she lisped.

Doris was asked to take her sister home. As they neared the house, Emma heard Doris uncharacteristically angry, and Mary sobbing with rage. Doris had to run back to school.

Eleanor lifted Mary onto her knee. 'Who will help me with baking now that Doris isn't here?'

Mary wriggled down. 'I don't want to bake.'

Eleanor, ever the teacher, sat Mary at the dining room table and suggested she do schoolwork there. Jim was soon at Mary's elbow, trying to climb onto Mary's chair.

'Nooo!' said Mary, putting her arm around her work. 'Mummy! Jimmy won't let me draw.'

Two places were set, with pencils and offcuts of paper, but Jim soon lost interest and toddled off.

Emma and Eleanor managed to keep Mary at home for the rest of the year. However, on a cool autumn morning the following year, elbows deep in the washing tub, Eleanor again wondered where Mary was. She left the clothes in the tub and quickly looked in the other rooms. 'I'm going to the school,' Eleanor told Emma.

A crying Mary and her mother soon arrived back home.

Agery Sunday School, courtesy, Rosemary Browning.
Back row, third left, standing, Charles W Bowden
Third row, first left, Ivan Bowden. Doris Bowden is fourth left,
with large white ribbons. Also Eleanor Bowden and Gerald Bowden.
Mary Bowden, front row, second child from left.

'Miss Barbary was sympathetic,' Emma said. 'She said she wished all her students were as keen. She said Mary could go to school tomorrow, and if she lasts the day and still wants to go, I should enrol her.'

There was no dissuading Mary, and she was enrolled in April, 1918.

Doris complained. 'It's so unfair, Granny. Mary answers questions meant for me. She'll soon be better than me.'

Emma remembered when her sisters learned to read and write, when she, Emma, was sure she would never learn. The shame of illiteracy was paralysing. Much later, poor Annie had suffered as well, learning amongst younger children. Doris was right; it wasn't fair.

'That's what my girls said, too,' Emma said. 'But you're a clever girl, Doris. And Mary really is too young. Miss Barbary told your Mama that you will always be ahead.'

'Are you sure?' Doris said, wiping her wispy hair from her eyes.

Emma hugged her. 'Of course, I am.'

'But Daddy is always telling me to work harder. And everyone teases me because I have red hair and freckles. I hate – school.'

It was only when Marjorie and Dorothy Eden befriended the two Bowden girls that Doris settled into school, and her confidence began to grow. The friends spent their days playing with their dolls when they weren't studying. Emma smiled when she heard how strict Doris and Mary were with their 'babies'. And their three-year-old brother, Jim, enjoyed a reprieve from his nagging sisters.

Emma never missed a Sunday at the little stone church and was disappointed many of her children no longer were regular worshippers. They always had plausible excuses like 'the sheep got out' or 'the baby kept us up all night'. But at least her grandchildren attended Sunday School. She loved to see the new generation taking part in the anniversary celebrations and Tea Treats.

As usual, the Agery Tea held afterwards was hugely attended. Emma, relieved of her tea duties, watched, amused as the hungry miners spread cream on their sandwiches, cream on their sausage rolls, and cream on their cakes.

One evening in 1918, Emma sat nodding by the fire. She stirred when Eleanor returned to the kitchen.

The telephone jangled. Eleanor put the flour back on the shelf, picked up the earpiece, sagged at the waist as though winded, but continued to listen. She finally replaced the phone and drew her robe around her.

'What is it, Len?'

'It's Mother. She's – collapsed. I must call Emily.'

'Sit for a minute and catch your breath.' Emma pulled a chair out for her. 'Do you want to leave the children with me? There's not a lot going on outside.'

'I couldn't, Ma. Doris and Mary, maybe. But not Jim.'

'I suppose,' Emma said. 'He could run off. Maybe Benjy and Isey will take him. Keith is their age.'

'You're right. Thank goodness for the telephone.' She called Emily and Isey. 'We won't get away tomorrow,' she said, after hanging up. 'Emily has an appointment.'

'Is Emily alright?'

'She says she is.'

Two days later, Bill and Wes drove Emily and Len to Balaklava.

After a couple of days away, Eleanor telephoned Emma and asked about Doris and Mary.

'They're fine, Len. Don't you worry.'

'We won't be long,' Len said, 'Mama is dying.' She began to cry. Emma waited.

'S-sorry. We are such a big family, and my brothers are arguing… Can you believe that? Thomas, he's the youngest, has always been jealous of Sammy. But this is not the time to fight over the blacksmith shop. Poor Daddy.'

Emma wondered about her siblings in Cornwall. She missed being part of the large expanding family over there. Hopefully, her children wouldn't fight about their small inheritances on her deathbed.

Mary-Grace Tunkin took her last breath on August 24.

After the funeral, Eleanor telephoned Emma again. 'Daddy is devastated. He always thought he would go first. Now he wants to come to live in Agery. He says he'll feel safe with us married and settled on farms. He'll stay with Emily and Bill first.'

Emma wondered where everyone would sleep. There were only three bedrooms in the farmhouse, two inside, and one in the closed-in lean-to at the back, where Doris and Mary slept. Jim still slept with his parents. Emma decided to offer to board with her other children.

Sam Tunkin was horrified. 'I'll not drive you out of your own home, Emma.'

'After forty-nine years, I can do with a change. My children often invite me to spend time with them. It will be lovely to get to know my other grandchildren like I know Doris, Mary, and Jim.'

At Christmas, Emma's children put together an itinerary for her. Firstly, she would go to Annie and Richard's cottage in East Moonta.

Although Emma's curls were heavily streaked with grey, her face radiated a wellness belying her seventy-three years. She hummed as she packed her few clothes. She felt like a child, excited about a sleepover.

'I'm so glad you're here,' Annie said. 'We can go shopping together in Moonta. Colin is never here now. He works long hours.'

Emma discovered that shopping three times a week in Moonta had its advantages. Many of the mining families had retired there, and there was much to catch up on. But it was tiring, and she was pleased when Eva rang, reminding her she was due to arrive in Kadina.

Richard drove Emma there, and Melva and Muriel, who were nine and five, greeted their grandmother with glee.

'Grandma. Do you want to see baby Vivian?' Melva asked.

They walked on tiptoes to their bedroom and pulled back the netting. He was fast asleep, just a head peeping from the bedclothes. 'Let's go,' Emma whispered. 'I don't suppose Mummy wants us to wake him.'

Emma joined Eva in the kitchen. 'What can I do for you?' she asked, putting on her apron.

'Relax. Have a holiday,' Eva said.

'I feel a bit lost – in a nice way. I've been working as long as I can remember.'

'So, now is your chance to have a rest.'

'Grandma, come see our tree house,' exclaimed Muriel.

Emma followed the girls to the large eucalypt in the garden. Melva shinned up a rudimentary ladder.

'Now you, Grandma,' Muriel said.

Emma had long since been warned not to climb ladders. But this one was nailed to the tree.

Melva called. 'Are you coming?'

Emma reached up with her right foot and gripped a tree branch with her hand. 'Oh, well,' she said, lifting up her other foot. Her legs shook a little, but she continued up.

'There you are,' Melva said, taking her grandmother's hand. 'You can sit here.'

The branch was sturdy, but Emma dared not lean back. There was nothing behind her.

Muriel made a pretend cup of tea and handed it to Emma. 'Isn't this fun?' she said. 'You can be Mummy if you like.'

'Thank you, dear.'

Richard spotted them up the tree. 'I won't ask,' he said, shaking his head. 'Girls, it's dinner time. Down you come. And you too, Ma.' He reached up to give his mother a hand.

Emma gratefully stood on firm ground again.

After dinner, Emma, still determined to pull her weight, made her way to the woodpile. She placed a small log on the large stump, and, swinging the axe, split the log.

Richard came out to investigate. 'Ma...' he protested.

'This I can do, Richard. It feels wonderful. I used to long for the freedom of it. And if I don't keep moving, my joints will seize up.' She chopped another stick.

Richard chuckled. 'Not much chance of that.'

Emma visited Benjy and Isabella next. Only one of the three older boys lived at home now, but it was still a busy house with the younger boys, Gerald, Mervyn, and Keith, aged from three years to twelve.

Emma continued her gypsy lifestyle in Adelaide, staying with Lizey and John at Torrensville, and Vera and Stephen at Hilton. While living with her daughters, Emma was conscious of keeping to safe subjects, such as the weather, and the wonders of the new education system. In the evenings, she introduced her grandchildren to some of her old games, such as *Jacks*, with the knucklebones she had collected for Lizey and Annie.

Her sojourns continued for almost twelve months, when, at long last, she returned to Constantine Farm, praying she wouldn't have to leave again. It was just so much easier, being at home.

Doris ran out to meet her. 'We missed you, Grandma, really, really.'

Emma had never seen the girl so enthusiastic.

Emma hugged Doris and Mary, and young Jim ran into them all.

'Whoa,' Emma said, teetering.

When the three children left Emma's side, Eleanor handed Emma a cup of tea.

'So how was it?'

'They fussed over me; I wasn't allowed to do much.'

'Good. You've earned a rest. It's called a holiday.'

On November 12, Bert arrived at Constantine Farm early one day and bounced into the dining room, waving the newspaper. 'It's over. The war. Can you believe it? Germany has signed the agreement. Listen to this: *Effective as of yesterday, the eleventh hour, the eleventh day of November...*'

'Is that today's paper?' Wes said.

Bert nodded and handed it over to him. 'I was in town early.'

Wes read aloud:

After a protracted night of agony, a glorious morning has dawned...

Let the bugles sound the Truce of God to the whole world forever.

'Praise the Lord,' Eleanor said, looking over Wes's shoulder.

When the troops finally returned home, they were given a royal welcome.

As with many farmers, the Bowden brothers assembled before

dark to be in Moonta early. They would forever be indebted to those who fought, and to those who lost their lives those terrible four years of battle.

By Christmas that year, Jack proclaimed to his family that he was going to marry Elsie Lovell. Emma had wondered, she had noticed a change in her son's demeanour. He was smiling more, and to her delight, was more likely to ignore his brothers' ribbing.

Bert was clearly surprised. 'The singer?'

'How did you manage that?' Wes blurted.

'Come on, boys,' Jack said. 'You've all met her. You were, after all, at the same musical evenings. And I am forty-five-years-old.'

'Congratulations,' Wes said.

'Elsie's an Adelaide woman,' Jack went on. 'And she has no equal when it comes to singing the Cherry Ripe Song. But she won't get many more appointments on the Peninsula, so she needs to return to Adelaide.'

'You won't see much of her, then,' Bert chuckled, 'not living up here.'

'That's what I'm trying to tell you. I'm putting the farm up for sale. I have my eye on a farm in Penfield, near the city.'

Jack and Elsie were married on a scorching February, 1919 day in Adelaide. Emma hid her disappointment; she would have loved to be there.

Bert offered to buy Jack's farm, leaving only Wes at Constantine Farm. 'I would like to buy Jack's place, too,' Wes told Bert and Emma over lunch, cutting his cold mutton into neat squares. 'But I haven't the money, and I have three children to support.'

'I don't have the money either,' said Bert. 'But I have a plan. All ten of us are going get a share of the farm one day, right?'

'I suppose…' Wes's brow furrowed.

'I'm hoping I can get my share from you now.'

'How am I supposed to do that?' Wes's voice rose. 'Sell a tenth of the farm? If I did that for everyone, there'd be no farm. I've put my all into this place. What use is a tenth to me?'

'Hold on,' said Bert. 'The others are all right at the moment. You can take out a small mortgage, just for me.'

Wes stood, his face reddening. 'A *small* mortgage? It's hard enough making ends meet as it is.'

'I know, Wes. But it's not our fault you haven't any money. You married too young. Don't get me wrong, Len's a beauty, and I'd have jumped at the chance too, but still.'

Emma pushed the pot off the boil and joined them. 'Settle down, boys. You both have a point. I have money that I was going to leave to you in my will. But I can loan Wes some of that now. To be fair, you'll have to pay it back – not to me, but to your brothers and sisters after I die.'

'I don't like that at all,' Wes said. 'Being in debt to everyone as well as the bank. That could turn nasty. But I don't suppose I have a choice.'

So, he and Bert took Emma to the bank to revise her will.

Mary, Jim, Wes and Doris with the new car

In September, Eleanor gave birth to her last child, Wesley Eustace Bowden. Eustace was a Tunkin family name.

Emma put away her knitting and was set to help Len with her other children, now aged eight, six, and four.

Wes purchased a horseless carriage, a new Model T Ford painted black, to bring Len and the baby home from Mrs Elliot's Nursing Home in Moonta.

'It raised a few eyebrows in Moonta,' Wes told them, 'but it was either purchase one, or a new sprung chaise. Horses and buggies don't come cheap, either.'

Emma had occasionally seen horseless carriages. Cadd's automobile was green, but it was quieter, running on steam. She had never been in one and, after she saw Wes swaying up the road, she was not inclined to try. It was Mary who finally convinced Emma to get into the car.

'Come on, Grandma,' she said, tilting her head. 'You're not scared, are you?'

Emma allowed Mary to lead her to the vehicle. Mary jumped in beside her and grinned. Wes shut the door, and Emma held onto the edge of the seat, closing her eyes. She insisted they only go to the church and back.

Weeks later, after being driven to Eva and Dick's for their annual bonfire, as well as to musical evenings and tennis parties, she realised how fast and convenient the new automatic carriage was, in all weathers. So, when Wes drove Emma and Eleanor into Moonta, Emma was ecstatic. The town was no longer a forbidding distance away. And as they drove past the mines and into George Street, she noted so much change. New facades, more outlets, and so many horseless carriages.

Not quite knowing where to start, Emma hurried from one establishment to another. To her delight, she met Mary Ann Vicary Warn. After catching up on family news, Emma apologised. 'If only I could do this every week, but I must go. Wes and Len will be ready to go back.'

Agery School, c. 1921, photo courtesy, Rosemary Browning,
Doris in second row, 3rd from left, and Mary 7th.

There were several musicians in the Bowden family, and, in 1920, when Doris and Mary were nine and seven, they began piano lessons. Charles Wesley greatly encouraged his daughters from the outset, and Eleanor and Emma happily listened to the girls faltering attempts to master the art.

After two years, the girls passed their examinations with honours. Wes's pride knew no bounds. He purchased a new Beale piano and arranged for the girls to learn from a more advanced teacher in Moonta. This prepared the girls for the London School of Music examinations. For their lessons, they left school early on Fridays.

Emma was sure that the new piano improved the sound. 'And it's a real joy to hear them play a whole tune without stopping,' she told Wes.

Doris practised more than Mary, but Mary played her pieces well enough by ear on the exam day.

'Everyone says Mary is so clever,' Doris grumbled. 'How can I compete with her when she started two years younger?'

Jim told his grandmother he also wanted to leave school early on Fridays. 'But I'll not play the piano, not for anything.' Emma laughed. With his head of blonde curls, Jim charmed his way through his early years.

Wes lauded his girls' accomplishments, and often asked them to play for visitors. The girls were not so enthusiastic. One day, Emma had overheard them complaining after playing for the new Wesleyan minister.

'I hate it,' said Mary.

'So embarrassing,' Doris agreed. 'When I leave home, I shall never play another note.'

Emma had almost accepted that thirty-nine-year-old Bert would never marry, until he became interested in Ethel Mahar, Annie's stepdaughter. Ethel, who was fourteen when Annie and Richard Maher married, was now thirty-one.

Bert was notably active in the church and Red Cross and was also a great favourite with his nephews and nieces. Six-year-old Jim had almost taken up residence on Bert's farm since Jim's little brother was born. Jim loved helping Uncle Bert, and it was Jim who told Emma that Uncle Bert was seeing 'the lady with the pink hair – pink like a pig.' Emma smothered her giggles and hoped no-one heard him. Ethel was a pretty woman with hair like spun gold.

After Bert asked Richard Mahar for Ethel's hand, Annie put on her stern older sister look. 'And you have to ask me, too,' she said, grinning.

The Kadina Methodist Church overflowed when Bert and Ethel married in June 29, 1921.

Annie, as both stepmother of the bride *and* sister of the groom, rose to the occasion with her usual style. Her lipstick was crimson and her heels even higher than usual. She stitched a marvellous gown adorned with lace and pin-tucks across her ample bosom, and a matching apron to protect her new dress.

Annie walked serenely into the church and sat at the front. When smoothing her skirt, she noticed her apron, and she flushed. She removed her hatpins, her hat, and slipped the offending article over her head. She replaced her hat and hissed to her mother. 'Is that all right?'

'Perfect.'

On December 6, 1921, Len's sister, Annie, married Bertram Dodgson, and Len, Wes, Bill, and Emily, travelled to Balaklava for the occasion.

In May, 1922, Bert and Hettie's first child, Dulcie Ethel, was born. Emma loved that Dulcie lived close by, so she could watch her grow and learn.

Near the end of that year, Emma stood in the gentle breeze and observed the new harvester as it ploughed through the field, leaving its striped carpet of straw. Wes was beaming by the day's end. If only Ben had lived to see the fruit of the harvest.

'I knew the wheat was good,' Wes said, 'but it is surely fifteen bushels this time – we used to average about eight. And the barley is unbelievable, too. It's going to be a good Christmas, Ma.'

'Thank goodness he'll be in a good mood,' Doris muttered to Mary. 'Maybe God is listening after all.'

There it was again, Emma thought, that niggle about their father. Then she remembered Annie and her temper, when Lizey got the teaching job, and Lizey not telling her the details of her baby's death.

On December 30, the telephone rang. Eleanor answered it, then sat, crying. 'Not Annie too… No, no, no.'

'What is it, Len?' Emma said, putting her hand to Len's shoulder.

'My sister Annie – she had her baby, but…' Len couldn't continue.

Annie Tunkin Dodgson had given birth to a daughter but had died the following day.

'First Cecelia and now Annie,' Eleanor said, steeling herself. 'And that poor motherless little baby.' Emma waited for Eleanor's tears to subside. 'Bertram has named the baby Annie,' Eleanor went on. 'Now he wants Emily and Bill to adopt her.'

Emily and Bill, still childless after eight years of marriage, agreed. Then followed a few days of intense planning, and stocking of necessities, before the baby was warmly welcomed by her new parents.

Two weeks later, quite coincidentally, Jack and Elsie, also childless, were invited to adopt a family baby girl as well.

Emma wondered if she was losing her mind. Had she imagined all that? But Eleanor explained to her about baby Lesley, the daughter of Elsie's sister-in-law, Dorothy, wife of Ralph Lovell. 'Unlike Annie, Dorothy didn't die in childbirth,' Eleanor said. 'But she is seriously ill and expects to die. Such an awful decision to have to make.'

'Won't Elsie and Jack worry that Dorothy will take her back?' Emma asked.

'They do, but the little thing needs a home, and Dorothy wants them to keep her.'

Arnold and Bell arrived in Agery in January, soon after the two babies were informally adopted. Explanations flew around the room – Arnold and Bell had been travelling for days and knew nothing of it.

The walls of Constantine Farm bulged, as the many families congregated there to introduce the new babies to Arnold and Bell, and to meet Arnold's three children: Muriel, five, Irene, three, and baby Reginald.

Doris handed Emma a cup of tea and sat beside her grandmother. 'Are you really grandma to all these children?'

'I believe so, dear. But don't ask me all their names.'

As the evening wore on, the tired children and parents, who lived locally, left for home. But many of them returned for lunch the following day, laden with trays of food.

Emma worried when Wes and Arnold appeared to be arguing. It was embarrassing, in front of the rest of the family.

Wes demanded of Arnold. 'You did what?'

'I purchased an eighteen-hundred-acre farm in New South Wales. It is called Hillview, at Kamarah.'

Wes looked blankly at his brother. 'Where?'

'Near Wagga Wagga,' Arny added.

'Eighteen hundred acres,' said Bert enviously. 'How did you manage that? Racehorses?'

'No,' Arny said. 'I told you land was cheaper there. It only cost three hundred pounds.'

'Three hundred?' Wes's face was bright red. 'We paid that for this place. And it's not even three hundred acres.'

Arnold continued. 'Before the first crop, I kept us afloat by building miles of fencing for the new soldier settlement. Then it all took off. We cleared seventy acres – so easy with tractors and machines.'

Emma looked at her son with disbelief. Ben had worked every hour of the day, killing himself over his 275 acres.

'Maybe it's just as well your father isn't alive,' Emma said. 'He would have been proud, son, but Wes is right; it's outrageous what we paid for this place.'

'And you don't want to know the rest,' said Arnold.

'There's more?' Wes said, arms folded.

'My first wheat crop fetched top prices after the war, and I paid the entire mortgage off in a year.'

'It's not the same, though,' Wes said. 'You haven't the comfort of a convict-free colony such as ours. Your children will likely be brought up with children of convicts, even taught by them.'

Bert agreed. 'Wes is right. You must be surrounded by the descendants of convicts. They say it is a permanent stain. Like Da always said, we are lucky here, not having to worry about them.'

'When you've all finished,' said Arny. 'The real truth is that hundreds of convicts escaped and live in South Australia.'

'Rubbish,' Wes said. 'That's only talk, Arny.'

Emma left the room. She couldn't listen anymore.

After Arnold and his family returned to Kamarah, his land holding was the talk of the neighbourhood. Agery men remembered well what they paid for their land, upwards of forty years ago.

Wes told Bert he was going to build a new house. 'I'll show Arny...' he muttered.

Emma thought it a big outlay just to show his brother, but she pretended not to hear.

Wes soon produced house plans for Eleanor and the children to view. And he explained again when Richard and Eva visited. 'See here. For a bit of style and colour, the windows and doorways are framed with red bricks. But for most of it we will use Donaldson's stone. Buy local, I always say.'

'Tell them about the veranda, Wes,' Eleanor said.

Doris and Mary were wide-eyed.

'Are we really going to have verandas, like Howletts?' Mary said, her blue eyes dancing.

'We are, my dear,' her father replied.

'Muriel, we're going to have verandas. Do you want to play skipping?' Mary took her cousin's hand, and they ran off.

3rd house at Agery

There was barely any rain to interfere with building, and to Emma it was like a dream. With the men working before and after the harvests, they completed the new house that same year, in 1923.

Emma stood back. 'It looks so fine,' she said to Wes, as he escorted Emma through it. 'It's really lovely.'

When Emma entered the long hallway, she gave a little gasp. There, in pride of place, was a large oval likeness of Ben. Taken on his sixtieth birthday.

The children rushed on ahead of Wes and Emma. Wes, stepped aside for them, and continued Emma's tour.

Wes and Eleanor's bedroom was at the front, and it opened onto a wide passageway. Opposite the bedroom was a spacious sitting room, with a piano. Emma admired the skylights. There were red leadlight panels either side of the main door. They gave off a glorious pink as the late afternoon sun lit up the hallway.

'Your bedroom,' Wes said, leading her further down the passageway, 'has two doors.' Wes opened the first door, and Emma opened the second one, which opened onto the side veranda. Wes had planted a little garden. Tears sprung to Emma's eyes, and he patted her shoulder. 'Come now, Ma, you've earned this.'

Emma's world, seventy-seven years on, began to unravel even more. In October, 1923, Benjy's third son, Ivan, a strapping dear lad of twenty, collapsed with severe abdominal pain.

He was admitted to Sister Jenkinson's Private Hospital in Kadina. The doctor operated, but Ivan's appendix had already ruptured, and three heart-breaking days later he died.

Emma wept on many fronts: for the child, his parents, and for herself.

Only weeks later, Emma's brother William, collapsed with pains in his chest. He was admitted to hospital in Wallaroo, not far from the farm. Emma breathed a sigh of relief when she saw William sitting up in his hospital bed. Wes shook his hand as William smiled.

'The doctor said it was only a minor heart attack,' William said.

'Are you sure?' Emma said as she kissed him and sat on the edge of the bed.

'Come on, Em. Even if it wasn't. What am I? Eighty-six?'

'Don't talk like that.'

'And what's this I hear,' William said, 'about young Arnold buying a huge farm?'

'It's in New South Wales, Uncle William,' Wes said. 'Convicts for neighbours? Not for me. Land isn't everything.'

William smiled and said, 'Mustn't be too quick to judge, Wes; we all make mistakes.' Wes looked at him curiously. 'I might have been a convict, you know.'

'Never!'

'Your father obviously didn't tell you. I broke the law at Moonta Mines. Remember that copper ore I found? The bonanza? I should have reported it straight away. But I was sick of living on the dangerous mining lease. The mine manager didn't notice, so we kept the news to ourselves. I could have gone to jail.'

Wes was speechless.

'Would you class me as an undesirable neighbour, a stain on your family's life?'

'Of course not,' Wes said. 'You're a hero.'

'Sometimes, there's not a lot of difference.' While Wes fell into contemplation, William continued. 'Then there was a man I hired early on. Named Moon. He was a hard worker, honest. Then he told me he was an escaped convict, and he had to move on. I was lost without his help!'

The handbell rang in the ward, and Emma rose and kissed her brother. William pressed something into Emma's hand. 'It's my lucky penny,' he told her. 'It has served me well.'

The doctors transferred William to the Royal Adelaide Hospital, but he died there, the following day, on November 1.

At Christmas, Emma felt uneasy when she saw Lizey, who was sallow, with deep circles under her eyes. Emma hadn't seen her for several months.

Lizey patted her arm. 'I'm all right, Ma. I'll see a doctor when I return to Adelaide.'

But Lizey had cancer, and a telephone call on February 5, 1924, confirmed that a sudden bleed had ended her life.

Emma moaned into her hands. 'Not my lovely girl. At fifty-six? That's not fair.'

'Sit down,' pleaded Eleanor. 'I'll call Wes.'

When Wes hurried in, Emma hugged him tightly. 'Why didn't He take me instead?' she said.

'It doesn't work that way...' Wes said.

Emma had thought she was the next to go. Now she understood more of what William's Eliza had gone through. It wouldn't be so bad, dying. She was after all, seventy-nine.

Still, she was glad of the distraction her grandchildren provided. The boys, at eight and four, were their own mixture of bravado and mischief, with plenty of arguments when their father wasn't around. Wessy hated that his brother was always four years older than him, but that wasn't going to change, as Emma often tried to explain to him.

At eleven, Mary, pretty, fair-haired, blue eyed and coquettish, was full of fun, and her prowess at singing and playing the piano increased with every year.

Thirteen-year-old Doris had graduated to the new high school in Kadina, billeting there during the week. Since beginning high school, the girl had quite grown up, and Emma loved to listen to her dry wit, and her way of summarising little bits of news from the week.

Wes brought Doris home on Friday nights, and one night, with her end of year exams coming soon, Doris worked quietly at the dining room table, pencil poised over what she called mathematics.

'The square of the hypotenuse...' Doris was mumbling.

Emma asked, 'What is that?' Doris smiled. She was tall and slender, with her fine auburn hair parted in the middle and drawn into a wispy bun. 'Is it something boring, dear?'

'Oh no, Grandma, I love it. And I like French and Latin too. I like everything but domestic arts.'

'Cooking and sewing?'

Doris nodded glumly.

'So much has changed,' Emma said. 'Those were all I knew when I was a girl. That, and cleaning silver.'

'Really?' Doris said. 'Tell me about it, Grandma? Your story. Could I use it for a composition?'

'I suppose you can, dear. But it's not terribly interesting…'

Doris stood. 'Wait. I'll get a notebook.' Returning, she said, 'So, let's start from the beginning. You were born in… 1844? What is your earliest memory?'

Talking about the past soothed Emma, and Doris wrote quickly. Doris proudly showed her grandmother her story when the school year ended. It had been marked *Excellent.*

'I think I'll keep writing,' Doris said. 'It's sooo interesting.'

'Is it, dear?'

While Emma had happily talked of Ben's many achievements, she was embarrassed talking about living on the mining lease. It was nothing to be proud of. And she didn't want to talk about leaving Cornwall because they had been so poor.

Emma and her grandchildren (1924); l. to r. back, Muriel, Mervyn, Claude, Emma, Melva, with baby Ken, Doris with Dulcie, Mary with Annie. Front Wessy, Jim, and Vivian

As the Bowdens gathered at Christmas, 1924, Annie and Wes planned a party for Emma's eightieth birthday, the following year. As they left, Benjy and Annie reminded everyone to keep the last weekend of November free.

'With eight children and twenty-seven grandchildren,' Annie said, 'it will be a grand re-union, and a fitting celebration of your life, Mama.'

However, as 1925 progressed, Emma began to wonder if she would live to see the day. It had been her worst year since Ben had gone, with two more of her children dying. It was staggering news, and, like Eliza had with her own children, Emma wanted to die with them.

First, it was Benjy. At age fifty-four, he was rushed to the Kadina Hospital with knife-like chest pain. He died almost immediately. And five-months later, fifty-two-year-old Jack's coronary arteries also failed him.

Emma cried to Annie, 'Are you all going to die and leave me?'

'I hope not,' Annie said, alarmed. 'I'm only sixty.'

'I can't believe it,' Emma said. 'My two boys. Gone.'

'They had good lives, Mama,' Annie said, taking her mother's hands and recounting some of the boys' escapades.

'I suppose they did have fun,' Emma conceded. 'A better life than my lost babies. But… that's no help.'

Three months after Jack's funeral, under a cornflower-blue sky, many motoring cars found their way to Agery for Emma's birthday party. The road still wasn't metalled, and the dust bucked up behind them until they finally turned into the Constantine Farm driveway. Excited voices became louder as the children ran ahead, up the few steps and under the shade of the veranda.

'Look at you,' Emma said to the little girls, gorgeous in their white lace trimmed frocks and white hair ribbons. 'And you,' she said, patting the boys' shiny hair.

The children giggled and played on the steps into the front garden. Some tackled the mulberry tree, while others jumped, competitively, from the veranda.

The older children and their parents carried covered trays to the dining room table, the kitchen being far too small to admit more than three or four at a time.

The day was hot, and wheat rippled all around them in the cooling breeze. Before tea was served, Wes asked for quiet so Doris could make her speech.

'We are so proud of you, Grandma. You are famous. If you and Grandpa hadn't been brave and emigrated, none of us would be here. Happy birthday!'

Everyone sang the birthday song. Len took snapshots, with her new box camera, of Emma, seated near the front steps, surrounded by her grandchildren. In some of them, the children made funny faces at the camera, or wore one another's hats. The photographs were printed after Christmas, and Eleanor made an album for Emma.

Emma fought tears as she slowly turned the pages. 'What a treasure,' she whispered. 'Can I keep this?'

'Of course,' said Wes, 'we made it for you.'

Emma spent many hours sitting on her veranda, gazing at the shiny grey and white photographs. They were so precious.

In 1926, after Annie's husband, Richard, had died aged age seventy-four, Annie asked her mother to move into the cottage in East Moonta with her. Emma thought about it, but not for long. She was tired, and Christmas would soon be upon them. She was defeated. And she didn't like the thought of Annie being alone. Young Colin had a job now.

After a few months with Annie, Emma realised there was little chance of her returning to Constantine Farm; Annie depended on her for company, especially on her shopping trips into Moonta. While Emma enjoyed being in the town, she didn't share Annie's passion for traipsing from shop to shop daily.

After two years in East Moonta, Emma, waiting for Annie, who was in her third drapery establishment for the morning, confided in Wes and Len. 'With the harvests and all, these trips are not easy to organise,' Emma said, her legs aching. 'If only we could live in the town. Then Annie could shop every day, and I can, well, just rest. Maybe I'm dreaming...'

Wes hesitated. 'Mm. Maybe not at eighty-three, Ma. Why shouldn't you rest? Surely the two of you could afford a cottage in town.'

'I'll pay for it,' Emma said. 'Annie will need money for her fashions.'

'Do you want me to look around for you?'

'We'd better ask Annie first,' Eleanor said.

Wes laughed. 'Ask Annie if she wants to live beside the shops in Moonta?'

'I know,' Eleanor said, 'but we'd better discuss it.'

Annie was soon squealing with delight. 'Live here? If you can find us a place, Wes, we'll move in the next day.' She looked at her mother. 'I mean, if that's alright with you.'

Her mother nodded.

Chappells Bootmakers, George Street, Moonta, c. 1880, courtesy, SLSA, B27808

When the weather cooled, Wes and Bert took several days to search for a suitable cottage. Bert arrived before Wes. He had the children Dulcie and Ross. who were now five and three.

'We've found a nice semi-detached cottage,' Wes announced to Annie and Emma. 'It's close to the town hall. It's number 64 George Street. Built by Dr Todman. It has three bedrooms, a kitchen, and a sitting room, and everywhere is within walking distance. It is only four houses to the butcher. Seven to the bank.'

The two proud women would be completely independent.

Emma was delighted with the cottage, with its popular lacy iron décor around the bull-nose veranda and its matching wrought iron fence. The lacy design reminded her of the many lacy viaducts spanning great valleys, all those years ago, on the Truro to Plymouth rail journey, on their way to Australia. She wondered how she could remember all that – when she often didn't know what day it was.

Wes opened the door. 'It has electricity, Ma, here…'

Emma tentatively pushed the switch on the wall. The room lit up. 'A tonic for my poor eyes,' she said.

Emma looked at the document in her hand. There it was, with her name on it. Who would have thought? She had owned the farm, but that was different; she had inherited it, and it really belonged to the boys. This cottage, on the other hand, would be purchased by her. It was her very own little freehold, adjacent to Queens Square fountain. Opposite, through the trees, was the magnificent, brand new Moonta Mehodist Church. It was perfect.

Moonta Methodist Church, c. 1927, courtesy, SLSA, B4384

22. 64 George Street, Moonta

George Street, c. 1896. The town hall and the square are on the left.
Emma lived opposite the square, courtesy, SLSA, B33886

In 1928, Emma's family helped Emma and Annie move into their Queen Square cottage. As the weeks went by, Emma often sat happily beside the front window, which looked out over the square and its pretty, white fountain amongst the trees. Her heart was full. She had long missed the convenience of a town.

Emma didn't avoid all of Annie's excursions. There were days when Annie's feet, crippled by her four-inch heels, pained her, and she leaned heavily on her mother.

Now, Emma and Annie could see their families more often, and even Arnold, Annabell, and their family came over from New South Wales.

'Remind me of the children's ages again, Annie,' Emma said, fanning herself vigorously.

'Muriel will be eleven, Irene nine...' Annie counted on her fingers.

'And the boys?'

'Reggie is seven, and Bruce – is almost three.'

Arny stood beside his shiny new Chevrolet automobile. 'My, my, you are close to everything. Bell will be envious.'

'I reckon,' Bell said. 'A drapery shop just a few houses away?'

Three of Arny's four children dutifully lined up, while Bruce wriggled to get out of his father's arms.

'Come inside,' Emma said to the children, 'Annie will get you some cake.' Her face softened as the children filed inside. She had missed them and hoped the spat between her sons had been resolved.

Wes and Bert showed no signs of animosity toward Arnold when they converted the George Street sitting room into a bedroom for the family from New South Wales.

The following morning, Annie was brushing Emma's curls when Arny and Bell surfaced.

Emma's curls

'Let me trim these ringlets, Mama,' Annie said. 'They're tangled. No one wears their hair on their shoulders nowadays It's just not fashionable.' She rolled her eyes at young Irene, who giggled.

'When did I ever care about fashion?' Emma said. 'My neck will be cold in winter. Isn't that right, Irene?'

'It will, Grandma. We got cold sleeping on the ground last night.'

'You slept on the ground?'

Irene crept closer. 'And we had picnics on a rug.'

Emma smiled at their earnest confiding.

Most of Emma's family called to the cottage over the following days, and Christmas was like a dream, with a long week of family visits and excursions to the seaside.

A global economic catastrophe had begun in 1929. Wes strode into the Moonta cottage with a grim expression. Eleanor looked concerned, and Doris and Mary slipped outside.

Wes sat heavily in the armchair. 'We're ruined. We get nothing for our wheat and wool, yet everything else is going up. Taxes, the cost of shipping, machinery, even fencing wire.'

Eleanor sat on the edge of the chair and put her arm around his shoulder. 'We'll be more careful, Wes. Doris is earning a tidy sum, teaching piano. And Mary is advertising for singing pupils...'

'I can lend you some money, Wes,' Emma said.

'Thanks, Ma. But it's a small miracle we need. The whole farming industry is about to collapse.'

It was true. The substantial fall in the price of wheat and wool worldwide was disastrous. Australia depended heavily on exporting both.

When Bill and Emily piled into the cottage, they too were full of woe.

Richard's Eva tried to cheer them up. 'You're looking better, Emily,' she said.

Emily was thin, and her eyes had dark shadows. And now they all knew; the Tunkin family was cursed with consumption.

'She'll soon be better,' Bill said. 'We are moving to Moonta Bay. The sea air is just what she needs. And I've just sold the farm. We are going to take over Cliff House.'

'Lucky you, selling before the crash,' Wes said. 'Perfect timing. How did you do it?'

'Too clever, I suppose,' Bill said. 'Actually, I had hoped for a better price for the farm. And we still have to make a living, so we're going to take in boarders.'

'It's a bit run down, and it's huge,' Richard said.

Emma remembered seeing the hotel from the beach, all those years ago. It was 'too expensive', they had said then.

'I'll just have to renovate as I go,' Bill said.

Eva whispered to Eleanor, 'We thought if we all give Bill a hand doing up the mansion, he might offer us an out-of-season holiday. You know, only in winter, when it's empty. And we'd all pitch in with cooking and cleaning.'

Eleanor replied, 'March or September would suit me. Imagine us all holidaying by the sea, our children amusing themselves on the sand, while we relax. Just like the rich.'

Wes looked at his clever wife. Nearly forty-three, and still as beautiful as ever.

'That will be a novelty,' Hettie said.

'Sounds like bliss,' Eva added.

The brothers gathered around Bill, and it was decided.

Later in the week, Bert, Wes, and Bill duly measured Cliff House for paint and materials, and soon began the work on the wide, lacy, iron verandas.

When Emma's sons called to see her, they were invariably covered with white paint, but the lift in their moods made her heart sing. And the women talked of little else except their upcoming holiday, certainly their first with their children – and by the sea.

'March fifteenth, Ma,' Bert said. 'Will we book you in, too?'

'It hardly has that many rooms, son.'

'It has ten bedrooms, two dining rooms, and two sitting rooms where the children will bunk in.'

'It will be cold,' Emma complained. 'You said the wind blows straight off the sea.'

'Ah, but there is a secret hiding place, just for you,' Bill said.

'Now you are teasing me.'

'No, truly, there is a glass-roofed inner courtyard. It is always warm. In fact, it is quite hot on a sunny day,' Bill said. 'Tell her, Wes.'

'Remarkably warm,' Wes nodded. 'And it was good enough for Superintendent Hancock. Did you know that, when he retired, he lived at Cliff House? He took it for his health.'

'Did he now?' Emma brightened. Memories of the mining manager surfaced. 'Well, then, if it was good enough for him...'

Emma's family laughed.

Wes was delighted; his mother's memory still served her well.

Moonta Bay and Cliff House, c. 1932, courtesy, SLSA, B8261

Their sea-side holiday, their first of many, was everything they had dreamed.

'It's a miracle,' Wes said, looking around at the sheltered bay. The water was clear and there were no rolling dangerous waves. The sand was white, and the outcrop of rocks were climbable for small children.

The men went fishing, and everyone enjoyed rare meals of fresh fish. The cousins ran down the cliff steps and path and played on the rocks, or on the sandy beach for hours, settling into little groups, some digging and others sailing hastily carved boats.

Emma, Eleanor, and Emily often sat on the veranda and listened to the laughter of the children echo up the cliffs. Sometimes, the smaller children played at their feet, and never far from Emily, was little Annie, now called Nan.

Nan (Annie) at Cliff House

'She's an imaginative child,' Emma said sleepily, watching the little girl's face framed by straight fair hair and a fringe.

Nan talked softly to her doll.

Emma allowed her memories to take over as the tide washed in and out. She could hardly believe she was at the seaside – and with her whole family.

Emma didn't always remember where she was, but it didn't matter, so long as her daughter, Annie was nearby. There were regular family visitors from Agery to the Moonta house, especially on Friday evenings or Saturday mornings, when the Bowden men drove their families to the Moonta shops. And they rarely left town without having tea with Annie and Emma. When Jim attended the Moonta School of Mines, he lived with Emma and Annie from Monday to Saturday. His cousin Dulcie also stayed there while her parents shopped.

Emma's face brightened when she saw the youngsters running through the doorway, and she often pressed into their hands a coin or a sweet treat.

Early in July, she remembered William's lucky penny and folded Jim's fingers around it. He gave her a quick smile and examined the treasure closely. He scratched at the green residue around the numbers, 1854.

'Victoria.' he read. 'She was our Queen, wasn't she?'

'Isn't she still?' Emma raised an eyebrow.

'No, it's King George now.'

'Oh… Your mother has taught you well.'

Jim leaned on the table, his fist supporting his jaw. 'She's always teaching us,' he said, pulling a funny face.

Emma giggled.

Emma continually thought about joining her loved ones in the great hereafter. And on that cool Friday evening, July 19, 1929, she did just that. She was in her eighty-fourth year.

It was a quiet unobtrusive moment. One minute she was laughing, the next she was quiet and still.

Annie touched her arm. 'Ma… Mama,' she said. Annie put her hand to her mouth. Then she smiled. Her dear mother was at peace at last, in her own home. She couldn't have done better than that.

But Annie was worried about seven-year-old Dulcie. She didn't want to explain death to the little girl.

'Dulcie, dear,' she said, putting her arm around the girl's shoulder and turning her away from Emma. 'Go next door and ask them to telephone for the doctor. Grandma isn't well. And I want you to stay there, dear. Will you do that for me? Don't come back here. Your daddy will pick you up from there.' Dulcie looked at the door and then at Annie. 'Jim, show her where to go.'

Obituary

Emma Bowden of Agery died quietly at her daughter Annie's dinner table in Moonta. She was one of the first pioneers of the district and…experienced many hardships, in facing which she showed a splendid example to her fellow settlers. Nor was she lacking in her effort to help in any good cause. She was a most ardent and diligent member of the Methodist Church and was a fine type of Christian woman. A family of ten children were reared to an adult age of whom there survives five sons, two daughters, twenty-seven grandchildren and eight great grandchildren. The funeral on Sunday afternoon was very largely attended and her remains interred beside those of her husband Ben at the Moonta Cemetery.

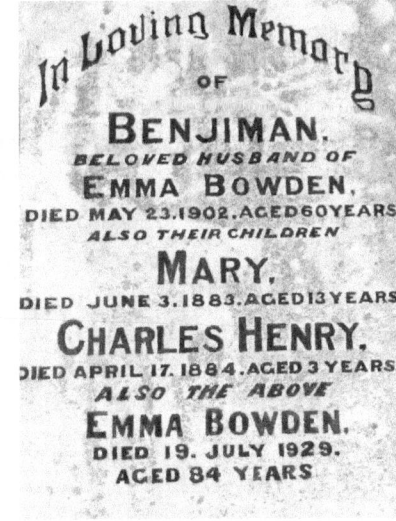

In Loving Memory
OF
BENJIMAN.
BELOVED HUSBAND OF
EMMA BOWDEN,
DIED MAY 23.1902. AGED 60 YEARS
ALSO THEIR CHILDREN
MARY,
DIED JUNE 3.1883. AGED 13 YEARS
CHARLES HENRY,
DIED APRIL 17.1884. AGED 3 YEARS.
ALSO THE ABOVE
EMMA BOWDEN,
DIED 19. JULY 1929.
AGED 84 YEARS

23. I Give and Bequeath

Emma's seven surviving children, Annie, William, Richard, Bert, Wes, Arnold, and Vera gathered at the offices in Ellen Street of Mr Leslie Bennett, Mayor of Moonta, and one of the two executors of Emma's will.

Annie hobbled in and sat in a chair against the wall. Vera and Eva joined her.

'We're not expecting a lot,' Eva said, removing her hat and laying it on her knee.

'There's so many of us, and there was never much to spare,' Annie added, speaking behind her hand, 'and the cost of these two lawyers will see most of it gone.'

Vera hoped they were wrong. Her Stephen had said the canny old lady was bound to have put some money aside.

Leslie Bennett's receptionist ushered them in.

John Symons, the other executor, sat at the head of the long, polished table. 'Good afternoon,' he said, scanning the pages. 'If everyone is here, let's begin.'

This is the last will and testament of me Emma Bowden, of

Agery...

His voice rose now.

I desire that all my just debts, funeral, and testamentary expenses shall be paid…
I GIVE AND BEQUEATH
– unto each of my daughters, Elizabeth Ann Mahar, Eliza Jane Trethowan, and Vera Mary Edwards, the sum of £50.

Annie smiled and nudged Vera.

– unto each of my sons, John Samuel Bowden, Ben George Bowden, and Richard Rowling Bowden, the sum of £100.
– to my son, Arnold Henry Bowden, £300.
– to my sons, William Trethowan Bowden, Lloyd Herbert Bowden, and Charles Wesley Bowden, each £485.

Wes's heart thumped. He elbowed Bert and whispered, 'Four hundred and eighty-five!'

'Mrs Bowden was an astute woman,' Leslie Bennett told them, 'quite remarkable really.'

Wes nodded. His mother had continued the age-old tradition of putting money aside from the good years, for the bad.

After the meeting, the family was jubilant as they returned to the George Street cottage.

'It's a bit of a miracle,' Bert said to Wes, steadying his voice. 'It couldn't have come at a – better time. I can't even grow wheat at four shillings a bushel. Now wool is down to ten pence, from twenty-seven pence! We were all but gone.' As Bill joined them, Bert said, 'Lucky you, Bill. Got out in the nick of time.'

'Not really,' Bill confided. 'I'd swap your money problems for a healthy wife any day. Better go,' he added. 'The Tossell girl is with Emily. It's been so cold, and her cough is worsening.'

Arnold put on his coat.

'Take care, Arny.' said Wes.

'Wes,' said Arnold, 'are you still going on about convicts?'

Bert stood beside Wes. 'Wes is right, Arny. I don't know how you sleep at night with those convicts all around you. No money is worth that.'

Arnold put his hand up. 'Stop it you two, before you make entire fools of yourselves. We aren't the only State with convicts. You obviously haven't heard that the great, convict-free, state of South Australia was planned by a convict! Mr Edward G Wakefield was in prison when he wrote his famous *Letter from Sydney*, with all of its recommendations for South Australia's convict-free settlement. He never was in Australia, but some of his cellmates were, and he learned from them.'

'Our Mr Wakefield?' Wes blustered.

'It's not a secret either. I came prepared this time.' Arnold waved the clippings. 'It's in all the newspapers. Which one will I start with?' He leafed through them and read out the headings: 'The Wakefield Bubble Pricked; Wakefield as a Fortune Hunter; Letters from Gaol; Champion of Landed Gentry; Wakefield Whitewashed. I like that one,' Arnold added.

Bert and Wes took the clippings in silence.

'*Labor Daily*, 1927?' Wes read aloud. 'You knew about this – before?'

'Of course,' Arnold said. 'But this is the crux of the matter, Wes. None of us are perfect. Wakefield made a mistake, a big one, yes, but he also came up with a brilliant plan for a non-convict Australia. He could see the benefits of attracting good, hard-working Christians to the country, people often destined for a dreadful life, or death, in the poorhouse.'

'So,' Wes said, 'like with Uncle William, when pushed to the limit, Wakefield was tempted.'

'That's right,' Arnold said, relaxing a bit. 'And Wakefield wasn't the only convict associated with South Australia. Hundreds made their way from New South Wales to South Australia.' Arnold was in full swing now, his voice getting louder. 'They are all around you, grubbing stumps, buying up farms; one ex-convict even made it to your Parliament!'

'Parliament!' Wes said, reddening. 'Father was so sure South Australia was superior. No one ever said…'

Arnold's laugh was hollow. 'Of course, they didn't.'

Wes stared through the window, remembering Uncle William, and his man, Moon.

'We wondered about the convicts, too,' Arnold said. 'But many of these so-called "villains" stole little more than bread to feed their family.' The room was quiet. 'Not to say it's right,' he continued. 'But petty thievery is just that, petty. We all make mistakes. No one's perfect. And look at the state the country is in now. We can't blame the convicts for that.'

'It's a pity the Improvement Societies were disbanded,' Wes said. He looked at Arnold and began to explain. 'In South Australia, just about every town had these – '

'Wes, I know what an Improvement Society is. We had them in New South Wales, too. In fact, they were all over Australia.' Arnold rolled his eyes. 'You still think I know nothing because I'm the youngest. Well, I give up. I'm leaving.'

'Wait…' Wes said, catching his arm. 'Wait. Sorry.'

'So, can I go?'

'Before that,' Wes said. 'Do you have any advice for us? Heaven knows, we farmers right now need all the help we can get.'

'You really want my opinion?' Arnold said. 'Where do I start? One of our biggest problems is we don't have control over the sale of our produce anymore. You are right about the AIMS, but more importantly, I think, we must resurrect the Wheat Board. We'll need all of our combined resources to get that back. And that's just the beginning. And shouldn't we diversify more? We can't just depend on wheat and wool.'

Wes was wide-eyed. 'You are right,' he said. 'Pity our Mr Hancock isn't around anymore.'

'But the college is still running,' Arnold said.

Wes and Arnold talked into the evening; their parents would have been proud. Arnold and his family left the following morning, with the Constantine Farm family waving, and the dust ballooning behind the car.

Arnold was right, Wes realised, gazing after them. Even though he, Wes, was a small farmer, he wasn't entirely powerless. Like his father, he was on several committees, not least, the Clinton District Council.

24. Nineteen Years Later (1948)

Charles Wesley and Eleanor Bowden, 1950

Kadina and Wallaroo Times June 25, 1948
Cr. Charles Wesley Bowden is seeking re-election for a
further term in the District Council of Clinton:
• He has served 22 years in the District Council of Clinton:
• Chairman of the Council for three years during the war peri-
od, including Chairman of Clinton Red Cross Circle.
Other public offices held by him:
• Chairman of Y.P. Local Government Association:
• Member of Agery School Committee for 28 years, during
which time, as secretary, saw the erection of a new school-
house.
• Chairman of this committee 1926-1940 and 1942-1946.
• Chairman of Back to Agery celebration in 1935.
• Chairman of Agery Memorial Park Committee; President of
the Moonta Veterinary Club, for a very long period.
• Chairman of local committee in connection with the District
War Agricultural Committee.
He is at present Chairman of Agery Branch of the S.A Wheat
and Woolgrowers' Association, member of the State Executive, and member of the Barley Committee of that organisa-
tion. For the past three seasons has represented the S.A. Bar-
ley Growers on the Classification Committee of the Australian
Barley Board.

25. Charles Wesley and Eleanor Bowden Travel to Cornwall (1950)

The People's Weekly, February 25.
Mr and Mrs CW Bowden of Agery will leave Adelaide on March 13, 1950, for Melbourne, where they will join the *SS Cyrenia* on their visit to England.

Mr Bowden has been appointed by the executive of the South Australian Wheat Growers' Association as a second delegate to the above council to meet in Stockholm, Sweden, on the May 29.

Wes, also a representative of the SA Barley Growers Classification Committee, is also deputed to enquire into future prospects in the United Kingdom for wheat and barley marketing, bulk handling, and any other matter of significance pertaining to Australian primary producers and the rural industry.

Charles Wesley and Eleanor Bowden disembarked at Genoa and set out for Milan. Met by a representative of Pozzani, Roscom & Co, clients of the Australian Barley Board, Pozzani and Roscom hosted them during their ten days in Italy.

Travelling overland, the intrepid pair finally arrived in Constantine, Cornwall, the birthplace of Ben and Emma Bowden, who left there March 16, 1864.

Here, Wes and Len were warmly welcomed by Wes's Cornish cousins, uncles, and aunts. Wes saw for himself Cornwall's gloriously green, rolling downs and valleys, and Brunel's magnificent viaducts. They also visited the numerous place names spoken of so often by his parents: Trengilly Wartha, Nancenoy, Polwheveral, Helston.

It rained more often than not, dressing the hedgerows with Queen Anne's Lace, Foxglove, Fuchsia, Honeysuckle, and much, much more. Over the next two months, Charles Wesley, and his wife, Eleanor, heard many a tale about Ben and Emma, and the family they had left behind. They recorded many of these stories in the booklet, *A History of Agery* (1966), one of the many documents, which inspired the author to research and write their story.

Another booklet, *Descendants of Ben and Emma Bowden*, also provided a wealth of information. It was compiled by Bronwyn and

Don Plowman and Rosalie Bowden, after a large family reunion in Adelaide in 1977. The author didn't attend this grand affair because she lived overseas. The reunion attendees were asked to bring lists of their family members, spouses, and descendants with relevant dates. These were pinned up for everyone to see and to add to family charts for future generations.

Trengilly Wartha, now a much awarded Inn

Author's Note

Charles Wesley Bowden was my grandfather. His oldest daughter, Alicia Doris Bowden, was my mother. She married Hartley Edwin Weyland (Jack) in 1939. I was born in 1941. I have five brothers and sisters, Jeffrey, John, Colleen, Helen, and Jill.

After Annie died, my grandfather gave the cottage to his daughter Doris, much to my father's chagrin, and we all lived at 64 George Street Moonta, from 1943 until 1953. This cottage in Moonta still stands.

In 1966, *A History of Agery* was published, and I left Australia to see Cornwall for myself, on the first of my several visits.

Appendix 1: Map of Cornwall

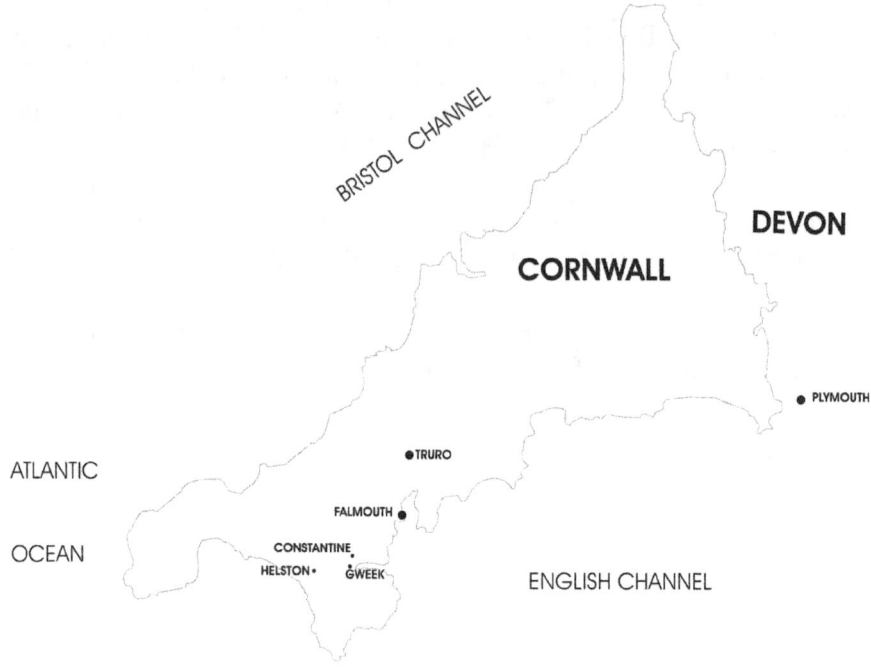

Appendix 2: Map of Tiparra

301 Matthews 1875	**300** Staples, G S 1875	**6** Morgan, 1873	**5** / **4** Cross PENANG CHURCH 1872 & SCHOOL	**13**	**12** Staples, J 1873	**446** Hancock, J 1883 **459**

301 Matthews 1875 · **300** Staples, G S 1875 · **6** Morgan, 1873 · **5** · **4** Cross 1872 · PENANG CHURCH & SCHOOL · **13** · **12** Staples, J 1873 · **446** Hancock, J 1883 · **459**

306 Nankivell, E Jr. 1875 · **308** Andrewartha, T 1875 · **7** · **8** 1868 · **14** Hilton 1872 · **15** Hilton 1872 · **445** Ortloff, W F 1883

314 Hancock, J 1875 · **315** Ingram 1876 Harvey, GM 1881

307 Stacey, W B 1875 · **310** Tiddy, James O 1876 · **309** Andrewartha, T 1875 · **313** Hancock, J 1875 · **316** Staples, G S 1875 Staples, Robert 1877 · **444** Merrifield, W 1880 Staples, G S · **425** Morgan, J L 1879

25ᴱ MOONTA

19 Howlett, Henry 1881 · **535** Stacey, W B 1876 · **317** Howlett, Henry 1875 · **311ˢ** · **317ᴱ** · **312** Gluyas, Thomas 1875 Tiddy, James O 1880 Eden, John 1892 · **423** Eden, John 1881 · **424ᵂ** Bowden, Ben 1881

18 · **318** Matters, George 1875 · **319** Bowden, Ben 1875 AGERY CHURCH & SCHOOL · **520** · Lomman, M 1888 · AGERY SWAMP · **422** Lomman, Matthew 1888 · **421** Lomman, Matthew 1880

456 Lomman, Matthew 1899 · **420** Triplett, Fred 1880

575 · **239ᴱ** · **579** · **580** · **241** Lomman, Peter 1883 Eden, John 1885 · **521** · **242** Bowden, Ben 1885 · **460** Triplett, J T 1886 · **461** Triplett, Richard 1879

247 · **246ᵂ** Lord, J 1883 · **246ᴱ** 1885 Lomman, P 1883 Bowden, Ben 1885 · **244** Denyer, J 1885 Trethowan, W J · **243** Denyer, J 1883 Trethowan, W J · Trethowan, W J 1881 · **395** · **396** King, Peter 1881

245

252 Philips. Jack Bowden. Bert Bowden. · **225** · **223** · **222** · **221** King, John 1880 · **393**

226

Map: The district of Agery, a part of the Hundred of Tippara.

Appendix 3: Bowden Family Genealogy

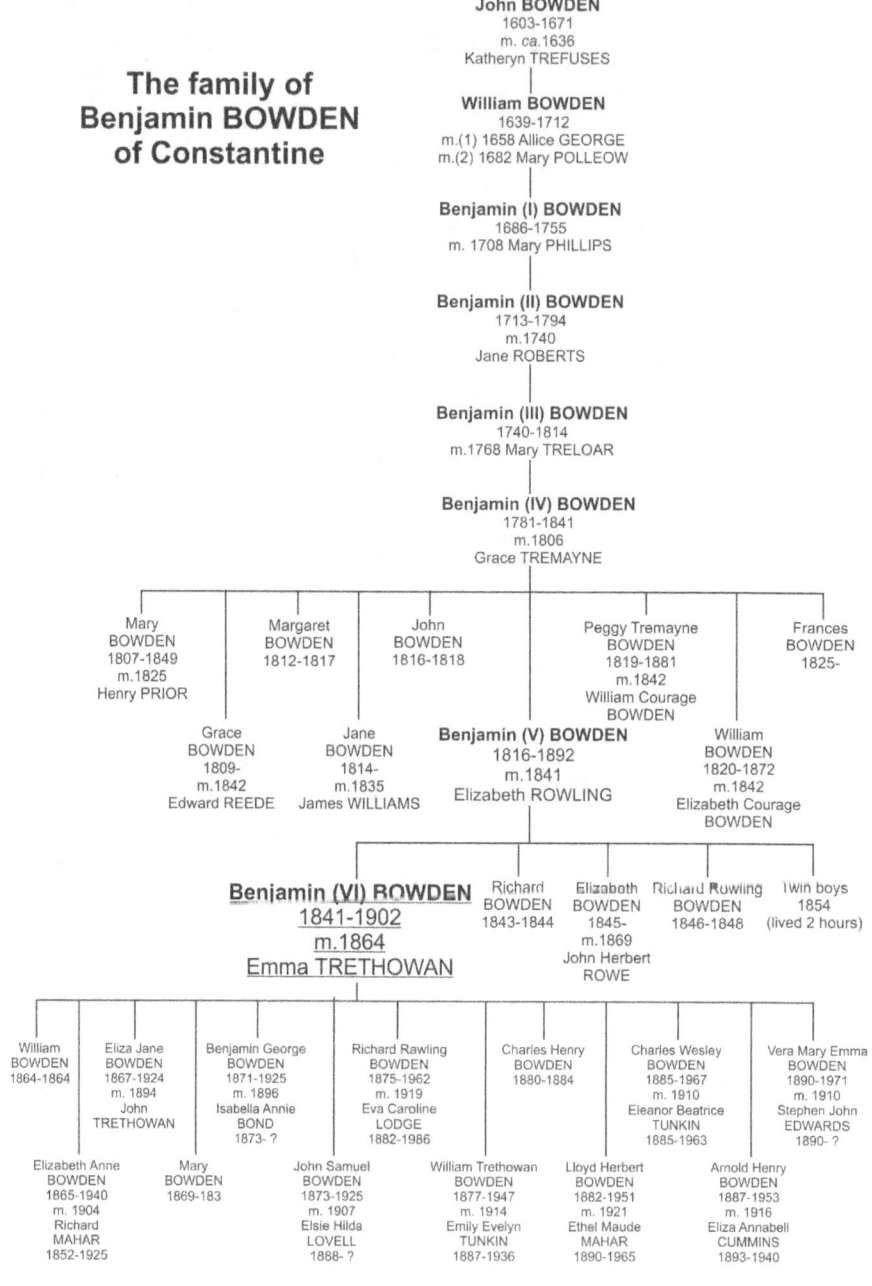

The family of Benjamin BOWDEN of Constantine

John BOWDEN
1603-1671
m. ca.1636
Katheryn TREFUSES

William BOWDEN
1639-1712
m.(1) 1658 Allice GEORGE
m.(2) 1682 Mary POLLEOW

Benjamin (I) BOWDEN
1686-1755
m. 1708 Mary PHILLIPS

Benjamin (II) BOWDEN
1713-1794
m.1740
Jane ROBERTS

Benjamin (III) BOWDEN
1740-1814
m.1768 Mary TRELOAR

Benjamin (IV) BOWDEN
1781-1841
m.1806
Grace TREMAYNE

Mary BOWDEN
1807-1849
m.1825
Henry PRIOR

Margaret BOWDEN
1812-1817

John BOWDEN
1816-1818

Peggy Tremayne BOWDEN
1819-1881
m.1842
William Courage BOWDEN

Frances BOWDEN
1825-

Grace BOWDEN
1809-
m.1842
Edward REEDE

Jane BOWDEN
1814-
m.1835
James WILLIAMS

Benjamin (V) BOWDEN
1816-1892
m.1841
Elizabeth ROWLING

William BOWDEN
1820-1872
m.1842
Elizabeth Courage BOWDEN

Benjamin (VI) BOWDEN
1841-1902
m.1864
Emma TRETHOWAN

Richard BOWDEN
1843-1844

Elizabeth BOWDEN
1845-
m.1869
John Herbert ROWE

Richard Rowling BOWDEN
1846-1848

Twin boys
1854
(lived 2 hours)

William BOWDEN
1864-1864

Eliza Jane BOWDEN
1867-1924
m. 1894
John TRETHOWAN

Benjamin George BOWDEN
1871-1925
m. 1896
Isabella Annie BOND
1873- ?

Richard Rawling BOWDEN
1875-1962
m. 1919
Eva Caroline LODGE
1882-1986

Charles Henry BOWDEN
1880-1884

Charles Wesley BOWDEN
1885-1967
m. 1910
Eleanor Beatrice TUNKIN
1885-1963

Vera Mary Emma BOWDEN
1890-1971
m. 1910
Stephen John EDWARDS
1890- ?

Elizabeth Anne BOWDEN
1865-1940
m. 1904
Richard MAHAR
1852-1925

Mary BOWDEN
1869-183

John Samuel BOWDEN
1873-1925
m. 1907
Elsie Hilda LOVELL
1888- ?

William Trethowan BOWDEN
1877-1947
m. 1914
Emily Evelyn TUNKIN
1887-1936

Lloyd Herbert BOWDEN
1882-1951
m. 1921
Ethel Maude MAHAR
1890-1965

Arnold Henry BOWDEN
1887-1953
m. 1916
Eliza Annabell CUMMINS
1893-1940

Appendix 4: Trethowan Family Genealogy

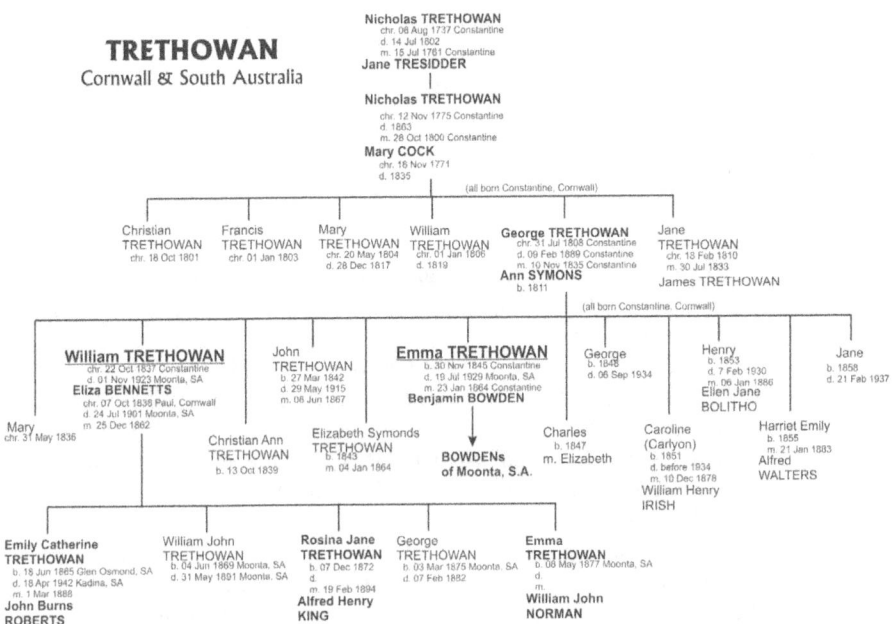

TRETHOWAN
Cornwall & South Australia

Nicholas TRETHOWAN
chr. 08 Aug 1737 Constantine
d. 14 Jul 1802
m. 15 Jul 1761 Constantine
Jane TRESIDDER

Nicholas TRETHOWAN
chr. 12 Nov 1775 Constantine
d. 1863
m. 28 Oct 1800 Constantine
Mary COCK
chr. 16 Nov 1771
d. 1835

(all born Constantine, Cornwall)

Christian
TRETHOWAN
chr. 18 Oct 1801

Francis
TRETHOWAN
chr. 01 Jan 1803

Mary
TRETHOWAN
chr. 20 May 1804
d. 28 Dec 1817

William
TRETHOWAN
chr. 01 Jan 1806
d. 1819

George TRETHOWAN
chr. 31 Jul 1808 Constantine
d. 09 Feb 1889 Constantine
m. 10 Nov 1835 Constantine
Ann SYMONS
b. 1811

Jane
TRETHOWAN
chr. 18 Feb 1810
m. 30 Jul 1833
James TRETHOWAN

(all born Constantine, Cornwall)

William TRETHOWAN
chr. 22 Oct 1837 Constantine
d. 01 Nov 1923 Moonta, SA
Eliza BENNETTS
chr. 07 Oct 1838 Paul, Cornwall
d. 24 Jul 1901 Moonta, SA
m. 25 Dec 1862

Mary
chr. 31 May 1836

John
TRETHOWAN
b. 27 Mar 1842
d. 29 May 1915
m. 06 Jun 1867

Christian Ann
TRETHOWAN
b. 13 Oct 1839

Emma TRETHOWAN
b. 30 Nov 1845 Constantine
d. 19 Jul 1929 Moonta, SA
m. 23 Jan 1864 Constantine
Benjamin BOWDEN

Elizabeth Symonds
TRETHOWAN
b. 1843
m. 04 Jan 1864

BOWDENs
of Moonta, S.A.

George
b. 1848
d. 06 Sep 1934

Charles
b. 1847
m. Elizabeth

Henry
b. 1853
d. 7 Feb 1930
m. 06 Jan 1886
Ellen Jane
BOLITHO

Caroline
(Carlyon)
b. 1851
d. before 1934
m. 10 Dec 1878
William Henry
IRISH

Jane
b. 1858
d. 21 Feb 1937

Harriet Emily
b. 1855
m. 21 Jan 1883
Alfred
WALTERS

Emily Catherine
TRETHOWAN
b. 18 Jun 1865 Glen Osmond, SA
d. 16 Apr 1942 Kadina, SA
m. 1 Mar 1888
John Burns
ROBERTS

William John
TRETHOWAN
b. 04 Jun 1869 Moonta, SA
d. 31 May 1891 Moonta, SA

Rosina Jane
TRETHOWAN
b. 07 Dec 1872
d.
m. 19 Feb 1894
Alfred Henry
KING

George
TRETHOWAN
b. 03 Mar 1875 Moonta, SA
d. 07 Feb 1882

Emma
TRETHOWAN
b. 06 May 1877 Moonta, SA
d.
m.
William John
NORMAN

Bibliography

Barnett, Gordon A. *Tunkin 1740-1988: A Family History*, Macquarie, ACT: self-published, 1989.

http://www.CORNISH-Lrootsweb.com UK Census data and anomalies. Birth, marriage and death registrations and rental documents.

Bowden, Charles Wesley. *History of Agery, Kadina & Moonta*, South Australia: The Farmer Press, 1966.

Davenport, Samuel. *Some New Industries For South Australia*. Adelaide: WC Rigby, 1864.

Duffy, Michael et al. *The New Maritime History of Devon, Vol 2: From the Late Eighteenth Century to the Present Day*, Devon, UK: Conway Maritime Press in association with the University of Exeter, 1994.

Faull, Jim. *The Cornish in Australia*, Melbourne: AE Press, 1983.

Gott, Robert. *South Australia*. Port Melbourne, VIC: Reed Educational & Professional Publishing, 1997.

Halliday, F.E.. *A History of Cornwall*, London: Gerald Duckworth & Co. Ltd, 1959.

Diary of Charles Marsden | State Library of South Australia
https://digital.collections.slsa.sa.gov.au›nodes›view
Diary of Charles Marsden, emigrant labourer of Stalybridge, Lancashire, on a voyage from Plymouth to Port Adelaide aboard the Eastern Empire, 16 March 1864.

Payton, Philip. *The Cornish farmer in Australia*, Cornwall, UK: Dyllansow Truran, 1987 & 1984.

Payton, Philip. *Pictorial History of Australia's Little Cornwall*, Adelaide: Rigby Ltd, 1978.

Payton, Phillip. *Making Moonta, the Invention of Australia's Little Cornwall*, Exeter, UK: University of Exeter Press, 2007.

Philbey, Marilyn, compiler. *Yorke Peninsula Records, Vol. 3, Obituaries and Death Notices, 1875*.

Plowman, Bronwyn & Bowden, Rosalie. *Descendants of Ben and Emma Bowden*, South Australia: self-published, 1978.

Simpson, ER, *Beaumont House, The land and its people*, Adelaide: Beaumont Press, 1993.

Unknown author. *Emigrant's Friend, or Authentic Guide to South Australia, 1848*. Surry Hills, NSW: Readers' Digest Services Pty Ltd, republished, 2010.

www.ingramcontent.com/pod-product-compliance
Lightning Source LLC
Chambersburg PA
CBHW070504030726
47503CB00004B/1159